MRS. PARKINGTON

Louis Bromfield

Thorndike Press • Thorndike, Maine

Library of Congress Cataloging in Publication Data:

Bromfield, Louis, 1896-1956.
Mrs. Parkington / Louis Bromfield.
p. cm.
ISBN 1-56054-354-X (alk. paper : lg. print)
1. Large type books. I. Title.
[PS3503.R66M519 1992] 91-46249
813'.52—dc20 CIP

Thorndike Press Large Print edition published in 1992
by arrangement with HarperCollins Publishers, Inc.

Cover design by James B. Murray.

The tree indicium is a trademark of Thorndike Press.

This book is printed on acid-free, high opacity paper. ∞

MRS. PARKINGTON

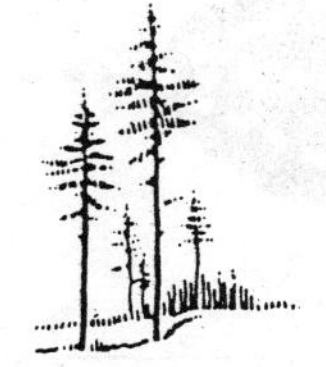

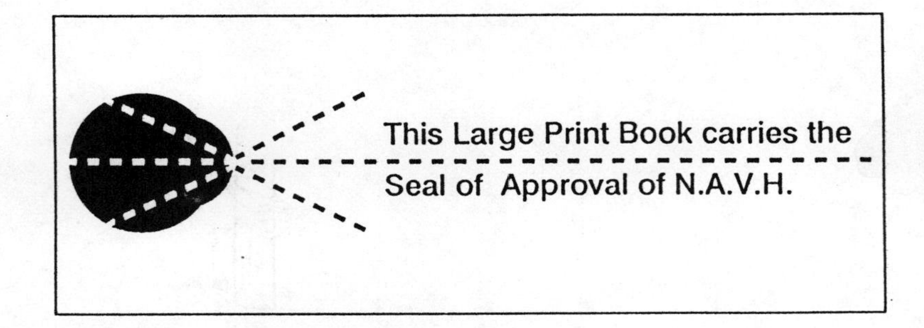
This Large Print Book carries the
Seal of Approval of N.A.V.H.

MRS. PARKINGTON

I

Outside the snow was falling, thickly in great wet flakes, so that the sound of the traffic on Park Avenue coming through the drawn curtains was muted and distant. Mrs. Parkington, seated before her mirror with a half-pint of champagne by her side, thought how nice it was to have a Christmas this year which seemed like Christmas. True, tomorrow the snow would be turned to slush, discolored by soot, and those great machines bought by the personable and bumptious mayor would be scooping it up and hauling it off to the North River; but snow — the mere idea of snow — was pleasant. Just the sight of it drifting down in soft white flakes through the bright auras of the street lights made you feel happy and content. And it summoned memories, very long memories, of the days when snow was not a nuisance in New York but brought out sleds and sleighs and there was racing in the park, and the sound of sleigh bells was heard everywhere in the city. Gus had loved the cutter racing; it suited his flamboyant nature. When one was eighty-four and in good health and spirits and had a half-pint of Lanson every evening just before dinner, one had a long memory. Long memories were perhaps common among widowed old ladies but memories so crammed with romance and excitement as that of Mrs. Parkington were rare.

She was doing her own hair, setting the waves exactly as they should be. She had always done her own hair and now at eighty-four she had no intention of giving it up. Ten years ago she had had it cut, not so much as a concession to fashion, as because it was simpler to do and less trouble to keep in order. She could not abide untidy women. Hair hanging down in strings at the nape of the neck implied some obscure weakness of character or an untidiness of mind.

She finished the last of the half-pint and suddenly called, "Mattie! Mattie!"

At the sound of her voice there appeared out of the adjoining bedroom the stout figure of a woman in her late sixties. She had a curious figure, almost round like the figures of those toys which return to an upright position no matter how often they are pushed over. In fact Mattie resembled such a toy in a great many ways. Her face was plump and round and with a snub nose. Her gray hair was done severely in a knot at the nape of her neck. She was dressed neatly in a gray dress with buttons down the front and a very full skirt. She was a Swede by birth and she was altogether a remarkable woman. She was masseuse, hairdresser, secretary and friend, and she knew with a devastating and intimate knowledge everything that had happened to Mrs. Parkington during the forty-one years of close association.

"Yes, Mrs. Parkington," said Mattie.

"Tell Taylor to bring up another half-pint."

Mattie looked at her silently for a moment. Then she said, "Do you think it wise, Mrs. Parkington? If you're having wine with dinner your acidity will be awful tomorrow. You'll be like a vinegar bottle."

Mrs. Parkington laughed, "I won't have wine for dinner. Do as I say!"

"Very well, Mrs. Parkington, only don't complain to me tomorrow. You know how you always feel after Christmas."

The old woman did not answer her and Mattie went out and in a little while Mrs. Parkington rose from the dressing table and went into her own small sitting-room. She had a spare figure, very straight with very pretty hands and feet. She wore a black evening dress with a great deal of black lace to hide the thinness of her throat and shoulders and blue-veined wrists. Her eyes were remarkable, blue and very bright, like the surface of a mountain lake glittering in the sun.

The sitting-room was small and cluttered by a great deal of furniture, many books and photographs and *bibelots* on little tables. All of the articles were obviously expensive and a great many of them were ugly but she was fond of each one of them. When she moved out of the great house on Fifth Avenue to make way for progress and a seventy-story skyscraper, she had collected for what Mattie described as the "boodwar," the things which she wished to keep about her because of the happy or sentimental associations they had for her. This room was the result, cozy and cluttered but warm. There were objects out of the "cozy corner" of the eighties and nineties, objects picked up during yachting expeditions in the Mediterranean and the Far East, two atrocious gilt chairs sold to her at a huge price as authentic sixty years ago before she learned about such things, a great many books, mostly obscure or forgotten novels in French and English, chosen not for their literary qualities but because they had attracted her by some character or incident; a chaise longue, a long "pier glass" with an ornate frame, and countless photographs of yachting parties and picnics at Newport, and shooting parties in Scotland and Austria.

Nearly all of them were group photographs, as if all her life had been spent among crowds. Scattered among them were a few portrait photographs — one of "Major" Parkington, her deceased husband, one each of her two dead sons, Eddie Herbert, one of her daughter, the Duchess, a signed portrait of Edward VII as the Prince of Wales, and one of the Princess, a daguerreotype, very yellowed and dimmed by age, of a sturdy-faced man standing with his hand on the shoulder of a small pretty woman clad in a severe black dress with a collar of white lace. The daguerreotype stood on her desk, framed like a valuable miniature, in a frame of onyx and diamonds. It bore in a faded gold script across the bottom the legend, Forsythe and Wicks, portraits, Leaping Rock, Nevada. And there was a small old-fashioned photograph, which in its own onyx and diamond frame seemed to have a special importance, of a rather ugly but very chic woman sitting up very straight. Across the face of it written in fading ink was the inscription — *à Ma Chère Amie Susie — Aspasie.*

Her granddaughter Madeleine — the one who chose a cowboy as her fourth husband, said the sitting-room looked like the nest of a pack rat, but Mrs. Parkington only laughed because very few people ever saw it, and in any case it had been a very long time since mockery or disapproval had had any power to touch her. Her sitting-room was her own where she went when she wanted to be alone, in those moments when she felt impelled to withdraw from all the crumbling world about her and retire into the warmth of memories of the days when everything was pleasant and there seemed to be no trouble in the world.

As she came into the room she went straight to the old pier glass and faced it to look at herself. The glass had long ago begun to show streaks and splotches from age but she had never troubled to have it resilvered. Now there was scarcely any reason to go to the trouble; it would last out her time and afterward no one would want it. It wasn't the sort of mirror which gained value with age; it was merely ugly and no one would ever buy it save as a freak, the way people now bought ugly Victorian things because they were becoming smart.

It was an odd thing about fashion. She had lived to see countless fashions in furniture, in architecture, in dress. Some of the changes she regretted but on the whole it seemed to her that the taste of Americans had improved immensely and that the present fashions were not only beautiful but simple and practical as well.

She stood for a moment looking at herself in the streaked mirror, thinking, You are old and withered, but you've stood time better than the mirror. Both of you have seen a good deal. And that is something for which both of you should be thankful.

The face was indeed immensely wrinkled, with many fine lines which had come of living, sometimes recklessly, sometimes sensibly, always extravagantly; but the extravagance, she thought, was not her fault. There had always been money, so much of it that it had ceased to have any value. She had always had whatever she wanted simply for the asking. Nowadays they said this person or that one was rich but they no longer knew what it was to be rich in the sense the Major had been rich. It had been an immense, almost incalculable wealth, with no income taxes to devour it before it ever reached you, and no reason to calculate here and there how you were to pay taxes and still have what you wanted.

She was still a very rich old woman, and as she had grown older she had wanted less and less of luxury and show, and so in a way she was still as rich as she had always been. In some ways it was good to have less money; for one thing it gave her an excuse to get rid of that vast absurd château, set among shops and skyscrapers on Fifth Avenue without trees or parks or even a blade of grass near it. The Major had wanted her to live there until she died and the children after her death, but he himself died before he knew what was happening to the world. He didn't live long enough to see this new America with laws which would have put him in jail for life for the very acts which in his day had been called, "developing the resources of the country." She had no illusions about her husband. He had built up a vast fortune, but at heart he had always been a bandit. She did even concede that perhaps in his day, when there were so many of his kind in America, it had never occurred to him that he was a thief, a swindler and a super-confidence man.

There was a knock at the door and Mattie came in. In and out of her skirts, like animated bundles of silken feathers, ran Bijou and Mignon, the Pekingese, yapping and barking. Directly behind her came Taylor carrying on a silver tray another half-pint of champagne and a glass. He looked as he always did, dignified to the point of grimness. He too had been with her for a long time, so long that his grimness and dignity sometimes filled her with a wild desire to laugh at him, considering how well they knew each other and how long they had been together. But she never did laugh because she knew that it would hurt him far more than any rebuke or sarcasm she might utter. Taylor had a frame and it was possible for him to live only so long as he kept within it. He was English but even in England frames were beginning at last to be smashed.

He put down the tray on the table beside the chaise longue and she said, "Thank you, Taylor."

He stood very stiffly as if he, like Mattie, disapproved of the second small bottle. "Is that all, madame?"

"That's all. No one has come yet?"

"No, madame."

"I'll be down directly to look at the flowers."

"I think they look very well, madame."

"I'm sure they do, but the florists' men always make them too stiff and perfect."

"Very well, madame."

It was an old story — this business of the flowers. The florist, like Taylor, had a frame and he always wanted to stay within it. And his flowers looked that way. You knew by the way he arranged them that he was a vulgar man. He had no feeling for flowers. He liked a "rich effect." Taylor was the same way. Taylor had never become reconciled to giving up the pomp and importance of the big house. Vulgarity, Mrs. Parkington reflected, was a strange thing, at once very simple and very complex. A few people were born with it. A great many learned by experience what it was and lost it. But most people were born vulgar and remained so to the end of their lives. And again there were so many varieties of vulgarity, not only ostentation, but hypocrisy and false simplicity, and pretentiousness . . . well, she would think about all that another time. Commonness she liked. People who were common never suffered from the unforgivable sin of pretentiousness.

They would begin arriving for dinner soon and she wanted to be there to receive them. All her life she had been punctual, standing before the fire to welcome them as they came in. It was very important to have good manners and to be punctual; that was one of the things she had learned. If you had great beauty or genius you could afford to be slack, but there was really no other excuse. And even that excuse was not a very good one.

She seated herself by the tray where Mattie was pouring out the champagne, skillfully as a waiter at the Paris Ritz. Mattie was really a remarkable woman. She knew how to do everything.

The two Pekingese jumped into Mrs. Parkington's lap and licked her hands and she caressed them for a second, her wrinkled face softening with affection. A great many people didn't like Pekingese, especially men, but that was because they did not understand them . . . that their courage and dignity and self-importance was too great for their small bodies and so they, like little men suffering the same lack of proportion, sometimes appeared to be merely boisterous and annoying.

She looked up at Mattie and said, "You take that glass, Mattie, and fetch me my own out of the dressing room."

Mattie looked at her directly out of her blue, ageless Swedish eyes, a look of reproof.

"You know I never drink champagne, madame."

The old woman laughed, "Well, tonight you're going to drink it. It's Christmas night. We're going to drink as old friends and I want no nonsense."

Mattie did not answer her but went quietly to fetch the other glass. Probably, thought Mrs. Parkington, she thinks I'm growing childish, and perhaps I am. But no matter. She could accept that too as she had accepted many things.

When Mattie returned they raised their glasses and Mrs. Parkington said, "Merry

Christmas and Happy New Year." And as she drank she thought, I may not be here next year — without fear or regret. She was no more alarmed at the thought of death than she was now of the tragedies she had encountered in her long life. She had had more than her share of them, so many tragedies and such violent ones that people sometimes said that she must be a woman with no heart to have endured and survived them. That was only because they did not understand; they did not know that through sorrow she had acquired peace and wisdom. Tonight on Christmas night she was quite ready to die but she had a curious feeling that she must go on living because there was some new tragedy impending. It was not a new feeling — this sense of foreboding. She had had it before, many times, since that first occasion long ago when she knew that there was no use in searching for her father and mother because they were already dead. The feeling of presentiment was very nearly infallible.

She put down her glass quickly and said, "Well, there we are, Mattie. Another Christmas nearly over." She crossed to the table and opened the jewel case and took out her diamond necklace. "Here, Mattie, fasten it," she said, "it will make me feel brighter tonight."

She needed the necklace just as she needed the extra glass of champagne. The prospect of meeting all the family wearied her. She could endure them separately but together they appalled her, all save her great-granddaughter Jane. The rest were dull, dull, dull. Oh, God, they were dull. Her granddaughter, Madeleine, it was true, sometimes made her laugh; Madeleine with all her husbands and now her cowboy, was common and sexy, as if the Major had been born again in woman's clothing.

Now she would have to face them all again at the annual Christmas party which had been going on for thirty years. She was tired of her offspring and their offspring and their offspring's offspring. She had felt very detached from them for a long time now, as if they were connected to her only by a slender thread which might be snipped off at any time, leaving her free.

When Mattie had fastened the diamond necklace she said, "Keep the dogs up here, Mattie. They make the Duchess nervous."

Mattie said, "Very good, madame." And then suddenly, "How is the Duchess, madame? It's been a long time since I've seen her."

"Not much changed."

It was odd how, although her daughter

Alice had been married twice since her divorce from the Duke, she and Mattie and the whole family still called her the Duchess . . . probably because Alice, even when she had had too much to drink, had dignity . . . a kind of blank and meaningless tragic dignity. She was a period piece out of the nineties when rich American girls had married impecunious peers.

With a sigh Mrs. Parkington went through the door Mattie held open for her. The servant did not close the door at once but stood in the open doorway watching until her mistress reached the lift and went inside closing the door behind her. She still remained standing there, in an attitude of intense listening until she heard the elevator stop two floors below and heard Taylor open the door. Then she went inside the door of the boudoir to turn down the bed and put the dressing table in order. Once during her work, she paused and stood looking at the photographs in the "boodwar" and at last she picked up a small photograph of Mrs. Parkington's two sons as boys. Eddie must have been about seventeen at the time and Herbert about nineteen. They stood in front of the stables at Newport each holding the bridle of a saddle horse, dressed in the funny old-fashioned clothes of the opening of the century.

After a long time Mattie put down the photograph, sighed and, turning, said, "Come Mignon! Come Bijou! We'll go and have some supper." But clearly she wasn't thinking of the dogs. Her round, well-polished face wore a look of pity and abstraction, as if she had lost herself in the maze of the long distant past.

In the small drawing-room, Mrs. Parkington went from vase to vase of flowers, setting them right, giving each great luxurious bouquet a touch or pat, just enough to disarrange the florist's rigid pattern and restore to the blossoms their right to existence as flowers. She loved flowers, not only as things of beauty but as symbols of the country and the open air and nature itself, from which she had been shut away all too much by the very circumstances of her life.

This room was quite different from the "pack rat's nest" above-stairs. It was a beautiful room, and she knew it was beautiful and secretly was proud of it as a kind of symbol of her own achievement — that she had begun life in a boardinghouse in Leaping Rock, Nevada, passed through period after period of monstrous taste and finally emerged with an extraordinary knowledge of periods and architecture and the history of painting and decoration. She had never had any education at all beyond learning to read and write and do sums, but all her life she had been clever and God had endowed her with a memory which never forgot anything, and now, at eighty-four, she spoke French and German and English and was an authority on many subjects. It was not schools which educated people: it was something inside themselves.

And it was not money alone which had made the beauty of this room, but knowledge and taste, things which could not, despite the Major's ideas to the contrary, be bought.

When she had finished with the flowers she went to the fireplace and stood beneath the Romney with her back to it enjoying the gentle warmth of the fire. The room before her seemed to her to have a kind of glow about it, of mahogany and jade and crystal and flowers.

Standing there she wondered who would be the first to arrive. She hoped it would not be "the Duchess." She felt ill at ease with her own daughter as if the girl who was herself now over sixty, were a stranger. And the sight of her was always distressing because Alice was a kind of symbol of a something which, even now after forty-five years, still had the power of making her blush and feel ashamed.

She was disappointed for in a moment Taylor opened the tall mahogany door and in his English statesman's voice, faintly deformed by the echo of a cockney youth, announced, "Mrs. Sanderson!" If Taylor had had his way, Mrs. Parkington knew, he would have ignored Alice's other no less unfortunate marriages, and announced "The Duchess de Brantès," but she had put an end to that snobbery long ago. Mrs. Parkington thought it silly to announce the guests at a family dinner but she had not the heart to deny Taylor a second pleasure and satisfaction.

Her daughter came in dressed in a gown which the old woman thought after the first glance, was much too young for her. Alice had never had any sense of choosing the proper clothes and she had stubbornly refused to allow anyone else to choose for her. She was wearing in her hair above her sallow face an absurd ornament of artificial flowers, sequins and tulle. Only a young and beautiful woman could have carried it off and Alice was neither. She looked like the Major's side of the house, big and touched by what the old lady felt must be a congenital and inherited blowziness. Her drinking contributed nothing toward greater neatness or chic. Her maid might send her out looking almost chic but very early in the course of the evening, sometimes even before she arrived at dinner, she began to go to pieces. Her hair grew untidy, her corsets slipped up, her stockings wrinkled. Lately she had taken to spilling things at table. It wasn't only Alice's congenital untidiness, Mrs. Parkington knew; drink made it much worse. Only last week Alice had fallen off her chair during the music after dinner at the Desmonds.

Now, as her daughter crossed the room toward her, she watched for the signs. There were none. Alice seemed to be quite, as her father put it in the old days, "on an even keel," but you could never tell how much she had had to drink in the bathroom out of the Listerine bottle. She was like her father that way, too, but the Major had had a prodigious head. Mrs. Parkington had seen him drink four times as much as the men around him who grew tipsy, without even showing any signs. It was an accomplishment he had used in business deals to make for him millions of dollars.

Alice was quite near now. She embraced her mother, kissing her on the wrinkled cheek and saying, "Merry Christmas, Mother." And although she turned away her head, it was no good. There was a smell of spices on her breath.

"Merry Christmas," said Mrs. Parkington,

"and thank you for the lovely silver box."

"It's old," said Alice abruptly, "Dutch, I should think. Is everyone coming tonight?"

"Everyone. It's the first time in years the whole family has been in New York at Christmas."

Alice said, "I want to see Madeleine's cowboy. She is certainly insatiable."

"She's merely healthy and a little spoiled."

"I hope he'll stand up under the strain better than the others. Madeleine's trouble is that she's congenitally moral. If she were more promiscuous and married less she wouldn't be in the papers so often."

"Alice!" said Mrs. Parkington.

"I only mean it in a kindly way. I hope he's good and strong for Madeleine's sake."

Talk of this sort always made Mrs. Parkington uneasy. It was "modern" she supposed but she had never grown quite used to it, and she did not like cattiness in women. But she knew that Alice had some right to talk thus; she remembered Madeleine's own epithets "the disappointed Duchess" and the "bathroom drinker." However Mrs. Parkington decided to veer away from the subject.

The Duchess sat down, wearily. You knew by the way she sat down that she was not only tired but she was bored, desperately bored. There was boredom in the weary eyelids, in the sagging throat. She had come to dinner because it was a ceremony, and because it was better than staying home alone. Her mother, watching her, reflected even while they talked how extraordinary it was that a woman who had had so much wealth and so many opportunities in life, should have so few resources. Alice did not even enjoy reading and she had no hobbies and was really interested in nothing whatever. It was extraordinary that she should seem older than her own mother.

There had never been much open sympathy or understanding between them. Mrs. Parkington could never find any means of keeping up a sustained conversation with her daughter. Their talk was always no more than a series of false starts which led nowhere. Now, in desperation, she said, "What have you been doing lately?"

"Nothing much. I went to the opera Friday in the Geraghty box."

"Odd people. There was never as much ermine in the world as Mrs. Geraghty wears."

"I suppose she needs to assert herself in some way. Oceans of ermine is as good as any other way. At least you can *buy* ermine if you have enough money."

Mrs. Parkington made no reply. She had seen a great many Mrs. Benjamin Franklin

Geraghtys come and go in her time. She wasn't even bored by them any longer, because for a long time she had been quietly eliminating from her existence people who had to buy ermine in order to assert themselves. Of course you couldn't eliminate your own family entirely, no matter how much they bored you.

The Duchess opened her evening bag and brought out an enameled box from which she took a small pellet, swallowing it quickly. Her mother saw the action without seeing it, out of the corner of her eye, wondering what it was Alice was taking — drugs or breath scent or one of those newfangled things like Benzedrine. Then she heard Taylor's voice announcing Mr. and Mrs. Swann, and all her senses quickened at the prospect of seeing her granddaughter Madeleine's latest husband.

She scarcely noticed Madeleine herself, coming toward her in that enthusiastic way she had of being a whole herd steers about to trample you. Some day, the old lady felt, Madeleine in one of her rushes would be unable to stop short and the results would be disastrous for someone. Her granddaughter was a big, coarse woman, of thirty-nine with bumptious good health and the appearance and manners of an aggressive cook.

The old lady's eyes were all for the husband and when she saw him, she thought, Anyway, he's better than the Argentine or the other two. He's a man and he's hard and maybe that's what Madeleine needs. They say little tough fellows like that are pretty good.

Madeleine did manage to pull up in time and gave her a heavy, rather wet and very enthusiastic kiss on the cheek. Mrs. Parkington was rather finicky and could not control a grimace of displeasure which Madeleine failed to notice as she said, with enthusiasm, "This, Grandmother, is my husband Al."

Al took her hand and said, "How d'you do, ma'am?" And the old lady thought, Hear! A professional cowboy! A dude rancher! But his big hand, common and outsized for his small stature, a workingman's hand, was horny, and she noticed that even his dinner jacket did not conceal that faintly protruding abdomen which cowboys no matter how young or thin, acquired from long slouching in a Mexican saddle.

Her first reaction was that he was common — incredibly common, but Madeleine with her concentration of purpose, would not of course, mind his commonness; on the contrary, with her strong tastes, she would doubtless find it an asset. He was spare, with a hatchet face, lined and leathery, but he had very nice eyes, very alive and blue, and a sensual but controlled mouth. The eyes and mouth made her like him.

"I'm very glad to know you," she said, meaning it.

Then Madeleine presented him to the Duchess, who had been watching all the while with a faint glint of humor in the tired, heavy-lidded over-made-up eyes.

Then Amory Stilham came in with his wife and son — the old lady's granddaughter and great-grandson. They came directly to her, and in her heart now she wanted nothing of them. With an effort she altered her features into a smile of welcome.

Helen, her granddaughter was not at all like her sister Madeleine. She was a thin, spare, nervous woman, with a mouth which sagged bitterly at the corners, as if she held a grudge against life because it had denied her something she wanted more than all the things which had been given her. You would have said that she had everything. She was married to one of the Stilhams, a big, handsome if stupid man, and she had wealth and a house in town and one in Westbury. She had horses and a yacht and two children, a boy and a girl. None the less, the thin mouth turned down at the corners. At times it turned down savagely.

Helen, it was true, was the only one in the family with brains — the kind of brains which could create or accomplish things, but she never seemed to accomplish anything more than to serve in a bored way on countless committees. There was no way of really communicating with Helen — Mrs. Parkington had discovered that long ago. Helen gave the impression of living inside a shell, one of those shells which required a knife and biceps to open. Her handclasp was flabby.

Then in the place of Helen's hand, the old lady felt in her hand, the big hand of Helen's husband Amory — St. Judes, Harvard, the Carnelian Club, descendant of the Stilham who had founded Barchester, Massachusetts. Mrs. Parkington had one strong reaction to her grandson-in-law and she had experienced it at once on the day long ago when he and Helen came into the immense drawing room of the old house on Fifth Avenue to tell her they were engaged to be married. He is vulgar, she thought then, incredibly vulgar. It always astonished her that Amory thought there was something distinguished about being a stockbroker. He was big and floridly handsome, but vulgar — far more vulgar than the Major had ever been, even in the flashy days when he liked wearing big diamonds. The Major had been common, with dash and color and personality, but Amory was just plain vulgar. It was odd, too, when all his background and training were popularly supposed to produce only distinction and taste.

He said, "Well, Grandma, you're a wonder. I never saw you looking younger. Why even the Duchess and your grandchildren look older than you!"

Mrs. Parkington's skin was suddenly covered by goose pimples, but she managed to say quietly, "I'll be eighty-five next month but I'm still in my right mind, Amory."

Then Amory's son made a little bow and took her hand, "Merry Christmas, Grandma," he said.

"Merry Christmas, Jack."

He was handsome in a decadent fashion. He looked, Mrs. Parkington thought, as if he should have more common sense than he had, always being photographed in night clubs and at Palm Beach with glamour girls. Apparently he had no sense. He was much more a Blair than a Parkington — a Blair crossed with a Stilham. What could you expect?

Quickly she said to Helen, "Where's Janie? She's coming, I hope."

"Oh, yes, she's coming. She was going some place for a cocktail on the way. I couldn't make out where. She's very mysterious lately." And as soon as she had finished speaking the mouth drooped again. She spoke, sententiously, as if there were worlds of mystery and disapproval behind her words.

Even while she spoke, Mrs. Parkington was astonished by the anxiety in her own voice. It was remarkable that at her age it should matter to her so much that an eighteen-year-old girl should not miss the Christmas party. In her heart she knew the reason. Janie meant more to her than all the others put together.

And almost at once Janie and Mrs. Parkington's old beau, Harry Van Diver, came in together. Harry always came to the Christmas parties as if he were a member of the family.

They were late and hurried across the room. Mrs. Parkington thought what an absurd contrast they made — the one so young and pretty, the other so old, so faded, out of another century, another world. Even at seventy-eight Harry still preserved his manner of being an old-fashioned Union Club cavalier.

A light came into the eyes of the old lady at sight of her great-granddaughter and when the girl kissed her there was warmth in the embrace.

"I'm sorry, Grandmother, but it's snowing and I couldn't find a taxi."

"It's all right, my dear, there's no hurry.

I always have dinner half an hour after people are asked."

She liked good food, Mrs. Parkington, and she had an excellent cook she did not wish to lose because people who thought more of cocktails than food were late.

"Well, Harry," she said, "What is your excuse?"

"The same as Janie's. You look wonderfully well, Susie."

"I've put on more rouge than usual."

Taylor approached them with the cocktails, his friend Albert, the footman, who came in to "help out," close behind him with the big silver tray of hors d'oeuvres. When she and Harry had each had a champagne cocktail and the servants had passed, she said, "I always like to look my best at the Christmas dinner. It annoys Amory." Then in a lowered voice, "I suspect he thinks I'm going to live forever."

Harry Van Diver chuckled. He liked Amory no more than old Mrs. Parkington liked him. Amory was of a generation when he-men were professional . . . a bad generation, Harry always said, the men who were now between forty and sixty-five. They learned nothing in college. They were always attending class reunions. Their talk was entirely of the stock market or how much they had drunk the night before. They were all, like Amory, perpetual adolescents who, if they did not die of drink or overwork by sixty, found themselves deserted and dreary. Harry himself was old enough to belong to a generation which went to Europe and collected pictures and lived preciously on their incomes and wore out their lives sitting in the back of opera boxes. Also, because he was a snob, he felt that Amory had betrayed his club and his class.

He glanced at Amory who was talking to the Duchess, thinking with satisfaction how it must annoy Amory to see Mrs. Parkington going on and on, healthy and energetic and strong, standing always between him and his share of the vast Parkington fortune. Harry Van Diver, thin, shriveled, elegant and fastidious, was a he-bitch. That was why Mrs. Parkington liked him, why she had kept him about for more than twenty years since the time she had given up forever all thoughts of vanity or love. Harry's bitter feminine tongue amused her, and he was safe. He had admired her for over forty years. There had never been any danger of Harry's growing "sexy."

As he watched Amory and the Duchess with his nearsighted malicious black eyes, so squinted that he looked monstrously like an elderly and clever monkey, Mrs. Parkington thought how long time was, how many things you could discover and learn in eighty-four years . . . and how many things some people never learned though they lived forever.

Then Taylor's pompous voice said, "Dinner is served, madame," and addressing all of them, rather with the air of a hen mothering a flock of foolish chicks, she said, "Come along! Come along!" and led the way on Harry's arm.

In the center of the great mahogany table stood a Christmas tree, lighted, with gifts for each member of the family and for Harry Van Diver, each one selected by Mrs. Parkington and Mattie during long days of earnest shopping.

Mrs. Parkington put Madeleine's cowboy husband on her right and Harry Van Diver on her left. She did this in a half-conscious desire to annoy Amory. Beside the cowboy she placed Janie so that she might have the girl as near her as possible, then Amory, then Madeleine. (There was faint malice in this too because Amory with his St. Judes-Harvard mentality looked upon Madeleine and her amorous recklessness as a family disgrace.) Then came her great-grandson and then the Duchess and next to Harry Van

Diver, Helen, with her bitter mouth and complaining eyes. It was not a good arrangement, she knew, but considering the material, as good as any other. At eighty-four, after a well-conducted life spent in entertaining, she had at last earned the right to the most entertaining company which, among the men, was certainly Harry and the cowboy.

She decided that she liked the cowboy. Now and then she forgot his name completely. Until Madeleine had had enough of him and divorced him, he would always be simply "the cowboy" to her as Madeleine's first husband had been "the Argentine," her second "that Racquet Club boy," the third, "the horse trainer." It was much simpler that way.

He sat there beside her eating and answering her questions with a polite "yes, ma'am" or "no, ma'am," eating such food as he had never tasted before, with the little finger of his big bony hand crooked a little in spite of anything he could do about it. Mrs. Parkington knew that Madeleine had spoken to him about crooking his finger because every now and then he would remember and bring it down again alongside his other fingers. But almost at once it would fly up again into a crooked position. She supposed he had acquired the cocked finger trick out of an effort to make himself feel an equal of the divorcées he had met in Reno.

What a world! she thought, when a decent fellow like that has his natural good manners corrupted for the sake of a lot of concupiscent sluts who don't know their own minds.

She had no use for what she referred to as legal and dishonest adultery.

Once or twice Harry Van Diver on her left attempted to claim her attention and force her to "shift" the table but she said sharply, "Leave me in peace, Harry. I'm enjoying myself. This is a family party."

There were many things she would have liked to discover about the cowboy — whether he had lived with other women like Madeleine, what he thought of this queer family gathering. There was nothing lascivious in this curiosity; she only wanted to know for the most profound and human of reasons. Her interest was almost coldly scientific. She was curious because she liked him, because she felt sorry for him sitting here in this big elegant room, his face red with the effort of wearing a dinner jacket and trying to behave as he thought people should behave in such a house, with Madeleine's eyes fastened on him, devouring him. She wanted to say to him, "Don't worry about any of this. It's all claptrap and most of these people, my descendants, are vulgar and pretentious and they are vulgar and pretentious because they're afraid and they're afraid because in their hearts they are aware they are inferior and that not even money can alter that. Don't worry and fuss. It's all right!" But she was also wise enough to know that he would not understand a word of what she was saying and that such a speech would only confuse him further. They could never find each other through all the clutter of rubbish which complicated all the human relationships here in this room — Amory's stupidity and pretentiousness, the Duchess's despair and weariness, Helen's discontent and fear, Madeleine's air of being a thwarted Venus Genetrix and all the vague hampering things which came of their all being too rich. Janie, she thought, glancing fondly at the girl, was different. It was still possible to save her.

And Mrs. Parkington knew suddenly through the conversation she was making why she was bored. These people all around her save for Janie and perhaps the cowboy with his big hands and his way of addressing her as "ma'am" were all dead. They were deader than she would be when she lay in her coffin. Nothing had ever happened to them, not even to the Duchess with her air of being a tired tragedienne, not even to Madeleine to whom love was a matter of mechanics, like one of those machines which kept swallowing up things. To Harry, on her left, nothing whatever had ever happened. His whole life had been spent collecting pictures or sitting in the back of a box at the opera. He was, she thought, the best "box-sitter" in the world, the best "filler-in," the best gossip. People had sometimes whispered about his indeterminate sex, but Mrs. Parkington was shrewd about things like that. Harry had never had any sex at all. That was why he suggested marriage to her only when he knew that it was perfectly safe.

No, none of them would be sitting at her table if they had not been related to her, most of them the very fruit of her womb. They were "living dead" like the strange people who inhabited places like Pasadena and Santa Barbara.

She kept listening to two or three conversations at once, catching fragments of this one or that one, hoping that some phrase or remark might strike fire, like steel striking against flint, to illuminate and annihilate that sensation of suffocation she felt stealing over her as she listened to Harry's small talk.

And suddenly she was rewarded. It was something the Duchess said. Amory had been holding forth against Mr. Roosevelt and all Democrats. It was a familiar harangue into which he would plunge at the slightest invitation.

He was saying, "And look at Wall Street now! It used to be a barometer of the state of the country's prosperity. As a barometer it is destroyed. You can't tell anything about prosperity any more from a stock market report."

And then the Duchess began to be bored. The alcohol or the drugs or whatever it was which brought her spasmodic life, had ceased to function, and the massive weight of Amory's dullness began to be unendurable. She struck then, like an asp. She said, looking at him under her dull, heavy-lidded eyes, "I've been thinking, Amory, that it would be a good idea for your club to have its reunion this year in Sing-Sing. It might be kinder to all the boys who won't be able to get out."

Then Mrs. Parkington saw Amory's face turn first white and then red, a fierce apoplectic red which made Mrs. Parkington know that that was how he would die one day if he were not mercifully run over by an automobile or crashed in a plane before then. He stammered for a second and then said, "That was a rude and mannerless thing to say, Alice. You know as well as I do that neither Bill Jennings nor Percy Harris are guilty of any crime. They've been persecuted. That's all, and you know it."

But the stimulus which was driving the Duchess still operated and she said, "I've sometimes thought that my father — the gentleman from whom all our money comes — would have spent all his life in jail by the laws which exist nowadays — along with all the big shots of his time. They were all crooks and ruthless, every one of them."

It was Amory's wife who took up the battle for him. She said, "That was a shocking thing to say, Alice, about your own father."

But the Duchess only said, "Do you really *know* anything about my father — except what you've read in that apotheosis of hogwash written by a hack writer who needed money to pay his rent?"

Then Mrs. Parkington by an effort of will spiritually absented herself from the conversation. If they chose to brawl among themselves, that was their privilege. She had no intention of interfering. At least something was happening.

She turned to Madeleine's cowboy husband and said suddenly, "I was born in Leaping Rock, Nevada. It was quite a town in those days. Lola Montez came there." And as she spoke she heard the music beginning in the hall, soft music which had very little to do with the quality of the party (What could Viennese music mean to a man like Amory or his droop-mouthed wife or the cowboy?

Each year for more than ten years now, she had had in musicians to play at the Christmas party, music like this, soft and romantic which coming from the distant hall could not annoy the others, but which helped to soothe her own nerves and dissipate a little her own boredom. She heard it now, groping in her mind to place the name of the waltz, while it carried one part of her back, back into the remote, and glittering past out of which there emerged, even while she talked of Leaping Rock to the cowboy, romantic and glittering images, like figures out of a mist.

When she spoke the word "Leaping Rock" she struck fire. The cowboy said, "Do I know Leaping Rock, ma'am? . . . like the back of my own hand. I was born in the hills not ten miles from there. When I was just a kid we used to dare each other to go alone into the Opera House. People said it was haunted."

"It probably was," said Mrs. Parkington. "Is it still there?"

"No, ma'am, the roof fell in five years ago."

Then suddenly while the cowboy was talking about Leaping Rock and the color of the dolomite peaks to the west of it in the early dawn when the sun came up beyond the range of mountains on the other side of the valley, she remembered the name of the waltz they were now playing; it was "The Music of the Spheres" and suddenly she forgot Leaping Rock and was in a baroque ballroom in Vienna. It was all peach pink and pale blue and gilt and someone was saying, ". . . *présenter le Comte Eric Wallstein.*" At the same time she was aware that the cowboy had come to life. Quite suddenly he was flesh and blood — very much flesh and blood, and no longer an automaton responding to strings held by Madeleine.

Then she heard Madeleine saying above the cowboy's talk about Nevada, "Grandmother, don't you think we should leave the table now?"

"Yes, my dear," said Mrs. Parkington, taking the napkin from her lap and rising. She hated to break off the talk with the cowboy. He was enjoying himself for the first time — perhaps for the first time since Madeleine had snatched him up and brought him east. His extraordinarily clear blue eyes were shining. The shyness was gone. He called her "ma'am" quite naturally now, and not like a Hollywood actor playing the role of a cowboy.

"You must come to see me while you're

here," she said as she rose from the table, "Come in to tea and we'll talk our fill about Nevada."

The rest of the evening passed for Mrs. Parkington in a cloud of weariness, save for two moments, one which happened as they left the dining-room when Amory came up to her side and said, "Could I speak to you privately, Grandmother?"

She looked up at him suddenly wondering what it was he wanted of her, and was struck again by the stupidity of his big, floridly handsome face. He had been told that he was a shrewd operator in the market, and he believed, she knew, that he was a shrewd operator. She thought, He is a fool beside the Major. There aren't any longer men of the Major's stature. He was the real thing.

She said, "Of course, Amory. Let's go into the small sitting-room."

He followed her into the room, closing the door behind him. It was a small room, intimate and feminine in its softness and elegance. Rather slyly she watched him and even by the dim light she saw that with the closing of the door his manner had changed. The air of confidence and conceit which approached arrogance, seemed to melt away. She knew that he was at his best with a crowd of men when he was acting the role of a "big shot." When he was left alone with her he grew uneasy and almost timid, and she wondered whether he behaved in the same fashion when he was alone with another man. She had never been taken in by him. All his defenses, concocted of family, of clubs, of snobbery and complacency, of wealth were down when he faced her, because she had no proper respect for any of these things when they were used as he used them.

Now as he closed the door and faced her, she had the impression that not only was he uneasy but frightened. He stood there for a single unbearable moment facing her in silence, until she sat down and said, "What is it, Amory?"

He too sat down and lighted a cigar, "It's about money, Grandmother."

There was something absurd about his addressing her as "Grandmother." He was himself over fifty and his pompousness made him seem older. In any case she disliked the habit of married relatives addressing in-laws as "Grandmother" and "Mother."

"What's wrong?" she asked. "I thought you'd weathered the storm. Everyone says you were remarkably clever during the crash."

He hesitated for a moment. "It isn't that.

We weathered that all right. It's only that a loan for a few weeks — six months at the most — would be a great help just now."

She did not answer him but sat waiting, with half-deliberate cruelty, putting the burden of the whole thing upon him. After a moment he said, "I'm a little short just now. I got in rather deeply on some utilities business which didn't turn out very well. The government has ruined the utilities market like everything else."

"I thought the government had put an end to that sort of gambling."

"It wasn't gambling," he said dully, and she was aware suddenly that be was not only afraid but tired. At the same time she remembered how he had snubbed the shy, nervous cowboy with the clear blue eyes.

"How much?" she asked bluntly.

He did not answer her at once. When he did answer he said, looking away from her, "About seven hundred thousand."

"That's a great deal of money."

Still looking away from her, he said, "I thought that . . . until it's paid, you could charge it up against my share of the inheritance."

The answer not only shocked her, but made it impossible for her to answer immediately.

After a moment she said, "I'm not in the

grave yet, Amory."

"I didn't mean that."

"In any case, it is your wife's inheritance, Amory. The Major left everything to me to dispose of as I saw fit."

"I'm sorry. I didn't mean to be tactless."

"Never mind," she sighed. "But seven hundred thousand is a great deal of money. When everything is washed up after I'm dead, Helen's share might not amount to that much."

He looked at her in surprise and alarm, and she added, "There are quite a number of heirs and a lot of inheritance taxes." She smiled, "Money isn't what it once was, you know."

"Who should know better than a stockbroker?"

She kept hearing the waltz played by the orchestra in the hall. She wanted to be done with Amory, to escape from him and everyone and everything like him, so she said, "In any case I couldn't lend even a much smaller amount without knowing the details."

She remembered that he had thrust out his lower lip. It gave him a sullen, almost evil expression — one which his wife must have seen many times. It occurred to her that perhaps that was one reason why Helen's mouth sagged at the corners. It was the expression of a spoiled willful boy who has been crossed. He had been born into a world with every possible advantage and taught that there was some special quality about all Stilhams and at fifty he still resented any doubt regarding himself or his ability or his remarkable gifts.

He said, "I can't tell you the details now."

"Can't you raise the money among your partners?"

"They haven't that much liquid cash."

"I have the others to consider. In a sense it's their money I should be lending you. Would you want me to go to them for their permission?"

"No. They wouldn't give it . . . certainly not Madeleine or 'the Duchess.' They've always disliked me for reasons I've never been able to understand."

She moved as if to rise, and said, "In any case I couldn't lend all that money without knowing everything about your financial circumstances. That's what bankers ask, isn't it?"

"Yes."

"Well, when you choose to tell me, Amory, we can consider its possibilities."

He was silent then and his silence made the old woman's restlessness and desire to escape being shut in with him almost unbearable.

He said, "If I find it's necessary I'll tell you everything. The circumstances may be desperate."

"Even if you failed, I should always see to it that Helen and the children are taken care of."

"Fail?" be echoed. "Me fail?"

She was aware of a gratifying sense of power and of a satisfaction in using it almost cruelly. But the man was a fool to think all he needed do was to ask for seven hundred thousand dollars and receive it. In any case the interview was getting nowhere. She stood up, impatient to return to the music.

"I'm sorry, Amory, to refuse you. You must have friends who can raise that amount of money — surely out of Wall Street and all the banks, and all your friends in Harvard."

"It isn't the way it used to be when the Major was alive. Money men aren't allowed to stand together nowadays. It's even against their God-damned New Deal laws for a friend to stand by a friend." He flushed and said, "Forgive me for swearing. I forgot myself."

She laughed. "I lived for forty years with the Major." Then she moved toward the door. "Well, if worse comes to worst and you see fit to explain everything to me, come back again."

He held the door open for her and she went out. Out of the small room she felt free again and relieved. The little band was playing the "Skater's Waltz" now. That music too was filled with memories, of another, a gayer, less strained and tormented world. She kept seeing the baroque ballroom in Vienna and the station platform in Salzburg.

She wasn't allowed to finish her conversation with the cowboy because Madeleine whisked him away a little while after she entered the room.

"We're taking a plane, Grandmother, for Nassau in the morning. I hope you'll forgive us."

"Of course, my dear."

The cowboy said, "Good night, ma'am, and thank you for a fine evening and a fine supper."

As his blue eyes met hers there was a twinkle in them which made her feel suddenly very young. It reminded her that the two of them shared a secret from all the others.

They knew the color of the peak on the far side of Leaping Rock when the sun came up over the range to the east. She must have been, she thought, at least fifty years old when the cowboy was born and she had not seen Leaping Rock in more than sixty years, but it did not matter. The peak would still be there when both of them were long dead and there would be others not yet conceived who would share their secret and feel about the great peak as they felt. It was very odd, she thought, that this cowboy born and brought up in Nevada, should, like "The Music of the Spheres," make her think of Eric.

She said, "Remember you promised to come to tea one day," . . . and softly with the coquetry of a young woman she added, "alone." Quickly she turned to Madeleine, "It's only because we wanted to talk about Leaping Rock and the old days."

"Sure, I understand," said Madeleine. "He's crazy about it out there. He doesn't even want to go to Nassau."

The other moment came at the end of the evening when as they all rose to leave, Janie said, "Granny, can I talk to you a minute after the others have gone?"

"Of course, my child."

"You aren't too tired?"

"Not in the least tired."

A moment before she bad been desperately tired but when Janie spoke, the weariness vanished. The child would scarcely understand that a woman of eighty-four could be flattered by so simple a thing as the request of a child of eighteen to talk to her.

Janie was not obviously pretty; she was at once something more and something less than that, with her fair hair and blue eyes and perfect skin. The mouth was too wide, the forehead too high, the nose too tilted for the accepted standard of banal American prettiness. It was the play of expression which made her extraordinarily attractive, the mobility of the intelligent wedge-shaped small face which at one moment could be dark and sullen and the next brilliant as the morning sun. She had the sort of looks which would make her a beauty at thirty-five when other women were just beginning to fade. She had, even at eighteen, what none of the others had ever had — the elements of distinction.

The girl asked her brother to wait for her in the hall below, and when they had all gone, she said, "Granny, I'm in love."

The old woman smiled, "In love . . . with whom?"

"You've never heard of him."

"Do your father and mother like that?"

"No, that's the trouble."

"Who is he?"

"Well, he works for the government. He is twenty-seven years old and he was born in South Bend, Indiana."

Mrs. Parkington smiled again, "Now I understand why your father objects."

"Mama is just as bad."

"How did you meet him?"

"That's it. I met him through Father. Father invited him to the country for a weekend on business. The funny thing is that Father seemed to like him very much at first and told me to be nice to him and give him a good time. So I did my best and then later on when I went out with him in New York they were both angry."

"What did they say?" asked Mrs. Parkington.

"They said he was a nobody. That he had no money and no future, and that I wasn't to see him because it might grow serious and at my age I wasn't capable of judging about things like that . . . all the kind of talk I've heard in movies and novels."

Mrs. Parkington's face grew serious. "Of course they may be right. What is he like?"

Janie looked away from her toward the fireplace as if she were trying to summon up a clear picture of the young man. Her great-grandmother watched her, thinking, How young she is! How odd that this thing should have skipped two generations only to appear again in the child of Helen and Amory! How very unlikely!

The girl was talking, saying, "Well, he's

tall. He has big hands but they're beautiful. He has very nice white teeth. He has black, rather wavy hair . . . plenty of it, and he's dark but not the sallow kind of darkness. It's the healthy kind." She laughed, "He has rosy cheeks and a nice voice." For a moment she felt about as if searching for something and then said, "And he's clean. He's so nice and clean."

Mrs. Parkington chuckled, "I didn't ask for a portrait in technicolor or a certificate of sanitation. I only meant why do you think you're in love?"

Now the girl looked at her and smiled. There was something about Janie's smile which could melt granite. When she smiled the big mouth curled up at the corners.

Now she said, smiling, "I don't know, Granny. That's a tough one. I love to be with him and I feel sure inside me that if I waited for fifty years I'd never find anyone I'd like better." Shyly she looked down at her hands, "I've even thought about the children I'm going to have, and I'd like to have him for the father."

Mrs. Parkington's face was serious as she watched the girl. "Well," she said, "those are very sound reasons and very modern. Is he serious?"

"Oh, he's very serious about some things,

but he has a sense of humor, a wonderful sense of humor."

"Where did he go to school?"

"To Wisconsin State and after that to law school at Columbia."

"I see. He belongs to the future rather than to the past."

Suddenly an extraordinary light came into the face of the girl. "That's it, Granny! That's what I feel, only I never was able to put it into words. It's very clever of you to understand."

"Maybe it's because of my age."

"He's not like any of the boys I know. I don't mean anything against them . . . the kind of boys Father and Mama would like to have me marry . . . only they always seem so . . . I don't know. They don't seem to want to go anywhere. There doesn't seem to be any place for them to go. They seem empty . . . and dead. I don't want that kind of life. I want it to be exciting. He makes everything . . . the present and the future seem exciting."

Mrs. Parkington sighed, "Yes, I know. I said that once, a long time ago. And it was exciting too. That's why you're here, my dear."

"You *do* know what I mean, Granny."

"Yes, I think I do." She rose and said,

"It's very late, my dear. I'll tell you what you do. You bring him to tea with me, some afternoon . . . soon."

"Oh, could I, Granny? That's sweet of you."

"Shall we say Thursday?"

"I'll ask him. He's awfully busy, but I'm sure he could get away early."

The old woman kissed her and then stood by the fire looking after the girl as she left the room and went down the stairway to join her brother. When she had gone, Mrs. Parkington touched the bell and while she waited for Taylor to appear, she thought how like Janie she must have been more than half a century ago in Leaping Rock — how extraordinary it was that she herself had come out of a mining camp and Janie out of this decadent world which had surrounded her tonight, a world as different from Leaping Rock as day from night. She had asked Janie to bring her young man to tea rather than to dinner because tea did not involve a whole evening. Janie might be wrong; he might be terrible. Mrs. Parkington knew a great deal about love and what it could do to you.

Then Taylor appeared and she said, "It's very late, Taylor. I shouldn't bother about clearing away tonight. I shall be out for lunch tomorrow and you'll have the whole day."

"Thank you, madame."

"Did you have a good Christmas?"

"Yes, madame. You're not tired?"

"No, Taylor." She started toward the door and he followed her. "There's no need," she said, "I'll walk up. I think I'd like to."

"Very good, madame."

She didn't know why she chose to climb the stairs, save that it suited her mood. She went slowly, thoughtfully, as if at each step she were climbing into another world, the world of memory, as if each step took her deeper and deeper into the past.

II

Each morning she stood by the window packing lunches as the sun came up behind the mountains. The spectacle began with the rosy light striking the great peak on the far side of the flat green valley long before the sun, hidden by the mountains, was itself visible. A river of clear water ran down the center of the valley, shallow and clean, wandering this way and that lazily in the sunshine of the dry season. Willows and cottonwoods and sedge grass, haunted by wild birds, grew along its flanks, and all the year round, even when there was no rain, the trees stayed green and brilliant against the yellow burnt grass of the valley and the red of the mountains across the wide valley from the boardinghouse.

For it was really a boardinghouse and not a hotel for all its high-sounding name, and it stood opposite the Wilder Gap Saloon on the long single street of Leaping Rock with its back turned toward the peak so that Susie, working in the kitchen, could look across the valley. At seventeen she did not understand why the view from the kitchen window made her heart sing. It was vast and free and open, so vast that the invasion of man could never alter nor wholly subdue its beauty, so filled with splendor that there were moments when it seemed to her a valley out of paradise. And as the day wore on, and the sun swung through the arc of heaven, it remained not one valley; it became many valleys, changing as the light altered, quivering at noon in an iridescent mirage of heat, deepening into cool rich purple as the night fell.

There was the early morning when all the gaudy, rough street of Leaping Rock, lined with brothels and saloons and gambling establishments, lay in a cool blue shadow while the rest of the valley warmed slowly to the pink glow of the sunrise. Then there was noon when all the valley was flooded with hot, clear, light which made the feathery leaves of the pepper trees in the dirty yard outside the window hang limply and the pale willows and the shining cottonwoods lining the river bed danced and swayed in the heat. And there was the afternoon, just before sunset, when the blue shadow of the great mountain crept across the flat land slowly, gently, inevitably, bathing the whole landscape in a blue dusk which at last engulfed Leaping Rock itself as the miners returned and the oil lights began to glow in the brothels and saloons and overhead the sky turned from red to flamingo pink to the blue of azure and at last to the deep blue of velvet and the stars came out like diamonds. The nights were best of all — the clear, dry cool nights when the air was like the champagne sold in the Opera House bar and the great vastness of the mountains melted away into darkness and there was only space and emptiness and a sense of freedom and an ecstasy of the spirit.

Susie always saw the sunrise because she and her mother got out of bed in the darkness to prepare the lunches for the men going off to the mines. While the pink light increased and the mountain walls emerged again from the darkness like a transparency at the Opera House, Susie and her mother packed the sandwiches and poured the coffee into containers. Her mother was a spare and active woman rather like a beautiful whippet with small blue eyes and a dimpled mouth and a twinkle. She was one of those women who worked hard through some fierce inner compulsion. Life without physical action, without hard work would have been intolerable to her, and in Susie's spare trim figure there was something of the same passionate restlessness and desperate need for activity. But in Susie these things were tempered by a romantic feeling which at moments seemed to hypnotize her into a kind of dreaming peace.

The Grand Hotel was the best establishment of its kind in the whole bawdy town. Its rooms and linen, kept by Chinese servants, were clean and fresh and cool. Its food was plain but good, and about the parlor and even the little drinking and smoking room there was an air of home, born out of the spirit of Susie's mother, who would, if it had been possible, have mothered the whole world.

From her mother Susie got her fineness of bone and the fineness of feature and the elusive look of race, and from her too Susie got the shrewdness and that curious objectivity which protected and carried her through all the shocks and tragedies of her life. It gave her the power to stand aside watching herself in the very midst of calamity, as if at times she were two persons, one herself and the other a kind of narrator in a Greek tragedy. People said sometimes that she was hardhearted and unfeeling, and toward the end of her life they sometimes said that only a hardhearted woman could have survived the tragedies which happened to her. But it was only that people did not understand. It was this quality, inherited from her mother and the product of her mother's stern training, which stood by her on the morning the whole life of Leaping Rock and the valley was shattered by catastrophe.

From her father, Susie reflected long afterward, she had gained nothing save perhaps the good humor and calmness of disposition which her mother had never known. Her mother fidgeted and worried and because of this the Grand Hotel was the best establishment in Leaping Rock. Her father never worried at all, and so everyone loved him although he never amounted to much and his family would have had hard going indeed but for his wife. Susie loved her father and she only respected her mother.

The knowledge of this curious fact troubled and sometimes distressed her as she stood at the window of the kitchen looking across the enchanted valley. It troubled her again and again through her long life — that so many people she respected she could not love at all and so many people she loved were not worth her respect.

That was one of the things which made her think a great deal about Augustus Parkington. She respected him and in a way she loved him, not the way of course in which she loved her father. At seventeen she was beginning to find out the different ways in which you could love people. Certainly they were not all alike. Her father she loved because he was gentle and humorous and never worried. Sometimes she thought she loved him because he was so utterly different from her mother who did everything well and thoroughly, who worried all day long and was never still from the time she rose as the dawn came up over the valley until the lights began to go out in the saloons and gambling houses along Nevada Street. Her father worked. He had a kind of job checking the men in and out of the mines; but he did not allow it to trouble him. He had no desire to become superintendent of the works or to go out prospecting in the hope of making a sudden great fortune like Augustus Parkington. He was simply content to sit in his little cage, smiling and swapping stories with the men as they went in and out, just as he liked sitting on the front porch of the Grand Hotel entertaining the guests. They, like Susie herself, always felt better at the sight of him, a big, rather soft man, with a twinkle in his gray eyes when he returned from the mines in the evening.

Augustus Parkington was very different. In the first place he came from the East, from New York, and he was what Susie's mother called "a flashy dresser." Even when he went up to the mines he wore his best clothes with shoes carefully polished by Sam Young, the Chinese boy, wearing the finest silk shirt with a purple cravat fastened with a diamond pin and a heavy gold watch chain across his checkered waistcoat. He wore a big diamond on the little finger. The only man Susie had ever seen who dressed nearly so richly was Aristides Vedder, the gambler, who made the circuit of Leadville, Virginia City and Leaping Rock over and over again many times a year. But of course the fine clothes worn by Aristides Vedder did not make the same effect as when worn by Augustus.

When Susie wasn't careful she found herself thinking of him as "Augustus" although she had no right to any such familiarity. He was, after all, a middle-aged man, thirty-three on his next birthday, and he was important. He owned half of the great Juno Mine which kept on and on pouring silver down the side of the great mountain on the opposite side of the valley. And people said he owned railroads in the East and was a big stock operator. They said he was a millionaire and that he didn't know how rich he was and didn't care, that he wasn't interested in money but in the making of it.

Susie didn't know much about the East so the stories about him had no very great reality. To her all the stories had a little of the fantastic quality of the *Thousand and One Nights.* She had never been east of Denver and the East seemed a foreign country and

New York a place filled with big restaurants and bright lights and beautiful women and rich men. While she worked about the kitchen with her mother, she thought a great deal about it and how she must some day go there, for Susie inside her small, trim body had bursting ambition. That was what made her resemble her mother rather than her father. Sometimes at night she couldn't sleep because the ambitions kept churning and rumbling about inside her, as if she had bad indigestion.

And the beauty of the rich valley didn't help her to stifle the yearnings. It was grand and splendrous, she was aware, but she also knew that it was barren. Leaping Rock held no future for herself. As she grew older she began to understand what it was that made her mother so restless and miserable and busy, so that all day long until late at night she hurried from one thing to another, making work for herself where before there had been none. All day, all night, until she fell asleep her mother was running away from something, and presently Susie understood what it was.

The discovery came to her one day in the very middle of the morning. Surprisingly, in the very middle of their work while they were dusting the parlor, her mother sat down abruptly and said, "Susie, there's something

I must say to you.

And Susie was frightened, because her mother had never before done anything like this. She lived perpetually shut in, behind a kind of wall which came between herself and Susie. And now Susie was aware with the sharp and puzzled instinct of an adolescent girl that the wall was down, that for the first time her mother meant to talk of what went on deep inside her behind that wall. She sat down on the edge of the horsehair sofa, her toes pointing in, filled with shyness. At first she thought her mother was going to tell her that she had some fatal malady and was about to die.

But it wasn't that. Her mother clasped her thin, hard hands together and said abruptly, "When you're eighteen, Susie, I'm going to send you away."

As if it cost her a great effort she said nothing more until Susie murmured, "Yes, Ma. Where?"

"To the East, Susie . . . to your Great Aunt Sapphira in Vermont."

And again Susie was frightened. She had never seen her Great Aunt Sapphira but she knew that her father always spoke of Sapphira as the family witch. Susie didn't even know then whether she wanted to go to Vermont. It was the East but not the East she had dreamed of. And she loved the valley. It was the valley and the great mountain she knew she would miss most of all . . . more even than her father.

But her mother was going on. "I want you to have things in life which I've never had, Susie. I wanted a great many things — power and satisfaction and money and diamonds. . . . " Her eyes flashed suddenly and she spoke with firmness, almost with shame, "Yes, diamonds and power. When I was your age I wanted to be somebody in the world, I thought it was going to be like that when I married your father, but it wasn't." She sighed and said, "Your father is a good man. He's never caused me any trouble or any unhappiness, but it just wasn't in him, I guess. He didn't want the things I wanted. They didn't signify. He didn't value them. I could have got them in my own way once — a woman's way — but I didn't and I don't regret it now . . . only sometimes. I want you to have all those things, Susie, that I didn't have. I want you to live nice and in a civilized world, not a place like Leaping Rock. There's nothing here for you. You're mighty pretty and it would be a shame if you were just to settle down and work and get hands like mine."

She watched Susie sitting on the edge of

the sofa. When she had finished Susie didn't say anything and her mother said, "Don't you want those things, Susie?"

After a moment the girl said, "Yes, maybe. I don't know. Only I don't like leaving you and Pa . . . and the valley."

She was only fourteen then and the things her mother talked about didn't mean much to her. Suddenly her mother stood up and resumed her dusting now, furiously as if she hated the prim shabby sofas and chairs. Then she said, "We'll never speak of it again."

They never did speak of it again, but as Susie grew older she began to understand about the things her mother talked of. The understanding came slowly, out of books and because the germs of the same ambition which tortured her defeated mother were there inside her own breast. But most of all, it was Augustus Parkington who made her understand. When he talked to her about the East and the great world outside the valley, in the purple evenings after the sun had disappeared behind the great mountain, the fabulous world of the East became alive and real, perhaps because he loved it so much or perhaps because his own immense vitality and enthusiasm swept you with him, as flood-water rushing down El Dorado Canyon in the spring carried everything before it. In Topeka and Chicago they said Augustus Parkington could sell a whore-house to a Baptist preacher.

He would sit there on the front porch of the Grand Hotel, big and handsome in his fine clothes and jewelry, talking in his rich deep voice — a voice which embraced and seduced you, man or woman, young or old — and presently you were completely under his spell and fearful that he would stop talking and go away because after he had gone the world about you for a long time afterward seemed a tired and empty place.

He liked Susie and he nearly always treated her like a little girl, even when she had turned seventeen and her figure filled out the calico dresses her mother made for her. But there were moments when Susie knew that something different had come into the relationship between them. It was something she did not understand and so it alarmed and at the same time excited her. Because she was intensely feminine she became aware as she grew older of the maleness of Major Parkington. His mere presence, on those yearly visits, made the whole hotel seem a more exciting place. She had, once or twice, overheard conversations in which people talked about Major Parkington and the way he had with women, but this did not mean much to her. She knew nothing about love at all and even less about sex, and the idea of marrying a man as old as Augustus Parkington was preposterous. A girl of seventeen marrying an old man of thirty-three! She only hoped that somehow, somewhere, some time she would meet a suitor her own age who was half as fine as the Major. Sometimes she wondered how he could be interested in talking to anyone so young and insignificant as herself.

It was only long afterward that she came to understand what he was doing on those evenings. She understood after she came to know him and his way with women. He had spent those hours talking to her because he could not help himself, because always in the big handsome body and mind was the urge to woo and seduce this young girl who was so simple and straightforward and lacking in feminine tricks. Her very lack of coquetry, her very simplicity at once defeated him and enticed him. And always at the back of his character was that disconcerting charm and niceness which kept him from carrying through so base a desire as the seduction of a nice girl and the daughter of so respectable and worthy a woman as the proprietress of the Grand Hotel. He was always like that, during all his life; at the very moment when you were prepared and reconciled forever to dismissing him as an unmitigated scoundrel he did something utterly disarming and generous and nice which confounded you and you found yourself in the position of beginning all over again.

Long afterward she understood what he was doing when he "wasted" his time talking to her. He was wooing her, making love to her, caressing her without once speaking of love or even touching her. He did it with his voice, his clear blue eyes, his manner. It was as if there were an aura about him which reached out and enveloped you, filling you with strange half-realized thoughts and desires.

A dozen times during the evening the face of her mother would appear in the window behind them and then disappear again like a ghost. And again it was only long afterward, years after her mother's death, that Susie understood what was in her mother's mind. She was thinking, If he wants her he must marry her. He could give her everything and Susie is smart enough to profit by what he can give her. But he will never marry her. She would be of help to him in what he wants from the world, but he isn't clever enough to understand that.

And so her mother kept watch, returning again and again to the window. Major Parkington was her mother's best boarder. If Susie could keep him at the Grand Hotel on his visits to Leaping Rock, it was all right so long as there was no monkey business. But he must never so much as touch her. . . .

It might never have happened but for the explosion. Long afterward Susie learned that many great things, many sweeping currents changing the whole of one's life came of isolated, sometimes small happenings, apparently unrelated to the events surrounding them.

On the morning of the explosion she was alone in the big kitchen peeling potatoes and watching the wide valley. Now and then a wagon or a man on horseback appeared on the thin ribbon of a road which ran from the town of Leaping Rock straight across to the great mountain where the mines were. It was a hot morning and at moments the waves of heat rising from the sandy floor of the valley would appear to lift the lone horseman or wagon from the road high into the air and turn him upside down. Then a sudden gust of wind would flatten the glittering tongues of heat and the horseman would appear again right side up on the road, moving toward the thread of river bordered by cottonwood trees. Presently the purple which veiled the bottom of the great mountain at sunrise was gone and with it the deep rose light that painted the very top, and then the whole mountain stood suddenly revealed in the blistering heat of midday, naked and bare and ugly, a terrifying mass of rock streaked with copper and silver. Up there on the face of the mountain, in the small cleft which looked as if it had been made by the tomahawk of some great Indian god, was the mine. Up there among the myriads of ants who were the Chinese and Irish who worked the mine, were her father sitting in his cage, telling stories, and her mother who had crossed the valley in the buckboard a little after sunrise to take food to her father and Major Augustus Parkington. They had stayed the night rather than cross the wide valley after dark.

Susie had finished the potatoes and was emptying the peelings into the slop bucket for the pigs when it occurred. As she straightened her body to close the door she saw, high up in the cleft, a sudden vast flower of smoke. At first it was like a ball of the cotton which they were trying to grow in the wide flat valley. Then slowly in the hot air it began to spread and at the same time the sound of the explosion entered the town. The windows rattled with the impact and

Susie felt herself thrown against the door and then from along the single street bordered by brothels and gambling houses and stores there came the confused sound of many frightened people. There were screams and shouts and the firing of guns and the brayings of donkeys and the neighing of horses all mingled together.

She thought dully, They are up there, Ma and Pa and the Major. They've all been killed. For it seemed to her as the smoke rose and spread like the opening of a gigantic flower, that no one in that narrow cleft could be alive.

And almost at once in the narrow straight road there appeared a hurrying procession of figures, some on horses, some on donkeys, some in buckboards and still others on foot, running. They were coming out from the town, crossing the valley toward the great mountain.

For a moment, standing there by the door, she felt a wild impulse to join the mob, and then a quiet voice deep inside her, the voice which was to speak to her again and again during her long life, said, "There is no use in your going. There is nothing you can do. You will be more useful here if you are calm and go about your work. They will be coming back after a time. They will want bandages and hot water and beds and food."

And so she went back again into the house and set to work preparing all the things which might be needed. She thought, Perhaps Ma and Pa and the Major are dead or maybe they are only hurt. All I can do now is to pray for them and work.

And as she worked she fought back both tears and terror. Her hands shook so that it was difficult for her to tear the old sheets into strips for bandages, and presently two of the harlots from Mrs. LaVerne's establishment came in, lost and terrified. They helped with the work and after that she felt better.

Presently from the cleft in the mountain on the opposite side of the valley, figures small as ants began to trickle down toward the valley and late in the afternoon, the first of the wounded and dying began to cross the hot valley, some walking, some on donkeyback and some in carts. But still there was no message or any news.

As she worked, Susie and the harlots sometimes talked and sometimes were silent but never did they speak of the mine or the disaster except to say now and then, "Someone will be coming soon."

And Susie who had never spoken to such women before, divined that they were human.

She learned that one of them was called Belle Slocomb and was born in Providence, Rhode Island. The other was a German girl called Minnie Oberland who came from Cincinnati. She was a little frightened at the prospect of her mother's returning to find the two girls in the hotel. Probably her mother would call them evil names and send them out of the house — that is, if she were not already dead. . . . But Susie on her own felt no special horror or strangeness about the two girls. They seemed a little loud and the color in their cheeks a little violent and Minnie Oberland's gold teeth a little strange and unnatural, but otherwise they were not much different from all the women she knew. They were not at all what she had expected women like them to be; smoke did not pour from their nostrils and they did not have tails. Minnie cried a good deal; it seemed that she was in love with one of the men who worked up there in the cleft of the great mountain. The one called Belle Slocomb did not cry, although her eyes at times seemed to glisten with an unnatural brightness. She said she had been in love once and that was enough and that she was finished with everything of that sort.

Then at the hour when the mountain, falling into the shadow cast by the setting sun seemed to sink down into a haze of blue shadow, Susie heard, during one of the silences that fell upon them, the sound of footsteps on the porch — a heavy man's footstep which in a moment she recognized. It was Major Parkington. It was odd that her heart should tell her who it was before his own big figure appeared in the doorway.

He had his arm in a sling and his wavy black hair was clotted with blood and his handsome face was streaked with dust. At sight of him one of the harlots — Belle Slocomb — said, "Just what happened, Gus?" She seemed, Susie thought, to know him very well.

He sat down heavily on the sofa as if he no longer had the strength to walk or to stand and the two harlots bent over him. Susie stood very still watching him. She wanted to do what the harlots had done. She wanted to touch him, to push the curly black hair back from his eyes; but it was as if she were paralyzed and could not move. He looked at her and when his blue eyes met hers she knew that her father and mother were dead.

He said to the harlots, "Go away, girls. I want to speak to Susie alone."

As if they understood what had happened, Belle said, "All right, Gus." Then she looked at Susie and crossed the room and putting her arms about her, kissed her. She didn't say anything, but turning away she put her arm about the shoulder of the German girl from Cincinnati and led her out of the room.

Then the Major looked again at Susie and Susie said, "Both?"

"Both."

Susie did not cry. No tears would come now, perhaps because she had known somehow from the moment of the explosion what he was telling her now. She had had moments like that before, moments of curious clairvoyance, and she was to have many more of them again and again at odd moments of crisis in her life.

She felt suddenly faint and would have fallen but for the Major's arm which slipped quickly around her small waist. It was a strong arm; they said in Leaping Rock that he was stronger than any of the miners.

When she opened her eyes she was lying on the sofa. The Major was sitting beside her and the two harlots, their faces soft now with sympathy, were near, the one holding a basin of water and the other an empty brandy glass.

The blonde one asked, "Are you all right now, honey?"

"I'm all right," Susie managed to say.

Then the Major said again, "Go away, girls. If I want you I'll call you. You might help downstairs, there'll be a lot of work to do down there."

They went away and when the door closed, the Major took her hand and said, "I'm going to take care of you now. You're going away with me, back to New York."

She didn't answer him but only lay with her eyes closed, pressing the palms of her hands against the eyeballs and trying to understand what had happened to her and what was to come next.

When she did not answer, he said again, "That's right, isn't it? You're going to let me take care of you?"

She made a great effort to pull herself back out of the fog which she felt gathering about her. She made a great effort to remember the good manners her mother had taught her and give him a polite answer.

"I'll take care of everything," he said, "You won't need to worry about anything."

She understood that he was trying to be kind, but also it seemed to her odd that he should be in such haste to settle everything. In spite of the harsh realities of Leaping Rock, there was about her a kind of innocence which remained with her to the end of her life, even at the Christmas dinner when she watched granddaughter Madeleine and the cowboy, knowing perfectly well what lay at the bottom of the relationship between them. As an old woman although there was no knowledge beyond her, she still kept the same purifying innocence of spirit.

Now without looking up at him she asked, "Do you mean . . . will I marry you?" And she heard him say, "Yes . . . why, yes . . . of course," followed by a cough as if he were astonished and embarrassed.

For a second, even in the midst of shock and sorrow, she found herself thinking, That would mean I could escape. Now Ma and Pa are dead there is nothing to keep me in Leaping Rock. I could see the world . . . I could do everything. . . . All the things she had dreamed of as she peeled potatoes and washed dishes looking out across the hot valley at the great pink and purple mountain. She had seen herself glittering with diamonds descending a great stairway. She had seen herself driving out in a carriage with wonderful black horses and a coachman and footman . . . sitting at the head of a table where there were ambassadors and millionaires . . . speaking French, buying her clothes in Paris . . . going to London and Washington.

In a flashing, glittering second all the silly

dreams darted, like fireflies, through her brain.

He was patting her hand gently now and the gesture irritated her. It was as if she were a pet dog he was consoling. Even in the heat she was aware of warmth in his hand. She said, "I don't know. Don't ask me now." And then the tears came flooding into her eyes so that she could not speak.

He stayed there with her until at last the sobbing ceased and, relaxed, she fell asleep. Then he went out and called the two harlots and told them to let her lie there until she wakened and go down to the kitchen and see that the supper was prepared for the boarders who had not been killed or injured in the disaster. Himself, he washed up and returned to the mine.

III

There were times when Mrs. Parkington grew bored and moments when she grew a little weary of the sloppy winter weather in New York. She was fastidious and hated slush and liquid soot under foot. But she preferred New York even in the depths of winter to going off to Florida or California. In the old days she occasionally went to Paris or London in winter, out of season. She liked cities out of season because they had for her an air of reality, not being overrun by strangers who did not belong there, who did not have jobs and roots and families. The Major had loved resorts, possibly because he was a gambler, and in the last years of his life she had had plenty of experience with resorts — surrounded always by what the Duchess called "international white trash." She had loved the Pyrenees and the blue Mediterranean and the damp rich fertility of the Norman countryside beyond the channel coast, but circumstances had never permitted her to develop any contact with them. She was always, wherever she went, Mrs. Parkington or Madame Parkington or Signora Parkington, the wife of the incredibly rich and handsome old Major Parkington who had come in on his yacht and was staying at the Splendide or the Carlton or the Hermitage, a robust old gentleman who ordered only the best food and champagne and rooms and lost fortunes at roulette and *chemin de fer*. Now and then she had managed to establish incognito some sort of contact with the people who lived in or near the great resorts — the small shopkeepers, the market gardeners, the farmers — but always very quickly they discovered her identity and then everything changed and neither the small people nor herself any longer had any reality. It was as if the money, all the great Parkington fortune, exerted a kind of evil enchantment, forcing her always back into the society of people who had at first amused her but whom she had come after a time to detest as frivolous and stupid and above all boring in their monotony. The Major, in his insensibility, had never seemed to be annoyed by them. He had gone on and on drinking and gambling and eating, carrying on business by cablegram, until the day at Cannes when he fell down dead as a turnip under extremely peculiar circumstances and set her free to live as she pleased. From that day on she avoided resorts and saw only the people for whom she felt affection or whose brains or talent she held in respect. It was a rule which she broke only once a year when she entertained her own family at Christmas dinner.

And so she stayed on in New York right through the winter in her own pleasant, luxurious house, the house which she had planned and furnished as a comfortable nest in which to die.

On Thursday after Christmas she came down for tea early, with impatience, because Janie was bringing her young man to call. She had made it a special occasion, with fresh flowers and shortbread and scones, and put on her new black dress from Bendel's and the new hat, the one with a stiff chic bow on the side, which sat pertly and with a youthful air on her white hair. She wanted to make a good impression upon Janie's young man. As she stood in her dressing-room regarding herself in the old cheval glass, she suddenly caught a glimpse of Mattie watching her with a curious smile on her broad Swedish face. As their eyes met, Mrs. Parkington turned and said, "What are you laughing at, Mattie?"

Mattie's face grew slowly red, and she replied, "Nothing, madame. I was only thinking how smart you looked and how young."

"I'll live to bury them all," said Mrs. Parkington.

That was an old joke but sometimes she

half-believed in the truth of it. As she picked up the handkerchief Mattie had put out for her, she knew there was much more behind that smile than Mattie had confessed. Mattie had a long memory. She was thinking of a time when her mistress had studied herself in the mirror for a half hour at a time before going out because she had wanted to please someone, more than she wanted anything else in all her life. It was odd that for more than forty years Mattie had known perfectly well that her mistress was an adulteress and had never betrayed even the faintest sign of the knowledge.

That, I suppose, thought Mrs. Parkington, is what is called being a perfect servant. But it's also being a perfect friend. But on second thought Mattie was in theory at least a wicked woman because she had connived at the adultery, giving silent approval and even encouraging it.

"Would you mind, madame," Mattie was saying, "If I peeked when Miss Janie's young man comes in?"

"No, Mattie. Take a good look. You could pretend to be doing something in the hall and I'll introduce you."

But Mattie, it seemed, did not think this was the proper procedure. She said, "No, madame. Not so soon. I might do it on the second or third time he comes."

"Very well. Suit yourself, Mattie."

She moved toward the door and again heard Mattie speaking. "Miss Janie's got to be a very pretty girl. I never thought she would be when she was little."

"She was too fat then and straightening her teeth made a great difference." She opened the door and then said, "I'll take the dogs with me . . . Come Bijou . . . come Mignon!"

The two Pekingese leapt from the sofa and, yapping with excitement, ran past her into the hall and down the curved stairway into the shadows of the hall as Taylor came forward with his false guardsman's walk to answer the bell which sounded distantly in the servant's hall.

At the top of the stairs Mrs. Parkington stopped for a moment to look at her watch. It wasn't five yet and Janie had said her young man could not leave his office until five. It couldn't be Janie yet.

As the door opened, the old lady leaned out over the rail in order to get a view of the hallway. For a moment the back of Taylor obscured her view. Then as he stood aside, she saw that the caller was the cowboy whom she thought was in Nassau with Madeleine.

She heard Taylor saying, "I'll see if Mrs. Parkington is in." And before he could ask the cowboy to sit down, she started down the stairway, calling out impatiently, "It's all right, Taylor. Tell Mr. Swann to come in."

She was astonished at seeing him, but very pleased. It was to be a pleasant late afternoon in the small sitting-room where she had had the brief unpleasant interview with Amory on Christmas night. She and the cowboy and Janie and her young man could shut the door and close out the rest of the world, all the unpleasant dull people and the slush and soot and dirt. The anticipation of pleasure made her feet light as she descended the stairs.

The cowboy had lost none of his shy awkwardness. He came up the three steps leading from the vestibule into the hall and then stood there shyly, his big hands clasped as if he did not know what to do with them, his face a little flushed, awed again by the elegance of the house. His blue eyes turned toward her; he waited as if uncertain what to do.

She came toward him, fluttering a little, even at the age of eighty-four. She was aware of this and a trifle ashamed that any man should still rouse in her heart a desire to please and attract. Yet she experienced too a flutter of pleasure. This man, so out of place here in the big hall, had a hard core of masculinity. It was like steel, unlike anything she had encountered in many years.

It was easy to see why Madeleine had made a fool of herself.

Her tiny blue-veined be-diamonded hand disappeared in his. A sudden smile broke out on his face — "broke out" she thought was exactly right, like the sun coming out from behind a cloud.

She said, "This is good luck. Where is Madeleine?"

He said, a little sheepishly, "She is still at the dressmaker's. I didn't like it much there."

"Come along in here," she said, leading him by the hand into the small sitting room.

The curtains were drawn and in the yellow marble fireplace there was a small wood fire. Beside it Taylor had placed the great Sheffield tray with all the heavy silver. As she rang a bell and then said, "Sit down here," one of the dogs leapt into her lap as she sat down and the other, the black one, curled on the rug with its nose against the fender, just below the Dresden china shepherdess.

Taylor appeared in the doorway and she said to the cowboy, "Would you like tea?"

He said, "Yes, ma'am," but shyly without enthusiasm, and she asked "Perhaps you'd prefer whisky."

His face brightened, "Yes, ma'am, bourbon, if you have it . . . straight, with water on the side."

"Have we any bourbon, Taylor?"
"Yes, madame."
"And tea for me."

She divined that Madeleine had not been allowing him bourbon. Madeleine probably thought it a vulgar drink.

When Taylor had gone, she said, "I didn't know you were still in town. I thought you'd gone to Nassau."

"No. Madeleine's clothes weren't ready." The grin broadened on his face. It was not exactly a handsome face, she thought, watching it slyly. It was a simple face — with a wide mouth, a straight nose, blue eyes surrounded by the tiny wrinkles which come of living always out of doors. The eyebrows were a little too heavy, and the hair a little too slicked. She guessed that he was ashamed of the natural wave for which most of the women she knew would give a couple of years of their lives.

He took out a gold and platinum cigarette case and asked, "May I smoke, ma'am?"

(The cigarette case would, of course, be a gift from Madeleine. He handled it with awe as if he were afraid of it.)

"Of course."

She fussed with the tea things while he lighted a cigarette, wanting to fill in the silence and make him feel at ease. She was aware that there was no barrier between him and her; he was simple and she had learned long ago that simplicity and directness were a great power and vastly important to the richness of life. It was "things" which got between them — this room, with its marble fireplace and the heavy silver and the naked Boucher drawings and the luxurious little dogs. Except that she had chosen all of them, they had very little to do with her. She would not care very much if they all vanished overnight.

"Are you enjoying New York?"

"Yes. It's quite a place for sight-seeing."

"Will you be sorry to leave?"

"No. It's all right, but it's not my kind of thing. A lot of the time I don't know what to do with myself." He grinned, "and I don't get enough sleep here."

She was not getting very far. There were so many things she wanted to know — how he had met Madeleine, how they had ever come close enough even to discuss marriage, which one had done the wooing, what he really thought of her granddaughter, how on earth he had ever come to marry her. But she knew that this afternoon at least, she would discover the answer to none of these things. This was a simple man and he had a simple code of decency and honor. It would take a long time for her to break down these barriers. The sight of him took her back a long way into the past, to Leaping Rock and the shadows of the great mountain. There she had once known men like this. In all the years in between she had met only one or two like him. The sort of life she had led had not brought men of this sort into the vortex of her existence. She regretted it now, but there was nothing to be done about it.

Suddenly she said, "Do you have a ranch of your own?"

"Yes, ma'am. Not a very big one. Only ten thousand acres but it's good grazing ground. It'll take care of a thousand head of Herefords in a good season. I'm hoping to spread out a bit."

She thought, Maybe he married Madeleine for money. But almost at once dismissed the idea. A man with a face like this wouldn't marry for money. You could tell by people's faces . . . so much . . . everything. To understand people's faces required years of experience and a fine sensitive instinct. She had a sudden idiotic impulse to say, "I'll buy you another hundred thousand acres, two hundred thousand acres, a million — whatever you want. I'll make it a wedding gift." But immediately she knew this was silly and that he would not accept. He would be frightened or think her mildly insane.

"How old are you?" she asked abruptly.

"Thirty-four."

(Then he was five years younger than Madeleine.)

"There's plenty of time to spread out. Does Madeleine like it out there?"

"Yes. For a while she's crazy about it but after a little she seems to get kind of bored.

"That's in her blood . . . both things," said Mrs. Parkington. And after a moment she added, "That's like her grandfather — Major Parkington."

Then Taylor came in followed by the footman with the tea and sandwiches and the bourbon and at the same time the doorbell sounded and Mrs. Parkington, bending over the tea tray, carefully, so as not to disturb the Pekingese, said, "That's probably Miss Janie and her young man. Bring them right in here, Taylor."

But it wasn't Janie. When the door opened, the Duchess came in. She was dressed badly again, Mrs. Parkington thought, in a violet walking suit trimmed with sable and a turban of mink which made her bored, weary, sallow face look rather like that of an impotent pasha.

She said, "Hello, Mother." And then as her nearsighted eyes discovered another figure in the room, she said, "Oh, I thought you were alone."

The cowboy stood up, uncertain as to whether or not to shake hands. The Duchess peered at him and then said, "Oh, it's you . . . Madeleine's husband," as if he weren't there at all, and then as if moved by an afterthought, "Glad to see you."

She sat down and said, "Could I have some of the bourbon?"

"Of course," said Mrs. Parkington. She had long ago given up trying to persuade Alice to drink less. She rang the bell and asked "How is your rheumatism?"

"Neither better nor worse," said the Duchess. "Sometimes I think it's neuralgia . . . sometimes acidity."

"I think it's acidity," said Mrs. Parkington, firmly and with significance.

The Duchess took out a cigarette and lighted it. She did it languidly as she did everything, as if long ago she had lost all interest in whatever she did and was only marking time until with utter indifference, she died. Mrs. Parkington saw that the clear blue eyes of Al Swann were watching her daughter and it occurred to her that he must find the whole assortment of his wife's relatives odd in the extreme.

Taylor arrived with another glass and the

Duchess took her Bourbon straight, like Al, and Mrs. Parkington, with an odd desire to chuckle, saw that the cowboy watched the performance with respect. Then Alice said, "If you're alone for dinner, Mother, I thought I might stay."

Mrs. Parkington did not want this. All the time in her heart she was hoping that Janie and her young man might not have an engagement and could be lured into staying for dinner or perhaps into going to the theater . . . that is, if the young man was really what Janie said he was. She wanted young people tonight, not someone tired like Alice to feed off her vitality. She pulled herself together and said, "If you have nothing better to do, stay by all means."

A sudden gleam came into her daughter's eye, a curious gleam of life as if an oyster had suddenly become animated. Alice said, "There is something important to discuss. I'd like to talk with you alone."

"Janie is coming," said Mrs. Parkington quickly, "She's bringing her young man. They may stay to dinner."

The gleam in the eye of the Duchess seemed to grow a little brighter. "That's luck. I've wanted to meet him. Janie never said anything about him to me. I only heard in a roundabout way."

Her voice trailed away drearily and Mrs. Parkington thought, She must not begin to whine. It's better that she drinks than to go about complaining all the while like Helen. And quickly she said, "Janie hasn't told anyone but me."

The Duchess rose quietly and with a curious dignity that was almost like a burlesque of dignity, walked three or four steps to the decanter which contained the Bourbon. Quietly, ignoring the eyes of Mrs. Parkington and Al Swann, she poured herself another measure of whisky.

Mrs. Parkington thought, Now she is going to spoil everything. I won't get a chance to get any nearer to Al and it's going to be difficult with Janie's young man.

She could not ask Alice not to take another drink. A kind of pride prevented her. She never had discussed the subject of drinking with Alice. Somehow she had never been able to do it. It was weak of her, she knew, but she was aware that to break someone of the habit of drinking, you had to offer him something. Alice drank out of despair; at sixty-five there was nothing which could be offered her to compensate for the solace of alcohol . . . nothing at all.

She was sitting down again, with the same unsteady travesty of dignity, as if she were balancing a coronet on the top of her head. Mrs. Parkington thought, With a train she would be like Beatrice Lillie doing a duchess at the coronation. But behind this reflection, there was a pang, for Mrs. Parkington suddenly remembered Alice, sitting there in the absurd violet walking costume, as she had been as a little girl, before anything had happened to her.

Quickly, abruptly, she said, "Mr. Swann . . . Al, I mean . . . was born in Leaping Rock, where I was born." And she saw that for a moment the name "Leaping Rock" meant nothing to her daughter. It lay too far back, before she was born, in a world of which she knew nothing at all save the stories her mother had told her as a child. And now Alice was sixty-five and between her and these stories there was a veil, a thick veil with a pattern confused and ugly, which obscured much.

"Oh, yes," she said and smiled the ordered practiced inane smile of one pretending interest from an eminence shrouded in fog. And Mrs. Parkington thought, It's awful now. Her dropping in has spoiled everything.

Then the bell sounded again and she said, aware that Al was uneasy, "That's Janie, I suppose," and in her excitement she stood up, taking the sleepy, indignant Pekingese from her lap and slipping it under her arm. She started toward the door leading into the hallway and then checked herself and moved toward the fireplace, standing with her back to the gentle flame as if she had meant to warm herself. A curious smile came over the face of the Duchess. It was difficult sometimes for Mrs. Parkington to discover how much her daughter observed, how much of what happened beneath the surface of things ever penetrated the haze in which she seemed to exist. Alice was secret as a turtle, yet at times as acutely sensitive as a gazelle.

Then something came into the room. It was as if the air had changed, as if the light had become more brilliant. It came in the door with Janie and her young man, and Mrs. Parkington knew at once that it was going to be all right. Janie was right. She must keep this young man.

He was tall, possibly over six feet, and good-looking, not handsome so much as healthy, with his dark hair and high color and blue eyes. He moved nicely as if he felt confidence in himself, not at all as if he were shy at meeting a formidable old lady who was very nearly legendary. Yet there was nothing arrogant or conceited or brazen in his manner. Mrs. Parkington thought, Oh, blessed young man who was born simple and direct. He must have been born so for he could not have learned the magic secret in so few years.

He was happy, it was clear, and Janie was happy. It was the happiness that came of being with each other. It was as simple as that.

Janie brought him straight over to her and as her great-granddaughter came nearer to her, Mrs. Parkington felt warmth stealing over her old body. Janie's face was flushed, her eyes brilliant.

She said, "This is Ned, Great-Grandmama. Ned Talbot."

He said quite simply, "I'm so glad to meet you, Mrs. Parkington."

He took her hand and she said, "I wanted to meet you too," Then she said, "This is my daughter, Mrs. Sanderson, and Mr. Swann . . . Al Swann who married my granddaughter Madeleine." She smiled, "There are a lot of us — quite a lot. Sometimes it seems very complicated."

The boy had nice manners. He shook hands with both the Duchess and Al and the Duchess took out a *lorgnon* to reinforce her weak eyes. She looked at him with frank concentration for a long time as, if making a study of a wax figure at Madame Tussaud's.

The conversation was not good. It could

not have been because the mixture of the people in the room was too preposterous. Al and his ranch, the Duchess with her dreary manner of splendor, and the two young people, so obviously in love. It was talk about the weather, about theaters, about books, about Washington, about everything in general and nothing in particular. Mrs. Parkington did not trouble to give it much of her attention, only enough to keep it going. She was watching the boy, discovering many things which experience had taught her could be discovered.

She noticed with pleasure the line of his square jaw. Janie, who had her share of the family instability, would have need of the firmness it indicated. She liked the full, rather sensual mouth and the large and beautiful hands. Janie was young and warm — the whole family had been like that, even the Duchess, long ago — and she would need a lover as well as a husband to bring her happiness. Big men should not have small tight mouths and small hands. That was Amory's trouble; that was one of the things which made his wife's mouth turn down so bitterly at the corners.

And she liked the large vigorous ears with their well-defined lobes and the line from the chin which was clear and straight, and the rather large feet and the square set of the shoulders. At fifty he would be heavier but never fat; there was too much energy in him, too much life in the eyes and the way the lips curled at the corners. He had humor too. There were fine lines about the eyes, not the deep creases that fringed the cowboy's eyes, but lines which came of good humor and health. Al was simple and direct; this boy was different. He was not simple, although he understood somehow the power of simplicity. He was complex — complicated. At times he would be tortured by his own variety of mood and intelligence. He might even be unfaithful to Janie, but he would, Mrs. Parkington thought, never allow her to discover it, and he would never be carried into disaster by the sweep of his own emotions.

Suddenly Mrs. Parkington laughed quietly, so quietly that the others did not even notice it. She had thought, I am looking him over as if he were a horse I was buying for Janie, as if I were telling his fortune.

He was talking now and she liked the sound of his voice. He was arguing with the Duchess some point of British politics, bewildering her heavy mind by the quickness of his own. He talked very rapidly as if his tongue could not keep pace with his mind.

When he had finished and made his point,

the Duchess agreed, won over more by his masculinity and vitality and charm than by his arguments which could scarcely make much impression on her tired befogged mind. She was displaying an extraordinary interest in him, looking at him directly now and then through the *lorgnon.* Once she even reached up and set her hat straight and took out a lipstick and made up her lips.

Janie obviously was very proud of him. She had clearly wanted to show him off. But the nice thing was that he was not showing off. His excitement over an idea was genuine. It even moved Al, who sitting forward a little in his chair, listening, could not have had the faintest idea of what they were talking about.

When Ned had finished, Al looked at his watch (from Cartier, thought Mrs. Parkington. Another gift from Madeleine) and said, "I must go. Madeleine's waiting for me at the hotel. I'm late already."

"Madeleine doesn't like to be kept waiting," said the Duchess with a perfectly blank expression. You did not know whether or not she spoke with malice, implying that Madeleine always bought her husbands and expected them to be punctual. Al looked at her sharply and Mrs. Parkington thought the color appeared for a second in his weathered face. She herself did not know whether or not Alice had been malicious. She had never been able, even after sixty-five years, to discover when Alice was being malicious and when she was simply being stupid and tactless. Perhaps it had something to do with the myopia of her hyperthyroid eyes. Nearsighted people very often had a curious blank expression which came of the effort to focus objects which were perpetually hazy.

Shyly, Al said good night and went out. Mrs. Parkington went with him as far as the hall, for she wanted to ask him to come back another time when they could have a good talk about Nevada. If she asked him in front of the others, she knew it would mean nothing and he might not return.

In the doorway, she asked him to come back.

"I'd like to, ma'am," he said.

"Telephone me and I'll fix it so that we can be alone and have a good talk."

"Yes. I'd like that."

He started to move away but she laid her hand on his arm. Suddenly she found herself saying, "Is it all right with Madeleine?"

For a second he was silent. Then the tanned face turned a mahogany red and the blue eyes looked past her. "Yes, Mrs. Parkington. It's all right."

She patted his arm and said, "I'm glad."

And he went away quickly as she thought, So, it's like that!

What a fool Madeleine was! But that was not her fault. It was a tragedy. Otherwise, Madeleine was the best of the family, save for Janie. She was big, healthy, pleasant and good-natured, but this thing was a disease.

As she re-entered the room, closing the door behind her, a sigh rose from deep inside her, taking utter possession of the trim, straight old body.

Consciously she thrust back the sigh and brightened herself in time to hear Alice saying, "I must say our new relative doesn't have much to say for himself."

"He hadn't much chance," said Mrs. Parkington.

But Alice had not finished. She said, "He does seem to be bearing up better than the others. Cowboys must have something."

Then suddenly, sharply, Mrs. Parkington made use of her dignity. It was a terrifying dignity which could chill and awe even her own descendants. It was as if she turned suddenly to ice, as if she became a sword of judgment, tempered with contempt.

She simply said, "Alice! That's enough of that!"

The dignity had invested her partly because she had grown fond of Al and did not mean to have him treated as a fool, and partly because the things implied by her daughter's remark had nothing to do with the two young people here in the room with them. Alice had been insensitive and vulgar, smirching somehow the brightness which Janie and Ned had brought into the room.

Purposely the old woman crossed near to the Duchess, saying fiercely as she passed, "Sometimes you are a bloody fool!" But Alice, cowering spiritually, merely stared at her in astonishment, wondering that her mother, who had no scruples at discussing anything on earth, should suddenly have turned prude.

But already her mother was saying brightly, too brightly, too eagerly, "Could you and Ned have dinner with me?" And before they could answer she said, "We're having pheasant your great-uncle Henry sent down from Rhinebeck."

Janie came over quickly and put her arm about her great-grandmother. "We can't, darling. We're dining with Ned's sister. She's here from South Bend for two days with her husband."

Something in Janie's voice took away the chill of disappointment. Mrs. Parkington thought, Janie knows. She knows how much I want them. That was what Janie had that none of her other descendants had ever had save her son Herbert and Herbert was dead, these fifty years, so long ago that lately the memory of him had come to seem nearer to her than the physical reality of the people about her. Janie *knew*, with that curious extra sense which she herself had.

She wanted suddenly to say, "Bring them too." But she did not, partly because she would have seemed too eager and partly out of worldly experience. The sister and her husband might turn out to be frightful and spoil everything.

"It's all right, my dear. Another time."

Ned said, "I'm very sorry, Mrs. Parkington. I should have liked staying. I'd put them off but I want Janie to meet my sister and it's the only time we could meet."

Then Janie kissed her and whispered, "Come into the hall, Granny. I want to ask you something."

So Mrs. Parkington went into the hall with them and Janie said to her young man, "Go along, get your hat, Ned. I want to speak to Granny."

She stood watching him go away and then she turned to Mrs. Parkington and said, "Isn't he nice, darling? Isn't he what you would like?"

Mrs. Parkington laughed, "It's a little late for that. But he is what I would have liked at your age." Then she kissed Janie and said, "Run along now."

She watched them go out the door and as she turned to re-enter the small sitting-room she felt suddenly tired and depressed and old. The feeling was like a cloud of mist enveloping her, dimming everything — the lights, the outlines of the familiar furniture, the figure of the Duchess in the absurd violet costume.

I am old, she thought. After all I am old. But at the same time she was aware that the weariness was born not so much of her body as of the weight of all that happened to her since she had gone out joyously to meet what life held for her. Oddly the weariness seemed to center about the figure of the Duchess. The violet walking costume lay at the very midst of the cloud.

With a great effort of will she straightened her body and smiled at Alice.

"He's a nice boy," she said, "and I should think, a clever one."

"Helen and Amory are not very pleased." She chuckled wickedly, "South Bend! They probably think South Bend is full of Indians and cowboys."

Mrs. Parkington was about to say, "If ever a family needed new blood, ours does." But Alice said it for her. So she rang for Taylor to clear away and said, "At least we're trying. Janie and her young man, Madeleine and her cowboy." Then she noticed the gleam again in the olive-colored eyes of the Duchess, and was certain now that her daughter had some tremendous piece of news which would make no one but herself happy.

Taylor came and Mrs. Parkington said, "Mrs. Sanderson and I will dine here by the fire." It would be better that way. She could not dine at the great table alone with Alice. Then she added, "Mrs. Sanderson would probably like a cocktail. What do you want, Alice?"

"A martini."

Taylor's face betrayed no emotion whatever. "Very good. Shall I bring it when I bring your champagne?"

"Yes. We'll be ready in half an hour. I'm going to freshen up."

She had hoped to escape Alice for a little while, but there was no escape. Alice rose and said, "I'll come up with you." And Mrs. Parkington resigned herself out of weariness.

In the boudoir abovestairs Alice lost herself among the objects — the chairs, photographs, sofas — that once had been a part of the monstrous house on Fifth Avenue. While Mrs. Parkington primped, thinking how gray her face looked, her daughter went about looking at the faded photographs, making comments, remembering things long forgotten. For a long time she held the photographs of her dead brothers, the two brothers who had always been so much more beautiful and brilliant than herself, peering at them in a near-sighted way, as if seeking to recapture something which perhaps was not happiness but something better than the grayness of her present existence.

Suddenly she turned and said, "How odd of Uncle Henry to send you pheasants. Do you ever hear from him?"

"He drops in now and then and sometimes sends eggs or capons or pheasants or something."

"I haven't seen him for years. What is he like now?"

"About the same — older . . . but not much changed . . ." she smiled, "Still a rip-snorter."

Then the conversation died away, leaving the shadow of Uncle Henry, the Major's younger brother, there in the room with them — Uncle Henry, the family black sheep whom they all looked upon as mad because he did what he pleased in life, married the daughter of one of his farm tenants and lived like a farm laborer. He hadn't been too mad, because he was a very rich man and had won several very profitable lawsuits against railroad companies and the estate of his own brother, the Major.

Presently Mrs. Parkington finished with her primping and said, "We'd better go down. Pheasant should not sit around waiting."

The revelation came about the middle of dinner when they were just finishing Uncle Henry's pheasant. Mrs. Parkington, to raise her spirits, had had two half-pints of champagne and the Duchess had had three martinis followed by a half-pint of Burgundy with the bird. But the wine had not raised Mrs. Parkington's spirits.

As Taylor took away the pheasant, the Duchess, the gleam returning to her eyes, said, "I heard something alarming about Amory last night."

Mrs. Parkington looked at her and said, "What? I knew there was something on your mind."

"He's in trouble."

"What about?"

"Money. There's something shady about it. I must say I was surprised — about Amory of all people."

Mrs. Parkington did not answer. The memory of the conversation with Amory concerning a loan returned to her. At the same time she thought, How stupid Alice is to say "Amory of all people." Why Amory was just the sort . . . a vestryman of St. Bart's, a pompous ass and a man cursed with the smugness which believes itself all-knowing.

"For heaven's sake," she asked, "what is it?"

But the Duchess took her time, seeming to relish the story. "It seems," she said, "that he has lost a great deal of money in the last ten years."

"I know that," said Mrs. Parkington.

"And lately he's been trying to gamble and get it back."

"Yes."

"But not with his own money . . . with the money and securities of other people . . . some of it belonging to his firm and some to his clients."

Mrs. Parkington frowned. She didn't want to hear the story tonight. She was too weary and depressed. But she had to hear, knowing that in some strange way she was looked upon as the head of the family and that in the end it would all come back upon her. There was never any escape. They all depended on her, even Amory. And in this case there was no stopping Alice.

Mrs. Parkington asked, "Where did you hear this?"

"Judge Everett told me. He came in for tea yesterday."

"I never thought of Judge Everett as a gossip."

"He didn't tell it as gossip. He thought perhaps you ought to know about it."

Tartly Mrs. Parkington asked, "Why didn't he come to me directly?"

"He said he didn't because he was not sure about details." Alice smiled suddenly. "And he was afraid to tell you without having the facts at hand. He was afraid that you'd tell him he was a fool."

"It may be that he is. It all sounds like gossip to me." But she knew it wasn't gossip. She sincerely wished it was. "In any case I wouldn't repeat it to anyone."

"Of course not, Mother. It isn't the sort of thing to go about telling about your niece's husband." When Mrs. Parkington, lost in thought, said nothing, her daughter asked, "What are you going to do about it?"

"Nothing! There's nothing I can do. It's up to Amory to get himself out of this. In any case, there may be nothing in it."

Alice was smiling now, a blank, slightly tipsy smile. She was pleased because she hated Amory and was none too fond of his wife with the drooping mouth. Mrs. Parkington wasn't thinking of either of them. She was thinking of their daughter, Janie, and the radiance she had taken with her out of the house. Nothing must happen to spoil Janie's happiness. She kept telling herself that such things did not happen to people like Amory — why, Amory had always been a monument of respectability — St. Bart School, Harvard, the best clubs, vestryman. Things like that didn't happen to people like Amory. But a quiet voice kept saying, "But they do happen. They've happened to people you've known well. A crook is a crook and times have changed. Big crooks get caught nowadays. They don't get away with it as they used to."

She saw that Alice would not mind the notoriety; she could no longer be touched by it. Once perhaps, long ago, the pictures in the papers, the raucous headlines had shocked and hurt her, but for a long time, perhaps twenty years, these things had no longer had any power to astonish or hurt her. There had been too many family headlines since the day Augustus Parkington brought back to New York a bride from Leaping Rock, Nevada. Only on extraordinary occasions did the Duchess ever emerge from the misty world in which she existed to read a newspaper. She would certainly not mind the notoriety. She would be unaware of it.

Then as she sat there, thinking, she became aware that the daughter opposite her had collapsed. Quite suddenly she seemed to have become weary and shattered. The eyes were closed, the head fallen a little on one side. For a second Mrs. Parkington thought, She is dead! For she had all the appearance of a dead person.

"Alice!" she said, and then in a stronger voice, "Alice! Alice!"

Then the tired head stirred, the dull eyes opened and peered at her. "Are you ill?"

"No, but I think I'll go home if you'll call a taxi."

When the taxi came, Taylor and Mrs. Parkington helped her to the door and Mrs. Parkington said, "I think you'd better go with her, Taylor."

The Duchess made a great effort at pulling herself together and said, "He doesn't need to come. I'm all right."

"Don't be a fool!" said Mrs. Parkington.

Taylor fetched his hat and supported her to the taxi while Mrs. Parkington stood in the doorway watching. It had begun to snow again and the flakes came down thinly, melting they struck the sidewalk. When the taxi drove off Mrs. Parkington closed the door and, followed by the two Pekingese, climbed the three shallow steps, and crossed the hall to the lift.

Upstairs she found Mattie waiting for her with the nightgown and peignoir laid out, her face expressionless. She was like Taylor, a good servant, a kind friend. She gave no sign of knowing that anything unusual had gone on belowstairs.

Mrs. Parkington said, "You can go to bed, Mattie. I'll read for a little while."

"Very good, madame."

She helped the old lady out of her clothes and then went away and Mrs. Parkington settled herself on the chaise longue with a French novel. It was an old novel by "Gyp" and she hoped that the memories it raised would dissipate the sense of depression and worry which had taken possession of her.

Old books, familiar scents, stray pieces of music took her, more and more frequently, into the remote past. For some time now she had fallen into the habit of tricking herself into slipping away from the present. It was a process of anesthesia, and made sleep possible on the nights when her mind alive, awake and glittering, flitted like a firefly from one anxiety to another.

But the old novel by "Gyp" failed as a means of escape. Suddenly she could not even keep her mind on it. She would read a whole page without being aware of what she was reading because the story the Duchess had told her kept returning, gnawing like a weasel at her consciousness. She kept thinking, The fool! Why did he do it? Whatever happened, it must be hushed up. Alone now she no longer pretended to doubt the truth of the rumor.

And suddenly she was grateful for one of the few times in her life that she was a very rich woman. If this were true about Amory — if he really was in trouble — she could pay off what he had stolen, she could even give him money to bribe his way out of everything. She hated bribery as she hated all corruption, all dishonesty, but she would stoop to it now, at eighty-four, if there was no other way, but not for Amory's sake, not to save Amory. For him she had little sympathy. If there must be dishonesty, if she had to accept it, she preferred the cynical, gangster dishonesty of her dead husband. In that, at least, there had been a kind of evil grandeur and romance. She hated Amory's hypocrisy. No, she would not lift a finger to help Amory himself, but there was Janie to think of and Janie's young man and what lay before them. All that money could be of use, if only to buy a clear way to happiness and decency for Janie. She would use it somehow to buy an escape for Janie from the blight which had touched the rest of the family.

But Amory must come to her and ask for help. She would not offer it, not to Amory who behaved when he married her granddaughter Helen as if he were conferring an honor upon the Parkington family. Amory must come on his knees to ask her.

In the old woman there had never been any strong instinct for vengeance. The humiliation of Amory would only be a payment, a kind of fine for the humbuggery of himself and all his background of privilege and snobbery.

The novel by "Gyp" slipped forgotten from her lap, startling Mignon, the Pekingese, into an outburst of yapping. When she had quieted the dog she rose and turning out the light went into her bedroom, hoping that she would be able to sleep. But sleep did not come. In the darkness she lay watching the snow falling thicker and thicker through the windows of light made by the street lamp. And presently the sight of the softly falling snow seemed to hypnotize her and after a time she slipped into a strange, blurred borderland between sleep and consciousness, and the snow seemed to be falling all about her in the room itself and through the snowstorm she drifted back and back through world after world to a winter night long ago and she was descending from a cab, helped by Major Augustus Parkington, into the falling snow through which the yellow gaslight was shining softly. A match seller came out of the snow and Gus gave her a coin, and then with a chuckle, lifted Mrs. Parkington, his bride, off her feet and holding her against his great barrel chest, carried her across the sloppy sidewalk and up the steps into the Brevoort Hotel from which the sound of music was coming.

IV

It was odd, Mrs. Parkington sometimes reflected, how small were the things which fixed themselves in the memory of the remote past. The two images which remained visually the most alive out of all that period of her life were the red curtains and the gold *baldaquins* in the parlor of the suite in the Brevoort where Gus took her, and Mademoiselle Conti's green gloves. There was too the music of the waltz from *La Grande Duchesse de Gerolstein* which the little band was playing in the dining-room as they arrived. It remained forever fixed in her mind together with the moment she stood in the hallway while the concierge in broken English congratulated Major Augustus Parkington on his marriage and complimented the bride. Always for the rest of her life when she heard Offenbach she was back again to the snowy evening when she and Gus had arrived at the Brevoort straight from Nevada.

On that night Gus had seemed happy and excited, filled to overflowing with that enormous vitality which made him different from other men. It was the vitality, that great animal good health, which made her love him, the same vitality which he did not hesitate to use without scruple, against anyone, to gain what he wanted. When all else had fallen away, when there were no longer any illusions, the vitality still had the power to warm and hold her.

And now, on this snowy night, he led the way up the stairs, accompanied by the concierge and three or four attendants. Major Parkington was rich and important and a great spender and no amount of attention was too much for him. It was the way Susie had hoped, during the hours she had sat by the window looking across the great valley, it would be. There was gas light and music and gaiety and people running after her rich and important husband.

And then the concierge stopped at a door at the far end of the hallway and unlocking it, stood aside for her and her husband to go in. Then it was she saw the red curtains and the gold *baldaquins*.

It was a big room with a red carpet and lots of frivolous gilt furniture in the flamboyant style of the Second Empire and there were roses everywhere in vases, white roses ordered by the Major, and on the table, champagne in a silver cooler. But something about the heavy gold *baldaquins* and the red curtains fascinated and delighted her. They were rich and full and expensive like something out of a fairy story, exactly as they should have been.

Then the porters brought up the baggage and Gus tipped them, three times as much as most people would have given, and told the concierge that he did not wish to be disturbed until he rang.

When they had gone Gus went to the door and locked it and then smiling at her, came across and kissed her and said, "Happy, sparrow?"

"Yes," she answered shyly.

"You *are* a little sparrow . . . all gray and soft in your funny old-fashioned clothes, but tomorrow you will be a bird of paradise."

Then he opened the champagne while she watched him, puzzled a little and bewildered but excited. She had never seen him like this. On the train during the long journey he had been quiet and respectful and kind, almost as if she were a child whom he had to protect. But now there was something boisterous and excited in his manner. He no longer seemed much older than herself. He was no age at all.

When he had opened the champagne he took off his coat and sat down and drew her down on his lap and kissed her throat and then, giving her a glass, he raised his own glass and said, "Come, my sparrow. Here's to the future. It's ours forever. We'll conquer the whole world. We'll have everything."

She drank the champagne and then he refilled her glass and kissed her again on the throat, let his head rest against her breast for a long time. And shyly her free hand stole up and her fingers, as if of their own accord, stole through the dark vigorous curls and caressed the back of the strong neck. His head pressed more tightly against her and she fancied that she heard him sob. Then suddenly he looked up at her again and the blue eyes were misty. She felt herself pressed against the great muscles of his strong thighs and heard him say, "Oh, sparrow! I'm happy! I was nobody and you're nobody but one day we'll be somebody."

They had another glass of champagne and for a long time he was silent, pressing his head against her while her fingers ran through his hair. She felt strangely excited and yet detached as if she were watching herself and him. This was different from what had happened before. From the moment the justice of the peace had spoken the last words of the marriage service, he had been quiet and respectful and kind. She herself had been frightened and shy and quiet, wondering at what had happened to her. And now suddenly all the fear and shyness were swept away. This man was new and different and she felt rising inside her a curious sense of abandon and ecstasy. It was as if, voluptuously, all these things which had held her back, which had made her nervous and tense and unresponsive, were dissolving into a warm mist. The scent of the white roses was very strong now. She could see the flowers, lovely half-opened buds, against the great red curtains. From belowstairs faintly came the sound of the music made by the little orchestra.

She thought, This is our wedding night. All that went before was nothing . . . nothing at all. This is the way I meant it to be even without ever knowing it.

And then she felt his fingers loosening one by one the tiny buttons of her basque and she heard his deep, warm voice saying, "I love you, sparrow. Oh, my Susie, I love you."

The champagne glass slipped out of her hand to the floor and he picked her up and carried her into the next room. For a moment she felt that she would faint, but the feel of his full lips on her throat brought back that strange feeling of ecstasy which swept everything before it. She thought, I love him. I did not know before what love was. I know now. I love him.

The big muscular hands were gentle with

a gentleness beyond her belief. Their touch filled her whole body with fire. She was like a blossom opening at the warmth of the sun and he became beautiful to her in a new way, with a profound direct primitive beauty that was like the godlike splendor of the great valley.

Afterward they had supper served by the maitre d'hôtel himself—*merlan frits*, pressed duck and Burgundy, salad and *paté de foie gras*. She always remembered the supper, a little because it was the first lesson he gave her in how to eat well, more because of the sense of happiness and fulfillment.

He said, "We'll not go downstairs until to-morrow, sparrow. Not until you can appear as a bird of paradise." He looked at her smiling, with that frank healthy look which made him irresistible. "Anyway, it's nicer to be alone now, isn't it?"

"It's very nice to be alone," she answered and then shyly "I love you, Gus. I know it now." It was the first time she had spoken the word "love."

"Have I made you happy?" he asked with a curious air of valor and pride.

"Very happy, Gus."

Beneath the table he pressed her knee between his, "Well go on being happy, always."

Twice more that night he made love to

her. Long afterward she understood that he had treated her not as a wife, but as a mistress. She was grateful to him always, even after she came to understand that for him women, even his wife, would always be mistresses because with his great vitality he loved women rather than any one woman.

The next day was the day of the green gloves, a day of which they seemed as much a symbol, as the red curtains and *baldaquins* and champagne had been a symbol of the warm voluptuous night.

Gus held open the door and the woman came in. She came in magnificently, walking very erect but gracefully, smiling as the light from between the red curtains struck her ugly face. That was what Susie thought of on first sight, that she was ugly. She had a large mouth and a rather too large nose with a pronounced arch at the bridge, and her eyes were set a trifle too near to each other. She was dark and about middle height, taller than Susie herself. It was impossible to judge her age. Her entrance was accompanied by the rustling of much taffeta. The effect was that of many muted violins accompanying a sonorous solo passage by the French horn.

Then Major Parkington closed the door and said, "Susie, this is Mademoiselle Conti." And to Mademoiselle Conti he said, "This is my wife." He spoke with curious pride as if he were proud to present Mademoiselle Conti to his wife and his wife to Mademoiselle Conti.

The stranger came across to shake Susie's hand and then she noticed for the first time the green gloves. They were of poison green velvet with long cuffs, pushed down carelessly about the wrists. Susie felt confused and shy and very nearly tripped over the rug which lay before the gilt commode with the marble top. The white roses had opened during the night and their heavy fragrance filled the room to suffocation.

Mademoiselle Conti said, "It is a pleasure to meet the wife of my very good friend Major Parkington."

She spoke formally in a deep warm voice and with an accent, slight but strong enough to add piquancy to her speech.

Susie said that it was a pleasure too to meet Mademoiselle Conti and Parkington said, "We are going to lunch here and after lunch Mademoiselle Conti is going with you to Madame de Thèbes to buy some clothes. She knows all about such things."

He need not have added the final sentence for Susie had remarked almost at once that Mademoiselle Conti knew all about clothes. Although it was the first time Susie had ever seen an example of real *chic,* she knew it when she saw it. It was there in the cut of the black frock, in the way Mademoiselle Conti wore the frock and carried herself. It was there in the tiny hat with three pert black ostrich feathers worn a little forward on her head. It was there in the cut of the basque and the jut of the bustle and the slight curve of the back. But most of all it was there in the green velvet gloves.

Mademoiselle Conti was a work of art.

The art was not confined to the costume; it was in the woman's manner as well. While Susie's husband sent for a waiter and ordered lunch Mademoiselle Conti threw off her fur jacket, laid aside her muff and settled down to chat with Susie.

All morning, from the moment Gus had said he was bringing Mademoiselle Conti to lunch, Susie had been miserable and shy, troubled over how she was to behave and what she would find to talk about with a strange Frenchwoman out of this glittering world of New York.

And now it was perfectly simple. Mademoiselle Conti had no airs and she had immense vitality. It was like the vitality of a steel spring. She took command of the conversation and saw to it that there was no awkward pause. But she saw to it as well that there was no shyness or awkwardness on the part of the new bride. As if it were a physical thing, utterly under her control, she turned on warmth and friendliness.

She was interested in the long trip from the West, in the mines, in Leaping Rock. She was full of plans for Susie's clothes, for the theater, for a thousand things.

Then the lunch came — terrapin amontillado with artichoke and salad and biscuit Tortoni. Susie's shyness was gone now. She was fascinated and tongue-tied. She had expected a strange and different world but not one like this in which Gus seemed to be a great man, knowing everything. Her heart sang for so many reasons — because of Gus, so big and handsome and full-blooded sitting opposite her, because of the memories of the night before, because of Mademoiselle Conti and the way she sat so upright in the gilt chair chattering and making Gus and herself laugh. And because she was aware of a kind of beauty, a civilized beauty, a visual beauty, which she had never before encountered — the beauty of ugly Mademoiselle Conti in the black frock, with the green gloves beside her, against the heavy red curtains with the gold *baldaquins*. She was happy in a way she had never been before. It was as if the air were filled with music.

* * *

Madame de Thèbes' establishment occupied a whole house in Sixteenth Street just off Fifth Avenue. Madame herself was a squat Frenchwoman who looked rather like a frog, with a hairy mole on her chin, but she went to Paris once a year and the most fashionable women of New York — those who lived in the great houses on Fifth Avenue, on Murray Hill, in Washington Square, as well as those who lived apart in their own world of Delmonico's and the French opera — bought their clothes there. On the outside of the red brick house near the door there was a discreet plaque which read simply *Madame de Thèbes. Couturière to the Empress Eugenie.*

Here Mademoiselle Conti brought Susie after the lunch at the Brevoort. The moment the colored boy opened the door it was clear that Mademoiselle Conti was also *someone.* Two saleswomen came forward and greeted her and when they had been seated in the *petit salon* reserved for favored customers, Madame de Thèbes herself came in. She and Mademoiselle Conti greeted each other with birdlike little cries, kissed each other and chattered in French of which Susie understood not a word. She gathered only that Mademoiselle Conti's Christian name was Aspasie and that Madame de Thèbes was known as Hortense. She sat there, suddenly miserable again, aware that her wool walking suit, bought in Denver, had nothing of that quality of the green gloves, none of that quality which even Madame de Thèbes, short and dumpy in her black alpaca dress, seemed to have.

Then the chatter was finished and Mademoiselle Conti said in English, "This is my friend Mrs. Parkington — the Major's wife. I have brought her to fit her out — practically everything."

"Plaisir," murmured Madame de Thèbes, and even as she spoke, Susie was aware that she was already being measured and fitted. The black eyes of the dressmaker glittered and she turned to Mademoiselle Conti and said something, quite a long speech in rapid French, which made Susie feel that she was less human than an inanimate object undergoing the process of appraisal.

What Madame de Thèbes said, partly in words, partly in thought was this — "She is a pretty little thing with a nice figure and she has lovely eyes and hair and complexion. We can do a great deal with her. She will be a fine advertisement. She will be seen about. She will go everywhere because the Major means to go everywhere and have everything in life."

For Madame de Thèbes knew the Major and was willing to speculate on his future. He was clever. He was rich. He was good-looking. He had paid for the clothes of many women. He was an *arriviste.* And above all he was ruthless.

And so Madame de Thèbes and Mademoiselle Conti set to work to dress Susie for New York.

It went on till long after the lamplighter had made his round of Sixteenth Street in the softly falling snow. Madame de Thèbes showed her dresses, some on the backs of proud young women, some on lay figures or simply thrown over the backs of sofas and chairs. Once when Susie leaned over and whispered to Mademoiselle Conti "What about prices?" Mademoiselle only shrugged her shoulders and said, "Leave that to me. Your husband has given me carte blanche." And once when Susie suggested than an evening frock showed too much of the bosom of the young woman who displayed it, Mademoiselle said, "Do not trouble yourself about that. You have a wonderful *poitrine.* A *belle poitrine* is nothing to be ashamed of."

It was nearly seven o'clock when Mademoiselle Conti pulled on the green gloves to show that the business had finally come to an end. Three ball gowns had been ordered and four frocks and two walking suits, as well as tippets and *pelisses* and muffs and an overall wrap of a dark soft fur with a hood attached. Madame de Thèbes would send round a ball gown and two frocks which Madame Parkington could wear until her own things were ready.

And that was not all, said Mademoiselle Conti. It was only the beginning. By the time they entered a cab to drive home, Susie felt weary and a little bewildered, but she felt also that Mademoiselle Conti and even Madame de Thèbes were already in some mysterious fashion, old friends. As they entered the Brevoort they met Major Parkington coming out of the bar and he would not let Mademoiselle Conti go until they had shared a bottle of champagne in the sitting room with the red curtains.

When she had gone he turned to Susie, kissed her, and said, "Well, my sparrow, did you buy a lot of pretty clothes?"

"Yes. Lovely clothes."

"Tired?"

"Yes."

"The champagne will make you feel better. Come, sit down."

He took her on his knee and kissed her again and then asked, "And Mademoiselle Conti? Do you like her?"

"Yes. Very much. She is very kind."

He laughed. "She is very clever. You listen to her and you'll be all right and you'll have nothing to be afraid of."

She wanted to ask him who Mademoiselle Conti was and how he had come to know her, a Frenchwoman, so well, but she was tired and she felt suddenly shy.

He said, "She is going to teach you to speak French and a lot of other things which are worth knowing. We are going a long way together, sparrow — as far as it's possible to go."

There was a knock at the door and when he opened it, there was Madame de Thèbes' colored doorman with two big boxes. When the boy had been tipped and sent away, the Major cut the strings on the boxes with a gold penknife and took off the lid. Inside was a cape of dark fur and a pale yellow ball gown and when they lifted them out of the boxes, they discovered a tiny white dove, wrapped in paper.

"What is that for?" she asked.

"To wear in your hair, sparrow. That was smart of Madame de Thèbes to think of you as a dove." Then he grinned at her and said, "Now I must see you in it. Tonight we will go down to dinner and perhaps afterward to Delmonico's."

He drew her down again on his knee and began unfastening the tiny buttons of her basque. Then he pressed his head against her breast and said, "I love you very much, sparrow. I love you very much . . . more than I ever thought I would love you or anyone."

Afterward she dressed in the ball dress of pale yellow and placed the dove in her hair, well forward on one side as Mademoiselle Conti had worn her little hat with the three plumes. He watched her dress and watched her regard herself in the mirror. He watched her attempt to pull the bodice higher without success. Then as she studied herself in the long gold framed glass, she saw suddenly his reflection behind her. She saw his arm rise and place about her throat a necklace of pearls, two strands of them. When he fastened them, they lay below her throat almost to the line which marked the division between her breasts. She saw his reflection smile at her and suddenly she began, tired and bewildered, to cry.

The next day they rose late. The Major did not go to his office on lower Broadway, but stayed with her, dawdling for a long time over breakfast. Already she had discovered that when he wakened, it was completely, with all his senses and intelligence alive. A little while after he wakened he would be singing and whistling and making rather bad affectionate jokes. Now he read his newspaper and talked to her at the same time. He had a remarkable capacity for doing several things at once; it was as if his mind were divided into compartments, each tightly sealed. He could open and close one compartment after another without confusion or leakage from one to the other. This, together with the health and vitality of a bull, made it possible for him to do the work of three or four men.

Now he sat across the breakfast table from her, watching her as he talked, his eyes bright with pride and love and amusement.

He said, "Did you like it last night, sparrow?"

"It was wonderful."

She was still a little bewildered, but out of her confusion she knew, without any doubts, that what had happened to her since they came up the steps through the snowstorm, was wonderful beyond anything she had dreamed of.

"It was wonderful," she repeated, "But don't make it happen too fast Gus. Give me a little time." And almost immediately she was aware that the voice which spoke was not hers at all but her mother's, the voice of her mother's common sense. The Major, she was beginning to discover, never did anything by halves and he wanted to do everything at once. But the spell of the evening before was still on her, as if she were still enchanted by the French opera and the great table at Delmonico's heaped with food and wine. The supper of the night before had been her wedding breakfast, alone at a table with Gus, in a big restaurant filled with people who kept coming up to the table to be introduced to her. That would be all the wedding breakfast she would ever have. And their love . . . she knew now that she was in love and it was something she had never even imagined.

Across the table from her the Major lighted a cigar (He knew already that she did not mind his smoking in her presence). Then he smiled at her with that curious look in the blue eyes which seemed to envelop and protect her, and said, "Miss Livingstone is coming to lunch with us. I think I had better explain to you about Miss Livingstone."

He cleared his throat and seemed to reflect for a moment and said abruptly as if it cost him a great effort, "I am a very rich man, sparrow."

"I guessed you were rich, Gus."

"And I mean to be richer still." He paused

again, looking at the tip of his cigar. Then he said, "But wealth isn't everything. I want a lot more than that. The world is filled with things and I guess I want everything. Money can buy much but not everything."

She did not answer him because she was a little frightened.

"I can take care of myself. A man can do it. But I want you to have everything too." His brow wrinkled and she thought that color came into his face. Then he said, "This is a tough place . . . New York. We'll have to fight for what we want. I've always had to fight. I don't mind for myself but I want to make it easy for you." He looked at her sharply, all the softness gone out of his eyes. "Do you understand what I am driving at?"

"Yes, Gus. I think I do."

"You'll have to help. I can't do it alone."

"I'll do anything you want, Gus." He was everything to her, everything now.

Then he seemed to relax again. "And that brings us to Miss Livingstone." He looked at her and smiled, the sensuous lips curling a little at the corners in mockery. "Miss Livingstone," he said, "is what is known as a 'lady in reduced circumstances.' She is a poor relation of everyone in New York who is what the papers call 'important.' "

Again he hesitated, as if it were difficult for him to find the words necessary for him to continue. He turned the cigar round and round in his strong fingers, and presently he said, "She is a dreary woman, I am afraid, but there is a great deal she can teach you . . . and me, too . . . that we will need to know."

"I don't know anything really, Gus. I was scared to death most of the time last night."

He laughed, "You were wonderful. You were exactly right. They wanted to see what I had brought out of the West. They found I had brought a dove . . . a lovely white innocent dove. Still, there are things to learn . . . how to behave and who are the right people and a lot of other things." Suddenly he leaned across the table and took her hands in his. "We're going on an adventure, sparrow. We're going to have a fight. If we stick together it will be all right because we're smart . . . a lot smarter than 98 per cent of the people in this town. We're going to have everything. Augustus Parkington and little Susie Graham are going to end up on the top of the heap. Understand?"

"Yes. I think so." But her voice was soft and trembled a little. She did not understand but she meant to learn.

* * *

Miss Livingstone turned out to be a dreary little woman. She dressed in gray with a shabby bonnet and a cape with a high collar which she appeared to use as a protection, as if she believed that when she ducked her head so that only her eyes were showing, she had managed to conceal the whole of herself. She was actually thirty-three, but resigned long ago to maidenhood, she made no effort and appeared ten years older than her age. She had a slight lisp and lived with her father in a small flat in Twelfth Street. Her eyes were brown and her complexion mole-flecked and rather muddy.

As they sat at lunch that day — the Major and Susie and Miss Livingstone — Susie felt sorry for her, why she did not know exactly, except that she seemed frightened and ashamed of herself, especially after she had taken off the cape and had no collar behind which to hide herself. Apparently she knew a good many of the people having lunch in the same dining room, but each time she bowed to one, dark color spread over her sallow face. To Susie it seemed that all her body must be only a mass of exposed nerve ends. It seemed to her too that the Major was aware of Miss Livingstone's uneasiness. He paid great attention to her, gently urging upon her one delicacy after another and asking after the health of her father. What Susie did not know was that this was the first time Miss Livingstone had even eaten in public in a "public house." And she did not know until long afterward that the blush which came over the sallow face of Miss Livingstone was occasioned not only by the consciousness of being seen in a public house but by being seen at the same table with the flamboyant Major Augustus Parkington.

Afterward the Major went away leaving the two women together. For a little while after they had gone back to the parlor of the apartment, there was an awkward sense of strain. For a moment they stood looking at each other and Susie thought, He has hired friends for me. I must make real friends of them. With Mademoiselle Conti, in spite of her being a foreigner, this was easy enough. Gray, shy Miss Livingstone was something else. Susie felt sorry for Miss Livingstone. It would be impossible for anyone to feel sorry for Mademoiselle Conti. But at the moment the problem was to ease the agonized shyness of Miss Livingstone and so Susie said, "What would you like to do?" And Miss Livingstone said quickly, "It's what you like, Mrs. Parkington. Major Parkington suggested that we go to see some of the shops. He said there were many things you might want."

So all that afternoon they went from shop to shop, staring and feeling and buying. Miss Livingstone was not like Mademoiselle Conti; she did not buy things wholesale with a lavish hand. It was Susie who had to take the lead. The most Miss Livingstone ever said was, "I think it would be nice for you to have these handkerchiefs" or "That is a pretty pair of slippers. Why not buy them?" There seemed to be no check placed upon money. Most of the shopkeepers and their assistants seemed to know Miss Livingstone or to have heard of her. And the Major's name appeared to be as magical as it had been at Madame de Thèbes'. And at each place Susie bought a small gift or two for Miss Livingstone, because she felt sorry for her. Miss Livingstone's clothes all seemed shabby. The ostrich feather on her hat had obviously been transferred from bonnet to bonnet for a period of years. The gray of the high-collared cape was not a fresh gray; Susie suspected that earlier it had seen service as a durable dress.

Miss Livingstone protested at first, but the pleasure the small gifts gave her showed itself in an unsuspected light in her eyes and the heightened color of her face. Susie said, "Please take them. It gives me so much pleasure."

When they came in after darkness had

fallen, Miss Livingstone seemed almost happy. Susie asked her to the apartment for a cup of tea, but Miss Livingstone said she must return to her father who always expected her to have tea with him. What she did not say was that her father did not know where she had been all the afternoon, or that she had been shopping with the wife of that vulgar adventurer Augustus Parkington. Miss Livingstone had told him a white lie — that she was spending the afternoon with the Ladies Guild of St. John's Church — because she needed the money paid her as companion to Augustus Parkington's bride, not only for herself but to make her father's life more comfortable.

So Miss Livingstone left her and went like a gray bird, quickly, softly away into the yellow light of the street lamps. She was carrying a little parcel containing a special French sachet Mrs. Parkington had bought her.

When she had gone, Susie went up the stairs of the Brevoort past the bowing servants to the parlor with the red curtains. As she moved along the corridor she heard presently the sound of voices which as she came nearer, became clearly those of Mademoiselle Conti and the Major. They were arguing about something. The voice of the Major was scarcely audible but that of Mademoiselle

Conti was excited and strongly accented. For a moment Susie waited at the door, hesitating. They both seemed so much older than herself, possessed of so much more authority. She heard Mademoiselle Conti say, "It was only because you wanted to show her off. Delmonico's was the last place you should have taken her. It was a bad beginning. A woman like me . . . yes . . . but not a young bride. *On ne fait pas ça.*"

Then Susie was filled with shame at the idea of eavesdropping and pushed open the door. Mademoiselle Conti was standing by the red curtains drawn up even more erectly than usual in a wine-colored dress and a bold hat with flaunting plumes. Her black eyes were flashing. Certainly she was not ugly now; there was something magnificent about her that sent a faint chill of admiration down Susie's spine.

The Major's face was serious and astonished as Susie came in. He rose from his chair and came toward her, smiling suddenly.

Whatever the reason for the quarrel had been, it faded quickly. Champagne was ordered and in a little while Mademoiselle Conti, after arranging for a second visit to Madame de Thèbes, went away, making a magnificent exit, standing for a moment in the doorway leaning against the door to wish them a Happy New Year.

Her manner with the Major was quite different from that of Miss Livingstone. It was almost as if she dominated him.

Day after day, week after week, faded one into another in a kind of fireworks display of amusement and luxury, spending and furs and jewelry. There were times when Susie did not know whether she was happy or not, times in the night when she wakened in the great French bed with the Major lying beside her, when she was frightened, by what she did not know. The money frightened her because there seemed to be so much of it; he never asked her to spend less but only whether there was not something she did not have which she wanted. It seemed to her absurd and preposterous and somehow wrong that her mother had worked so hard in the Grand Hotel in Leaping Rock to save in a year what she spent in a few hours. It seemed odd and wrong that poor Miss Livingstone had so little. Neither of them was less intelligent than Gus; in some ways both were more intelligent. But Gus seemed to have ways of turning everything to gold, ways she did not understand or attempt to understand.

And she was frightened by the size of the city and its confusion, and the feeling she had of having no place in it but of being whirled about in a kind of maelstrom of luxury and gaiety. She thought, Some day perhaps, I shall have friends and a home. I must speak to Gus about it.

But never was she quite able to bring herself to the point of speaking to him.

And she was frightened by the slow discovery that there was a part of her husband which she did not know at all and which he was determined she should not know. Of what happened to him, what he was like, what he did from the time he left in the morning until he returned in the evening, she knew nothing at all. Twice in a newspaper she had discovered articles which abused him and called him all names short of that of thief; and then she noticed that that particular newspaper never again appeared in their rooms. In other papers she frequently saw his name, always in the part of the paper dealing with business which bored her. She read what was written about him; it had always to do with railroads and mines but she understood very little of what was written about Major Augustus Parkington.

She knew only that she loved him for his strength and the curious tenderness which accompanied it, for his vitality and his boisterous good humor, for the charm which could melt a bronze statue if he chose to use it. She knew, even then, that she had been fortunate in the love circumstance had given her. But even the love and the knowledge had no power to stifle the dread she sometimes felt in the night.

And then one day, timidly, she said, "Gus, can we have a house of our own some day?"

"Sure, sparrow."

"And I'd like to meet people . . . the kind of people who become friends."

"Sure, sparrow, you will." Then he put his arms about her and said, "That's coming. We must do one thing at a time. I had a surprise for you, but I'll tell you now. You're going to have a house . . . a fine beautiful house on Thirty-fourth Street just off Fifth Avenue. It's bought and it's being redecorated."

"But can't I help with it, Gus?"

"It's nearly finished now." She wanted suddenly to cry but she controlled herself.

"You mustn't feel badly. It's a beautiful house. There isn't a finer house in the whole of New York. It's so near finished now, it would be a pity to spoil the surprise by showing it to you. You can wait, can't you?"

"Yes. I guess so."

And the next Sunday he said abruptly while they were having breakfast, "We're going to church this morning."

They went to St. John's Church on Fifth Avenue a little way from the hotel and as they went in, a little while before the service began, Susie was aware that their entrance created excitement in the congregation. A man whom the Major seemed to know took them down the long central aisle to a pew three rows from the front, and as they advanced, the Major even taller and straighter than ever, a little wave of excitement and whispering followed them.

It was a big church, famous for its music and Susie sat quietly with her eyes straight before her, aware in every nerve that for some reason she and the big man beside her were the center of all interest. It was as if the glances of the people behind her bored through Madame de Thèbes' rich furs and frock. From time to time waves of color swept over her face and her whole body seemed painfully warm.

When the service was finished they walked slowly down the aisle again, but most of the congregation seemed already to have gone or to be entering the carriages drawn up outside at the curb. The man who had showed them their pew was waiting, hat in hand, and the Major introduced him as Mr. Agnew. The rector was also there and a few other people who bowed from a distance. Mr. Agnew was a small, thin, frail man, with rather weaselly eyes.

"Mr. Agnew and I," explained the Major, "are in business together."

"It's a pleasure to meet you, ma'am," said Mr. Agnew. "The Major has been telling me about you."

Then the rector interrupted saying, "I presume this is Mrs. Parkington." He was a handsome man, too handsome, Susie thought, with a high color, dark eyelashes and wavy black hair. He had scarcely any lips at all, and there were deep sharp lines at the corners of the mouth. "Reverend Mr. Burchard," the Major murmured.

He pressed Susie's hand warmly and said, "We are indeed glad to welcome you among us. I am delighted to meet Major Parkington's wife. I hope you will think of St. John's as your home."

He held Susie's hand a little too long and pressed it a trifle too warmly. Something about him made her feel a little unclean. He was, she felt, paying her special attention, not because she was a woman, young and pretty, but for other reasons. What they were she was unable to divine.

"Mrs. Burchard," he continued, "was saying only the other day that she wanted to call on Major Parkington's wife."

By the time they had finished chatting the rest of the congregation, save Mr. Agnew, had gone. He waited to accompany them through the small churchyard to the street where, standing with his head bare, he said good-bye.

As they walked toward the hotel, Susie said, "You never told me you had a partner called Mr. Agnew."

The Major laughed, "He's not a partner. I just helped him out of a hole and made some money for him." He chuckled again, "He's just a squirt. Did you like the service?"

"It was too long and the church was cold."

"It won't be much longer," said the Major, "I've just bought a new heating plant for it. And the rector, Mr. Burchard — did you like him?"

"No."

"Why?"

"I don't know. I had a feeling about him. He's not my idea of a minister."

Again the Major chuckled. "I think he'll go a long way. He's certain to become a bishop. There's no stopping him. He knows what he wants and he knows all the tricks."

Presently out of the first confusion and impact of lights and people and clothes and rich food and money, one thing at least became clear to Susie: it was the knowledge that her husband meant what he had said when half mockingly, as if he were a little ashamed, he had declared that he meant for both of them to have everything life could give him. She began to understand why he had brought Mademoiselle Conti and Miss Livingstone into her existence. She began to understand their value to her, and she was grateful to the Major for the delicacy with which, in the beginning, he had managed to introduce the two women into her daily life. He might have said, "You are young and awkward and provincial. Before you can go about and take a place in the life of New York you will need to learn many things — among them, simply how to dress and behave." But he did not do this. Quietly he had allowed her to understand and adapt herself to them.

They became slowly not alone her only friends but very close friends indeed. Wisely, by instinct, she kept them apart. Almost from the beginning she understood that they were different elements which no power on earth could bring together, and after a time, although she sometimes spoke of Miss Livingstone to Mademoiselle Conti, she never mentioned Mademoiselle Conti in the presence of Miss Livingstone.

Mademoiselle Conti, always with tact and brilliance, taught her many things — how to walk erectly and with an air of dominating those about her, how to put on a hat or a frock, how to make conversation about nothing whatever, how to make the best feminine use of a fan or a muff, how to destroy the slight nasal quality in her voice. There were, too, the French lessons which went remarkably well and the books which Mademoiselle Conti gave her to read, sometimes in French. She taught her things about music and opera and took her to concerts where they attracted much notice — the ugly, smart Frenchwoman and the small, pretty, smartly dressed American one.

Long afterward it seemed to her that the source of most of her education came neither from books nor precepts but from the fortunate fact that both Mademoiselle Conti and Miss Livingstone, in their very different ways, were inveterate gossips. People, their doings, their scandals, their tragedies, their defeats and triumphs, were of the most passionate interest to both women. It was true that their gossip was of worlds widely apart and unconnected in any way, at least on the surface, but it was also true that between them they covered very nearly the whole of the world in which the Major had decided Susie was to move.

Mademoiselle Conti seemed to know everything which went on in the world of artists and singers, dancers and actresses and politicians and rich men. It was a world which fascinated Susie and she could never have enough of Mademoiselle Conti's stories, not only of New York but of London and Paris as well. Sometimes at Madame de Thèbes' or in a restaurant Mademoiselle Conti pointed out to her people she read about in the papers or about whom Mademoiselle Conti had told her stories — actresses and concubines, people like Jim Fiske and Josie Mansfield and La Belle Otero.

Miss Livingstone knew none of these people and until she became Susie's companion, she never frequented even the fringes of the world in which they moved. Miss Livingstone came out of a world which did not live in public, which was rarely seen and whose women lived a seraglio-like existence behind closed doors in great houses which stood in Washington Square and lower Fifth Avenue, on Murray Hill and in a cluster about the region of Thirty-fourth Street. One great marble house, belonging to an eccentric called Mrs. Morton Ogden, stood far north of the others in the area above the reservoir occupied largely by squatters. Mrs. Ogden, Miss Livingstone said, occupied a curious position in New York society. Her father, immensely rich but a vulgar self-made man, had married a Van Cortlandt out of a house on Washington Square, so Mrs. Morton Ogden had the advantages both of blue blood and enormous wealth. The invitations she sent out for her first reception in the huge marble house were written in red ink and since then Mrs. Morton Ogden had been known in New York society as "Bloody Mary."

Susie discovered before long that Miss Livingstone was indeed what was called "a poor relation." It was true that she knew the women who lived behind the closed doors of the great houses; she was related to many of them. The drab gray costume with the high-collared cape had come down to her from Mrs. Morton Ogden's aunt on the Van Cortlandt side. Until the Major came along and engaged her as companion, she and her father had existed in a three-room flat upon an allowance from a cousin.

Miss Livingstone talked a great deal about her father. He seemed to dominate her whole existence. She had to be home at five to make his tea. On days when he did not feel as well as usual she sent messages to say that she must stay at home. Bit by bit, out of Miss Livingstone's incessant small references to her invalid parent, he began to have a reality for Susie, and as slowly he emerged, it became clear to her that "dear Father" was a kind of monster who had destroyed, carefully and deliberately, all possibility of Miss Livingstone's having a normal existence.

One day Miss Livingstone confessed that she had given up her one chance of marrying because her father needed her. She told the story naïvely with tears in her pale eyes, tears partly of pity for herself and partly for "dear Papa." The admirer had been, Susie gathered, neither young nor very desirable, but Miss Livingstone had been fond of him. When she could not bring herself to say that she would leave her father and marry him, he had gone away.

Susie asked, "Have you ever heard from him, my dear?"

"Yes. Sometimes at Christmas I have a card from him. Once I saw him on the street. He didn't see me."

She began to cry and Susie put an arm about her shoulder and found herself crying suddenly. "Do you mind if I call you Harriette? It seems silly to go on calling you Miss Livingstone."

For a little time Miss Livingstone could not answer for sobbing, but at last she managed to say, "Yes . . . please do . . . it would make me very happy."

And so after that they were Harriette and Susie to each other and something seemed to happen to Miss Livingstone. With the money the Major paid her — and he paid her richly because he too felt sorry for her in his big-handed generous way — she began to buy herself small gewgaws and clothes that were no longer a dusty gray or an ugly brown. Even the Major noticed the difference. One night he asked, "What has come over Miss Livingstone? She's beginning to look like a fast woman."

"Don't make fun of her, Gus."

"I'm not making fun of her. It must be something you've done to her." He kissed her suddenly, one of those deep embraces which seemed to take utter possession of her. "You're a nice girl, sparrow, and I'm beginning to think you're a clever one."

She did not think herself clever . . . it was only that she liked people. She liked people and there was no spitefulness in her nature. What he meant by the remark, she did not understand until much later, and the Major, clever in his own way, did not trouble to explain. What he meant was that she had won the fanatic loyalty not only of Miss Livingstone but of Mademoiselle Conti as well, something infinitely more difficult to achieve. Even then he knew, far better than Susie herself, how profound and enduring was the devotion of Aspasie Conti.

He knew, too, that from Miss Livingstone Susie was learning exactly what he had meant her to learn. Without any special effort or consciousness, she was beginning to know very nearly everything about all those families, the powerful families living in the big ugly houses, who were connected with Miss Livingstone by blood and tradition. They were Miss Livingstone's whole world and she had very few other subjects of conversation. It was inevitable that Susie should acquire the knowledge of them which he meant her to acquire; later on she would have need of that knowledge. Those families were very important in the plans of Major Parkington, the adventurer, who had determined to become respectable and solid and even distinguished.

There were, of course, other people who touched her life, mostly men, but never more than superficially, occasional business acquaintances whom the Major brought to dine, one or two actors. And there were women who bowed from across the room to the Major but did not come to their table. Once, when he saw a hurt look in her eyes, he said, "My dear, they do not come to the table because I am with my wife. They aren't the sort a man introduces to his wife."

"Oh," she said.

"You understand?"

"Yes. Yes." But it did seem odd that he knew so many of these women. Among them were many of the women Mademoiselle Conti pointed out to her from time to time. It seemed that Mademoiselle Conti also knew most of them.

Then one afternoon after Miss Livingstone had left her to go home to tea with her father, Susie walked into the hotel to find the wife of Reverend Mr. Burchard inquiring if Mrs. Parkington was in.

The wife of the rector of St. John's was a tall, rather raw-boned woman, with a face like a Percheron mare, the daughter of a bishop. The concierge pointed out Susie as she came in and Mrs. Burchard, with an iron professional smile on her face, came quickly toward her, too quickly so that Susie felt suddenly frightened as if this were a female sheriff bearing down upon her.

"My dear Mrs. Parkington," she said, "I'm Mrs. Burchard, the rector's wife."

Susie asked her to the parlor of the suite for a cup of tea, and upstairs in the room with the scarlet curtains, they sat opposite each other and chatted. "Chatted" was the proper word, Susie thought afterward, for there was a brittle insincerity about everything they said. Mrs. Burchard said she had been meaning to call for ever so long but that the duties of a rector's wife with five children were such that she was forever behind schedule. Susie, watching Mrs. Burchard, with a detachment and objectivity natural to her but also considerably developed by contact with Mademoiselle Conti, found herself startled by the word children. It scarcely seemed possible that this woman could be a mother, and when there rose in her memory the grim, hard-lipped face of the Reverend Burchard, the possibility of children seemed even more startling. And suddenly she felt a wild hysterical desire to laugh because all unwanted, all undesired, there came into her imagination the picture of these two people in the act of making love. It seemed scarcely credible. She could not keep herself from thinking that the act must have required a considerable amount of grim concentration on the part of both of them. She wondered how the rector could have married this mare-faced woman, and then saw again his face with the lipless mouth and the hard lines on either side of it, and thought, It is the face of a man who would marry a monstrosity if it would help him in his career.

The thought rather astonished her. She was beginning to understand many things about life she did not understand a year ago.

But Mrs. Burchard was talking on and on. "Poor Harriette Livingstone," she was saying, "How nice it must be for her to have you as a friend! She has had a dreary life . . . always so selfless, caring for her poor invalid father."

Susie wanted to say, "The old devil" but did not.

Mrs. Burchard said, "She must be a great help too on her side . . . with you coming as a stranger to New York and Major Parkington not knowing many people . . . practically a stranger here himself."

Even while Susie sat there she was learning a lesson — that in the world you must not always say what first came into your head. There might come a day when she could say it, but not yet. So she only said, with false primness, "I am very fond of Harriette. Sometimes I think it would be a good thing if her father would die. He can't have much pleasure in life and if he died Harriette could be free. She's not too old yet to enjoy life."

"Harriette must be thirty-three. The best part of her life is over. I'm sure God will reward her for her devotion."

This time Susie answered her rather tartly, "I'm sure the Lord owes her a big debt. He'll have a lot to make up for."

But before Mrs. Burchard had time to pretend shock, the door opened and the Major came in. He greeted Mrs. Burchard warmly, so warmly and with such *empressement* that for a moment the horse-faced woman softened and even trembled a little as if she were a seductive woman. Again Susie felt a wild desire to laugh and again she controlled herself.

To the Major Mrs. Burchard said, "Dear me, I had no idea it was so late. Your wife and I were having such a pleasant chat the time must have flown. I must go now. The rector and I always hear the children's prayers before they go to bed."

The Major urged her not to hurry off, but without any very great sincerity, and she went away saying that she expected Mrs. Parkington without fail at the gathering of the sewing circle on Wednesday.

The Major held open the door for her and when she had gone, he closed it and looked at Susie and said, "Well?"

There was a wonderful humorous look in his blue eyes, a look which made her love him with a sudden rush of love.

"She is an awful woman!" said Susie.

"Kiss me first and then we'll talk about her."

He kissed her and she asked, "Why did she call on me?"

The Major chuckled, "The church has a heavy debt. It's been buying real estate really on speculation, and the others are not so generous as Augustus Parkington."

"Oh, Gus, I think that's awful . . . for a church to be run like that."

He said, "St. John's my dear, is a fashionable church. It would rather surprise Jesus Himself."

He looked at her again with that humorous look of utter understanding that was like a caress from his great strong hands. "You're learning a lot of things, aren't you, sparrow? Are you going to the sewing circle?"

"I don't want to."

He put his arm about her waist. "You'd better go. It may not be pleasant. It may even be frightening, but it will be good experience. You'd better go."

"Do I have to?"

The look in his eyes suddenly became grave, "I think you'd better." Then he kissed her again. "You mustn't mind. Remember, honey, the future belongs to us . . . everything. Nobody has as much as we have."

"All right, Gus." She looked up at him.

"I think I'd do anything you ask."

"That's my sparrow. Take Miss Livingstone with you. She'll know all the women there."

Then at dinner he said suddenly, "Tomorrow you can see the surprise. The house is finished. We'll be moving on Monday."

"Oh Gus!" A sudden wave of pleasure and excitement swept over her, making her feel a little dizzy.

"I'll come home early and we can go to see it at teatime I'll carry you over the doorstep."

But it didn't turn out quite as he planned. The next afternoon Mademoiselle Conti went with her to Madame de Thèbes. She looked gray and tired despite the rouge which she used, artificially and decoratively, as a Frenchwoman. Under the great black eyes there were dark circles. For two or three days she had looked badly and something was gone of the old dashing erectness of her carriage. For the first time Susie suspected that she was perhaps older than she appeared to be. When Susie had asked if Mademoiselle Conti did not feel well, she only said, "Eet is nothing. You understand."

All the way from Madame de Thèbes to the hotel, Mademoiselle Conti, always so vivacious, was silent, and when they arrived at the door, she said, "May I come up for a cup of tea? I must speak to you of something."

Once they were inside the door of the scarlet curtained parlor, Mademoiselle Conti said, "Don't order tea until I have talked to you. We must not be interrupted."

Susie took off her cape and bonnet and said, "Take off your jacket, mademoiselle."

But Mademoiselle Conti in her deep voice said, "No, I shall be going at once."

She had not seated herself, but stood beside the gilt and marble-topped commode, looking pale and tragic, very erect again like a great actress. She wore the green gloves and one hand with the green fingers outstretched was pressed against the cold white marble. The pose remained forever in Susie's memory and years afterward she saw it again in Sargent's portrait of "Madame X" and recognized it at once.

"But you must have cup of tea," said Susie.

"No. I must go away quickly and I am not coming back. It is not *au revoir* . . . it is good-bye."

"But why? Have I done anything?" She was aware, desperately, that she did not want Mademoiselle Conti to go away.

"It is nothing you have done. It is something I did long ago. I do not want to go away. It is the last thing I wish."

"Then why must you go?"

"I cannot tell you that."

Although her voice had not changed its tragic quality, tears glittered in the great black eyes. Watching her, a curious thing happened to Susie. She became aware that Mademoiselle Conti, whether consciously or not, was giving a great performance, and as if hypnotized, she felt a sudden necessity deep within herself to give a performance on her side worthy of that of Mademoiselle Conti.

She moved nearer to the tragic invincible figure and put her arm about Mademoiselle Conti's waist. "But you can't do that. We are friends. It may be something which makes no difference. It may be something of no importance whatever."

"I have been fighting against it for three days and now I must go away because of the evil of someone . . . a woman who has threatened me."

"What has that to do with us?" asked Susie.

Suddenly the hand in the poison green glove moved from the marble-topped commode to wrench Susie's hand from her waist.

"It has everything to do with us. You must not embrace me. You must not touch me!" She started toward the door but Susie reached it before her and stood against it.

"No Aspasie! You must not . . . You see, I called you Aspasie without thinking. Tell me! Then if you must go, you must go."

Mademoiselle Conti suddenly covered her face with the green gloves. For a long time she was silent, and then with her eyes still covered, she said in a curious dead voice, "Veree well. I will tell you then."

She was silent for a moment and then, dropping her hands from her face but turning so that she did not look at Susie, she said, "It is this. I was once your husband's mistress. Another woman . . . another actress who hates me . . . has been saying she would tell you if I did not pay her money. It is all over. It was all over long ago between him and me. We are good friends. We respect each other — that is all."

She looked suddenly, quickly at Susie and then looked away again, her black eyes filled with tears.

Susie had really heard only the words, "I was once your husband's mistress." The rest came to her dimly over the monstrous shock of those six words. She heard Mademoiselle Conti saying, "I will go now," and herself saying, "No. Not yet. I must think. I must think!"

She felt suddenly faint and slipped to the

arm of the chair beside her. One thought after another went quickly through her brain churning each other round and round. She was aware that Mademoiselle Conti had not gone away but was still standing by the commode. The thoughts kept saying, Of course he has had many mistresses. He is not in love with her now. He cannot be. She is old. I like her. She is a friend. Of course he has had mistresses before . . . a man like him . . . it couldn't be otherwise . . . that is why he knows how to make love so well . . . No doubt she is the one who taught him . . . A fire of jealousy scorched her brain and quickly burned itself out. That is silly. There is nothing to be jealous of. He loves only you. You are young and pretty. He no longer loves her. No, I don't want her to go away. I don't want her to go away. I like her. If she goes away everything will be different for you. You'll be alone. You need her. You love her. You will never again find anyone quite like her. Don't be a silly sentimental fool!

Then she found herself looking at Mademoiselle Conti and saying, "You mustn't go away, Aspasie. We shall never speak of it again. It will be as if it hadn't happened. I believe you when you say that it is finished. It doesn't matter. Only you mustn't go away.

I promise we will never speak of it again. It will be as if it had not happened."

She found herself holding both the green-gloved hands. Then Mademoiselle Conti was crying and they were embracing each other, Mademoiselle Conti kissing her French fashion, on both cheeks. She was saying, "Susie, you are a wonderful woman . . . a wise woman . . . *a femme du monde.*" And suddenly she understood that Mademoiselle Conti was paying her a great compliment and that it filled her with extraordinary pride to be called *une femme du monde*. It meant that she was wise and logical and human and mature and clever. It meant too that she was beginning to learn the things Gus meant her to learn.

That was how she and Mademoiselle Conti came to call each other Aspasie and Susie.

"And now," said Mademoiselle Conti with sudden briskness, "I think I need some champagne."

So when the Major returned he found his wife and Aspasie Conti sharing a bottle of champagne. They seemed gay. Susie had a third glass for him.

She said, "Aspasie and I are drinking to the new house." The word "Aspasie" gave him a shock that was apparent even in a face trained to conceal emotion. He took the glass of champagne Susie poured for him and murmured, "To the new house." The three of them raised their glasses and then Susie said, "I've invited Aspasie to go with us. She's dying of curiosity."

It was clear that he found himself at a loss for words. The shadow of disappointment came into his eyes, but after moment he said, "I think that's a wonderful idea. She gave me a great many suggestions and some good advice. She'll like to see how they were carried out."

There was a shade of mockery in his voice but Susie chose to ignore it and if Mademoiselle Conti noticed it, she gave no sign. Something very curious had happened suddenly. It was as if the two women were in alliance against him. With his immense sexual awareness, he divined it and suddenly grinned. Something, he was aware, had happened which altered the relationship among the three of them, but of what it was he had no idea.

When they had finished the champagne he said quickly, "Come along! I'm trying out a new pair of horses and they're not good at waiting."

So in the end he did not carry Susie over the doorstep. The butler was expecting them and flung open the great mahogany doors as the three of them got down from the carriage and came up the stoop. As they crossed the threshold, Susie's arm was linked in Aspasie's and there was a very grim look on the Major's face. Each of the women was having her small revenge for something. He still did not know what it was. When women came together as a sex against a man, a man had no chance. That was an old rule which he knew from a wide experience.

In the center of the great hall there was an immense gas-lit crystal chandelier, blazing and glittering. Beyond it Susie saw a huge stairway with a marble balustrade. The floor too was of marble and in the corners of the hall stood four huge porcelain vases and numbers of potted palms. She felt a sudden sharp pang of disappointment. This was not the house, the "home" she had dreamed of. It was more like a hotel.

She managed to say, as he watched, "Oh, Gus, it's wonderful!" She even managed to look as if she meant the words she spoke. Mademoiselle Conti herself could scarcely have given a better performance.

V

Mrs. Parkington herself went out to get the flowers. She felt remarkably young again because Harry was coming and Harry belonged to that part of her life which had brilliant memories, when for a long period, save for the ugly business of Norah Ebbsworth and the tragedy of "the terrible summer," her life had been untroubled, when every day had seemed bright and each morning filled with expectancy of things to come. He belonged to that part of her life in which nothing had seemed to matter but enjoyment. The Duchess was eighteen and unmarried and the boys were at school and she had learned not to be hurt by the Major's infidelities and that a flirtation could be entertaining and that one would not go to hell afterward. Harry was thirty-five then and younger than herself and a friend of the Prince and a gambler and very attractive. He had wanted more than she was willing to give him but he did not hold that against her. He simply remained hopeful. He had been hopeful for a great many years. His hope revived each time she returned to England until she was middle-aged and he had a wife and five children of his own, and even after that he always gallantly pretended that she was still the most desirable woman he had ever met and also the coldest.

Looking back now as she drove to the flower shop she knew that she had refused him, not because she was cold but because she didn't like things that way, on such a casual basis. Even now she could not altogether understand or forgive the promiscuity she sometimes encountered in fashionable English country houses. And after the thing had happened in Bad Gastein she knew that she was right. If she hadn't felt as she did, she would never have had that happiness. Nevertheless there were moments when, even as an old lady, she felt a faint regret over Harry. And she would be grateful to him always and forever, for what he had done in the business of Norah Ebbsworth.

And now here he was in New York, sent over in charge of documents and special treasures which had been shipped to America for safekeeping against the possible danger of capture by the Germans. It was very difficult to believe in the reality of such a situation — that the English should ever be in danger of defeat, that London itself should be threatened. She sighed, thinking how much she had seen in her lifetime, and thought, It was Harry and people like him who brought England to the danger she faces today. It was all very gay in the past and a few people had everything and a great many were miserable and hungry, standing toothless and undernourished to cheer every time royalty or a procession of peers passed by on the street. She thought, Now they are paying for it.

Then the car stopped in front of the florist's and Hicks, the driver, was holding the door open for her.

"A lovely day, madame," he was saying. "Like the first day of spring."

The snow was gone and the sidewalks were dripping. The flowers in the window looked brighter, as if they felt the sun and stood up a little straighter.

Inside, the proprietor greeted her, saying, "You look very well, Mrs. Parkington. I thought you'd have gone south long before now."

Tiresome, she thought, He treats me as if I were an aged broken-down invalid. Aloud she said, "No, I preferred to stay here. There is so much going on, nowadays. Florida can be very chilly and very dull." She moved toward a great vase of the first mimosa of the year, drawn by the beauty of its powdery gold and all the memories which the sight of it aroused. "I'll have some of that — about a dozen sprays." It made her think again of Harry and the villa at Monte Carlo and the parties Gus was always giving on the yacht.

Then very carefully she selected some blue Siberian iris and a lot of jonquils and two great bunches of Freesia for the perfume, and two bunches of violets which made her think suddenly of the Princess of Wales. Alexandra — the one who would always be the only Princess of Wales.

"I'll take them with me," she said, "I want them for this afternoon."

While the florist and his assistant wrapped them in sheafs of waxed paper, she went from one great bunch of flowers to another, smelling them, touching them as if she could somehow reach their very essence by a closer contact. The greenhouse was the only thing she missed about the house at Newport. When she still had the place there, flowers were sent down three times a week to the great house on Fifth Avenue. The flowers had taken the curse off the ugly house, destroying its vast pompous ornateness. Now she had to buy flowers and she no longer had a great plot of jonquils and tulips and other spring flowers laid out each year at the Flower Show by Ferguson and his assistants.

The flowers were ready and Hicks came in to help carry them to the car where he and the florists piled them about her on the seat and on the floor. I feel laid out like a corpse, she thought, but did not say it for fear of embarrassing Hicks and the florist.

As the florist closed the door, she called out, "Thanks, Mr. Wilks," and then Hicks drove off up Madison Avenue toward the house.

Once inside the door she had Taylor take the flowers to the pantry and then rang for Mattie to help. In a little while Mattie came down in the lift looking sleepy and a little disgruntled and Mrs. Parkington thought, Mattie is getting old. That was what came of letting yourself get too heavy. She only hoped that Mattie outlasted her. It was much easier to put up with Mattie's sly disapproval and complaints than to get adjusted to some-one new. And losing Mattie would be like losing her closest friend.

She knew why Mattie was disgruntled. Helping with the flowers was really Taylor's job, but Taylor was stupid about flowers. He had a way of turning the gayest bouquet into a set-piece funereal offering.

"It's a lovely day, Mattie," she said with exaggerated brightness, hoping that a little of her own mood might brush off like the pollen of the Golden Mimosa onto Mattie.

"Yes, madame," said Mattie firmly.

"I've brought back quite a lot of flowers — the first mimosa. I'll need some help with them."

"Of course, madame." She took Mrs. Parkington's hat and coat. "Mimosa," she said priggishly, "always seems a waste. It dries up right away."

"But it's gay while it lasts. I wanted the house to look nice for Lord Haxton."

Mattie did not answer her. She only sniffed and Mrs. Parkington knew that Mattie was being disapproving. She thought it was silly to be excited by the visit of an old man, an old man whom Mattie had never approved of even forty years earlier. Forty years ago she had thought him fast and disreputable and her opinion had never changed although now Harry was certainly old and harmless.

Mrs. Parkington began to hum to show that she was taking no notice of Mattie's mood.

Then Taylor appeared and said, "Mr. Stilham called, madame. He said it was important and he would come in after dinner unless he heard from you."

"It's all right, Taylor. Just call back and say I'll expect him about eight o'clock."

She stopped humming and frowned a little. It was tiresome the way they all came to her when they were in trouble; as if none of them had any common sense. All the fun and excitement suddenly drained out of her, leaving her feeling old and worried. Mattie was laying out the flowers on newspapers spread on a table in the dressing room by the main door, but their colors seemed dim now and their glory vanished, all because a long time ago her granddaughter had chosen to marry a prig and a fool who was in trouble now.

On the night before when Janie and Ned left Mrs. Parkington's house, they walked to Fifth Avenue and found a taxi. Ned said to the driver, "The Waldorf-Astoria," and when they were inside he took her hand and she asked, "What did you think of my great-grandmother?"

He was a sober young man and he was thoughtful for a moment. Then he answered, "She is a remarkable old lady . . . very charming and very bright. She didn't seem to be any age at all. And she was very kind to me."

"I wanted you to like her. I love her very much." She almost said, "Much more than I love my mother, much more than I love anyone in the family," but she kept silent for fear of shocking him. She was in love and love frightened her. She had never thought about falling in love and everything about the experience astonished her — that anyone should become very dear to her quite suddenly, that it should make her happy to sit with her hand in the hand of a young man of whose very existence she had been unaware only six months ago, that when she was with him, the world should seem so changed, the sun brighter, the stars more brilliant. But most of all she found it astonishing that one could be made so happy by the mere presence or the mere thought of another person.

There was no ignorance in her but she had innocence; she would very likely have it until she died. Great-grandmother Parkington was like that. Despite all she had known and experienced in a long rich life, she was at eighty-four, still innocent. She still anticipated with pleasure any new experience. She still liked the adventure of new people; each one was for her a new world opening and blossoming like a flower. It was innocence that kept her so young and so gay; it was the kind of innocence with which, out of all the family, Janie alone was blessed.

Now in the darkness the girl found that she was smiling as she said, "My great-grandmother has had an extraordinary life. Now and then she has told me bits of it. She is fascinating when you can get her to talk. She's been very lucky. She's lived through so many different worlds. We'll never have that chance."

In the darkness Ned chuckled, "I wouldn't say that. The world doesn't change as much as that, honey."

"But our world will always be more or less the same. We never knew what Europe was like before the first war and we never knew it between that war and this one, and if this one is ever finished, it will never be the same."

"I wouldn't worry too much about that. There'll be plenty to keep us busy just putting the pieces together again."

"I was only thinking how much she has seen. She told me the other day that she was seven years old when the Civil War was finished. Think of that!"

"Yes. That's something!"

They were silent for a moment and then she said, "You're really not listening. You're thinking of something else."

Very quickly he answered, "That's true. I was listening but I was also thinking about my sister and her husband and hoping you like them. They aren't brilliant but they're nice."

"Wouldn't it be wonderful if people like us didn't have to think at all about relations and friends and things like that? Wouldn't it be wonderful if we could just be alone in the world, the two of us, until afterward when we were married and settled and everything." She pressed his hand, "I don't mean anything about your sister and her husband. I'm sure they couldn't be nicer . . . I only mean that you're worrying about what I'll think of them and I'm worrying about what you really think of all my relatives. Some of mine are pretty awful."

She was thinking of the Duchess with her dull, slightly bewildered appraising eye and Aunt Madeleine and her divorces and even her brother Jack.

Ned answered, "I'm not marrying your relatives, honey."

But he had lied to her when he said he was thinking about his sister; he had really been thinking about her father and what he had heard only a few hours earlier, but he couldn't tell her anything about that. He kept hoping that he might never have to tell her, that what seemed certain now would in the end never happen. She had already asked him if he liked her father and he had lied, saying that he liked him very much which was not at all the truth. Even in his few years of experience, he had met too many men like Amory Stilham, and not one of them he knew was to be trusted. His work had brought him into contact with them, the kind of men who believed astonishingly that privilege placed them above the moral laws of the average citizen. They were, he had decided, a special product of a special era in American life; they were born of a period undistinguished by morals and distinguished principally by an undue respect for success, no matter how it was achieved. But they were, too, types that were eternal. The knowledge he had picked up during the afternoon kept gnawing at his brain like a worm . . . Amory Stilham would be tried and very likely go to jail and Amory Stilham was Janie's father. It was a horrible thing because it would hurt her.

The taxicab stopped at the doorway of the hotel. Everything seemed suddenly false and hideous to him, the bright lights of the canopy, the wide carpeted stairs, the people in the huge lobby. The monstrous size of the hotel — the last tribute to an age which believed there could be virtue or beauty merely in size or ostentation.

Then from among the crowd emerged the figures of his sister and brother-in-law. There was something real and solid about them which brought him comfort.

Janie liked them at once. His sister was called Mary and she was older than himself

. . . thirty-five, Ned told her, but the difference in age had not made any great difference. They were very close to each other because their mother had died when he was seven years old and Mary had been partly mother to him as well as sister. She was very proud of his record at the University of Wisconsin and the way he had gotten on since then. She was a big handsome woman dressed smartly in a mink coat and a small black hat with stiff green feathers. There was warmth about her, not the continual fiery warmth which Janie felt in Ned himself, something reserved and set aside for those toward whom he felt tenderness, but a big enveloping warmth. She was a woman who clearly loved her husband and two children, who kept her house well and enjoyed an occasional Rabelaisian joke because she was healthy and liked people. Even disappointments and disillusionments would not change her.

Her husband, whose name was Charlie Evans, was a good-looking successful fellow. You could tell he was successful by the brightness of the steel-rimmed spectacles he wore, by his extraordinary appearance of neatness and the twinkle in his brown eyes and the curl of his lips. Everything had gone well for Charlie Evans since the day he was born.

He had wanted a wife he loved, children, prosperity and he had all of them.

As they came toward her Janie liked them, but more than liking and far more profound was the feeling that they were warm and frank and friendly, that they meant to take her into their lives without reservations because Ned had chosen her and they loved Ned and would be loyal to him no matter what he did. It was a curious sensation, like the comfort of a warm bath after being chilled. It was something she had never met before in her world, except with Great-Grandmother Parkington, and there it was scarcely impressive since it was so familiar.

She and Mary had two cocktails and the men had three and then they went to dinner at "21." In the taxicab gaiety joined them and Ned's air of preoccupation seemed to fade away. He asked questions about Charlie's factory and the children and people called Hutchinson and Hoffman in South Bend who were old friends and then Mary said, suddenly, "That's enough, Ned. This is Janie's evening too."

Janie was grateful to her although she had neither felt bored nor excluded from their conversation. On the contrary all their talk made her feel pleasant and intimate and in a curious way it made her feel that through

Ned she belonged to something, that somehow she had already acquired solidity and roots, simply by being in love with him.

At "21" Janie bowed to Foxworthy the playwright and two actresses and a girl who had been at boarding school with her. Ned bowed across the room to a thin man with gray hair who he said was a man from the department in Washington.

This world was Janie's territory. She had invaded it to escape from the world into which she was born as the child of Amory and Helen Stilham, a fact which had bred in her a sense both of futility and inferiority, for all the things which an earlier generation had regarded as the greatest of advantages, appeared to Janie only as handicaps. As a child of fifteen she had become aware that she was imprisoned by circumstances — by being rich and the great-granddaughter of Mrs. Parkington, by being the daughter of Amory Stilham, by the very schools where she had received a not too sketchy education, by the certainty that wherever she went men with cameras seemed to appear magically out of walls to photograph her. And the knowledge had produced in her a kind of sadness, as if there were a curse upon her, as if some spell placed on her by a wicked fairy had made it impossible ever to exist as herself, to live as her great-grandmother had been able, despite everything, to live the whole of her long life. Because she was a thoughtful child she was aware too that there were whole worlds, unknown, unexplained, which were barred to her, shut away from her by all her "advantages."

That was why Ned had seemed wonderful to her — because he came from a world outside her own, and that was why tonight the presence of Mary and Charlie made her happy. This very restaurant, which to her was a commonplace affair, was to them exciting. Ned had suggested dining here because there would be people, famous or notorious, whom Mary and Charlie would find "interesting." That was what she liked about Mary and Charlie — they would be excited and gay tonight and tomorrow they would forget all the people they had seen because they had a life of their own which was perfectly satisfactory and pleasant. They were amused by the people she pointed out to them as they would be amused by animals in a zoo, and they would be honestly and simply impressed and then afterward in their own very real world they would forget all about them.

A world like that in which Mary and Charlie lived was a world Janie had never known but it seemed to her the most wonderful thing in the world. There were times when her own world seemed out of scale, dwarfing her, filling her with a sense of insignificance and futility. There were times when it seemed to her that she was only a ghost moving in shadows.

But Ned was real. Watching him across the table, she knew how real he was. There were times when she felt much older and wiser than he and times when she felt like a child beside him, a child for whom he felt great solicitude and tenderness. It seemed to her that the wisdom and knowledge which gave her the feeling of maturity were wisdom and knowledge that were destructive because they were tired and old and came out of a weary world. Sometimes it seemed to her that it was a world in which there was no faith in anything, but only a kind of deadness which oppressed her own spirit, so that nothing she did appeared to be worth doing and whatever lay ahead seemed only monotonous and dull.

Ned, she knew, trying not to look at him with too much adoration, had changed all that. His mere presence made whatever happened take on an exciting quality. When he was with her the whole world acquired a kind of brilliant coloration. When he was gone it turned drab again, infected by a dull and embalmed quality of monotonous security.

And this, her sad adolescent wisdom told her, was not simply because she was in love. There was a quiet, hidden animal vitality in him that manifested itself in odd sporadic ways, in abrupt chuckles, in sudden violent enthusiasms, in the very way he carried himself. But above all he had faith; he believed in what he was doing; he wanted ardently to make the world in which he lived a better, richer, more exciting place — not for himself alone but for all people — the common ones, the dull ones, the stupid ones, the underprivileged ones. That was something she had never encountered in a world upholstered in wealth and security and stagnation. It was something she could not hope to explain to her own mother and father. Only Great-Grandmother Parkington might understand, but in the presence of Granny she never felt able to speak of such things lest before the old woman's vast wisdom and experience, she should seem shy and childish.

Across the table from her, Ned watched her, conscious of her happiness, and pleased because it was clear that she liked his sister and brother-in-law and that they liked her. In some ways she was, he knew, older than any of them, but in others she was a baby. That, more than anything else, was what made him love her; her sad precocious wisdom fascinated him and her childishness filled him with a desire to cherish and protect her.

He was an ardent young man, but less simple than he seemed, and he had been endowed by God and nature with a kind of creative imagination. It was inclined to take hold of a situation and then build it toward a dramatic conclusion. This imagination helped to give him brilliance as a lawyer and to make his mind attractive to other people, but it also made him the victim of worry and the anticipation of tragedies and disasters which rarely achieved reality. It made of him a worrier, and that was what he was doing now — worrying madly, almost insanely over Janie and the future. Even the champagne did nothing to dull the leaping, vaulting imagination.

The knowledge about her father which he shared with none of the others, kept gnawing at his happiness, keeping him outside the gaiety of the others. The figure of Janie's father, the embezzler, the swindler, the sanctimonious crook, cast its shadow over the whole evening, while one part of his mind kept working, active as flame, creating a future of suffering which might never become reality. There was no possibility of doubt any longer regarding the guilt of Amory Stilham. He knew, perhaps better than anyone, because he had collected much of the evidence which had closed the trap.

Watching Jane, gay and happy, free from the melancholy which so often obscured her from him, he turned the doomed future over and over again in his mind, speculating whether he should prepare her for the horror that was to come or to let someone else tell her. For a wild moment it occurred to him that she might refuse to marry him because he had played a part in the investigation or because she felt, fantastically, that she could not bring upon him the disgrace of marrying the daughter of a swindler.

It was all a nasty, complicated business of which he and Janie were victims. There had been, he knew well enough, a moment just after he had gone to spend the week end at Amory Stilham's house in the country, when he could have turned back, when he could have forced himself not to see Janie again. And he knew too that such a course would have been much wiser. It would have been easier for him, it would have been better for his own future. But he was aware too that he was not like that; he understood that the very health and vigor which made his brain a brilliant, successful instrument, made him fall in love, recklessly, with all the violence of a lusty nature. He knew that by all the rules, Janie was not the right person for him. There was her name and her wealth and the unwelcome and snobbish attention of newspapers and public, and there was the curious background of enchanted stability which had surrounded her since she was born. There were so many things she did not know, about people, about the world, about how things worked in life, because her own life had never had any relation to the reality of people but only to the reality of a world, coddled and protected, wrapped in cotton wool, a world which was utterly doomed. Even her faint childish efforts to escape had only brought her into the borders of a world that was equally false, a world of writers and actors and idlers which fed upon itself, continually devouring its own entrails and consuming its own vitality. She was wrong, by all the dictates of his very clever reason, but this reason was bereft of authority because he loved her and felt a passionate need to rescue her, for he was still young enough to believe in St. George and the Dragon. Wisdom had not yet dulled ardor nor had experience made him crafty. He was young and he was in love and as with Janie herself, there was a part of him that was very wise and a part of him that was very young. There was, for neither of them, any escaping their own muddled generation.

His sister, knowing him so well, was aware throughout the evening that he was troubled and suffering, but knowing him well, she also knew that there was nothing she could do to help him. Whatever the trouble was he would have to fight his way out of it, for he was like that. He had always been since he was a stubborn little boy.

After dinner they went to see a musical play of Cole Porter's and then to Monte Carlo and El Morocco and the Stork where people knew Janie and a few knew Ned and none of them knew his sister and her husband. It was a conventional evening, the most conventional in the world, and in a way the emptiest and deadliest in the world, but Ned's sister and her husband loved it and in South Bend they would talk of it for a little time after they returned. It was for them the evening had been arranged and they had enjoyed themselves, making Janie happy although to her it was old stuff and tiresome. Before the evening was over their enjoyment had dulled even the edge of Ned's private misery.

When they had left Ned's sister and brother-in-law at the Waldorf, they drove in a taxicab to Janie's house in Sixty-eighth Street. On the way Ned took her hand again.

"They are nice, aren't they?" he asked, a little strained and nervous, because to him it made so great a difference.

"I think they're lovely. I think they're the nicest people I ever met."

"You needn't say that."

"But I mean it, honey."

They were silent then for a little while and happy with the simple happiness of being together. And presently he said, "You wouldn't let anything come between us, would you?" And he was aware of the banality and the inadequacy of his words.

"No, honey. Why do you ask that?"

"For no reason at all . . . only because I'm afraid sometimes."

"You know I wouldn't."

"Would you marry me tomorrow? Would you run away?"

"I would if it was necessary . . . if it really had to be done. But I'd rather wait. You see, my mother would like a wedding and my great-grandmother too. There's been so much in our family that was irregular, my mother makes a fetish of what is regular. She'd want everything done right." She laughed suddenly. "And I'd rather like it myself. I hope I'm only going to be married once."

At the door he said "Good night" and kissed

her, but there was no satisfaction, no pleasure in it, because the shadow of his worry came between them. She said suddenly, "What is it, darling? There's something wrong?"

He laughed, "No, nothing. I'm tired. I'm not used to staying out all night."

"Call me tomorrow before noon."

"Yes."

She went inside and closed the door and as she did so depression settled over her. It came down like a veil dimming the world all about her — the big hallway, the great stairway, the shadowy spaces of the over-elegant drawing room. She was aware as she started up the stairway of the sound of music, very faint and muffled, and thought, Mother must be awake.

Often in the night she wakened to hear the same sound and always it meant that her mother was suffering from insomnia and was lying awake on the sofa in the little sitting-room beside the bedroom she still shared with her husband. It happened more and more frequently of late . . . the faint sound of music joined with the coming of gray winter dawn.

On the second floor she walked along the hall to the sitting-room and knocked. Her mother's fretful voice said, "Come in," and as she opened the door Janie saw her lying on the chaise longue in a peignoir, a Shetland shawl about her shoulders. As Janie entered she put down her book, took off her horn-rimmed reading glasses and said, "Oh, it's you, dear. You're very late."

"It's only about four o'clock."

"It doesn't matter," said her mother, "Who did you go out with tonight?"

She divined that her mother probably knew all along that she had spent the evening with Ned. Both of them had avoided speaking his name for a long time now. She went on, "His sister was here from South Bend with her husband."

"What were they like?" The mother spoke as if she expected her to say they were something out of a zoo.

"They were very nice," Janie said, "I liked them very much." Then irritably she heard herself saying, "I wish you'd get up-to-date, Mother. Nearly all your friends are. Granny is much more up-to-date than you."

"I know," said Mrs. Stilham, "Your great-grandmother is always perfection."

"Why don't you take something to make you sleep?"

"No, thank you. We've enough trouble with that in the family." And Janie knew that her mother meant the Duchess. She went on, "I think I'm going to make this into a bedroom. I might sleep better if I could be alone. Your father is restless and snores."

"I think it would be more civilized," said Janie. Then she wished quickly that she had not spoken, for her mother, looking at her sharply, said, "What do you mean by that?"

"I don't know. Nothing at all." But she did mean something. She meant that it seemed evil for two people who hated each other to go on sharing a room. For she knew that her mother and father had hated each other for a long time in the most dreadful way, pretending that they did not hate each other, even sharing a room as if painfully to convince themselves that the truth was not true. It was a curious fetish, Janie sometimes thought, this worship of the idea of marital fidelity and happiness in a day when it no longer really mattered very much to anyone but the persons themselves. It must be awful to wake in the night and find yourself alone in the same room with someone you hated . . . night after night, on and on, forever, until you died.

Moved by a sudden pity for the tired woman with the drooping mouth, she said, "Is there anything I can get you, Mother? A glass of warm milk or something?"

"No. Nothing."

"Then I'll go to bed."

She started toward the door but her mother said, "Wait a moment, Janie. There's something I want to ask you."

"Yes, Mother."

"Sit down, please."

"Yes," said Janie, and sat down on the edge of a Louis Quinze armchair.

"It's about this Ned. I should like to know what is going on. You see a great deal of him. You seem to have dropped everybody . . . everything else."

"Yes."

"Are you in love with him?"

Quietly Janie said, "Yes."

"Seriously?"

"Yes."

A curious look came into her mother's face. "Nothing else has been going on?"

Janie felt suddenly angry, not at the suspicion but at the look in her mother's eye and the tone of her voice. "No. Why do you ask that?"

"Young people are so very odd nowadays."

"You talk as if you were a hundred years old."

"Sometimes I feel as if I were."

Janie was thinking, It might as well be now. I'll tell her now and get it over with. So aloud she said, "I'm going to marry him."

Her mother took the news with apparent

indifference. She was silent for a moment and then asked, "You're sure about it? It's not just an idea?"

"No."

Again her mother was thoughtful. Then she said, "I hope you understand how great a disappointment this will be to your father?"

"I don't see why it should be."

"You know perfectly well. Your father wanted you to marry someone he knew, someone out of your own world. I feel the same way although that's probably of no importance either to him or you."

"I'm sorry if he feels like that."

She was aware that her mother was behaving as she knew she would behave. She would never say, "You must not do this. I forbid it." She did not even grow angry. But she would work against it for the rest of her life, quietly, unscrupulously, insidiously, spreading doubts, tearing down confidence and happiness. Suddenly Janie felt very tired, as if the long slow discontent and unhappiness of this rich house had become an unbearable burden. Her mother was still talking, "I hope you realize what this means . . . that you'll have to give up all your friends, that you'll probably have to live in some outlandish place, with outlandish people. It won't be at all the way you think it will be."

"I've thought how it will be," said Janie, "And it's exactly what I want."

"You're a child, Janie. You don't know how it will be. You've been given all the things most people want most in the world and now you want to throw them all away."

Janie did not answer at once. When she spoke, she asked, "Were you in love with Father when you married him?"

"Yes, of course I was."

"It wasn't just the suitable thing to do?"

"I was very lucky. Your father was also considered an excellent match . . . and rightly."

"An excellent match," Janie repeated quietly, as if speaking to herself.

"That's what I said," repeated her mother. "And don't deceive yourself. In the long run that means something." Janie didn't answer her. Her mother said, "I only ask one thing. Don't hurry into this. It seems to me that Ned might have told your father and me."

"He didn't," said Janie, "because I asked him not to."

She was suddenly angry now, for the sake of Ned and the fashion in which her mother spoke of him. She said, "I wanted to spare him an idiotic conversation."

"And what, pray, do you mean by that rude remark?"

"I mean that neither of you could possibly understand about Ned or what he is."

"I think that I understand very well . . . only too well. He is a Red, a Communist. He's working for all the things which aim to tear down what has taken your father and men like him their lifetimes to build up."

Janie stood up. "You see, Mother, it's quite useless trying to talk about it."

"Of course," said her mother, "If you are determined to go through with it we'll back you up and have a wedding and put the best face possible on the whole thing."

And now Janie was really angry. "You needn't bother about the wedding. You needn't trouble yourself to put any face on at all." She stood up and walked toward the door, "I don't give a damn what you feel about it. I only know I've got to get out of this God-damned bedeviled house."

She went out the door, aware that her mother was rising to follow her. When she was halfway up the stairs, to her own room, she heard her mother's voice calling plaintively, "Janie, Janie!" But she paid no heed and presently she heard the door of her mother's sitting-room close again, and going into her own room she threw herself on her bed in the darkness and began to cry. She cried out of weariness, out of anger and partly out of pity for the tired, discontented woman with the drooping mouth belowstairs who could not sleep.

When she stopped crying and began to take off her clothes, the light of morning was already coming through the windows. The distant faint music from the radio belowstairs went on and on.

When Ned called in the morning she did not tell him anything of the conversation with her mother. He had, he said, to go to Washington by the one o'clock train. How long he would be there he did not know but he would send her a wire as soon as he discovered. His sister and brother-in-law were leaving at noon. They sent her their love. They had enjoyed the party the night before. They wanted her to pay them a visit in South Bend. His voice was deep and alive and the sound of it drove away the sense of gray depression.

He said, "I don't like to speak of it for fear it won't come true but they may have sent for me to give me a promotion."

"Oh Ned! How wonderful!"

"It might mean that I'd have to leave New York and go to San Francisco or Chicago.

Would you mind that?"

"How do you mean — would I mind it?"

"Would you mind going to one of those places with me?"

"Mind it, Ned? It would be wonderful."

"If that's what it is, I'll wire you. It would probably mean that I would have to go right away. You'd have to give up the idea of a big wedding."

"That would be all right too."

"Well, take good care of yourself."

"And you, honey."

"Good-bye."

"Good-bye."

But when his voice was cut off the loneliness and sense of depression returned. The whole house, even her own room, had acquired a kind of hatefulness, as houses do in which there exists long, persistent, dull unhappiness. Lying there in the bed, it seemed to her that she had first become aware of its hatefulness when she was twelve years old after she had gone to visit a school friend who lived in the country in Maryland. She and the friend had long since drifted apart so that the very appearance and personality of the friend had become something vague and hazy, but the memory of the house remained clear and bright — a roomy, rambling house full of soiled and faded chintz where there were very many dogs, a house with a hodgepodge of nondescript but friendly furniture with geraniums growing in pots in the windows. It was a house in which there was happiness and it had seemed bright and filled with sunlight even in the wet muddy days of January.

After that visit when she returned to the house in Sixty-eighth Street, it became forever a gloomy and depressing place, dark and filled with shadows, even when there was brilliant sunlight in the streets outside. It was a stuffy house, a luxurious house filled with expensive pictures and furniture which never seemed possessed either of life or of order. The effect was that of extravagant confusion, like that of a luxurious antique shop, as if between them, her parents had sought to buy or achieve by force something they neither possessed nor understood and which somehow would forever elude them.

Lying there in her bed, she permitted her mind to examine lazily the subject of houses and almost at once she thought of her great-grandmother's house. The things with which it was furnished were quite as expensive as the things in this great dreary house where people went in and out day after day, living, eating, sleeping sometimes without ever seeing each other. Yet the effect of Mrs.

Parkington's house was quite different. It was a cosy, happy place like the dark warm nest of a weaver bird or an oriole. In it one had not only a sense of happiness but of warmth and utter security. Inside its walls women, even the Duchess, took on a new beauty and brilliance and seemed more attractive. One did not think on looking at a chair, What a priceless piece of furniture; one thought, What a beautiful and friendly and inviting chair. Even the flowers had a different appearance and aura, not only because Mrs. Parkington had taste and sensitivity where flowers were concerned but because the flowers in her house seemed happy, as if they belonged there.

And again as had happened many times before, Janie felt a wild and passionate desire to live and grow old as her great-grandmother had done. To be like Mrs. Parkington seemed to her the greatest achievement one could desire. And suddenly her day became clear. She would have some lunch and go out quietly while her mother was still asleep to the British War Relief headquarters to do what there was to do there. And afterward she would go to Mrs. Parkington's for tea and perhaps Granny would ask her to stay for dinner.

She was dressing when there was a knock

at the door and her brother's voice said, "May I come in?"

When she saw him she thought, What a good-looking boy he is and how ill he looks!

He had the kind of lean overbred look that one finds sometimes in the portraits of El Greco, a lean face with soft beautiful eyes, contradicted by the narrowness and cruelty of the mouth. He was not at all a Parkington. His looks, his great-grandmother said, came from the Blair blood whence, she added, very likely came his recklessness and taste for dissipation. It was nearly forty years since Mrs. Parkington's son had married a Blair against her wishes. One could marry the daughter of a healthy truck driver, she had said, but not into a family where eccentricity constantly hovered on the borders of insanity. And now forty years after the marriage a Blair and not a Parkington came into Janie's bedroom.

Girls usually liked him, for the way he wore his clothes, for his glib conversation, for his reckless approach, for the beauty of his hands and hair and eyelashes. Janie saw his points but there were times when in the depths of her heart she knew he was perverse and defeated nearly to the point of insanity. Lately she had begun to feel that she was immensely older than he and to treat him like a child.

He flung himself down in a chair and said,

"Did you have a good time last night?"

"Yes. Wonderful."

"Who were the fresh looking couple?"

"Ned's sister and brother-in-law."

"From the Corn Belt too?"

"Yes."

"I saw you in the Champagne Room."

"Why didn't you join us?"

He grinned, "I didn't think Maisie would mix too well."

Janie sat in front of her dressing-table and began arranging her hair. In the mirror she could see the reflection of his face. Suddenly she asked, "Are you keeping Maisie?"

He grinned again, "No, I don't have to keep her."

"You cad," said Janie, with indifference.

"Why not let someone else do the paying?"

"I must say that's not a very nice point of view."

"Not nice but convenient and practical."

"Is she a nice girl . . . you know what I mean?"

The question seemed to puzzle him for a moment, "Yes," he said after a while, "we understand each other."

"Does she bore you?"

"Sometimes, but when she gets boring I run away. What made you think of that?"

Janie laughed, "I don't know. I've always

thought that would be the trouble in a situation of that kind . . . the long stretches of boredom in between."

He laughed, "It is . . . but then it must be true of married life too. Look at Mother and Father."

"It needn't be," said Janie, "if you marry the right person.

"Are you going to marry this Ned what's-his-name?"

"His name is Ned Talbot and you might as well start remembering it as he's going to be your brother-in-law."

He sat up in the chair, looking at her sharply.

"What are you looking at?" she asked.

"You sounded exactly like Granny Parkington and with your hair that way you look exactly like her in the picture that's in the library."

"Thanks. You couldn't pay me a greater compliment." She crossed the room to take a fur jacket out of the cupboard. "How's the work getting on?" she asked over her shoulder.

"All right."

"You don't seem to get to the office very early."

"There's no use going to the office. Your friend Ned and his boy friends have killed all the business in Wall Street."

Janie put on her jacket and took down a hat. "I guess it would have died anyway. But I should think Father would like to have you show up at least."

"He doesn't notice. The old bastard seems awfully busy nowadays . . . I don't know what about."

She turned toward him, the hat still in her hand, "I don't think that's funny!"

"Hoity Toity," said Jack.

"It's just vulgar and bad manners and fresh."

Jack yawned and stood up, "Well, he *is* an old bastard. If I didn't have my own trust fund money, he'd let me starve. He hates me and is ashamed of me." After a second he added, "And vice versa."

"You might go to work." She put on her hat, looked at herself in the glass and then took up her gloves, "I certainly don't envy you the end you're headed for."

"Don't worry, honey, I'll pull myself together before it's too late." He kissed her suddenly, "You're mighty pretty. This Ned guy is lucky."

"He's not half as lucky as I am."

"That's the way to talk."

She felt a sudden swift anger, at what she really did not know. Perhaps it was nerves as much as anything. But she said, "I'm lucky to get out of here — out of this bloody house."

"You bet you are," he said, "I'd get out too but the address is good and it saves me from paying rent. Maybe I'll scram anyway if it gets much worse."

At the door she said, "Really, Jack, you stink!"

"Thanks."

"And don't think that I'm kidding."

"It's despair, honey . . . cosmic despair. What's there to do but enjoy yourself nowadays . . . nothing to do, nothing to interest you."

"Nothing! Nothing! Nothing!" said Janie. "That's it. That's what's the matter with this bloody house."

As she went out the door she heard him saying, "You're right. A nihilist! That's what I am! A nihilist! I learned about that last year in Harvard. That's about all I learned there."

She ran down the stairs and out into the street as if she were followed by something unseen, like a child in a dark hallway.

Outside it was better. The clouds were gone and there was the warm sunshine of false spring which can turn New York suddenly in the midst of January into a summer city.

Yet Janie, walking rapidly toward Fifty-seventh Street, was unaware of the sunshine and the balminess of the air. The thing no longer followed her, but its presence had left her spirits dulled and troubled.

It was the thought of Jack which disturbed her, for she was fond of him and sometimes he made her laugh and he was nearer to her than either of her parents perhaps because he understood as well as herself the gray emptiness of their existence. But at the moment she was angry at him.

It was as if he had dragged something sordid into the peace of her own room and left it there. It would be there when she returned; it might always be there. It was as if he had spoiled for her the one room in all the house which was endurable. It had upset her that he had referred to their father as "the old bastard," not so much because of the cheap irreverence of the epithet — she was aware that her father had no special right to reverence — but because life in that house, disagreeable as it was, would become unbearable if some sort of facade were not preserved. You had sometimes to pretend if life were to be endured; you had sometimes to be respectable if you were to have any self-respect, and without self-respect the days became intolerable.

The spectacle of the hatred between her father and brother was always painful. It was as if they were no relation to each other, as if Jack were the result of some affair her mother had had with another man, an affair which, knowing her mother so well, she knew was not only improbable but impossible. Perhaps, she thought suddenly, it would have been better for her and for all of us. Perhaps it would have made her happier. Jack would have been somebody else . . . not a Blair, mixed up with the Stilhams blighted from birth by indolence and lack of all balance. Again she thought that perhaps Jack was mad; certainly he was unbalanced with the kind of irresponsible quality which was only a shade off madness.

As she walked she speculated about Maisie. The knowledge that Jack was living with Maisie did not disturb her profoundly; it was the quality of Maisie which disturbed her — that Maisie was everything that her mother and father openly detested, everything that was abhorrent to them. Her father, she thought, might have a mistress — indeed there were times when she was certain of it — but no one would ever know about it. He would return every night and share a room with his wife who bored him; he would keep up the farce of devotion to her in public.

No one would ever find out about it. There was something ugly and evil about Jack and Maisie, as if the boy had taken up with her out of hatred for his own father and the whole world he had been trained to respect. They had never liked each other. From the time the boy had been old enough to walk and talk, her father had treated him with contempt, because there was in him the Blair liking for music and books and pictures and the theater. (The Blairs might be crazy, she admitted to herself, but they were also gifted and civilized.) And as Jack grew older the distaste of father and son grew stronger, but the real hatred came into full bloom when Jack failed to make his father's club at Harvard, "the" club which always seemed so idiotically important to her father, more important than love or honesty or achievement. When Jack came home for the Easter holidays, her father would scarcely speak to him. It was as if he had been guilty of some unnamable crime for which he was disowned.

She thought, If Jack had a stronger character he would have run away from home. It would have made a man of him. But he was not strong and he had not run away. He had compromised until he was twenty-one when he came into the money from the Blair trust fund and became modestly independent.

He had gone on living in the gloomy house simply to annoy his father. Indeed every act of Jack's seemed designed as part of the wild, half-mad revolt . . . even Maisie. He certainly did not love Maisie. During the unpleasant interim in Janie's room he had said that she bored him.

There wasn't, she knew, anything very terrible about Maisie. She was simply incorrigible and uncivilized and amoral with a talent for getting into night club brawls and appearing in gossip columns. Maisie wasn't revolting against anything; she was just a very pretty manifestation of nature who called herself Maisie Bernard and had somehow got from a backwoods town in North Carolina to New York. She wouldn't have minded Maisie at all except that she sometimes got Jack into gossip columns and headlines by her escapades.

No, it was all very difficult and complicated. It was like being weighed down perpetually by a boredom that was too heavy, which you couldn't escape. But she was going to escape.

She was opposite the statue of General Sherman when a dreadful thought came to her. What if something happened between Ned and me? What if something happened to me? So that I couldn't escape. Then I might revolt too. Then I might get to be like Jack. For she felt somehow that she was not strong enough to escape alone. There were too many things — the bad Blair blood, the dreariness of the great house, the dislike for her father and mother, the awful sense of fatality and despair which sometimes annihilated all her strength.

In the midst of the traffic at Fifty-ninth Street, she found herself praying, Oh, God! Don't let anything happen. Don't! Please God!

At the British War Relief office there were things to do and other women to talk to, some of them, like herself, come there to escape from themselves. She gossiped and sold wool and poured tea and had a scotch and soda and listened on the radio to the progress of the campaign in Libya, upset and tense, as if she sought by her own will to change the news of the retreat toward Egypt. And once she thought again, This is a cursed world, in which to be young, for it seemed to her that it was a world in the process of going to pieces, disintegrating all about her before her very eyes. The world which she had been brought up to believe was made for her and would exist forever was already smashed and gone. All that remained of it were small broken pieces integrated and held together by illusion and hatred of all that was superseding it. The big gloomy house was like that and her father's firm and Wall Street itself. One found the shattered pieces of that broken world in clubs, on Long Island, in dinner parties at big houses like her own — a world saturated and corroded with hatred and defeat. Without knowing quite what she did, she avoided these broken fragments because they were depressing and stupid and to her young mind they were frightening because they were already dead. They whined without fighting at all. And she searched with equal blindness for the new world which was to take the place of the old one without ever finding it, perhaps because the new world was not yet integrated, perhaps because her own education had been so bad and so stupid that she had not the vision that was necessary to discover it.

Ned, she knew, was a part of that new world. He talked to her about it — a new world which would be a great step forward in civilization and the development of democracy. But it was not yet here; there was nothing even which she might grasp and touch and feel, savoring it as she savored the remnants of the broken world, nothing which had reality, to which she could attach herself.

She did not talk of these things to the other

women for she had discovered long ago that most of them either understood nothing or were untroubled by their lack of understanding or simply grew angry and called her a Red. It was not in this background, she knew, that one would find the beginnings of the new world.

And so she talked of trivial things and gossiped until five-thirty, when she took down her coat and said good afternoon and went in search of her great-grandmother. She had great need of the old lady and her tremendous sense of peace and security. There were times, it seemed to her, when Mrs. Parkington seemed utterly indestructible, through some force that came not of her great wealth but from inside herself.

She had not called earlier to say that she was coming because Mrs. Parkington was always at home at teatime. As she stepped out of the taxi, she was troubled to discover at the curb a battered old station wagon with the words *Dutch Harbor Farm* painted on the side. That meant Great-Uncle Henry would be there and the thought of Uncle Henry made her feel uncomfortable as drunken or mad people made her feel. It was worse because the time had been so long since she had seen him.

For a moment she debated the question of going away again and finally thought, Perhaps he will be leaving soon and Granny will ask me to stay to dinner with her.

Taylor opened the door and when she asked, "Is Mrs. Parkington alone?" he said, "No, Miss Janie, Mr. Henry Parkington is there and Lord Haxton."

Again the desire to run away swept over her, and she said, "Perhaps I'd better go away and come back tomorrow."

"No, Miss Janie. I wouldn't. I'm sure Mrs. Parkington would feel very hurt and I'm sure she'd like you to meet Lord Haxton." Then he added with the faintest glint of humor, "Mr. Henry is very quiet today."

"You'd better announce me. She wasn't expecting me."

He went away and while she was making up her face to look her best for Mrs. Parkington's friends, Mrs. Parkington herself came out of the small sitting-room followed by Taylor. The old lady came toward her and kissed her and suddenly Janie felt warm and secure again.

"Well, my dear, I'm glad you came," she said. "I telephoned your house but they didn't know where to find you. There's a very old friend of mine here I wanted you to meet." Then as they walked along the hall, Mrs.

Parkington said, "It's Lord Haxton. He's over here on some sort of mission that has to do with the war."

In the small sitting-room Uncle Henry was standing before the fire with his back to it, a big, heavy, bearded vigorous old man of nearly eighty. He was dressed in rough farmers' clothes, corduroy trousers, plaid flannel shirt and a nondescript woolen jacket. With the heat from the fire, he gave off the faint, clean odor of stables. The flames behind him lighted up his thick white hair so that he appeared to have a halo about his rugged sunburnt face.

Seated in a big chair by the fire was the stranger who must be Lord Haxton. As they came into the room be stood up.

He was old too with silvery white hair, but very thin and straight with a look of extraordinary distinction. It was a very handsome face with finely cut nose and chin, high forehead, flat temples and high cheek-bones. It was fine without being feminine, the last flowering of a type before it went too fine and fell into decadence. The eyes were of a bright blue which looked brighter in the healthy pinkness of the face. He was, thought Janie suddenly, the handsomest man she had ever seen.

Her great-grandmother said, "This is Lord

Haxton. He's a very old friend. I haven't seen him for years until today."

He shook hands with Janie and said that he was glad to know her. Then she had to kiss Uncle Henry because he always expected it and might grow very angry if she refused. Uncle Henry, she knew, liked kissing young girls and that only made it worse. He had been in some sort of trouble when he was in his sixties. No one ever spoke of it in the family save in whispers, but everyone knew about it. She hated the feel of his beard but she liked the smell of soap and horses which hung about him. He was really her great-uncle, the old Major's younger brother by a different mother, and he never seemed to belong to the family.

She knew her great-grandmother was watching her and she carried off Uncle Henry's kiss as gracefully as possible. Then her great-grandmother said, "You shouldn't drive after dark, Henry. Neither of us is as young as we once were."

"I couldn't feel younger, Susie. You needn't worry about me."

"You are certainly very spry." He was indeed, marrying again and happily, when he was past seventy. The original Parkingtons were certainly prodigious.

"As I was saying," continued Uncle Henry,

addressing Lord Haxton, "if England would adopt proper agricultural methods she could feed herself . . . but get an Englishman to change his ways! Never! That's what is the matter!" He moved away from the fireplace a little and thrust his hands into his trousers pockets, rocking a little on the balls of his feet like a young vigorous man of thirty. "Now, I've got only four hundred acres — none of it too good and ninety acres of it in timber but I produce enough on it to feed a village."

As he talked, Lord Haxton seemed to shrivel, to become more fragile and overbred. Beside Uncle Henry he seemed delicate and very old.

Mrs. Parkington, watching them, thought, Harry is bored and he is wrong to be bored. He should listen because Henry is a prodigious fellow and is talking sense.

Harry was sitting there, listening with a kind of superior politeness, cushioned by a security which had once produced and protected him, but which no longer existed. He was the answer to so much that was happening, to the falling apart of the British Empire, to the shattering of that bright secure luxurious world of which the violets had suddenly reminded her earlier in the day. No, he should be listening to Henry who loved his four hundred acres and liked common people and the power of all his money and produced a specimen son at the age of seventy-one.

Without willing it, she sighed, thinking of Henry's other four children by his first wife, who was the daughter of a neighboring market gardener, and his grandchildren and how different they all were from her own descendants. And her mind wandered back a long way to the time when she had first seen Henry, on the day the Major brought his boy-brother to the Brevoort, a rugged, awkward lad of fifteen, twenty years younger then the Major himself, with a different mother. And she remembered suddenly the news of Henry's marriage ten years later to the gardener's daughter and the scandal it had made and the Major's fury. But Henry was right and the Major was wrong. The Major had wanted to "be somebody," to have his daughter marry a duke, to have a great house on Fifth Avenue and a yacht and to know kings. The Parkingtons were common and earthy and the Major had tried to escape his own destiny. But he had failed and had remained common, thank God, until the sordid end in the hotel in Cannes.

That was his great quality and he had not been able to escape it, as none of us, thought

Mrs. Parkington, can escape the molding thumb of destiny. But Henry was right. People called him eccentric and even crazy, but he was not in the least crazy. Like herself he had lived long enough to see all the others who had called him crazy, melt and decay and disappear along with all their fortunes and ambitions. He had lived through the whole of the indecent era, going his own way like a peasant, beyond destruction. And look at him now, standing there like a young man. His children and grandchildren hadn't made "good matches" watering the blood with each generation. He hadn't allowed them to. And look at him now!

Janie, listening, felt bored with Uncle Henry's talk of "concentrated farming" and rotations and fertilizers and soils. Yet she could not help feeling the feminine stimulus of his vigor and masculinity. She suspected that perhaps he had spoiled her great-grandmother's afternoon by bouncing in without warning. He had taken over Lord Haxton for himself. The signs were there in Mrs. Parkington's dress and the flamboyant flower she had pinned coquettishly on her shoulder. Granny had meant to have tea with an old beau, talking about the old days and now it was all spoiled by herself and Uncle Henry. She thought, I ought to go away, but even if I went away it wouldn't make any difference because Uncle Henry won't go until he's ready to. He's come for a "visit" with Granny and he doesn't mean to go until he's had his fill. And now that he had got going on Lord Haxton, there was no telling when he would leave. She was glad of the excuse to stay. It was very pleasant here, and secure and warm. If she went away there would be no place to go but back to the dreary house with all the expensive furniture.

Opposite her, behind the tea tray, Mrs. Parkington had virtually ceased listening to the discussion between the two men. She managed out of her worldly experience to hear enough of their conversation to follow its trend and permit her, now and then, to put in a sentence or two which gave the illusion of participation, but her mind lingered in another world, of boredom and disillusionment and weariness. She was aware now, and honest with herself about it, that the call of Harry was a failure; it had been a failure even before Henry arrived. To be quite honest, Henry had made it better by bouncing in, ruddy and smelling of horse manure.

She supposed that one should never try to take up old friendships after so many years. Too many things happened in between, to yourself and to the world. Certainly too many things had happened since she last saw Harry . . . things which he seemed unaware of, upholstered in his conceit and trust in his own security. He still talked as if there were no danger; he still quoted John Donne and Milton and Spenser, rather sententiously, as he had always done long ago in a different world. He still talked as if, at most, this war was not serious really, but only an annoyance. Harry like half of England, she thought, went to Munich with Chamberlain and his umbrella and he learned no more there than Chamberlain learned.

She saw now, quite clearly, that Harry was a fool, and that he had always been a fool, for all his record long ago at Oxford and his brilliant career. She wondered suddenly what that career would have been if Harry had had to make it on his own as the Major had done, without privilege and position and friends. Like so many Englishmen of his kind, his career had been a long record of brilliant failure, going from office to office, from post to post, without ever achieving anything beyond being witty and intelligent and knowing everyone in Europe. Sometimes he had been responsible for tragic blunders but he had gone on and on just the same because, despite the shallowness, he was what the English called "a gentleman."

Henry was really going to town now, in his blunt, vigorous way. He was saying, "In fact there has really been no British Empire since the passing of the Statutes of Westminister. It is dead but it has refused to lie down."

It always astonished her how much Henry knew. You thought of him as eccentric and blunt and uncouth and ignorant and all the time he kept hidden a vast amount of information, facts and hard thinking. And she heard Harry saying, "But, my dear sir, you don't understand the intricacies of British politics," and suddenly she felt a really vicious contempt toward him. Those damned intricacies they always fell back upon. They talked the same way forty years ago. Only then you could afford intricacies as you could afford "brilliant failures" like Harry. You couldn't afford them any longer. Something was loose in the world, something exasperated, something infuriated which would snuff all the Harrys and the "intricacies" out of existence. It was loose in Russia, in Germany, in England, in America, in India and the islands of the East. Even before the Major died, he had known it, the way he had known when it was a good time to sell wheat or cotton or railroad shares. That was why he put everything into nontaxable securities and left it all to her. But those damned English like Harry who thought their politics something special and precious which other people, even more civilized people like the French could not understand! There was an end in sight to "blundering through."

And for no reason at all, she wanted suddenly to cry, partly because she remembered the Major with sudden clearness as he had been in the beginning in the red and gold room at the Brevoort. Henry always made her think of him. And with the memory was the knowledge that out of all the women he had known, he had loved her best of all. He had loved her and trusted her. It was there in every sentence of the long and intricate will. Again and again he had written in it, "to my beloved wife who will understand my purpose," or "to my beloved wife who may be trusted to carry out my wishes." And she wanted to cry too out of some cosmic sadness at the vanity and folly of the whole human race.

And suddenly she wanted Harry to go away and never return, because he had become, while he sat there arguing feebly with Henry, a symbol of all the years in her life which might have been rich but were, she saw now, only glittering and empty and wasted. Henry had done a much better job, farming and leading his warm, solid existence, with a dull healthy wife, wise and concupiscent and uxorious in the Parkington way.

She thought, I must be getting old . . . dozing like this and wandering away into the past. And she was aware that Harry was rising, lifting his slim overbred elegance out of the depths of his chair. He looked beautiful but fragile. I will outlast him, she thought with the triumphant feeling of very old people, although he is eight years younger than I. It was better to think of him as he had been forty years ago. He seemed to have flowered and gone to seed in futility.

"In any case," he was saying to Henry, "I am glad to hear the American point of view."

"It is not the American point of view," said Henry, "It is my own. The American people do not understand what is happening in the world. They don't think very far although they are great for feeling and have a remarkable instinct about things."

Then Harry did that remarkable thing which people of his station in life in his country had a way of doing. He turned away from Henry and came toward Mrs. Parkington and as he did so, he seemed to eliminate Uncle Henry from existence, as a child might wipe the chalk words from a slate. Henry did not seem to mind or even to notice for he was already talking to Janie. Mrs. Parkington thought, That is what they have been doing for too long. That is what they are still doing. Oh, the fools! The bloody fools! That's why they're where they are today.

She smiled at him but there was no feeling in the smile. It caused her pain.

"I'll go with you as far as the door," she said and they went out together, Mrs. Parkington feeling dry and withered and old. In the hallway, Harry said, "Your brother-in-law is quite a fellow."

"He is indeed."

"There is something about him that is very like Gus."

"Yes . . . a great deal. What are your plans?" She asked then out of politeness although she had not the least interest.

"I go to Washington . . . after that home, I suppose."

She did not say, "I must see you again," or, "Let me know when you pass through." She had not the least interest. This was very likely the last time they would ever see each other.

"Well. Good luck on your trip."

Taylor had helped him on with his coat and was holding out his hat for him.

"It has been very nice seeing you," said

Harry, "You were always a wonderful woman. You still are."

"Thank you, Harry. Good-bye again and good luck."

She stood at the top of the three low steps until the door closed behind him. Then slowly she went back again to the sitting-room, thinking how extraordinary it was that the past and the present and even the future were sometimes so intricately entangled, and she wished that she might not die but live on and on to see what was coming. Harry had not changed at all. He was the same Harry, older and more tired, she had known at Sandringham, in London, at Monte Carlo, at Oriander. It was herself who had changed. Harry, it seemed to her, was no more than a wraith out of a world which no longer existed. But once long ago he had done her a great kindness in the case of Norah Ebbsworth. That was something she would never forget.

When she returned Henry was already leaving. He kissed Janie again and then pressed his white beard against Mrs. Parkington's cheek and with the scent of cologne water and tobacco and horses, her spirits rose again.

She said, "Henry, I am going to drive up and see you when the weather is better."

"It's about time. You haven't been there

since just after Gus died."

"I didn't realize it was so long."

He turned and smiled at Janie. "Why don't you bring her too?" he said to Mrs. Parkington. "She's never seen her new cousin, Johnny."

"How old is he?" asked Mrs. Parkington.

"He'll be four his next birthday."

Janie laughed, "I've never been able to figure out his relationship — the son of my great-grandfather's brother."

"Cousin, I suppose," said Henry. "The Parkingtons are a remarkable family."

"I'll come," said Janie. "I'd love to."

Then he went away and when he had gone, the smile still remained on Janie's face. "I haven't seen him since I was a little girl. I never knew he was like that. Mama always said he was crazy."

"I'm afraid your mother doesn't understand Henry's quality," said Mrs. Parkington, and she too smiled as if she shared a secret with Janie which none of the others knew.

Then Taylor appeared to take away the tea tray. He said, "Mr. Stilham called, madame. He said be would be here about eight o'clock."

She looked at Janie slyly and then picked up the black Pekingese and began rubbing its ears. She thought, The child doesn't know anything. If it's really serious who is to tell her? And she knew that of course, the burden would fall upon her, because you couldn't trust the others to make it as easy as possible for Janie.

When Amory came in she noticed that his eyes were bloodshot and that his face was more high-colored than usual and she thought, It must be bad. He has been drinking. She had never known Amory to drink too much, save perhaps at college reunions and club dinners. There was, she knew, a sort of relief in such drinking for men like Amory who had never really grown up or learned anything. They drank because they wanted somehow to escape from a life which baffled and thwarted them back into the world of adolescence. She thought too, Amory is the kind of man who becomes a nasty drunk, and as if to prepare herself she stiffened her thin body a little and put down her coffee cup.

"Good evening, Amory," she said. "I'm just finishing my coffee. Would you like some?"

"No, thanks, Granny. But I could do with a glass of brandy."

She pushed the bell beside her and flushed. Nothing irritated her so much as to have Amory call her Granny — a great, grown, stupid man patronizing her. Now, since he was drunk, it was particularly offensive. The thing was beginning all wrong. In its essence, she knew, the interview would be one of the most unpleasant she had ever known, but his drinking and surliness made it worse.

Taylor appeared and she told him to take away the coffee and bring the brandy for Mr. Stilham. Then Mattie appeared and took away the Pekingese for their supper and Taylor returned with the brandy and poured a glass and served it to Amory. He said, "Thank you, Taylor." He had not even said good evening to Mattie.

To Taylor Mrs. Parkington said, "Don't disturb us, Taylor. If anyone calls, take the message."

"Yes, madame." His face showed no sign of anything at all.

As the door closed, she said, "Janie was here this afternoon and Uncle Henry."

"Crazy, as usual, I suppose," said Amory.

"Henry's not very crazy," she said quietly. "In the end he's turned out better than most of us."

She knew that Amory thought Henry vulgar and one of the many liabilities of the family. It was extraordinary how vulgar people were unable ever to understand what vulgarity was. It was like the uncanny ability of bores to recognize bores.

"I haven't seen Janie since the Christmas party," Amory said, "She's never at home any more. She comes in about five in the morning and never gets up till afternoon."

"She looked very well and happy."

He did not answer but only finished his brandy and asked, "May I have another glass?"

"Yes, of course." She wanted to say, "You are a grown man. You should know best if you should have another glass." But she held her tongue.

He stood up and went to the decanter and poured himself a second glass of brandy. Then he leaned against the yellow marble mantelpiece sliding his elbow along it to steady himself. She knew what was going to happen and knew that she could not prevent it. His elbow touched the shepherdess in Dresden china and gently, slowly in a kind of enchanted inevitable movement, pushed it over the edge. Mrs. Parkington gave a faint cry and started up out of her chair. The shepherdess struck the marble slab below and shattered, and she heard herself saying peevishly, "Oh, Amory! How could you?"

What she saw in the movement of the crash was not the death of the shepherdess but the death of the shepherd which had been her companion and was shattered long ago in the house on Thirty-fourth Street with the huge chandelier and the great hall with the oriental vases and the marble stairway.

For the death of the shepherd had been a more violent death, although there was at least dignity in it. The shepherd had not been thrust to destruction by a drunken man but hurled all the way across the ballroom by a man who was very nearly insane with fury.

VI

She had cried out almost the same words to the Major, "Oh, Gus. How could you?" And had begun to cry.

Aspasie Conti was in the room and Harriette Livingstone and Mrs. Morton Ogden and Gus had shouted, "I'll be God-damned if I'll take it lying down. I'll make the bastards pay for it!"

In the eyes of Harriette, there was a look of shock and alarm, because it was probably that in all her life she had never before heard words like "God damn" or "bastard," but in the eyes of Aspasie and Mrs. Morton Ogden there was a bright look, such as comes into the eyes of feminine women at the glorious sight of an angry man whose fury is not directed at them. Aspasie was dressed in a chic but demure dress of black with a white fichu, which made her ugliness and handsome figure seem tall and tragic. She wore it because earlier in the evening she had been reciting a great scene from Phèdre and the long speech of Célimène from *Le Misanthrope* for the guests. And Mrs. Morton Ogden was upholstered in purple velvet wearing the most famous necklace of diamonds in New York and an aigrette in her hair. Harriette was in gray taffeta, dressed like a mouse. As the shepherdess fell from the mantelpiece the whole scene returned to Mrs. Parkington in utter clarity, as if it were happening at that moment and not sixty years earlier.

The shepherd and shepherdess had been a pair until Gus smashed the shepherd. They were pretty and delicate and expensive and she had admired them in the window of Tiffany's shop and a little later Aspasie had bought them and the Major had presented them to her on her birthday. And now Gus had hurled the poor shepherd across the room and shattered him beyond repair against the wall of the ballroom.

She heard Mrs. Morton Ogden say, "You shouldn't have done that, Gus. The evening has already been bad enough for poor Susie. You should have considered her condition."

Then she felt Gus' arms about her and his voice, the rage suddenly melted out of it, saying, "I'm sorry, sparrow. Forgive me. I'll buy you ten shepherds tomorrow or fifty if you like, only don't cry. It wasn't you I was angry at."

"Vous êtes brut" Aspasie said in the same angry voice Susie had heard once through the door of the red and gold room at the Brevoort.

"Take her to bed," said Mrs. Morton Ogden, and Gus still with his arm about her said, "Come along, sparrow," and led her out of the ballroom past the dining-room where the men from Delmonico's were putting into big wicker panniers all the rich food which had not been eaten by the guests who had not come. The sight made her feel sick with humiliation.

At the foot of the stairs Gus picked her up and carried her past the palms and the lilies and red roses and garlands of smilax. Halfway up the stairs, he stopped and kissed her throat and for a moment she forgot all about the party and what had happened. Then he said, "They'll pay for it!"

"No, Gus. You mustn't feel like that," she whispered. "It doesn't matter. It really doesn't matter at all. I didn't cry because of that. I swear I didn't . . . It was because I'm tired."

He did not answer her but carried her the rest of the way up the stairs and placed her on the great double bed of ebony inlaid with mother-of-pearl which he had bought at the Paris Exposition. Then he called in her maid. It was long before the day of Mattie and the maid was an Alsatian girl called Thérèse, a nice girl, sympathetic and very professional. He said to the maid, "Will you see that Madame is put to bed at once and then go to the kitchen and bring her some hot milk." He kissed her again and said, "I must go downstairs now and say good night to Mrs. Ogden. I have one or two things to discuss with her."

When he had gone away Thérèse helped her out of Madame de Thèbes' loops and garlands of pale yellow satin and white roses and she went into the next room to look at the children. She went in so softly that she did not even waken the nurse who snored on while she stood looking down at them in their small cots. Alice was sleeping with one hand thrown across her face, her straight dark hair rolled in the *bigoudis* which produced the sausagelike curls the nurse thought were fashionable. Herbert lay on his side, his face pressed into the pillow, his blond curls damp, his clear skin beautiful even in the dim light that came through the door of the bedroom. She stood longer at the side of Herbert, because he was beautiful and the sight of him always brought a pang, half of satisfaction, half of fear. Alice was a nice child, docile and good, but she was sallow and dank without the radiance of her small brother. Susie admitted these things in the darkness, alone, secretly, but in the daylight she always treated Alice as if she were a beauty.

Now, looking down at them, she found herself praying — that they would have a decent, good life, that they would understand how to live and know the value of things that were good and simple as she knew them, in spite even of Gus and all his flamboyance and generosity. She prayed out of a fear which she herself did not quite understand.

What went on belowstairs she did not know until years afterward when Mrs. Morton Ogden told her just before she died in the great marble house at Fifty-seventh Street. And even then, long afterward, she was able to reconstruct the scene, and because she knew the participants so well she was able to see it in her imagination and even divine what they had said and the part each played in the peculiar council of war.

After they had dispatched Miss Livingstone to her invalid father in the Parkington brougham, the three of them — the Major and Mrs. Morton Ogden and Aspasie went into the small gold sitting-room with the Italian scenes painted on the walls and sat down with a bottle of iced champagne. The men from Delmonico's had gone and the servants were sent to bed and all the lights were out save the gas flames inside the cut-glass globes of the great chandelier in the hall. Mrs. Morton Ogden sent home her own brougham which had been standing in the snow for an hour and awaited the return of the Parkington brougham from Miss Livingstone's flat in Eighth Street. None of them had discussed the business of shipping Harriette off; they all knew that she was not a fit listener to what they meant to discuss. A mouse had no place at a conference of eagles.

In the hearts of each of them sitting in the ornate little room there was fury. In the heart of Aspasie was the fury of a baffled performer. She had expected to perform before a large and fashionable audience, the cream of New York society, and on the gold chairs after dinner she found herself confronted by thirty or forty stockbrokers, speculators, Tammany politicians and their wives, not one of whom understood a word of the long sonorous passages of Racine nor the wit of Molière. She had gone on heroically reading in her deep passionate voice while her audience stirred and grew glassy-eyed on the gold chairs, bewildered by spectacle of an ugly woman grimacing and making inexplicable and extraordinary sounds in a tongue of which not one of them understood anything.

But she was enraged too because the *bourgeoisie* — she could not dignify their provinciality by the word *mondaine* — had insulted her darling Susie. Many of them had refused the invitations. That was understandable. But most of them had accepted, perhaps out of fear of the Major's power and then failed to appear. The ones who had come were the "wrong people" but friends of the Major, some of them disreputable, whom he had insisted upon inviting. "They are my friends," he said. "I see no reason why people should not mix. It is a civilized and intelligent thing for people of all sorts to know each other." The only ones from St. John's parish and the fashionable world were those who came because they dared not refuse the Major anything, people like the rector and his horse-faced wife and Mr. Agnew and his wife. But those who did not appear had insulted the "*plus charmante femme du monde, ma chère* Susie!"

Opposite her in purple velvet and diamonds, tightly corseted and slightly red in the face from champagne and the long pressure of her stays, Mrs. Morton Ogden enjoyed a special fury of her own. She rather liked what she called "having the furies" because otherwise life in New York in the seventies became boring beyond the point of endurance. And at heart, Mrs. Morton Ogden was a tyrant and a dictator. She was furious now because by the insult to Gus and Susie Parkington, she too had been insulted — or worse, she had been slapped in the face by scores of people whom in her heart she regarded with only faintly concealed contempt. They had insulted Susie Parkington and Susie Parkington was her protégée, whom she had chosen partly because Susie was pretty and charming, but more because her husband was a challenge, one of the worst challenges. He was flamboyant and irrepressible. He had a way of laughing at things which the women who dwelt behind the closed doors cherished most. He was a gambler and reckless and had a way with women, and disturbed many a respectable lady's imagination in a way she had not believed possible until the moment he began talking to her. He was a buccaneer, a nobody who had made an immense fortune by none too scrupulous methods even in a day when scruples were of no great value. He was indeed a challenge, but Mrs. Morton Ogden's perversity enjoyed challenges and she had made up her mind that she would "put over" the Parkingtons.

It was not wise to cross Mrs. Morton Ogden if you wished to survive. She had immense power and she was perfectly aware of her power. It was compounded of many things. She had immense wealth come to her out of the original fortune of a grandfather who dealt in cattle and land, and of this wealth she had complete control, being a widow and childless. She managed it admirably and was not above investing in adventures with Major Parkington whose touch appeared to turn everything into profits of one hundred to two hundred per cent and sometimes more. She had with Gus Parkington a perfect understanding.

But she had more, too, than wealth; she had an impeccable position with an ancestry on her grandmother's side studded like plush with cairngorms with Livingstones and Van Rensselaers and Suydams and other members of heavy Dutch families which had come over to New Amsterdam to get on in the world. Her wit and her vigor, she knew well enough, had not come from them but from her grandfather, the rich cattle drover. But they had their place in the scheme of things; she did not undervalue those heavy names any more than she undervalued the millions and vigor that had come down from her grandfather.

She had a great marble house far uptown on Fifty-seventh Street — within sight of the squatters and their goats and she had lived much abroad and when ambassadors and princes and dukes came to flatter the middle-class snobbery of her fellow citizens, they stayed with Mrs. Morton Ogden or were introduced to society and entertained in her house. And Mrs. Ogden had the courage of her own beliefs — that New York was dull and provincial and stuffy and that among those who constituted the *bon ton* there were no brains and very little cultivation. She would have preferred living in Paris or Rome but two things held her back — one her greed for more and more money and the other a deep-dyed, deeply rooted patriotism which she concealed almost shyly. She had no patience either for the precious delicate souls who had fled the shopkeepers paradise of New York for Europe. She had an idea, indeed a kind of mission, that she could civilize New York and teach it how to use its money. She would say again and again, "By God, I'll civilize them, if it's the last thing I do!"

And so she forced many things down the throats of the already gorged, gouty and upholstered world of fashion; among them her parties which were different from any other parties. Her food was the best food in the city but she did not bring it on by wagon-loads; she did not have five or six courses of meat, game and fish, interrupted by Roman punch to provide the guests with an opportunity to recover their breath. And after dinner the men were not permitted to stay for two hours swilling brandy and telling dirty stories or talking about the stock market. After dinner she frequently had singers from the French opera or recitations — Aspasie had read many times in her great marble house — and most horrible of all she invited the artists not only to sit at table with other guests but encouraged them to mingle as well. Only Mrs. Morton Ogden could achieve all these things. The others lacked the daring or the intelligence and sometimes both.

She had taken up the Parkingtons as she had taken up the singers from the French Opera, partly as a diversion from plush boredom, partly because of genuine fondness for Susie and admiration for Gus (whom she looked upon as a kind of picturesque bandit whose friendship was immensely profitable) and partly out of utter perversity and exasperation. She made them a cause, and they could not have found a more powerful friend.

This, then, was Mrs. Morton Ogden, a free woman unhampered by conventions or complexes, who now sat with Aspasie and the Major in the gold room with the Italian pictures. While she listened to the conversation and occasionally put in a word, she was compiling a list of those who had defied her espousal of the Parkingtons and who would again pass the doors of her house. Among them were many people on the way up (they were always the worst snobs) to whom this privilege meant almost as much as life itself and some others who considered themselves the Old Guard and strong enough to defy her. There were ways of humbling them as well. If anyone knew how, it was Mrs. Malvina Ogden. She had not only prestige; she had what in that world was a supreme power — she did not even know how rich she was.

Aspasie was inclined to be a little hysterical. She cried out, "It is a conspiracy! They came together and agreed upon it."

Mrs. Ogden was not of that opinion. A few perhaps had conspired but most of them had simply done it deliberately thinking that on the next day they could say, "Did *you* go to the Parkington ball? We didn't. Impossible people! One has to draw the line somewhere!" But they would live to regret that.

The Major said very little, but he too thought a great deal. He too was making lists of names which must not be forgotten. For very nearly the first time in his life, he was tired with a weariness born of the interminable, agonizing evening. There had been a curious kind of torturing humiliation about it as the hour grew later and later and only about half the guests who had accepted appeared, slowly it became clear that it was, with one or two exceptions, the "wrong" half which came in. For a long time he had held on to the belief that they were late only because it was a snowy night, with icy streets over which the horses would have to move slowly. After the program of recitation and singing began, he gave up hope and sat near the back of the half-empty ballroom, miserably, on a stiff gold chair, carrying off the humiliation with a frozen face, checking over and over again those who had come and resolving that he would never forget their loyalty — the politicians, the hangers on, the speculators. A dozen men in the room, without even knowing it, were started that night on their various ways to becoming rich men. Two or three, years later, were saved from jail because Augustus Parkington intervened with power and money. He was not a man to forget either a friend or an enemy.

It was for Susie that he suffered most. For himself he was not sensitive. He had managed very well for himself and had no doubts about the future, but the humiliation for Susie was not to be borne. He suffered, never once understanding or believing that Susie did not care very much, that she would have preferred not giving a ball at all, that in her heart she did not even like the big house.

As the guests left, he said good-bye to them with an air of cordiality but the eyes were cold, like marble, and the lips drawn tight in a hard, brutal line. It was only when the last guest had gone and there was only Susie, Aspasie and Harriette and Mrs. Ogden that his temper broke and he smashed the poor Dresden shepherd.

But now in the room with the Italian pictures he was cold again, with the icy coldness which Susie never knew, but which terrified other people. When he turned cold Major Augustus Parkington could be sadistic, criminal and ruthless. And when he turned cold he was silent with a frightening silence. Aspasie was frightened and Mrs. Ogden was interested but unmoved because she was herself a little like Gus Parkington and understood him, and because she always felt quite able to take care of herself.

The butler appeared presently and said the carriage had returned and Mrs. Ogden rose and left with Aspasie. In the hall she said to the Major, "Thank you for the evening. I'll expect you at tea tomorrow . . . without Susie. By God, I'll civilize them or know the reason why."

When they had gone the Major wearily climbed the white marble stairs. He undressed in the darkness so as not to disturb Susie and all that night she slept with his arms about her, as if he would protect her thus forever.

In the morning after he had gone away, she felt suddenly ill and Harriette sent for Dr. Westbrook, but by the time he arrived it was too late to do anything. She lost her third baby and for a long time afterward was very ill.

When she was well enough, the Major took a house for her in Long Branch and sent her and the children and nurse there for the summer. The house was not a big house; it was much smaller than the Major would have liked but there was nothing else available. It was the kind of house Susie liked, rather worn and lived in. In it she felt safe and hidden away. There was no necessity for going out to restaurants nor any for having people to dinner. There was in it no marble and no statuary and no palms. For the first time it seemed to her that she had a home.

The Major came down on Friday and stayed until Tuesday and long afterward it seemed to her that in the ugly red house under the maple trees, they were happier than they had ever been before or afterward. It was not the wild happiness of those first passionate days at the Brevoort, but a warm, easy happiness in which they were used to each other, in which neither of them felt the need or desire for anyone else in the world. It was as if the Major's impulse to protect and shelter her had become a passion.

Sometimes during the week Aspasie came down to stay, for Aspasie was by now like one of the family. Usually she arrived on Tuesday after the Major had left and returned to the city on Friday before he had come back. All during the week they talked together in French because Susie wanted to speak the language perfectly and because by now, it was very nearly as natural for her to speak French as to speak English. She began to read French books and poetry and plays. When the weather was fine they took the children with them and picnicked on the beach beneath a great parasol.

Harriette did not come down at all since she could not leave her poor father and there was really no need for her, since there were no engagements, no meetings, no housekeeping which could cause any worry. Her father knew now about her connection with Major Parkington and he had become reconciled almost with pleasure to the shocking connection because it meant that he lived now almost in luxury in a new flat and no longer had to write once a month to three or four rich relatives to remind them that their contributions to his upkeep were overdue. Major Parkington took care of everything, lavishly. It was extraordinary; Harriette's father discovered how useful money could be.

The absences of the Major seemed to make him only the more devoted. He never again spoke of the ball to which people had not come and Susie was thankful for that. It was an ugly thing, and she saw no reason to embrace ugly things unless one was forced to face them. Nor did Aspasie ever speak of it. All that summer it was as if the ugly thing had never happened. The summer itself passed lazily with the Major spending the evenings at home and sometimes going out late at night after she was asleep to go to the gambling casino. The city seemed far away, like something Susie had dreamed, and presently as the summer wore on, she came to begrudge the passing not only of each day but each hour. At last she ceased even reading the newspapers, although Aspasie with her French mind could not pass a day without reading her *journal* from cover to cover. But Aspasie did not trouble to read or repeat any but the most sensational of the paragraphs she encountered. That was how Susie came to hear of Radnor Beaumont's suicide.

There it was spread in a great headline in two inch type across the whole front of the paper, because Radnor Beaumont was a rich man and an important man in New York, not only in finance but in the fashionable and sporting world as well.

Susie and Aspasie had been sitting under the parasol while the nurse and children walked along the edge of the surf collecting shells, and when Aspasie took the newspaper out of her bag and opened it and read the headline, the name Radnor Beaumont meant not very much to Susie, little more at first than simply the dim image of a big heavy man with gray hair and a pompous manner and a tall thin wife whom she had met at one of Mrs. Morton Ogden's *soirées*. She remembered them as being a disagreeable couple to whom the Major had presented her with pride. They had not seemed impressed and had turned away after talking for a little time about nothing at all.

She went on sewing, her mind filled with images of the Beaumonts, while Aspasie went on reading. Aspasie had hoped, clearly, that the suicide was *une affaire passionelle* and when she discovered that it had only to do with money, the interest went out of her voice. The account of the tragedy was not an inspiring story. Radnor Beaumont had inherited a large part of his wealth and influence, and so like most conservatives, not being at all certain that he could replace it once it was lost, he had been a careful man. The news that he had plunged and that he was a ruined man and a bankrupt was probably more shocking to his friends than the actual fact of his suicide. He had hung himself to a hook in the wardrobe of his own dressing-room in the house on Fifth Avenue and no one had found the body until many hours after the act. (In these details Aspasie's voice betrayed her interest.) There was a note which stated simply that he was ruined, and could not possibly hope to meet his debts.

When she had finished reading, Aspasie folded the newspaper and laid it across her knees and sat looking out at the sea. When she did not speak for a long time Susie looked up from her sewing at the strong fierce profile and in a sudden swift wave of intuition, she thought, Aspasie is thinking that Radnor Beaumont was one of those who accepted for dinner and the ball and then did not appear. For the profile of Aspasie against the blue of the Atlantic was set and hard with no pity in it. But neither of them spoke of the ball.

Presently Aspasie said, "I did not like him. He was a vulgar, provincial man who put on airs."

Two days later a letter came from Mrs. Morton Ogden. She was at Newport, she wrote, and the weather was very bad with much fog. She hoped that Susie had recovered and was feeling herself again. If she felt strong enough it might be a good idea to leave the children and come to Newport for a short visit. She was certain Gus would not object; in fact she had discussed it with Gus when they had met recently at a directors' meeting. No doubt, she added, Susie had heard of Radnor Beaumont's ruin and suicide.

I do not think (she wrote), *that he will be greatly missed. He no longer really had any place in the financial life of New York. The city is no longer a small town closed corporation, belonging to a few people whose money grew out of real estate. He was behind the times — small frog in what is becoming a big puddle. One day New York will be the banking center of the world. I understand his wife has collapsed completely and after the funeral will go away for a "rest cure."*

Susie did not go to Newport. She wanted simply to stay on and on forever at Long Branch. She answered that while she could think of nothing more enjoyable than a visit with Mrs. Ogden, the doctor advised against it.

She did not like the idea of the friendship

between Gus and Mrs. Ogden, nor the fact that they had been seeing each other during the summer. It was not that she had any physical jealousy of Mrs. Ogden; Susie was not by nature a jealous woman and it would certainly have been preposterous to suppose that the Major, with his liking for young pretty women, could find anything physical to admire in a war horse like Malvina Ogden. The jealousy was of another kind — because she divined that Gus talked to Mrs. Ogden about such things as politics and railroads and mines and banks, and never mentioned them to his own wife, treating her as if she were too frivolous or too stupid to understand. And her instinct told her that they were bad for each other because they were too much alike — energetic, ruthless, willful and contemptuous of others. The ambitions of both were insatiable. Gus was bad enough on his own, without being stimulated by someone like Mrs. Ogden.

That was one of her small worries. She had another too about little Alice. She was a good child who never cried or soiled her frocks, who even at three, had good manners. It was as if, already, she understood that she was sallow and dull and must somehow make up for it by being gentle and agreeable. When people passed the children on the boardwalk or the beach they always overlooked Alice and spoke to her brother, sitting up, golden haired and blue-eyed in his end of the pram. They would say that he was an angel and charming and beautiful and touch his curls. And if they noticed Alice at all it was to say, "She is a nice child too. How do you do, little girl?" And Alice would answer politely, "Very well, thank you."

The awful thing was that Susie herself, in her heart, deep inside her, felt like the people on the beach. At sight of little Herbert her own heart leapt with delight; at sight of Alice she felt nothing at all with her heart. Her head told her, You must be doubly nice to Alice to make up for the difference. Sometimes, almost in anguish, she thought, Oh, why couldn't Alice had have Herbert's looks. It doesn't matter what a boy looks like. A boy can take care of himself. Alice was so dull and good and little Herbert even at two was high-spirited and willful and naughty. Sometimes she wondered where Alice had come from, for she seemed to have in her looks and manner nothing of either herself or the Major. Even her looks would not have mattered so much if she had not been so listless and dull. Aspasie was an ugly woman but after a few moments of conversation with her one forgot her looks entirely and thought of her as handsome.

She was thinking of all these things one morning for the thousandth time as she watched the two children playing with their buckets and shovels in the sand, when Aspasie began again reading aloud from her newspaper.

There had been, it seemed, a whole epidemic of failures in New York. Radnor Beaumont was the first and three other solid firms had followed in quick succession. The partners of one of them, James Bradish and Alister Alsop, had been arrested. More arrests, predicted the newspaper, would probably follow. Again when she had finished reading, Aspasie folded her paper carefully in her thrifty French way and looked out to sea, and again Susie remembered that James Bradish and Alister Alsop and their wives were among those who had accepted but had not come to the ball. Of this neither Aspasie nor herself said anything. Again when she looked at Aspasie, the Frenchwoman was looking out toward the sea, her profile fierce as an eagle. Then for the first time a strange suspicion came to Susie, a suspicion so fantastic as to be scarcely believable. She looked again at Aspasie and said suddenly, "What are you thinking, Aspasie?" The Frenchwoman sighed and without turning toward her she said, "I'm thinking what a remarkable man your husband is. He should have been a general like Bonaparte."

When they arrived home from the hot beach, there was a telegram from New York on the table in the hall. Telegrams were not common in those days and the sight of it alarmed Susie. No one telegraphed unless they had something terribly important to say. As she tore it open she thought of Gus. Nothing must happen to Gus!

But it did not concern Gus. It was from Harriette Livingstone. It read, "Am arriving by afternoon train. Hope it will not inconvenience you but need is urgent. Lovingly, Harriette."

How could Harriette leave her father? How could Harriette who never traveled at all come all the way to Long Branch alone?

Susie and Aspasie drove to the little pitch-roofed, shingled, red station and brought her back to the house through the hot afternoon sun. Harriette was tremulous and full of apology.

"I know Aspasie will forgive me if I don't say why I have come. I would not have troubled you but it was so important. It is something very secret." She laid a gray-gloved hand on the hand of Aspasie and said, "You will forgive me, won't you? I know you will understand. Some day I'll be able to tell you."

"Of course," said Aspasie, politely, but Susie knew that curiosity was already devouring Aspasie like a cancer and she thought, Probably it's nothing at all . . . Harriette's sense of proportion is so grotesque. Very likely it is nothing at all. She kept telling herself this because she was really troubled lest what Harriette had to tell her concerned Gus.

She did not deceive herself; she had known for a long time that sooner or later someone would come to her and say, "Have you heard that your husband is keeping an actress?" Gus, she knew well enough, was like that. A wife wasn't enough for Gus. There was too much of him, too much vitality, too much gusto, too much of an appetite for parties and gaiety and low life. He had to have a lot of things a wife could not give him, things indeed which he would not permit a wife to give him because if she was like that he would no longer want her as his wife. For a long time she had known that one day she would know about his other life. She had worked to prepare herself for the discovery, yet now as she drove back to the little house with Harriette and Aspasie, she knew that when the time came it would be no easier for her than if the news had come to her, unprepared, out of the blue.

The horses stopped beneath the big maples and the three of them got down.

"What a pretty house!" said Harriette, "And such a pretty lawn and trees! It's what the French would call *très coquette!*"

"It is nice," said Susie, thinking that at times Harriette's gentleness and simplicity approached the borders of half-wittedness. There were times when she doubted that Harriette minded very much having been jilted, or being an old maid, or having to take care of her father. Sometimes she thought it was useless to waste pity on someone who had no profound feelings of any kind. She remembered something Gus had once said — that to be capable of tragedy, you must be of tragic stature to begin with.

Inside the house, she led Harriette to her own bedroom, to "freshen up" but Harriette could not even wait for that. The moment the door was closed she stood with her back against it and said, "It is a great favor I have to ask from you."

Susie felt suddenly weak with relief and sat down on the big bed; it wasn't then what she thought, it wasn't that Gus was unfaithful. She was aware that Harriette was experiencing a kind of perverse enjoyment in the excitement of the moment. Harriette was blossoming since she had come to know spectacular people. She was no longer the old pathetic, persecuted Harriette.

Susie said, "What is it, Harriette?"

"It's about my cousin, Goodhue Blair." She moved away from the door and sat on the bed beside Susie. "He came to the flat last night. He was a little intoxicated and said that if I could not help him there was only one thing to do and that was to kill himself. Goodhue is a very respectable man. I never saw him like that before. He said that he knew I was a friend of yours . . . I hope he was not exaggerating."

Susie made a deprecating gesture but did not interrupt Harriette. She continued, "He said that whether or not he killed himself was a matter entirely in the hands of Major Parkington."

"How could that possibly be?" asked Susie.

"I'm afraid I don't understand myself," said Harriette, "I'm not very good about things which have to do with money, but it seems that Goodhue's firm is in great difficulty and that the Major could save it and Goodhue. It is a very good firm, very old and well-established. When he asked me to come to you, I could not well refuse. I hope you don't think I am presuming."

Susie laid her hand on Harriette's gray-gloved one, "Of course not. You have been very kind to me. I don't quite understand but I will speak to the Major."

"I have never seen my cousin Goodhue in such a state before. He said he had appealed to Major Parkington himself but that he had refused to help him. Goodhue is a very proud man. I think he must have drunk too much in order to get up his courage. There is not much time, he said. Only until tomorrow evening at the latest."

Harriette had neither the tact nor the intelligence of Aspasie and now she plunged full into the fire, "I know Goodhue and his wife did not come to the party, but I think he meant to come. He said that Esther — that's his wife — was ill in bed with kidney complaint. She's never been quite right since her last child was born. I think he was telling the truth."

Susie felt the color rising in her cheeks and said quickly, "I'm sure that all this has nothing to do with whether they came to the party or not, Harriette. The Major isn't like that. I'll explain it as best I can to him. I'm sure he'll know more about it than either of us do."

"You're very good to me," said Harriette, "You've always been so good to me. You are really an angel, Susie."

"Never mind that. Will you be spending the night?"

"No, that I couldn't do. Father will be expecting me. There is a train tonight, isn't there? They told me there was."

"There's a train at six-ten. Aspasie is going back on it. If you'd like to stay, I'm sure we'd be delighted to have you."

"No. I'll go back with Aspasie." Suddenly she began to cry. "I love you and the Major so much," she said, "Your kindness has made all the difference to Father and me."

"It's nothing," said Susie, and with a remarkable degree of clairvoyance she divined that the "Harriette period" was coming to an end. Gus would arrange for her and her father, but gradually, in a kindly way, Harriette would have to go out of the picture. She was not only becoming tiresome but silly as well. The dreary Harriette had been much preferable to this sentimental one. Thank God there was no sentimentality in Aspasie.

Susie rose from the bed and said, "There is just time for you to have tea and a sandwich before the train leaves. Come along."

She held the door open for Harriette and followed her as she went out. Already she had forgotten Harriette's tiresomeness because she knew now that her suspicion was true. Gus had deliberately set about ruining the people who had humiliated them. He had been responsible for Radnor Beaumont's suicide and the arrest of James Bradish and Alister Alsop. And now there was Goodhue Blair and many others. And in the background was Mrs. Ogden . . . She saw it all clearly now. Between them they had planned this revenge. The knowledge made her suddenly and violently ill.

After Aspasie and Harriette had gone to the train she went to her own room and lay on the bed preparing herself for what she should say when the Major arrived on the evening train. At first as she listened to Harriette's fluttering muddled appeal, she had experienced only a swift sense of relief that what Harriette had come to tell her was not what she dreaded; but now the feeling of relief was gone and there remained only the knowledge of what Gus had done — that he was responsible for Radnor Beaumont's death and the ruin of a dozen other men because they had dared to humiliate him.

The fact itself had very little reality for her; what shocked her was the knowledge that her husband whom she loved could be so vindictive, so bitter, so ruthless. For a little time she tried to persuade herself that Harriette, being so addlepated, had got the whole story muddled, but she could not quite accomplish this because she remembered the look in the Major's eye as he hurled the Dresden shepherd across the ballroom. It was a Gus she had never seen before although people had told her he could be like that. And she remembered the cold glint in Mrs. Ogden's eyes. These were powerful, ruthless people who struck with violence and calculation. She had her own fashion of getting what she wanted; sometimes she achieved it even against the force of people like the Major and Mrs. Ogden. There were soft ways of wearing people down, of tricking them into doing what you wanted. She was herself no innocent and cooing dove. But the other two could be terrifying.

She heard her carriage come in the drive and heard the Major descend and climb the steps and open the door, and still she thought, He cannot be like that! Harriette must be crazy!

Always she was glad when he returned and was at the door to be kissed by him, but tonight she could not bring herself to meet him because she herself experienced a curious feeling of shame, as if she had unwittingly been involved in something disgraceful. And what Harriette told her had made her feel more acutely than ever that there was a part of the Major she did not know at all and had never known, all that part which had to do with his mines and banks and railroads. That part of him he had always kept hidden, thrusting her aside when she sought to penetrate the mystery and understand him, all of him. She felt now that when she saw him, there would be in her feelings as in her manner, a strangeness, almost a hostility, which had never been there before.

Then she heard his voice calling, "Susie! Susie! Where are you?" and she opened the door and went to the stair rail and said, weakly, "Here I am, Gus. Could you come up here?"

He came up the stairs three steps at a time but when he saw her, something in her face chilled him and he stopped in the doorway and said, like a small boy, "What is it, sparrow? What's the matter? Why weren't you there to meet me?"

She sat down on the bed, confused and unhappy. At sight of him, the old rush of love swept over her and when it had passed, she thought, He is the one who did that. He was mean and spiteful and small and vengeful. But she managed to say, "Something happened. I meant to be at the door but I couldn't."

"What happened?"

"Harriette was here. She stayed only an hour or two. She told me about Goodhue Blair . . . and all the others."

He did not answer her at once. He took a chair from against the wall and placed it beside the bed. Then he sat down and looked at her, distantly, with a coldness she had never before encountered in him. And she thought, This is how he is outside, with other people. That is why they are afraid of him, for she herself was suddenly frightened.

"So Harriette has been telling tales," he said.

"No. She didn't come for that. She came to ask me to ask you a favor . . . not to ruin her cousin. She said it was entirely in your hands and that her cousin would kill himself like Radnor Beaumont if you didn't help him."

"Goodhue Blair won't kill himself. He hasn't the guts. The worst he could do would be to drink himself to death." The contempt in his voice was like ice.

He moved a little nearer and after a moment said, "Do you know what you are talking about, Susie?"

"No. Only what I've been told and what I guessed. You never let me know anything. I'm not a fool, you know, Gus. I've plenty of brains. My brains might even be useful to you. That's the only thing I've ever resented . . . that you treated me always like a fool in these things."

"Business has nothing to do with women . . . it's ugly."

"But Mrs. Ogden . . ."

"Malvina Ogden is not a woman. She's much smarter than most men. Tell me, what is it that you guessed?"

She looked away from him, filled again with a curious sense of shame, for him. She said, "That you ruined a score of men and their families because they didn't come to a ball we gave . . . and you caused one man at least to kill himself."

Slowly she forced herself to look at him. His head was bent. He was looking at the heavy gold watch chain which he wore across his waistcoat, turning it round and round with his long strong fingers.

"Yes," he said, "That's true. People can't do a thing like that to my wife. I might have had another son but for them."

"No," she said quickly, "That's not true. I had a fall. That was what caused it." But she knew that he would never believe her, not until the day he died.

"But that's not all the story," he was saying, without looking at her. "There's much more to it, much more than you will ever understand. It's not woman's business but I'll try to explain it to you. Those same men would have ruined me just as ruthlessly. They were trying to do it, but they weren't strong enough. They weren't clever enough, not all of them together. I can tell you one thing — that if they had succeeded I wouldn't have hung myself in a cupboard. I'd have gone back to work and made another fortune and got them in the end. They weren't only my enemies, they were the enemies as well of the whole country."

She could not imagine what he meant but she was aware of a change in his manner. The anger was gone; he was calm and serious. Even the quality of his voice had changed.

"Do you know what this country is?" he asked rhetorically, "It's the biggest thing there has ever been on this earth. It's got everything. Did you ever think about the coal, the oil, the mines, the good fertile soil, the forests? We haven't even scratched the surface yet. There aren't ten people in this country who understand what is ahead of us, what this nation can become. I'm one of the ten people, Susie. It's so big that I can't even believe it myself. It needs big men to go ahead and build it up — not men like Radnor Beaumont and Goodhue Blair. They're New Yorkers and small-town men. Why, they've never even seen this country. What can men like that know about a place like Leaping Rock? What can they know about the West when they stick around New York and worry about whose parties they should go to or not go to. Do you know where they made their money? They inherited most of it and it didn't even take much brains on the part of their fathers and grandfathers to make it. They just sat and watched their land turn into money because other people developed factories and business and made it valuable for them. All they had to do was hang on to what they had. Always remember one thing, Susie, that the people who inherit money are always the tightest with it. They're afraid that if they lost it they'd never be able to make it again. That's why Radnor Beaumont hung himself — because he knew in his heart that once he was ruined he was ruined for good. There wasn't any coming back."

As if to help him make clear what he was trying to tell her, he stood up and began walking up and down. "Those men were trying to run the country — this great God-damned wonderful country they don't know anything about. They were' trying to make it into a closed corporation for themselves — the country they didn't know anything about at all. They were trying to buy it all for themselves and they're pygmies — that's what they are — pygmies. They did their best to ruin us. They thought we were nobodies, upstarts. They thought because they had hung on to what was given them, that they were smart with their two-penny tight little minds.

He whirled about suddenly, "They'd have ruined the country! They'd have let it stagnate! All they wanted was to keep it for themselves. They wanted to stop all progress, to keep it the small tight world they'd always known." He came over and stood at the foot of the bed, "They had to go just as all little people all through history have to go. There's a new world coming, a world so big most people can't even understand it and it needs a new kind of men who can take chances and think big . . . big as the great valley at Leaping Rock. This tight little world is busting open. There's a new sort of men who are big enough to break it wide open and make it into something . . . Gould and Harriman and Vanderbilt and a lot of others and myself. In another twenty-five years all the Goodhue Blairs and Radnor Beaumonts will be living in houses on back streets if they won't learn."

He bent over the end of the bed and took her hand, "Listen, sparrow. Did you ever know what I think about this country? I wouldn't trade Texas for the whole of Europe. Texas you can do something with. You can build into the future. Europe is stuck in a groove. It's all developed and finished. No, these little fellows tried to drive us out, to smash us. They tried to block us every way they could. They're not going to count much longer. If you're to get ahead as a banker you've got to be big and think big from now on. Nobody'll ever miss 'em. They had to go. The rest of us have a job to do. A big job that takes big, wide-open thinking and men who don't invest for a three per cent sure thing."

She was dazzled by his eloquence and the look of fire in his blue eyes. She had never thought of him like this. Even all his gusto and pleasure in life had seemed to her no more than a natural phenomenon, without direction. Now she began to understand many things.

"It happened to work two ways," he said. "It killed two birds with one stone . . . because it killed off a lot of birds who were rude to you." He took her hand between his two big hands and said, "You see? I'm sorry you thought me so small that I'd do something like that just out of revenge."

"I didn't think that . . . really. I didn't know."

"We're set now. The world belongs to us." He came round the end of the bed and sat down beside her. "I'll take care of Goodhue Blair," he said, "if it means so much to Harriette. I'll leave him with enough to live on but not enough to ever again be dangerous."

"Thank you, Gus. I'll telegraph to Harriette." And then out of her immense curiosity, she asked, "And Mrs. Ogden?"

"What do you mean — Mrs. Ogden?"

"Was she in on it?"

"Yes. She's one of the ones who understands how big this country is." He grinned. "And you remember she always said, 'I'll civilize 'em or know the reason why!' Do you understand and will you forgive me?"

"Yes, Gus."

Then he kissed her and she forgot all her anxieties for the moment.

"It wasn't so bad losing the baby, Gus," she said. "I'm going to have another."

It was all right now, save for one little sadness. She knew now that the little red house was no more than a dream. She was never to have a home — the kind of home she wanted. A home didn't fit in with what Gus had been talking about as he paced up and down her bedroom, illuminated by the passion and excitement of his ambitions, of his vast and curious dream.

VII

In the moment she stood there watching Amory, red-faced and clumsy, trying to pick up the pieces of the shattered shepherdess, it had all come back to her — the painful memory of the ball and the figures of Aspasie and Harriette, Mrs. Ogden and the Major. Of late the past returned to her in sudden unexpected flashes of memory, very clear and compressed, as if in a capsule containing only the essence and the significance of what had happened. And things which had occurred long ago began to fall into place in the pattern of her long existence, so that she understood how each apparently isolated episode had grown out of the past and in turn had its influence upon the future — that future which for a long time now had become the past. Time she found was a curious thing which people had not yet explored deeply enough to fathom its meaning and operation in relation to man. She thought suddenly of the simple description of relativity which her friend Dr. Salveminni had given her — that if you went along a river in a boat the landscape unfolded bit by bit in succession but that if you saw the same landscape from an airplane, you saw it all at once. She was beginning now to see her whole life as a whole, as if she saw it all at once from an airplane, rather than strung out, incident by incident, like the pearls of a necklace. She did not doubt the toughness and agility of her mind. In some ways it was brighter and quicker than it had ever been, alive with intuition and a kind of clairvoyance, darting this way and that like a firefly, and in a way it was stronger than it had ever been because it had wisdom for a base.

But relativity, philosophy, were not the concern of the moment. It was Amory, stooping and holding on to the yellow marble fireplace, while he struggled to pick up the shattered fragments of the shepherdess.

She said, "Let it go, Amory, Taylor will clear it away later. You may fall into the fireplace and burn yourself."

Relieved, Amory stood erect and said, "I'm very sorry, Granny. I don't know how it happened."

The word "Granny" infuriated her again but she still held her peace. She thought, If he is to make any sense, he must have a moderately clear head and aloud she said, "I think some coffee would help you," and relighted the flame under the silver coffee urn.

He went over to a chair and sat for a time

with his elbow on his knees, his head in his hands. When the coffee was hot, she poured a cup and carried it over to him. "It will be better without cream and sugar," she said.

Then he looked up at her suddenly as if he saw her face for the first time and she was aware that he was afraid and that this was why he had been drinking. The look in his eyes softened her and brought a quick, sudden understanding. She thought, It is really not his fault. He was born above his station. He is a dull fellow, not very bright, and he was taught all sorts of false things in school and at home, among them that any Stilham was a superior and privileged creature, that the world somehow depended on what he and his friend did and thought. Things were expected of him that were far beyond his capabilities. They tried to make a silk purse out of a sow's ear. And he himself had believed it all until now . . . now when he had at last overstrained in his effort to convince himself that he is what he is supposed to be.

He drank the coffee and she said, gently, as if to help him back to clarity, "You wanted to talk to me, Amory. What was it about?"

"It was about the money," he said, "You told me you would consider loaning it if I told you all the circumstances."

"Yes. That's right."

He said nothing more for a moment but sat staring into space as if making a gargantuan effort to regain possession of himself.

"More coffee?" she asked.

"Yes, please." He came over to her and she refilled the cup.

When he sat down again he said, without looking at her, "You never liked me much, did you?" He was saying things now that it would never have occurred to him to say if he were completely sober.

"No, Amory. Although it wasn't exactly dislike. I thought you were the wrong person for Helen and wrong in our family and I did not think you and Helen loved each other enough to make up for all that."

"Maybe you were right. Sometimes I think you were."

"Let's not bother with that," she said. "It's all water under the bridge."

He sighed and she knew what was behind the sigh — a desire to go back and begin over again, to go back to his early youth when, like Harry, he had lived in an enchanted world which seemed to have been constructed only for his pleasure and success. There were so many American men like that, huddling together in their clubs like refugees, going back to class reunions and club dinners to recapture what could not be recaptured save in the hazy illusion of alcohol.

"What do you want this money for?" she asked, and bluntly he said, "To pay back what I have stolen."

"It's as bad as that?"

"Yes."

Wonderingly, she asked, "Why did you do it? You had plenty of money. You knew there was more, much more, in the background. You had only to wait until I died. I had already given Helen a great deal."

"All that hasn't much to do with why I did it. I wanted to make more money. I wanted to be successful."

"There are so many things you could have done, so many things in this world to be interested in." And into her mind came a childish jingle she remembered out of nowhere: *The world is so full of a number of things, I'm sure we should all be as happy as kings.* But Amory was unaware of all that. All his expensive education hadn't taught him anything, least of all how to live the short span of time allotted to man. At fifty he had a child's mind without a child's curiosity or enthusiasm. Somewhere, sometime, something had gone wrong. There were too many men like him in America, so many that there must be some deep-rooted colossal fault in the very foundations of the whole structure.

"What I did wasn't really wrong," Amory was saying, "I used clients' securities as collateral on loans. It's been done many times before, by people we all know in Wall Street. If things had gone as I expected there wouldn't have been any trouble. I'd have replaced it all. But the government began to meddle and pry into the books. After all, we are a reputable firm. It wasn't as if it was done by a nobody. They might have left me alone. We haven't any rights left, even in our private lives."

She did not answer him at once. She was trying to see his point of view — that what he had done was all right since it was done by Amory Stilham. It was a curious point of view and he, she knew, was not the only one who shared it. They all had been brought up to believe things like that. The Major had, in his lifetime, been guilty of all sorts of skullduggery, things as bad as this and worse, but he had been clever enough to get away with them and he had never pretended that he deserved special privileges or that what he did was anything but crooked. His only rule was the frank one, that the end justified the means; if you got away with it, everything was all right. Amory was stupid.

"It's the interference of the government

which has ruined everything," he was saying. "It's killed all our business. It's made it impossible to operate."

It was a curious point of view, leading nowhere but backward. She saw, quite clearly, that he did not feel himself guilty of wrongdoing because he was Amory Stilham and a broker and that as such he should suffer no interference. There was no use going on with it.

She asked, "How much did you tell me you'd need?"

"About seven hundred and fifty thousand dollars." She caught her breath, "That, Amory, is a great deal of money. If I gave it to you, it would have to come out of Helen's share. Does she agree to that?"

He moved uneasily in his chair, "I don't know. She knows nothing about it."

"There is another thing," she said. "If I gave it to you to pay back your clients, would it stop the whole thing?"

"I don't know."

"That is something you had better find out."

He did not answer her.

"How soon," she asked, "would this have to be done?"

"Now . . . as soon as possible. It's about to come before the Grand Jury."

"Why didn't you tell me sooner? Now it

may be too late."

"I hoped to get money from partners and friends and hush the whole thing up."

"And they didn't give it to you?"

"No. A lot of them didn't have it . . . with taxes and restrictions and all this New Deal rot."

"And if the thing can't be stopped?"

"I shall have to stand trial."

"And then?"

"If they find me guilty . . ." He looked away from her without finishing the sentence and she felt a sudden chill come over her whole body. "Prison" was what he had not said. She had felt the chill, the same sort of awful dead, cold, chill years ago when a reform campaign and the law had very nearly caught up with Gus and they had had to live out of New York State for a whole year while he bribed himself out of the hole. It was only a little while after Eddie was born. That was how he had come to be born in Wilmington instead of New York City, because the shadow of prison hung over his father. Bribery! That was how Gus had done it. He had bought his way out. Perhaps it could be done again now, half a century later, in the case of Amory. She was not afraid for herself, she was beyond being touched by scandal, nor was she afraid for Amory. What happened to him was of no importance. It was only for the sake of Janie and her young man.

She said, "I will have to talk to Judge Everett before I can do anything. Does he know anything about it?"

"I don't know."

"He mentioned the possibility of some kind of trouble to Alice."

The color came into Amory's ace. The mutual hatred of the Duchess and Amory was of long standing in the family, "Why did he tell *her* of all people."

"I don't know."

"When can I have an answer? It must be quick or it will be too late to do any good. Once it's in the papers they'll all be after me just because I'm Amory Stilham and in Wall Street."

Very calmly she said, "That has nothing to do with it, Amory. It's exactly as if you were a little bank clerk who stole money out of the till to gamble with at the races."

He looked at her in astonishment, "I don't see any likeness at all," he said. "I'm a respectable and prominent businessman with a good deal of background and connections." Quite suddenly he was sober again. Still there was no use in trying to make him understand what she meant.

"Are you going to tell Helen and the children?"

"If it can be settled, there will be no need to tell anyone." Bitterness corroded his voice. "Sometimes lately I think that what happened to me wouldn't matter much to the children. They're like strangers to me."

She did not deny this. She only said, "If I can arrange this I want only one promise . . . that I'm to be allowed to tell Janie."

"It would make it easier for me."

She was suddenly weary of him and said, "I think the best thing for you would be to go home and get some sleep."

"I don't sleep."

"And Helen?"

"She doesn't sleep either. She hasn't slept for months."

He rose and said, "Could I have another glass of brandy? It's the only thing that keeps me going."

"Of course, but I wouldn't depend on it." As he poured the glass she added, "The Major always had a remarkable rule. When things were going well he could and did drink many a man under the table. When things went badly, he never drank anything at all."

Amory drained the glass and said, "The Major was a remarkable man. I could never hope to emulate him." He said it simply without sarcasm and with a touch of admiration.

She looked at him sharply, "The Major was a remarkable man," she said. "But in many ways not an admirable one. I should advise anyone against emulating his morals in these days. They would spend most of their lives in jail."

He looked at her in astonishment, a little shocked by her honesty. "But you were devoted to him?"

"I was devoted only to a part of him. I felt only contempt for the rest. I have, I think, never said that before. I wanted you to know. He caused much unhappiness and tragedy through his ambition. That is unforgivable in anyone. I have lived a long time, Amory. That is the unforgivable crime. It is something to contemplate."

But she was getting beyond his depth and she drew back. "If you don't mind, I'll go to bed. I'll need a lot of strength for to-morrow."

He flushed, "Of course. I'm sorry. But before I go there's one thing I'd like to say." She waited without speaking and he went on. "It's about Janie. I wish you could persuade Janie to stop seeing this young man she's lost her head over. You're the only one who has any influence with her."

"What's wrong with him? He seems a very

nice young man."

"He hasn't anything to offer her." Again she didn't answer him and he said, "Besides it's very embarrassing for me. He was the one who uncovered the trouble."

"But I thought she met him in your house, Amory."

"That's true. He did come out for a week-end."

"Why?"

The bluntness of the question startled him. Again the color swept the big, handsome, empty face. "I wanted to see whether there was some way of inducing him to call the thing off before he found out too much."

"Was there?" she asked bluntly.

"No. He's a damned fanatic, a Red, filled with crackpot ideas."

She smiled and moved toward the bell to summon Taylor. Amory followed her and a moment before Taylor appeared he said, "You have been very good and understanding. Thank you."

"I'll do all I can, Amory."

Then Taylor came in and Amory said Good night and left. She saw that Taylor noticed at once the shattered fragments of the shepherdess, and she said, "Mr. Stilham accidentally knocked the piece of Dresden off the mantel."

"Shall I save the pieces and have it mended, madame?"

"No. It's not worth it. Throw them out."

She knew suddenly that she was glad to be rid of the shepherdess. There had been something ill-omened about the Dresden pair. Each had been shattered at a moment of great unhappiness, almost of disaster.

Taylor said, "Judge Everett called, madame. He said he would call again in the morning."

"Thank you, Taylor and good night."

She went out thinking, If he called, it must be bad enough for him to offer to help. In any case he knows. It will save me the trouble of having to explain.

She did not go to sleep at once. After Mattie had gone away, she tried to read but the great, red, handsome face of Amory kept getting between her and the pages, so that the words on them meant nothing. She kept thinking too of other things — all the nonsense Amory had been taught and believed, all the folly and shabbiness of the world out of which he had come. It seemed to her, thinking of the war and what was going on in Europe as she lay there quietly in her bed, that the folly of the human race was beyond comprehension, that it was bent upon destroying itself through stupidity as the great dinosaurs and Brontosaurus had done. The human race seemed to have developed very little common sense and virtually no sense of value at all. She could not, honestly, exempt herself since again and again in her lifetime she had yielded to the common vanities and stupidity. Perhaps, she thought, addressing herself, you did acquire wisdom only through experience and by the time you had acquired wisdom you were too old to put it to any good use. It was a poor thing to belong to the human race; being a dog like Bijou was much more satisfactory. Even the most maltreated dog had a better time in life than many people in Europe were having at the moment.

Presently she put aside the book altogether and turned out the light, but still sleep did not come. The darkness seemed to make it worse; her mind went round like a carrousel, always in movement, always returning to the same place — this ugly business of Amory. She thought bitterly that it was pretentious of him to believe that he could be a crook and get away with it; he wasn't clever enough. The Major had certainly done many shady things but they were conceived on a grand scale involving millions, and somehow, curiously enough, people and even the nation itself had drawn great wealth and benefits from his operations. There seemed to be no men like him any longer; there hadn't been for a long time. And it was not true — what Amory whined — that they no longer had the opportunity. The opportunity was still there, in a different way, for the grandeur of vision which the Major had had.

And she thought how pitiful it was — that American rule of shirt sleeves to shirt sleeves in three generations — and how true, except that it wasn't really shirt sleeves to shirt sleeves, it was shirt sleeves to soiled and shabby silks.

She began to plan her day — that she would see Judge Everett — and find out what had happened and how really serious the whole thing was, and after that she would get in touch with Janie's young man and have a talk with him. That, she knew, would be painful. There were many things she would discover, perhaps without his being aware of it, although he was clever enough. She would try anything to get Amory out of the mess, not for his sake but for Janie's.

But Judge Everett would come first. She fell asleep thinking about the first time she had ever seen him, when he had come to Newport as a young lawyer to see the Major about the Consolidated Mills and Ore business. She remembered him at dinner in the yellow marble dining-room and the sound of the surf on the beach below the cliffs. By that time the Major had got what he wanted. Nobody stayed away from his parties any longer. He had got what he wanted without making concessions, bludgeoning his way through, helped by a wife who seemed made by God to suit his purpose. He had remained common and vigorous and Rabelaisian, only by that time people called it eccentricity and genius because they had to find excuses for themselves and their acceptance of him, to cover up their own vanity and weakness. That, she thought, was the root of whatever greatness he had, not that he had made great fortunes and changed the whole face of the continent, but that he remained the same to the very end, the same man who had come to the Grand Hotel of Leaping Rock in a checked suit and purple tie with a diamond in it.

And as she fell asleep she remembered Judge Everett as the first man whom she had ever heard openly defy the Major. After dinner while the two men sat in the next room having their cigars and brandy and she worked at her needlepoint, she overheard, shamelessly and with great interest, fragments of their conversation. As it progressed, it turned louder and more violent in tone as the disagreement grew stronger, and, listening, she discovered an admiration for the young man who dared defy a man so powerful as the Major, who might make or break the whole career of a young lawyer.

Toward the end, as the argument grew in violence, she heard the young lawyer say, "I'll have nothing to do with the whole affair and I'll advise my firm not to touch it. There are some limits, and I think, sir, that you have passed them in this business."

Then the Major said something she could not hear and she heard the young man saying, "Some day there will be a reckoning. It may not happen in your time but it is certain to come and when it comes it will be very nearly a revolution against you and all your kind. People will rise up and put an end to this kind of thing and you and your class will have to pay for it."

Then she heard the Major speaking and knew that he had risen from his chair. This time she could hear what he said, very clearly, "You talk like an anarchist, young man, but there may be something in what you say."

"Anarchist" was an odd old-fashioned word. In those days Gus had used it the way Amory used the word "Red" to designate anyone who opposed him.

Then quietly she had slipped out to the piazza overlooking the sea and when the two men came into the room where she had been sitting, she made an ostentatiously innocent entrance from the piazza as if she had been there all the time and had heard nothing. But the young lawyer seemed a new man to her and she thought, If I had married someone like that it would have been better in spite of everything and Alice wouldn't be marrying a week from now a dissolute and shabby young man who wants her money as much as she wants to be a duchess.

She marked the young man, then, thinking, If Gus dies before me I shall take him as my lawyer. It will make me feel respectable again. And now as she fell asleep she remembered the speech about the revolution and people catching up with men like the Major. It had happened too late to capture the Major; it had caught instead his grandson-in-law who was only a pitiful imitation of the old Titan.

When the judge called in the morning about ten o'clock he said that he had something serious to discuss with her and at once she said, "I know what it is. Amory was here last night. Is it as bad as I suspect?"

"It is pretty serious. We'll discuss it when

I come over. It's not a thing to talk about over the telephone."

After she had hung up she sat for a time staring out of the window at the dull façade of the apartment across the street. While she was sitting there, Mattie knocked and came into the "boodwar." Mrs. Parkington was aware of her presence but it lay somewhere outside the realm of actual consciousness, as if she were hypnotized by the façade opposite, although she really did not see it at all. It was the certainty that Mattie was staring at her which roused her. She turned and said, "Mattie. What is it?"

The honest, petulant, round face was filled with concern. Mattie said, "You slept badly last night."

"How do you know that?"

"By the way the bed looked. When you sleep well, the bed hardly looks as if it were slept in. It's very rumpled this morning . . . worse than I've ever seen it."

She knew that Mattie was trying to pry from her some hint of what was wrong. It was possible that she had overheard her conversation with the judge, even though the door between the rooms was closed.

"It was nothing," she said. "As we get older, Mattie, we need less sleep."

"You look very badly," said the implacable

Mattie. "You have great circles under your eyes like oysters."

"Never mind!" Mrs. Parkington said, tartly. "I always have circles in the morning. Go about your work."

"I only spoke of it for your own good, madame," said Mattie. She rarely used the word "madame" unless she was angry about something. Then she said,: "Mr. Amory had no right to keep you so late, telling you things to worry you."

"How do you know what he told me?"

"I don't know, but I can guess," said Mattie, her voice dropping with insinuation. Mrs. Parkington remembered that Amory had not greeted Mattie when she came into the room for the dogs. He had given no sign of being aware of her presence. That was unwise of him since Mattie was really like one of the family, in some ways more like one of the family than her family itself.

"Well, it was nothing. He told me nothing to worry me."

Mattie sniffed a sniff more eloquent than if she had said, "You needn't try to get away with lying to me." Then she went out, artfully leaving the door ajar, but not artfully enough for the maneuver to escape Mrs. Parkington's notice. Eavesdropping she considered an invasion of privacy although she herself had been guilty of it in the past. She called out angrily, "Please close the door, Mattie," and the door was closed without any further comment than the violence with which wood struck wood.

Then she picked up the telephone and called Amory's house and asked for Janie. The sound of the girl's voice excited and delighted her, as if somehow the quality of it gave her strength.

She said, "I want to talk to Ned, my dear. Where can I reach him?"

Janie gave her the telephone number and said, "He won't be in until eleven. He's flying up from Washington. He has wonderful news, Granny. He's been promoted. He's going to San Francisco in the autumn."

"Will you like that?"

"Yes. I'll love it."

"You haven't yet decided when you're going to be married?"

"Sometime in September."

"That's fine." There was a pause because Mrs. Parkington, knowing what she knew, for once could not think of anything to say. Presently she said, "I just wanted to talk to Ned about some business . . . about the law and certain securities I have."

"He'll know everything about that."

"I'm sure he will. Drop in to see me soon."

The judge appeared at eleven-thirty. He had always been punctual. Busy people always were; only idlers and those who had nothing on their minds could afford to waste the little time allotted to a lifetime.

He was a tall, thin man with white hair and mustaches and a rosy skin, who carried himself very erect with an air of pride. In this Mrs. Parkington thought him justified since he had been an ambassador and a cabinet member, but above all he had led an honorable life and done much good. Always, even as far back as the night she had overheard him facing down the Major, there had been a kind of spark, a kind of secret understanding between them. It was as if they knew something that others did not know; when they were together they could go directly to the heart of anything, without preliminaries, without hemming and hawing or pretense or explanations of any kind. That was why she did not dread his visit now but rather welcomed it. His advice would be good and very likely she would find that he believed her judgment correct.

When he saw her, he said, "It's a long time since you have sent for me, Susie. Much too long."

"There was nothing to prevent your coming in for tea now and then. I don't bother much with dinners any more. There seems so much to do nowadays."

She asked after his wife who, he said, was well except that she could not get wholly over her arthritis. The interest was one of politeness which deceived neither of them; he had, they both knew, married too young when his mind had had little to do with his choice. His wife was both dull and frivolous but he had stuck by her because there were three children, although there were times, even now, when she exasperated him to the point of violence. Mrs. Parkington knew this and she knew that he was aware of her knowledge, although neither of them had ever spoken of it. She knew too that she herself in some ways was nearer to him in understanding than his wife had ever been.

When they had gone through the whole of his family, she said, "This business of Amory is pretty bad?"

"I'm afraid it is."

"I don't know how bad it is or whether anything can be done. He seems very vague about the whole business. I might as well explain my side of the situation." She picked up one of the dogs and continued, "I'll be quite frank. I've never admired Amory. We never got on very well, even in the beginning."

"I think," the judge smiled, "that was apparent to a good many people. Certainly it was to me."

"He was always arrogant without having anything to be arrogant about. However, that has nothing to do with the present situation or very little at least. The point is that I want to do whatever I can to help. Above all, I should like to hush it up before it ever gets out at all. It is not a question of money. I'm prepared for that. If paying back the whole amount will help at all I'm perfectly willing."

There was no use in going into detail with him. He was her lawyer. He knew how enormous was her wealth and that even the loss of seven hundred and fifty thousand dollars would scarcely be noticed.

The judge said, "I don't know, Susie, how far it has gone or whether it can be mended now. Until now it has been officially none of my business. What I know I have only heard through channels which are not exactly public. However, it is beginning to get around." He took out his wallet and from it he took a newspaper clipping. He handed it to her and said, "You see? It is marked."

She put on her reading glasses and found the sentence he had marked. It was a gossip column and the sentence read, *Keep watch for a scandal concerning money in which one of New York's richest, most prominent clubmen with powerful connections is involved. If worse comes to worst he may have to join some of our other financiers up the river.*

As she came to the end she felt suddenly sick. Trying to control herself, she said, "Those damned columnists!"

"If it becomes known at all, there'll be no stopping it. The temper of the country isn't what it used to be." He did not add, "In the Major's day," but there was no need to say it.

She said, "Do you read the gossip columns regularly?" "I read everything. I discovered long ago that it was the best way to understand this fantastic country of ours."

"Whose securities has he used?" she asked.

"I don't know all the names. Some of them you will know. They are friends of yours."

"In a way that makes it worse."

She heard the telephone ringing distantly and thought bitterly, I suppose there is more trouble.

"What do you advise me to do, John?" she asked.

"Sit tight. I will go to work on it. If anything can be done I should be able to manage it."

Then there was a knock at the door and

when she answered it Taylor came in, "It is Mrs. Sanderson's maid, madame," he said, "She wants to speak to you. It is urgent, she said."

Mrs. Parkington took up the telephone beside her and heard the hysterical voice of the maid. "There's something the matter with Mrs. Sanderson, madame. I can't waken her. She just lies there. She won't speak or open her eyes."

Mrs. Parkington thought quickly, Then she isn't dead, and aloud she said, "Call Dr. Thursby at once. I'll give you his number." She picked up the address book beside the telephone and found the number, aware that the maid was still talking wildly into the telephone but hearing nothing she said.

"Listen to me," she said into the telephone. "Please be quiet for a moment. Call Dr. Thursby and ask him to come over at once. I will come immediately." She gave the number and said, "Have you got it right? Please repeat it." The maid repeated the number and she added, "If Dr. Thursby is out tell them to send someone else. And put hot-water bottles at her feet and wrap her in blankets. I shall be over immediately."

She put down the telephone and said, "It's Alice. The maid can't waken her. She's been taking things to make her sleep and very likely took too much."

The judge stood up, "I can drop you. My car is outside."

Then she rang for Mattie and Mattie, tiresomely, insisted upon going with her. There was no preventing her. Mattie said firmly, "If you don't take me, I shall run along behind the car. Maybe you would like that?"

In the car Mattie insisted on sitting in front with the driver. The judge and Mrs. Parkington sat side by side in silence, neither of them feeling any need for talk. The judge, knowing all about the Duchess and her drug taking, was thinking, It is extraordinary — the things that have happened to Susie, the tragedies and troubles. She is a remarkable woman to have survived them.

And in her corner Mrs. Parkington was thinking about her daughter Alice, not as she was now, insensible, lying in her bed, a tired woman of sixty-five, but as she had been a long time ago before she had married and gone to France to live.

It was as if there had always been a kind of blight upon Alice, from that summer long ago in Long Branch when she had worried because Alice was not as attractive as her brother Herbert. There were times when Mrs. Parkington came near to a belief in astrology since it seemed to offer the only explanation to the strangeness and diversity in the lives of people. How otherwise could one's life be as dull and futile as Alice's whole life had been? Why was it then that her own life had been a long record of the spectacular? — certainly not because she herself had sought the spectacular. All she had ever wanted, in her heart, was a quiet home and a pleasant unspectacular existence.

It seemed to her that the whole trouble had really begun with Mrs. Ogden and her espousal of Alice, her determination that Alice should be attractive and make a good match. It all began with Malvina Ogden's determination to give a great ball for Alice when she was eighteen, to push her forward, to make something of her when there was no material in Alice from which to make a brilliant career. If Malvina had only left her in peace she might have been an old maid or had a dull but respectable husband, which very clearly was the fate designed for her by nature.

The worst of it was that Alice had always known she was unattractive from the very beginning when people stopped the pram and admired extravagantly the golden-haired younger brother. Separated from her brother by school, it had been no better. It was not only that she had a sallow skin and was inclined to be pimply, but that there was no fire inside her which might have compensated for these things. She had not wanted any of the things which were given her so lavishly, neither the fashionable schools nor the clothes nor the parties; she had wanted only to be left in peace to become a nurse.

It was the Major who in the beginning had started the long misery. In his egotism and exuberance his children and even his wife were mere appendages and trappings of his success. No daughter of his would become so humble a thing as a trained nurse; *his* daughter must make a great match and make a glorious success in her life. It did not matter that his daughter had none of the qualities this demanded — neither the looks, nor the brilliance, nor the hardness. She was only a plain, dull, sentimental girl, immensely rich, who wished only to sink out of sight.

Mrs. Parkington remembered well the quarrels, the violence, that marked the whole period. It was the only real violence, they were the only real quarrels she and the Major had ever known, because she took Alice's side. But always there was pitted against her not only Gus but Mrs. Ogden who had made of Alice one of her *causes*.

And then Alice herself had deserted her mother. Some odd thing happened to her, something which even now Mrs. Parkington had never understood. The girl had said suddenly, “Very well! I shall go to parties and wear fine clothes and do all the things Father wishes.” And after that, her dullness took on a quality of chillness and indifference. Gus and Mrs. Ogden had their way, and at the great ball given by Mrs. Ogden, Alice wore a gown from Worth and the pearls her father had given her which reached halfway to her knees, and she had dozens of bouquets and her dance card was filled far in advance of the ball, but she had never believed in her own success. She knew that the flowers and the invitations came only because she was Major Parkington’s daughter and Mrs. Ogden’s protégée and because no one dared oppose so formidable a combination. Also because she was very rich . . .

And so when the Duke came to New York to stay with Malvina Ogden, clearly looking for a rich wife, poor Alice was the obvious victim, waiting like a sacrificial heifer in Worth clothes and pearls, to become the Duchess de Brantès. There was nothing Mrs. Parkington could do, for the girl herself wanted it, perhaps because she could, by becoming a duchess, stifle her own sense of her dreariness and compensate for past humiliations.

In the back of the judge's car, Mrs. Parkington sighed heavily, so heavily that the judge looked at her without being noticed at all. It was as if Alice had been doomed from the beginning, and now she was perhaps dying, having suffered much unhappiness and countless indignities without ever having lived at all.

Suddenly the car was at the door of the apartment house and the judge got down to help her out and Mattie got down from beside the driver. Mrs. Parkington felt suddenly weary and filled with despair. It had gone on and on like this for years now. They all turned to her when ill or in trouble and they were all God-damned dull and tiresome and scarcely worth the trouble. When Gus died, she thought she could do as she pleased, but it had only turned out to be worse than when he was alive. She thought, If only Herbert or Eddie had lived, I would have had someone . . . One could have forgiven them many things because they were handsome and gay and alive and attractive. But all the others, all except Janie, had no brightness. They had no right to call upon her.

She pulled herself together and managed to say goodbye to the judge and went into the apartment house on the arm of Mattie. On the way in she thought, apparently for no reason at all, of the cowboy Al, and felt a sudden intense desire to see him again, as if somehow his simplicity and quietness could give her the strength she needed.

The doctor was already there, a short grave humorless man of sixty with a small goatee and very shiny eyeglasses. There was no need of pretense between him and Mrs. Parkington. The Duchess was one of his charges and Mrs. Parkington paid him well — a yearly salary — to care for her daughter.

After they had exchanged greetings, he said, "She has taken an overdose of sleeping stuff. I think she will be all right. She has a very strong heart and a good constitution."

It was odd how perverse nature could be, to give to Alice the physique and constitution of ox, when Alice did not care whether she lived or died and had not cared for many years.

"Have you sent for a nurse?" asked Mrs. Parkington.

"Yes. She should be here in half an hour."

"I'm wondering whether it would not be wise to keep a nurse permanently."

The doctor looked at her. "You mean it might prevent this happening again?"

"Yes."

"It might be a good idea if Mrs. Sanderson would consent."

"I think she will consent," said Mrs. Parkington, "My daughter is rather careless. Shall I leave it for you to arrange?"

"If you like."

"I think a middle-aged woman, rather gossipy, would be best. It might help divert Mrs. Sanderson."

"I think I know just the woman," he said. "If that's all, I'll go to her room."

"That's all. I'll wait until the nurse arrives."

Mrs. Parkington crossed to the hallway leading to the bedroom. In the doorway she turned and said, "Thank you, Doctor. Thank you for everything."

He only bowed without answering her.

It was extraordinary how they had held a whole conversation without mentioning what lay at the root of it — that Alice had taken an overdose of sleeping medicine, not because she meant to take her life but only because she had been drinking alone, in her own flat. She was not the temperament to be tempted by suicide; drunkards seldom were. Each time they drink, they escape from life into a little death.

Emily, the maid, was sitting bolt upright on a chair by the bed, ostentatiously keeping watch over her mistress. Emily was a thin parched virgin, both hysterical and calculating. Mrs. Parkington was an immensely rich woman who might die leaving her daughter in the care of her maid and Emily wanted no mistake made concerning the fact of her devotion. There might be legacies to faithful servants and devoted retainers, of the sort Emily had read about in the newspaper accounts of the wills of rich and fashionable people like Mrs. Parkington. She might have chosen a comfortable chair, but the effect would not have been so good, so eloquent of Emily's vigilance and devotion.

Mrs. Parkington was not deceived by Emily's charades. She said, "Good morning," briskly and then said, looking at Alice who lay on her back breathing through her mouth, "How did it happen, Emily?"

Emily, already on her feet, said, "I don't know, madame. Mrs. Sanderson told me to go out to the pictures. She was alone here and already asleep when I came in."

If things had been different and they were more sympathetic, Alice might have been dining at home with her mother instead of drinking alone in her own flat. Mrs. Parkington sighed, thinking how yellow her daughter's skin looked against the white pillow. She reproached herself for not having made enough effort with Alice, although she could not think what more she could have done. It was difficult to deal with people who were both dull and bitter. Alice had been like that since she was seventeen.

"You needn't wait here," said Mrs. Parkington to Emily, "I'll stay until she comes round. Ask cook if she has a chop or a couple of eggs."

Then Emily went out leaving Mrs. Parkington alone with her daughter. When the maid had gone the old woman opened the window a little wider to let in the soft spring air and then seated herself in a comfortable chair where she could watch her daughter.

The weariness and boredom seemed gone from the face now, almost as if Alice were dead and had achieved that peace which comes to some people only in death. Beneath the flabbiness there were other faces, very clear in the memory of Mrs. Parkington — the face of Alice as a young girl on the day she married the Duke when, for a little time, she was happy because as a rich bride marrying a famous name she was for once genuinely important and envied by girls much prettier and more attractive than herself. All that had meant a great deal to Alice.

And there was the face of Alice when everything was finished and she had returned home from France with bitter lines about her mouth and a dull look of suffering in the hyperthyroid eyes. And the face of Alice when she married that cheap English remittance man who kept other women out of the allowance she gave him. And the aging middle-aged face that married for the third time a middle-aged, sexless widower called Sanderson, from Pasadena. He was not even attractive. He collected stained glass, played the organ and had halitosis. Each time it was money which had made Alice desirable; each time it was money which betrayed her into an unhappy marriage. Each time the man was a little less attractive. With all his faults the Duke was the best of the lot. All three marriages had ended only in disaster and humiliation.

Quietly, as she waited, she fell to thinking of the Duke. She had not really thought of him for many years, save when the papers recorded his death at the age of fifty in the Battle of Verdun. Until then he had written to her once or twice a year, as if the whole misery of his marriage to Alice had never happened at all. Sometimes she acknowledged the letters with a formal line or two as a woman of the world, but more often she left them unanswered. But it had made no difference. He went on writing to her just the same, charming letters, filled with wit and flattery, very Gallic, faintly impudent letters in which at times he seemed almost to be wooing her. Once he had written, "It can be a tragedy for a plain daughter to have a mother who is pretty and charming. It has, in fact, been a tragedy in more than one life."

The letter had made her unhappy for it revealed suddenly something which she had never considered until then and which now became clear to her — that Alice had been jealous of her because Gus had loved her so deeply, that she had been jealous of her because her brothers had adored their mother, and because they themselves were so much brighter and more handsome. It made her understand many things like the sullenness and defiance of Alice as a young girl and her sudden almost joyous submission to the will and schemes of Mrs. Morton Ogden.

VIII

Presently, wondering why the nurse had not yet come, Mrs. Parkington fell into a doze in which the past and present were hopelessly mixed. She was in Newport again in the great marble house, in June when Newport was loveliest, and the house and piazzas were hung with flowers and there were people about everywhere, caterers and florists and men hanging garlands of Chinese lanterns among the flowering trees, for Gus was making a typical Parkington effort. His daughter was about to marry a peer of France, to become a duchess, and this was to be the greatest wedding anyone had ever seen.

Herbert and Eddie were very good about it, although Eddie who was seventeen, thought it was all a lot of tripe and said so. And the Blair girl, Amélie, was there staying in the house because Herbert seemed unable to live without her. She was nineteen, Herbert's own age, a tall, slim girl, a little mad like all the Blairs — you never knew when or how the Blair eccentricities would break out. Thus far Amélie had done nothing worse than dress like a Botticelli and wear fresh flowers in her hair, which made her at times seem more like Ophelia than a Botticelli spring. Mrs. Parkington hoped the attraction was puppy love because it wasn't a good thing for anyone to marry a Blair. She did not try to oppose it openly for fear of turning Herbert against herself — and Herbert was more to her than any of the children, a fact which she acknowledged to herself but hid away shamefully in the deepest part of her. He was still in a way the beautiful baby in the pram whom everyone stopped to admire. There was something clear and bright about him with his fair hair and blue eyes and the vigor of his father. It was that vigor which kept him always in trouble, driving him on and on without relief, since he, unlike his father at the same age, already had everything. And so it was girls and pleasure, and now it was the Blair girl who moved about and spoke in an affected voice. It was odd, Mrs. Parkington thought, how life went round and round, turning up the most unlikely happenings. Amélie Blair was the granddaughter of Goodhue Blair whom Gus had saved from ruin because Harriette came all the way to Long Branch that hot summer afternoon to intercede for him.

Eddie, who was born a little while after that visit, was wild and precocious and good-looking. Already he had been sent home from

St. Bart's for bringing a case of beer into the dormitory. His father planned to send him out West into one of the mines "to straighten him out," but secretly Gus admired his wild adolescent young son because he was like himself. "I was only sixteen when I got a girl into trouble," he had boasted once to Susie. He would never see that his case and the cases of his sons were not in the least alike. A young man without a penny and colossal fierce ambitions could be as wild as he liked without harm because the fierceness of his ambitions would keep him going straight. It was different with two boys who already had all the things their father wanted. Their very good looks conspired to ruin them. But Gus would never listen to her. He wanted his children to have all the things he had never had as a boy, and always his sons were, in a way, merely an extension of his ego; they must be brilliant and clever because they were *his* sons. Their successes, their good looks, their marriages, were only a part of his own immense and complicated pattern of success. Gus wanted to swallow the whole world; that it did not wreck him meant only that he had the vigor, the hardness and constitution of a mythical figure.

That day of the wedding was not a happy one. All day Susie worried and fretted, not about the details of the wedding which she left to Aspasie with her French talent for such things, but about her own family and this marriage which depressed her.

And then about noon, the Duke appeared at the house to have a look at all the confusion. He was a neatly made young man of twenty-nine, overbred, with a rather lean face and dark, passionate eyes and a faintly effeminate manner, good-humored and agreeable enough but decidedly not what Susie in her wisdom would have chosen for a son-in-law. When he was with Gus, Susie felt a persistent wild desire to burst into laughter, because there was so little of understanding between them. The very air seemed to crackle with absurdity.

And now the Duke had come to pay his respects to her before lunch and with revulsion she faced what she had determined to do before he sailed with Alice on the "Carpathia" for London. She had to do it because there existed between her husband and her future son-in-law no ground whatever on which they might discuss the intimate things which troubled her.

She took him into her small sitting-room overlooking the sea and sent for sherry and when they were served, she said boldly, "Jacques, this is the last time we shall see each other before the wedding. There are one or two things I should like to say."

"Yes, *belle-mère*," he said, smiling.

"Alice is not a beautiful girl."

He frowned suddenly, "She is not a beauty, but she is pleasant-looking — *jolie-laide*."

Susie did not deceive herself. This was flattery and also an effort to convince himself that Alice was not so plain or poor-spirited a bride. To be a *jolie-laide* one had to have spirit and brains. Aspasie was a *jolie-laide* if you like, even now when she was over fifty.

"I want you to be good to her for that reason."

"Of course I shall be good to her, *belle-mère*." He said it glibly. He was altogether too smooth and cynical for her taste.

"I think I understand the basis of this marriage," she said, and without blushing he answered, "Yes."

The terms were good, thought Susie. Gus had seen to that. There was a fund set up which would give the Duke one hundred thousand a year so long as he lived, half of it for the upkeep of the estates; half for himself.

"What I am trying to say is painful," she continued, forcing the words out with a great effort. "To be quite honest I was always against the marriage but Alice wanted it and Mrs. Ogden and my husband. I do not believe in this sort of marriage."

He started to speak but she raised her hand, "Let me finish," she said. "It will be easier that way." He sank back in his chair and the passionate mocking eyes turned cold.

"I am not asking you to love Alice. I cannot even ask you the impossible — to be faithful to her. I am only asking you to be kind and considerate of her and not to make her more unhappy than she is already. If and when you are unfaithful, I only ask you to be discreet about it and never let her know or let her be humiliated by the knowledge that other people know. Treat her with the dignity as your wife and possibly the mother of your children. I do not think she is a demanding girl. Only be kind and considerate."

Even as she spoke she felt the force going out of her so the speech ended weakly. She had the impression he was not listening at all or that if he were listening it was with mockery and cynicism, believing that she was very naïve and bourgeois.

Then he said, surprisingly, "I will take very good care of your daughter, *belle-mère*. You need not worry. You seem to be a wise woman and a very frank one. I have sometimes wished I was marrying you instead of Alice. Your husband is a very fortunate man."

It was a strange thing to say, but she

thanked him for it. It seemed very odd to her that she should be talking like an old woman to this man who was only eight years younger than herself and in some ways immensely older and more tired than she would ever be.

Then they talked of other things and presently Aspasie knocked on the door and came in and said that Alice wanted to see her. The Duke went out and for a moment Aspasie stood looking after him, the proud firm profile outlined against the brilliant blue of the June sea. Susie watched her and after a moment she asked, "What are you thinking?"

Aspasie, looking handsome as she always did when she was angry, said, "There is no reason why I should not be honest. I was thinking what a *voyou* he is."

There was certainly no reason why she and Aspasie should not be honest with each other, considering how long and close their friendship had been and the strange circumstances in which it had been born.

"Alice is hysterical," she said. "Now she doesn't want to go through with the wedding. You'll have to force her."

"I don't know whether she is not right."

"She may be right but one can't behave like that," said Aspasie simply, "Let her marry him. It does not matter. If she does not marry him, it will be another like him. She is a doomed girl."

So she went down and quieted Alice who had suddenly taken an unreasonable and passionate dislike to the Duke, and as she sat with the girl, she saw through the window the figures of Malvina Ogden and her maid arriving in the victoria. Mrs. Ogden sat bolt upright, triumphantly. She had grown immensely heavy so that her side of the victoria sagged. Her horselike ugliness was emphasized by the green traveling costume she wore. She looks, thought Susie, as if this were her day — as if it were her daughter who was being married. In a way it was. She had "put over" the Parkingtons. No one would stay away from this party. There were even people who through Harriette and Aspasie had begged for invitations. Gus had what he wanted and Mrs. Ogden. It was odd that even after years of apparent intimacy, she could never think of the woman as "Malvina" but only as "Mrs. Ogden."

Then in another victoria Harriette arrived. She looked ruddy and well and was dressed, despite her thick middle-aged figure, in a frilly costume much too young for her. Her "poor father" had been dead for seven years now, and with the money Gus gave her she had founded a home for stray cats and dogs and was happy and blooming. It was strange, thought Susie, what curious and diverse satisfactions people demanded from life.

For the rest of the day Harriette bustled about the house, feeling important as a friend of the rich and fashionable Mrs. Parkington, distracting the servants and strewing confusion wherever she went. She had gone a long way since that first evening at the Brevoort when she had blushed at being seen dining with the notorious Major Augustus Parkington and his bride.

And there was Henry Parkington come down from the Genesee Valley with his bride, the farmer's daughter, dressed, both of them, carelessly and awkwardly. Their presence didn't please Gus but it gave Susie, amid all the flowers and decorations and hubbub, a sudden sense of having some contact with reality. Henry's wife was pregnant and showed it but it seemed to trouble neither Henry nor herself. Already people were beginning to say that Henry was crazy, but Susie didn't think so; it seemed to her that there was an old-fashioned common sense about him and his wife, the kind of sense which had begun to disappear utterly from the lives of herself and Gus in spite of anything she could do.

She took Henry's wife, whose name was Ida, under her wing and saw to it that, amid all the confusion, she had rest and quiet — something for which Ida did not appear to have any need or any desire. But it left Henry free to wander about staring at guests and decorations and making rude remarks. He was irrepressible, like a handsome young stallion, turned into pasture. Herbert's girl, Amélie Blair, took a great liking for him and Aspasie herself took him over at the end of the day. Susie knew that he couldn't be crazy if Aspasie approved of him. She had never been wrong about anyone.

And then as Mrs. Parkington was watching Aspasie and Henry talking in an alcove hung with smilax, she heard the sound of taxi horns in a day when there were no taxis and opened her eyes suddenly to find herself in Alice's room with the sound of the taxi horns coming in the open window from Park Avenue, and Alice, an old woman, unconscious, was lying on the bed. Before Mrs. Parkington was standing Emily, the maid, who said that the nurse had arrived at last and that lunch was served. Would she still like it on a tray or in the dining-room?

IX

The nurse was a big woman of about forty called Mrs. Dodsworth, with a kindly face. Mrs. Parkington thought she might do very well for a permanent companion for Alice. Time would tell.

The memories of Newport and the wedding stayed with her, pleasantly, as memories have a way of doing with old people who have lived a full rich life, and it was not until the middle of lunch that she remembered Amory and his trouble and that she had forgotten to call Ned Talbot who was so important in the whole affair. She sent Emily to get the number for her and, although it was in the midst of the lunch hour, Ned was in.

The sound of his voice gave her a feeling of pleasure and reassurance. He said, "I have just come back from Washington." And when she asked if he could come in at teatime to see her about something important, he said, "I have arranged to meet Janie. May I bring her?"

"No. I think better not. We had better be alone."

"All right. I'll call her. I'm sure she won't mind."

About three o'clock the Duchess opened her eyes and the nurse came to tell Mrs. Parkington who was reading in the drawing room.

"I'd like to see her alone," said Mrs. Parkington.

"Of course," replied Mrs. Dodsworth and Mrs. Parkington thought, She is going to be all right. She's not a fool like Emily.

At first the Duchess only stared at her mother out of the nearsighted eyes, not recognizing her. Then as she heard her voice, she said, "I'm sorry to have bothered you, Mother. How long have you been here?"

"It's no trouble, my dear. I'm only happy it wasn't more serious. I've been here since this morning."

Mrs. Parkington drew up a chair beside the bed and the Duchess made a faint effort to sit up and then gave it up and lay back again, "How long have I been asleep?" she asked.

"Since last night. How do you feel?"

"A little woozy. I cannot imagine how it happened. The nurse said I took too much sleeping stuff."

"Yes. The doctor is coming again at four."

Then the Duchess closed her eyes again, with a sigh of infinite weariness, and said, "It was very pleasant. I don't remember anything at all."

Her mother thought, She mustn't get that idea or she'll be trying suicide. Aloud she said, "It's very bad for you, very depressing physically. If I were you I'd try to go back to sleep and come out of it easily." She didn't speak about keeping on the nurse. That could wait. Now, it might only disturb her.

"I'll go now and you go back to sleep. I have a business appointment at five and I'll try to come back later."

She rose from the chair and Alice did not appear to hear or notice her. She had slipped back again into that world of peace and oblivion where there were no memories and no unhappiness and nothing at all happened.

The doctor returned at four and said she would be all right now and Mrs. Parkington went home with an odd feeling that her daughter had been snatched from death against her will. This raised in her mind a moral issue — should not people be allowed to die, if they chose. Their lives belonged to them alone. It should be their right to die if they preferred it, just as if they willed to go from one room into another. Sometimes it was a kind of torture to force them to go on living. It was a little like that with Alice. Alice was already dead. She walked and created a semblance of life but already she was dead. She had really been dead for a long time. There were few memories even to which she would want to return. In England, Mrs. Parkington remembered, they arrested people for attempting suicide. That, surely, was the height of absurdity.

England made her think again of Harry Haxton and all his class, in fact all the Conservative Party. They had been committing mass suicide for more than a quarter of a century, ever since she and Gus knew them well in the days of their friendship with the Prince.

Sometimes it seemed to her that the era in which she and Gus lived had been made especially for them — a wide-open, hell-bent-for-leather time in which a man like Gus could go all out, wide open, on a career so ambitious that most men would have trembled even to contemplate it. If he had been born earlier, the opportunity of a whole rich continent opening up would not have existed. If he had come to full flower in this new crumbling world he would have spent half his life in jail. Even the Prince with his liking for horse racing and Jews and actresses and Americans and all the wrong people had been made for Gus. It was extraordinary how Gus and the Prince had got on, how well the son of Queen Victoria and the millionaire-adventurer on the make, had understood each other. They had been friends from that very first poker game in the house in Park Lane.

But all that world was vanished now, swept away, shattered in the dustbins of time. She had the present to deal with and the future. Ned would be waiting for her.

Taylor had taken him into the small sitting-room, observing that Mrs. Parkington would certainly be in very shortly as she was always on time for appointments. Ned looked at his watch and said. "It doesn't matter. In any case, I'm early."

He was early because all the afternoon he had been tormented by speculations as to why she had sent for him and why she wanted to see him alone. The old imagination, the source of most of his unhappiness, had leaped into action, creating worry after worry — that the old lady was opposed to his marriage with Janie, that she had discovered his small part in uncovering the crime of Janie's father and was angry; that she meant to use him in some obscure fashion. From each of these worries sprang smaller ones, so that by the time he reached Mrs. Parkington's small sitting-room he was prepared for anything at all. He sat on the edge of the chair listening for some sound of her arrival.

It came at last, the sound of the motor,

after an interminable time of waiting. And after he heard the sound of the footsteps of the butler opening the door, hours again seemed to pass before Mrs. Parkington herself stood in the doorway, smiling at him the curious, crinkled wise smile which had made him trust her when he had seen her before. He thought, It isn't what I feared most of all. She isn't against me.

She came toward him holding out her hand and saying, "I'm sorry if I'm late. My whole day has been upset and confused. Everything seems to go wrong. When one starts off a day being late one is apt to grow later and later as the day advances." Then she turned to Taylor and asked him to bring tea. "Unless," she said to Ned, "You'd like something stronger."

"No, thank you. Tea will do."

She seated herself by the fire and said, "It was very good of you to change your plans and come. I hope Janie wasn't disappointed."

"No. That's all right. We're dining together in any case. And I had good news for her. I've been promoted in the service. I'm being sent to San Francisco."

"I'm delighted to hear that," said Mrs. Parkington and thought, That's fine. It will take her away from New York, out of everything into a new world.

Then Taylor brought the tea and she asked him to close the door. There was a little silence while her small blue-veined hands covered with rings moved about the silver and porcelain on the tea tray and as he watched her Ned thought, She looks so fragile and weak, but she isn't fragile or weak. She's tough as nails and strong as a lion. It was the kind of strength born, he thought, of experience and wisdom and a perfect adjustment to life. People felt the strength in her; that was why they came to her when they were in trouble.

He heard her saying, "I've forgotten how you like it. I'm never very good about things like that."

"Milk and one lump, please."

He rose to take the cup from her, feeling for no reason at all suddenly very young and awkward. He thought, As a young woman she must have bean fascinating — gentle and pretty but clever and strong. It was extraordinary that even at her age she gave you a strong sense of her femininity and charm. And then it occurred to him that when she was a young girl she must have been very like Janie . . . Janie without that sadness which clung to her even when she laughed.

When he had reached his chair again and sat down, she said abruptly, "I suppose you've been wondering why I was so serious about our seeing each other alone. It's because I had to talk to you about my grandson-in-law, Amory."

So that was it, after all. Someone had told her.

"He was here last night. He told me the whole story. You probably know as much of it as he does."

"Yes," said Ned gravely. She was making it easier than be had hoped. Her voice was very quiet and sure and above all, casual.

"He has a strange point of view about the whole thing . . . as if what he did was not wrong because he was the one who did it. I don't suppose you're very used to that kind of attitude. It grows out of his background and upbringing."

He could not think exactly how to answer this. He managed to say, "It is a strange point of view. I've run into it more often than you'd suppose. It's a kind of class attitude."

"My husband had the same attitude but with him it was a kind of grotesque egoism, and individuality . . . rugged, I believe they used to call it . . . rugged individualism. He was always alone — an individual. He never belonged to any class. On the other hand he accomplished a great many remarkable and stupendous things."

Ned thought, She doesn't deceive herself there. She knows he was a robber and a crook.

"But you must not be too narrow about a man like Major Parkington. He was a character. There were a lot of characters in those days." She turned down the flame beneath the silver kettle. "It's classes and class feeling that are dangerous in a democracy," she said. "If ever our people congeal into classes, then our democracy is lost. Individuals may be as bad as they like without too much harm. It's only when they gang up that they become dangerous. You see Amory isn't really an individual like the Major. He goes about in gangs — his old school, his old college, his clubs and stockbroker friends, his industrial associates. They gang together out of a mental need to reinforce each other, because none of them is big enough to stand alone. They keep telling each other that they have greater advantages than most people, that because they run this or that business or factory they are God-sent geniuses, that because they have the knack of making a little money, they are privileged and above law or control, that they know better than anyone about everything. And so a large part of the time they hover near to the edge of what is dishonest and criminal, and at the same time they don't accomplish very much — nothing like building the railroads and opening up the West. It's a singular, hypocritical and corrupt point of view, but Amory believes in it. In his heart he thinks he is right and the law is wrong."

She smiled and made a clucking sound, "Well, well, I've delivered quite a lecture on something you have perhaps thought out for yourself. I only venture to speak because I lived through so much at very close range. I've known most of the old giants — they were always in the house — and I know a good many of these others who huddle together like bison for protection. That's what rotted England. It's what produced men like Chamberlain and Sam Hoare and John Simon — a gang of Brahmins conspiring to keep the world under control for their own little group. Queen Elizabeth thought first of the glory of England — so did Pitt and Melbourne and Gladstone and Disraeli. No, the point of view of people like Amory alarms me. There are too many of them. They added up to the ruin of France as well — the little men who sold out to protect their own property."

She laughed and said, "I can't seem to stop myself but I don't often have an opportunity to talk to someone like you. Most of the people I see are old and belong to another world that doesn't exist any more, or they belong to Amory's tight, blind, doomed little world. I don't have much chance to exercise my brains, such as they are."

Opposite her, the young man had fallen into a state of utter quiescence and receptivity, willing to listen without speaking. He knew now why Janie said that it was difficult to get Mrs. Parkington to talk much about any but trivial things, but that when she did talk the conversation was stimulating. There was so much she could tell if she ever chose to tell, so much she knew which she could share if she chose to share it. He found it extraordinary that even at eighty-four her mind was not only alert but that it continued to grow and adapt itself, instead of turning set and bitter as happened so often to the minds of rich old people.

By way of response he said, "I've tried to think out a lot of these things but of course I'm always hampered by lack of experience. You read this and that about people like Major Parkington, but it's never the same as having known them. The people who write of them always manage to inject their own personalities into the picture. Either they are muckrakers who find no good in them or they are paid to whitewash them by the family which sets out to prove they were saints."

Mrs. Parkington laughed, "They certainly

weren't saints, but they weren't as evil as the reformers would have you believe. We have a book like that about Major Parkington. I didn't pay to have it written but some of his friends did — I think in the hope that some of the whitewash applied to the Major would spatter them at the same time. That was what they wanted."

She gave him another cup of tea and said a little wearily, "Of course it's about Amory's case I wanted to talk. I think to begin with you'd better understand my point of view. I've no special interest in Amory himself. I've never liked him but that's beside the point. When you get to my age and are still reasonably in possession of your faculties, you acquire, if you have any sense, a certain objectivity, even about the members of your own family. When your glands begin to slow down, you begin to acquire wisdom rather than to practice emotion. I don't much care what happens to Amory. He deserves whatever happens, but I want to do all I can to help him for only one reason and that is Janie. Perhaps you guessed that."

For a moment he couldn't answer her. Moisture came into his eyes and a lump into his throat and at the same time he thought, *That* is glands, damn it! Then he managed to say, "Thank you, because Janie means a lot to me."

"You can help Janie," she said. "You can take her away. You can give her a chance. If you don't she may just marry anybody and turn out like all the others, God help her. And I think you had better do it quickly."

He felt suddenly embarrassed and shy. It was not that she had complimented him extravagantly in words, it was what she implied. What he did not understand was the liking, very close to maternal love, which she had felt for him at sight, and the thought that had come to her not once but many times — that if things had been different, her own sons might have been like this, the sons who had been dead for nearly forty years, who had never really had any chance.

She was saying, "I had better make my point of view clear. I mean to pay back what Amory has taken. If we can't save him from jail, we can at least prevent people from saying that Janie's father robbed them. I should like to prevent his going to jail, even from being indicted. Do you think it is too late to prevent that?"

He was silent for a moment. Then he said, "I don't know. I'm no longer close enough to the case. I had very little to do with the whole thing beyond the original investigation. That's my part of the job, not the prosecution. But I should think the whole thing has gone too far to be stopped now. The case is a very clear one — almost hopelessly clear and simple." He put down his cup and said, "You have been very honest with me. May I be as honest with you?"

"It's the only way we shall get anywhere."

"Mr. Stilham must be a very stupid man to think he could get away in these days with what he tried to do."

She sighed and said, "I am afraid he *is* a very stupid man."

"You see, he even tried to buy me off. That was how I came meet Janie, the weekend he asked me to the country. He proposed paying me ten thousand dollars to turn in a report which covered him up. That too was very stupid of him. It proved that he had no understanding of what was going on in the world. In any case my report was almost finished. Too many people in the department knew of it. Even if I had been dishonest, I could not have done it. It was too late."

Then he hesitated for a moment looking down at his hands, as if considering whether he dared to say all he meant to say. Mrs. Parkington sat watching him, without speaking, liking his reasonableness and the clearness of his mind, that he did not say priggishly that he had turned down the offer of a bribe because he was virtuous, but only that in any case it was too late for him to accept it. She knew well enough from the face that he was not the kind that could be bribed. Amory, if he had had any instinct or wisdom, could have known it.

The boy was talking again, "He was very angry with me, as if I were in the wrong for what I had done. He talked about interference with private rights and spying and persecution. He seemed obsessed by the idea of persecution of himself and his class."

"He talked to me in exactly the same way."

"There is something in the persecution angle — very little — but something, and even that something Mr. Stilham does not understand. He doesn't understand that he and 'his class' have been put into a strait jacket because of the lawlessness of the generation or two before him. Because they were so crooked, the whole thing became intolerable and so the revolution came. That is why so little can be done to help him now. It is political now, not merely a question of bribing or honesty. No one would dare to help him in the face of public feeling. In a way, he and a lot of others like him are sacrifices of atonement for the sins of men who are already gone.

"For Major Parkington and his friends," she said.

"Yes, that's true."

Mrs. Parkington looked at her watch, "What time were you meeting Janie?"

"As near six-thirty as possible. It doesn't matter. She'll wait."

"No. Don't keep her waiting. Before you go there's one more thing I wanted to say. . . ." He waited and saw the color rising in Mrs. Parkington's face. She frowned a little and then said, "It's just this. If there's any way of buying Amory out of this . . . if there's anyone susceptible, you need only mention it to me, quite casually. The money doesn't make any difference."

"I don't know of any way. I'd do almost anything to help Janie out of this, Mrs. Parkington. I hope you understand that."

"I do."

"It's too late and anyway I doubt that any of those concerned could be bought off."

"It's different from my husband's day. I'm aware of that. He bought his way in and out of a great many things. Always it was a good investment." Then very quietly she added, "It was profitable for himself. But he destroyed the souls of two or three men who might otherwise have died honorably and two or three went to prison because of him. And a lot of women and children suffered. The curious thing is that so far as he was concerned, there seemed to have been no retribution."

"No. It has fallen on the second and third generation. The whole country has had to pay for it."

She stood up and said, "Now, I'm going to send you along to Janie." He rose too and came across the room. She continued speaking, "Does she have any suspicion about any of this?"

"No. Not yet. I'm sure she would have spoken to me about it."

She laid one hand on his shoulder and looked up into his face. "There's one more thing I want to ask you and that is, when and if it becomes necessary, you'll let me do the talking. I am old enough to understand a lot of things. I think I can do it better than anyone else, with less hurt."

"Sometimes," he said, "I've thought I should be the one to do the telling."

"No. Things like that leave scars that can never be got rid of, no matter how hard you try. Believe me, I know. And she might get some ideas that she ought not to marry you because she was ruining your career. She's fantastic in some ways. You'll promise to let me do the telling? You'll promise, won't you? Believe me, I'm being wise about it. It mustn't spoil things between the two of you. That is worth saving. All the rest, all the others are mere rubbish."

He was thoughtful for a moment, looking away from her. Then he said, "Very well. I'll leave it to you . . ."

She turned toward the door and as they walked, side by side, the very old woman and the very young man, she said, "This afternoon was the first time in eighty-four years I ever attempted to bribe anyone. It cost me a great deal to say what I did, but what things cost me does not matter any longer."

At the door, she said, "It was very strange of you to go on seeing Janie when you knew what you did. I wondered why you did it."

They were alone now in the hall. She did not ring for Taylor to help him on with his coat. She did not want the understanding between them broken, even by the presence of a mute servant.

He said, "I felt sorry for Janie. Then that weekend we went for long walks and while we were together I began to understand what was inside Janie and that she was unhappy and there was something between us which I'd never felt with any other girl. We kind of understood each other without saying anything as if we were meant for each other. And when I went away I kept thinking of her and then one afternoon I called her up and asked her to dine. And when she saw me she said, 'I was afraid you had forgotten all about me. I was hoping you hadn't.' I knew what I was doing. There was a moment when I could have pulled out, but I didn't. We'll make out all right — no matter what happens."

He had never said any of this before, even to Janie. Mrs. Parkington standing here, small and very straight, with her hands clasped behind her back, made it easy for him.

"It's going to be tough for Janie. You'll have to help me."

"You can count on me." She took his hand and held it between her two thin beringed hands, "You're a good boy. Good-bye and good luck."

After he had gone out the door, she stood for a little time staring at nothing at all, thinking of her own boys and that perhaps now, as a very old woman, she had, at last, found someone to take their place. But for Gus — but for all the things which had come between her and them, despite anything she could do. . . .

Then she turned and walked toward the

elevator. It was too late now to think about all that, too late by forty years. . . .

She had meant to return to the flat of the Duchess after dinner but when she went to her own room to spruce up a bit she found Mattie blocking her way. Mattie had been turning down the bed and when she saw Mrs. Parkington at the door of the cupboard which contained her hats, Mattie said abruptly, "I hope you are not thinking of going out, madame."

That she used the word "madame" instead of addressing her mistress as Mrs. Parkington set the tone of the encounter. Mrs. Parkington said with as much firmness as possible, "I am going over to Mrs. Sanderson's."

Mattie said, "Have you looked at yourself in the mirror? You look as if you had been dragged through a knothole."

Mrs. Parkington went on firmly selecting a hat without answering, but Mattie continued, "Bags under your eyes, madame, and a yellow face. You should go to bed early and not leave the house. Mrs. Sanderson is probably all right. I will get the nurse on the telephone. If you need to go over, I'll go with you."

As Mrs. Parkington took down a hat and turned from the cupboard, Mattie was already dialing a number. The sight angered her as much as she was able to be angered by Mattie. She said, "Leave that telephone alone, Mattie. I am still able to decide things for myself."

But Mattie ignored her. She finished dialing and got the number. The silly maid, Emily, answered but Mattie would have none of her. She asked for the nurse.

During the waiting, Mrs. Parkington sat down at her dressing table and put on her hat and at the same time it gave her an excuse to study her face in the glass. It did look saggy and tired and yellow. It certainly did. Then she heard Mattie lying over the telephone. "Just a moment. Mrs. Parkington asked me to call you. She is right here." She carried the telephone to the dressing table and put it down before mistress.

The voice of the nurse came over the wire, warm and confident and pleasing to Mrs. Parkington. As she listened, Mrs. Parkington thought, Very likely she will do. It will only be necessary to persuade Alice that she must keep her on.

Mrs. Sanderson, the nurse said, was sleeping. The doctor reported that she would be all right now. "There's no need to come over, Mrs. Parkington. She'll be able to see you in the morning."

As she put down the telephone, she realized

that Mattie was standing very near — near enough to hear what the nurse said, so that her mistress wouldn't be able to lie and cheat about the conversation.

"You see," said Mattie. "There's no use killing yourself for nothing."

Mrs. Parkington felt a slight sense of irritation at defeat by Mattie's superior tactics. She lifted the hat from her head and said, "Please go about your work, Mattie, and stop haggling me."

Mattie only said, "Now take off your clothes and get into bed. I'll bring you some warm milk in a thermos jug and you can have a good rest."

But the nagging was not yet finished. Mattie went into the bedroom while Mrs. Parkington undressed, but after a moment she returned to hang up the clothes and put away the hat and as she went about the tasks she said, "I think it's a shame the way the family imposes on you. They're certainly old enough to take care of themselves when they get into trouble. There's no use in their always running in and out of the house to put their worries on you."

Mrs. Parkington glanced at her, suspicious that Mattie knew something about Amory, but Mattie's round, plump face was perfectly blank save for the fine lines born of her irritation about the mouth and eyes. She kept right on talking, "Sometime I'm going to break out and speak my mind. I think it's awful — the way they all hang on you."

She brought a nightdress and dressing gown and laid them on the arm of the chair beside her mistress, asserting herself by a faint snort of rage. Mrs. Parkington did not answer her and was not worried by the threat. For twenty years or more Mattie had been threatening to "break out" at the people she said imposed on her mistress, but never yet had she done so.

Then she said, "The bed is turned over. I'll go and fetch the milk."

When Mattie had gone, Mrs. Parkington got into bed and adjusted the reading light. She was glad now that Mattie had bullied her into staying at home for it meant that she would have the whole evening alone, without family, without committees, without all the people who were always wanting things from her. Solitude was the most precious thing in the world if you knew how to employ it. It built up your endurance, and permitted you to see yourself coldly, with all your faults and virtues; it allowed you to get some sort of perspective on things. It made it possible to face and to endure many things which otherwise would have been unendurable. If you suffered in solitude, there was no need to parade your suffering shamefully in public.

Solitude was something Gus had never understood. He liked people, crowds of them. They did not sap his boisterous vitality; on the contrary he seemed to absorb fresh and inordinate supplies of vitality by mere contact with people. Some he had destroyed temporarily; a few, among them the people who worked for him, he destroyed permanently. Even when he was alone, his whole mind and body, untouched by reflection, were occupied and absorbed by planning fresh actions calculated to realize his vast ambitions or promote and feed the monstrous appetite of his egotism. When Gus was alone in a room behind locked doors, there was no solitude; alone on a desert island there would have been none, for the very air was always infested by the shadows of people, of plans, of plots, of tremendous events.

He had never understood her own hunger for occasional solitude, that there were times when, out of the complicated and artificial life into which he had thrust her, it was necessary to disappear, to be alone for a time, in order to go on living. He had been hurt when, after they had moved from the house on Thirty-fourth Street to the great mausoleum next door to Mrs. Ogden, she had insisted that she have a bedroom of her own in order now and then to have a little solitude. He had gone on being hurt for the rest of his life, believing to the very end that she had demanded her own room because she had been offended by the discovery of his infidelities. He had never understood why, after "the terrible summer," she had firmly gone off to the Rockingham Hotel in Portsmouth, to stay for a time under a different name where she would see no one she knew. He could never understand that this was the only thing which made it possible to go on living after the deaths of Herbert and Eddie.

The novel lay on the bed beside her, unopened, perhaps because the plot, the characters, the situations were all far less absorbing than the things she had lived through, the people she had known, the curious quality of suppressed melodrama that had always surrounded her from the very moment the mine had blown up and Gus had been trapped into marrying her; for she knew now as she had known for nearly forty years that he had never meant to ask her to marry him. He had merely meant to take her for his mistress; it was her own naïveté and innocence which had trapped him, these things and perhaps his own desire and his gambler's temperament which told him, "I might as well marry her as anyone else. Something can be made of her." Gus himself had admitted it during the nasty business over Mrs. Ebbsworth at the beginning of "the terrible summer."

Then the door opened and Mattie came in with the warm milk and some biscuits on a tray. Silently she crossed to the bedside table and put them down.

"Thank you, Mattie," said Mrs. Parkington. "That's everything I'll need."

But Mattie didn't go away. She stood there at the foot of the bed, respectfully but firmly, looking down at Mrs. Parkington. The old lady smiled, "Go on, Mattie. Say it! There's something on your mind. There's no use in our holding back anything from each other."

Mattie coughed and looked down at the footboard, "It's about Mr. Amory, Mrs. Parkington. I've been hearing some strange things. I thought maybe he had been troubling you . . . that was why he was coming here." Before Mrs. Parkington could answer, she said, "I've thought you should go away somewhere — make a trip, maybe."

"It might be a good idea, Mattie, but I couldn't go away yet . . . not until Mr. Stilham is out of his trouble. You see that, don't you, Mattie?"

The servant considered this for a moment. "No, Mrs. Parkington," she said, "I don't.

I've lived with you for a long time now. I hope I can say we are friends . . . more than just servant and mistress, although it's not perhaps for me to say. I've lived with you for a long time and I've see you put upon by people all those years. I think you've taken enough of that. You've a right to have some peace. God knows you've earned it. I don't see why you have to stay and face Mr. Amory's trouble. You didn't ask for it. You didn't do it. He's no blood relation of yours. I don't even think you like him. I think you ought to go away somewhere."

Mrs. Parkington listened, trying to stop the tears that kept coming into her eyes. She knew that her eyes were misted because she was tired and because she felt, perhaps more than she had ever felt it, the depth of Mattie's friendship and their closeness to each other. Mattie was an extraordinary woman; it was even more extraordinary that a woman of such character had gone on for years putting up patiently with a wilful woman like herself.

Going away on a trip somewhere *was* a good idea; it would be a good idea for Mattie as well as herself — Mattie who rarely went out of the house, even to take the air by walking round the block. Mattie had been getting into a rut, more and more lately. Mattie certainly deserved a change, but not now.

"I like what you said about being friends, Mattie," she said. "I think we don't even need to talk about that. And I think going away is a good idea but I can't go until this trouble is straightened out. Did you ever think how many people are going to be upset by it . . . their whole lives upset . . . and they won't know what to do — not Janie or Mrs. Stilham or Jack or even Mr. Amory himself. They just aren't made that way."

Mattie was watching her with resentment in the clear blue eyes. She wasn't being convinced. When she chose to be stubborn, Mattie could be simply colossal. Lots of Swedes were like that. So, craftily, exercising that peculiar beguiling charm which had always been her greatest and ultimate weapon, she said to Mattie, "Come Mattie. Sit down here on the edge of the bed."

She was being unscrupulous because she didn't want Mattie to leave her in a resentful mood and because she could not help herself. Mattie, she knew, would not be deceived by what she was doing. She would see through it but she would like it. She knew her mistress so well that she would know she was being victimized and enjoy it; sometimes Mattie could be very like a man. She came over and sat on the edge of the bed with a determined air of detachment and respect, so Mrs. Parkington had to go further. She reached out and took Mattie's hand. At the touch, the elderly maid relaxed a little.

"You see, Mattie, there's something I've only figured out lately. It took a long time to discover it . . . years and years. It's this . . . that some people are well provided by God with strength and common sense. In a way they're the lucky ones. Most people are fools or afraid or they run away from things. They're always coming to the well-provided people and unloading their burdens. I've come to the conclusion that I must be one of the tough ones who can take very nearly anything. That's the price I've had to pay for the great things that God gave me . . . and He gave me a great deal. Don't ever forget it . . . no matter what has happened to me in the past. You see, if someone like me runs away he's ducking his job and if he ducks his job something happens to him . . . something destructive and evil happens. All the strength goes out of you if you're that kind of person. If you go on doing it, you destroy yourself, because some kind of God-made or natural law operates like that. Don't you see that if I ran out on this now . . . it couldn't be any rest for me? I'd be miserable all the time thinking about the thing I was running away from and worrying about what was happening to Janie and Jack and Mrs. Stilham and even Mr. Amory. Janie and Jack aren't old enough yet to know how to behave if Mr. Amory should go to prison and neither he nor Mrs. Stilham have enough sense to know what to do. God or nature or something was ungenerous to them. It isn't their fault. I shan't try to tell them what to do but they'll come to me just the way they always have — all of them and a lot of others the minute they are in trouble. Because it's a kind of law. It just works that way. You can't do anything about it."

Mattie was looking at the floor but she was listening. Mrs. Parkington knew it by the very stillness of Mattie's plump fingers. When Mattie said nothing she continued, "And you must remember another thing, Mattie . . . that if you're one of the strong people you get stronger and calloused and hard, and the older you get, the more people lean on you, the wiser you get. You get so that you can take almost anything. You get so that, as Janie says, you know all the answers." She pressed Mattie's hand and said, "You're worrying about how this disgrace of Mr. Amory is going to affect me. I'll tell you something, Mattie, I wouldn't tell anyone else I know. What happens to Mr. Amory doesn't affect me at all. It's just part of a story in which I've lived for a long time — a story in which very little affects or shocks me any longer. It's like something I'm reading . . . something that exists at a great distance from me. None of it really touches me at all, but it touches Mrs. Stilham and the children terribly because they don't know how to deal with it, and I couldn't go away knowing that they were bewildered and suffering. They need someone to tell them what to do, to cheer them up, to give them a sense of perspective. Do you see what I mean, Mattie? Do you understand? You must, because you yourself are always having people coming to you. If you hadn't been like that yourself, you wouldn't have given your sister the money to come to America when her husband was killed. You wouldn't have volunteered to pay for your cousin Helga's baby when she got into trouble. You wouldn't be bothering to look after an old woman like me, worrying about whether I'm tired or not. You wouldn't go up to Cook's room every night to massage her back and look after that awful brat Hicks leaves with you on Thursdays when his wife has to visit her mother at the asylum. You know exactly what I mean, Mattie. Your body's being tired doesn't matter much. If you betray yourself then it's much more than weariness . . . it's destruction. It's something you can no more do than can I. God didn't ask us if we wanted the job. He just gave it to us — to both of us. You do see, Mattie, don't you?"

For the first time Mattie looked at her. She pressed Mrs. Parkington's thin hand and said, "Yes, Mrs. Parkington, I do . . . I'm afraid I do. Sometimes I don't think that it's very fair of God."

"Sometimes I've thought the same thing, Mattie. I used to think it a long time ago when so many terrible things happened to me. And then I began to see that in a way there was a plan in it all . . . it still seems a pretty muddled confused plan but it does seem that it works out to make life better for us. When it all adds up you and I have got something that the others never knew. We've got a kind of love and respect from people that they never knew and never will know and most of all we've got pretty clear consciences. When we die we'll be willing to die because we've had so much, we won't die feeling . . . well, unfinished. It's a great thing that God gave the strong ones. Because God was so generous to us in making us strong, I can afford to say it now without seeming smug because I've got a kind of detachment about things, even about myself.

I wouldn't dream of saying any of these things to anyone else in the world."

She released Mattie's hand, "As soon as all this is settled, you and I will go for a trip. Where would you like to go?"

Mattie blew her nose firmly and said, "There's not very many places left. We can't go to Europe or the East."

"I've got a kind of hankering to make a trip West, Mattie. You've never really seen the West except from the train on the way to California. If you haven't seen the West in some ways you haven't seen anything."

"I'd like that," said Mattie, simply.

"We'll go in the car and take Hicks along and we'll stop at funny hotels and maybe at trailer camps and something they call by the silly name of Motels."

Mattie rose heavily from the bed and Mrs. Parkington said, "There's one thing I'd like to ask you. Where did you hear all this about Mr. Amory?"

"Cook heard it from another cook at market . . . you know, that shop that sells *pâté de foie gras* and such stuff. It was Mrs. Everett's cook."

So that was it. Judge Everett had been talking in front of the servants at lunch. It was extraordinary how many things servants knew and how much they repeated. Well, very shortly it probably would not matter. Everyone would know about it.

Before Mattie could pry further, she said, "I think I'll go to sleep now, Mattie. Call me at seven forty-five."

Mattie looked at her sourly again. "That's very foolish, madame. You know you have the Symphony Board tomorrow and the Bellevue Guild and with having to see Mrs. Sanderson and this worrisome business about Mr. Amory . . ."

Mrs. Parkington interrupted the catalogue, "How am I to get all that done if I don't get up early?"

"It's too early, madame."

"It's much less tiring to get up a little earlier than to have to hurry all day from one thing to another always being late. Besides, there was a time when I got up before daylight and helped get breakfast for thirty-eight men."

Mattie sniffed, "That, madame, was about seventy-five years ago."

"I still want to be called at seven forty-five," said Mrs. Parkington. "Good night, Mattie."

"Good night, Mrs. Parkington."

She went out, closing the door very quietly behind her. Mrs. Parkington was glad that she had addressed her by her name instead of saying, "madame."

When Mattie had gone, Mrs. Parkington turned out the light, partly because she knew that Mattie would not go to sleep otherwise but would return again and again to look for darkness instead of a thread of light beneath her door and partly because she knew that the talk with Mattie had roused a whole rush of memories that would not permit her to read in any case. She would simply turn the pages without knowing what she was trying to read, because her memories were, in a way, more improbable than the contents of most books.

Somehow "the terrible summer" kept coming back to her thoughts. First Amory's trouble and then the Duchess' "illness" had revived it. It had been there, in the background of all the talk with Mattie.

In the darkness, lying awake because she was too tired to sleep, "the terrible summer" came alive again, quietly like a very distant landscape enveloped in a cold winter mist, and out of it she saw the figures of Norah Ebbsworth and Gus crossing the lawn from the stables beneath the Cedars of Lebanon at Oriander.

X

It was the week the Prince had come to stay. The Prince and Mrs. Keppner and the Baron Rothschild and Harry Haxton were with her on the terrace. They had been talking about a horse called Arreau owned by Monsieur Blanc of Monte Carlo, which had just won the Grand Prix, and all the time she had been watching the figures of Norah Ebbsworth and Gus as they crossed the lawn, and hating Norah. It wasn't that she was jealous of Norah; she wasn't really a jealous woman. It was simply that she hated Norah as Norah — as a well-born penniless, unscrupulous woman — a whore born in the midst of a world where everyone was privileged and protected, a whore without the deceit qualities or the courage of a whore. Norah was tall and dark, with blue eyes and a fair skin, a beauty whose loveliness had been spoiled long ago by the hardness of the mouth and eyes. She was a good gambler and gay in a bitter fashion.

Lying in the darkness, it seemed to her that Norah was the only person in the world she had ever really hated because Norah was the only person she had ever known who seemed to her to be wholly evil. Norah was not content with the evil inside herself; she sought to spread it by corrupting all about her. It seemed to her now that with Norah began the degeneration of Gus's taste in women. After that episode it had grown progressively worse until the sordid end in Cannes. Norah corrupted him as she had corrupted so many others. It was no satisfaction to know that she had died long ago, an old bitter woman, in squalor in a *pension* in Genoa. She still hated Norah Ebbsworth because she was Norah Ebbsworth, without warmth or generosity or kindliness.

And while on the terrace they talked about Arreau, she was watching the pair coming across the lawn, with Norah, probably telling some vulgar, strong story, turning to Gus and laughing as they walked. And as they neared the terrace and saw the others sitting there, Norah put her arm through Gus's arm, waved to them and threw back her head and laughed. It was exactly as if she had cried out, "See I've taken him away from Susie! I've got him! He's mine!"

And Susie couldn't any longer hear the conversation about her. She rose quietly and slipped into the big Georgian house to go up to her room and sit there very stiffly upright on a chair, trying to think what she should do.

There had been other women before Norah. She had come long ago to accept that, understanding that this was something Gus could not help because he was made like that, because there was so much of the animal in him that no one woman could ever keep him for herself. He just didn't fit into a tame, domestic scheme of things. She had come to believe, partly to salve the hurt to her own vanity, that what she did not know could not hurt her.

But this business of Norah Ebbsworth was different. It had happened in her own house, at her own table, before her eyes and in the presence of people staying with them. She remembered Gus's saying once that no wise man ever had an affair with a woman who would by any chance ever sit at the same table with his wife. And now he had broken the rule. She did not hold it against him; Norah, doubtless, had outmaneuvered him, and had come on the house party against his wishes.

She could fight back; belowstairs, on the terrace, Harry Haxton was only waiting for her to accept the proposals he was forever making; but this she could not bring herself to do since the tactics of cheating in revenge had always seemed to her not only vulgar but foolish, all the more so since Harry seemed to her amusing and pleasant but no more than that. Sitting bolt upright she tried to reason coldly what she should do since it was clear that it was impossible to stay on in the same house with Norah flaunting her triumph, telling everyone by every action, every gesture, every glance, that she had got what she wanted — the big good-looking, rich American. With Norah it wasn't simply the question of a week-end affair. With the evil there was in her, she wouldn't let it rest on that. She would want money . . . more money. That was why she had set her trap for Gus. If he hadn't been so rich the whole thing would never have happened. There were always women, hordes of them, in pursuit of Gus not only because he was big and attractive, but because he was rich and generous. In a way he was a victim but unfortunately a victim who himself enjoyed thoroughly and with gusto the sacrifice. Luckily his pocket could afford it.

For a time as she sat there in this strange, beautiful house which they had rented for the summer, she thought, Maybe it will be worse from now on. Maybe I should leave him now. Maybe I should go back to America and have my own life. Maybe it is not too late to have some of the things I have always wanted. The boys are grown now and Herbert is married with two children of his own. I'm only forty-three years old and I'm still attractive.

But she could not bring herself to go away. She thought, No, I cannot go now, not until I've beaten Norah. If it had been an ordinary woman, she would not have minded so much going off and leaving her with Gus. That sort of thing never lasted for long; he always came back quickly. But Norah was different. Because she was evil she would follow him, trying to blackmail him. She would show him off wherever she went.

Presently when she had pulled herself together she rang for her maid. The girl was Swedish, a well-trained girl, pretty too in a robust peasant fashion. Susie had grown very fond of her, but there was another stronger bond between them; in all the world only Mattie knew what had happened in Salzburg. Only Mattie knew about those ten days in the hotel at Bad Gastein. And Mattie had never betrayed her by so much as a word or a look of understanding. She had behaved, always, as if she were unaware that anything had happened there.

And now the sight of Mattie brought it all back and eased a little the pain and humiliation of this other thing. There were times when it seemed to her that what had happened in those ten days was something which could never have happened to her, like something she had dreamed, but now suddenly the memory was very real and gave her a curious, deep satisfaction. It was something Gus had never known, something he never would know because she would never tell him. There was a kind of satisfaction in his not knowing. She could watch him across the table beside Norah and think, You are not the only one!

And now the Swedish maid was asking her what she would wear for dinner and when she suggested a simple dress, Mattie said, "If you will forgive me, madame, I'd suggest that you wear the new black Worth gown and your diamonds."

Susie turned to look at her, astonished that she should have made such a suggestion. The girl's face was quite blank, so deliberately blank of all expression that Susie divined that she must know about Gus and Norah Ebbsworth. Mattie, she understood suddenly, was on her side but she was being discreet. She understood what it was Mattie wanted her to do. She wanted her to be brilliant and glittering and outshine Norah Ebbsworth which she could do, not only because she was clever enough but because she looked young enough to wear black and diamonds and still seem softer and younger than Norah with her hard mouth and eyes.

So she said quietly, "Very well, Mattie, although it seems a little odd as a summer dress."

"There is no summer in England, madame," said Mattie, "And in any case it is a large dinner and the Prince is here. Formality will flatter the Prince."

While she was dressing Gus came in. He stood behind her watching her reflection in the glass as she and Mattie worked over her hair. Without looking at him directly, she could watch him.

He said, "Well, sparrow. We missed you on the terrace."

He was pretending, she knew, trying to make himself believe that she did not know what was going on.

"I came up to lie down for a time. I suddenly felt very tired. You had better dress. There's not much time."

He bent over suddenly and kissed the back of her neck. Mattie stood aside stiffly in order to permit the caress. He took no notice of Mattie. He had no shyness.

Then he said, "I'll be ready," and went out. When he had gone Susie was aware that her heart was beating more rapidly and that the color had come into her face and she thought how handsome he was and what a remarkable man for fifty-six years. She was aware that the unexpected caress was not simply a spontaneous action. He had been telling her something. He had been saying, "I know I'm in the wrong. I'm ashamed too because Norah is a bitch. Forgive me. She does not matter at all beside you . . . no one does, no one ever has or ever will."

The kiss somehow took all the strength, all the resentment out of her because it made her remember suddenly that night at the Brevoort before they went out to Delmonico's when, standing behind her, he had clasped the pearls about her throat and kissed her.

The Swedish girl went on silently fixing the complicated waves and curls which were fashionable that year, and Susie knew that she could never leave him, and that what happened at Bad Gastein had been of no importance, however strange and wonderful it had seemed at the time.

When she went downstairs to the big drawing-room, Harry was already there and she knew at once that he had come down earlier than the others expressly to talk to her. His presence made her nervous and unhappy. She was fond of him and did not want to hurt him, but she was aware that she could not help herself, for the kiss had roused all her old feeling for Gus and with Gus in her very blood, Harry's good looks seemed pale and decadent and soft.

He said, "You look dazzling tonight."

"Thank you." She went about touching the flowers, loosening them, letting them breathe, and as she went from vase to vase, he said, "You have a hand of magic."

"Flowers must look like flowers, not like funeral offerings."

She knew he was watching her. She never doubted that he knew all about Gus and Norah. There was something feminine about Harry which made him a gossip, an intriguer and a very fine minor poet. He knew things before they happened.

He said suddenly, "I can't bear to see you hurt, Susie."

She knew it was stupid to say, "What makes you think I'm hurt?" It would not deceive him in the least. So she said nothing at all.

"Norah is a foul bitch. I have scores of my own to settle with her."

"It doesn't matter," she said, "Gus belongs to me, really. He's like that. But it doesn't mean anything."

"I'm going to get married."

She had redone the last of the flowers and

she turned toward him to say, "I'm very glad. I think it's much better that way."

"I've told no one yet."

"Who is the girl?"

"I doubt that you know her. She's young and she's very rich and I think she likes me. Her father is a rich builder, one of the richest in London."

"So it's that kind of a match?"

"Yes. You wouldn't be hurting her. She'd never know anything about it. It's rather our last chance, Susie. You'll be going back to America and I'll be getting married." He looked out of the window. "You've never believed how much I really love you. You'll never believe it because I can't make you believe it. I don't know how. But you *are* a woman, *what* a woman, my dear. If nothing ever happens between us, I'll die feeling that I've missed what is the most wonderful thing that could ever have happened to me."

"Thank you, Harry."

"I could arrange it. I could arrange to leave Gus with Norah when you came to stay with me."

She thought, Now is my chance if I wanted revenge on Gus. But she still did not want such a thing. She took Harry's hand and said, "It wouldn't be any good, Harry. It would only be a disappointment to you and it would violate something in me. I'm very fond of you but not that much. I'm not like Norah and so many other women over here. A thing like that for me isn't just like shaking hands. The answer, my dear, is 'no.' You get married to your rich young girl. It's much better that way."

Still no one came down the great stairway. He looked away from her and said, "It's odd how your saying 'no' makes you all the more desirable. I'm not used to women like you. Very few women have ever said 'no' to me." He walked over to the window and said, "You'd be something to win and possess and keep. I think I've always known that since the beginning. If ever there is anything I can do for you, even the least thing, you have only to ask me. I know that sounds like bad Tennyson, and consequently to say it, costs me more than you can ever know, but it's true." Then he turned toward her again. "I'll never speak of it again but there's one thing for you to remember — that I shall always be waiting for you somewhere until I die."

She started to speak but found no words with which to answer him and after a moment he said, "You must get Gus away from Norah. She is a cheat and a blackmailer."

With a curious pride she answered, "She'll have to be very clever to cope with Gus."

Then the Baron came downstairs and Lady

Woolsey and from the drive outside the window came the coughing explosions of Lord Hinchcombe's deLaunay-Belleville, and suddenly the room was filled with people — all the brilliant, fashionable people the world read about and envied and admired and hated and imitated. It was a world that was theatrical and witty and gay and above all secure but it had never brought Susie any happiness.

At dinner she sat on the right of the Prince with Harry on the other side. Deliberately she had put Norah beside Gus. Norah wore a bright poison green dress cut very low but Susie saw that the dress was a mistake. Choosing it was the gesture of a woman "forcing" her youth. It only made her seem harder. While Susie talked to Harry or the Prince she used unscrupulously that softness and charm which she had learned to summon up when she was tired or determined to gain something she wanted. The Prince was very fond of her and she knew that the fondness or even the sometimes frank manifestations of it did not alarm Gus, but it annoyed the snob in Norah, that special sort of snobbishness that was peculiar to England. To be "on the inside with the Prince" — to be called by him "Norah" instead of merely being called "Mrs. Ebbsworth" — she would gladly have given up Gus. Each time the Prince addressed her as "Susie" she knew that it was like the thrust of a knife in Norah's back. Susie was shrewd enough to know all that. She hated Norah because Norah was evil. For Norah she felt no mercy.

The scene happened in the card room just after the men had joined the ladies. It was a cool evening and around the fire had gathered a little group which included Harry and Norah, Lord Hinchcombe, the Baron, Mrs. Keppner and Mrs. Pulsifer, the American wife of a London banker, waiting for the Prince to give the word for starting the poker. He already sat at the table laying out cards and playing patience while he talked to Gus about some American investments. Susie had just finished giving orders to the butler and was closing one of the tall windows giving on to the terrace when she heard Harry saying, "It will be warmer in Biarritz. It's lovely there now and the Prince is very fond of it. He was delighted with the idea."

"Who's going?" Norah asked boldly.

"All the men," said Harry, "And Susie and Anne perhaps."

"What about me?"

"No, my dear, you're not going. This holiday is to be a rest. The party includes only quiet sensitive people."

There was a little edge of mockery in

Harry's voice which Susie knew very well. Never had it been directed at her, but she had seen the mockery grow and sometimes turn into something terrible. It always meant that Harry was laying a trap for someone. The very timbre of his voice should have warned Norah. As soon as she heard Norah speak again, she knew that Norah had fallen into the trap. She turned away and took down a book of sporting prints from the shelf near her and pretended to be looking for some special print; actually she did not see the book at all for she was listening, straining every nerve to hear.

Norah said, "That's very rude of you, Harry. I'd no intention of going in any case."

"I didn't mean to be rude. Only a precaution, Norah. You're a disrupting influence wherever you turn up."

Then Norah said, "I doubt that Gus will want to go. He's planning to go to Southampton yachting."

She heard again Harry's cold, level voice, "As a matter of fact it is Gus's idea as much as anyone's. He proposed it."

When Norah spoke again there was fury in her voice. Harry was making an exhibition of her, showing everyone in the group about the fire that she did not in the least possess Gus, giving the lie to all her actions, all the bold implications that he was hers. Susie waited, her heart beating rapidly.

"I'm surprised that you wanted Gus. I should think he would be in the way."

With her back to them, still turning the pages of the book Susie thought, It's going to happen. She is a fool to lose her temper. For the first time she understood a little how desperate Norah was, how necessary it was for her to keep possession of Gus. For a second Susie almost felt pity for her.

"I've no idea what you mean by that," said Harry.

The Baron said, "Norah thinks you're trying to cut her out of something."

"I think nothing of the sort," said Norah. "If you want to know what I think, I'm surprised that Harry and Susie don't want to keep Gus out of the picture."

Then Susie heard Gus' voice and the moment she heard it she knew that the quick ferocious temper had flared up. She wanted to check him but she still had to pretend that she was absorbed in the book and had heard nothing.

Gus said, "What did you mean by that, Norah?" Susie knew without turning how he looked, the face crimson, the vein in the forehead throbbing.

Norah was a fool not to be frightened, but

there was in her the sluttish hardness of a pub prostitute. She said coldly, "Only what everybody knows already."

Then Susie could no longer resist looking. As she turned, she saw that Gus, in his anger, had left the table where he had been talking to the Prince. The Prince had stopped playing his absentminded game of patience. He held the pack of cards in one hand and with the other he stroked his beard. Gus stood in front of Norah now. He was shaking and for a moment quite incapable of speech. Susie heard herself calling out, "Gus! Please! Gus!"

Gus without turning to her said, "Leave this to me." And then to Norah, he said, "What you implied about my wife is untrue. Admit now that it is untrue."

Norah's mouth, painted in a day when paint was not common on women, was hard and ugly. She said, "You're a fool, Gus, if you don't believe it."

Then an extraordinary thing happened. The Prince rose and said, "Never mind, Gus. No one believes it. No one could believe anything but good of Susie."

Gus recovered his temper with that suddenness which accompanied its ferocity. He said, "I beg your pardon, sir, for making a scene in my own house and in your presence."

"If there is an apology owing," the Prince

said, "I think it is to Susie."

Then he turned to Norah and said, "I think Mrs. Ebbsworth must be overtired. It might be a good idea for her to go up to her room and rest before going back to London."

The humiliation was complete. Nothing remained for Norah but to leave. She began to speak and then thought better of it and turning quickly, she walked the length of the card room and out of the door. She had lost both Gus and the favor of the Prince. Never again would she be invited to any house in which he was present.

Susie, standing there, humiliated but triumphant, knew that it was not possible to follow Norah. It was not possible even to see her again before she left the house.

The prince said, "Come. Let's get on with the poker," and seated himself at the table. When they were all seated Susie went to Anne Pulsifer and asked her to go up and speak to Norah and discover her plans.

When Mrs. Pulsifer had gone she said to Harry, "Thank you."

Harry said, "There is no sluttishness like that of an English slut who should know better."

Then he turned quickly to the game and Susie went to stand by the fireplace, looking into the fire, filled with a sudden happiness that frightened her.

Gus did not come to her room that night although she lay awake for a long time hoping he would come. There were times when he had sudden surprising flashes of tact and fine feelings and she knew that he had gone directly to his own room because it would have seemed both vulgar and sloppy to have staged a great reconciliation immediately after the scene with Norah. Susie knew that it was all over. Very likely Gus would never speak of the scene; probably he would never again speak Norah's name. He was like that.

When Mattie came in she said, "I have a message for you, madame. The housekeeper said to tell you that Mrs. Ebbsworth had been called up to London. She'll be leaving early in the morning."

While Mattie helped her undress, Susie said suddenly, "Do they know in the servant's room what happened in the card room?"

"Yes," said the girl. "They know something about it. There was quite a quarrel over it between the housekeeper and Mrs. Ebbsworth's maid."

"You mustn't speak of it outside, Mattie. It's the kind of story that will go everywhere once it's started. You mustn't speak of it because of His Royal Highness."

"Of course, madame," said Mattie. "I

wouldn't think of telling it about."

"I'll speak to the housekeeper and the others in the morning."

Susie got into bed, and it was only after the clothes had been put away and the dressing-room in order that Mattie spoke again. She asked, "Is there anything more I can do for you?"

"No, Mattie, thank you. Good night."

"Good night, madame. I am glad you had such a success. I was sure the black dress was the one to wear."

It was the first time Mattie had ever "presumed" — the first of what were to be countless times. She closed the door before Susie could answer, but she left her mistress smiling in the darkness. It was good to have friends like Harry and the Prince and Mattie.

When she opened her eyes the room was full of morning light and Gus was standing beside the bed. Like all alert people, Susie wakened suddenly, and she knew almost at once that something terrible had happened. She knew by the look in Gus's eyes and by the touch of his hand, stroking her hair, very quietly. In his other hand he held a bit of paper which she recognized at once as a telegraph form.

Gus said, "Take it easy, sparrow. Take your time. Wake up."

She was awake as she always was on opening her eyes, and she asked, "What is it, Gus? It's something bad."

He sat down on the edge of the bed, stopped stroking her hair and took her hand. "It's bad news," he said. "About Herbert."

She knew by his voice what he was feeling and she knew too that the news was the worst possible. She said what immediately came into her mind, "It couldn't be Herbert" . . . not Herbert, her bright, shining Herbert, the boy in the pram, whom everyone stopped to admire. People like Herbert couldn't die young. They brought too much into the world. Their beauty and charm were too great to be wasted or destroyed.

"It is Herbert," said Gus, quietly. "There was an accident on the road from Newport to Narragansett. The automobile got out of control and went off a bridge."

She only thought, That damned automobile! I never wanted him to buy one until they made better ones. That damned automobile! She was aware of a kind of numbness in which she felt nothing at all.

Gus said, "Aspasie sent the cable. It's a long one. She has told everything. I think the funeral will be on Thursday. There will be a memorial service when we get home."

But Susie's mind had already leapt far beyond such things as funerals and memorial services. Herbert was dead. She said, "Those poor children with no one to bring them up but that crazy Blair girl!"

"Yes," said Gus, "that's bad." Then he leaned down and put his arm about her and said, "Cry, sparrow! Go on. Cry! I'll hold you. I'll take care of you."

And then the tears came, in a wild rush, not so much then as the death of Herbert as at the sudden tenderness of Gus. The tears for Herbert would come later. They would always be there in her heart until she died.

It was curious how Aspasie was always at hand in every terrible moment of her life. There was an efficiency about Aspasie, a human efficiency, which few Americans understood. Americans, who thought of efficiency in terms of machinery, said the French were inefficient, and consequently few of them understood people like Aspasie whose life was founded upon common sense and eternal human values. And there was in Aspasie the formalism of the French which, like that of the Chinese, clothed naked human relationships with the cloak of civilization. The Chinese hire mourners who wail and cry at the head of a funeral procession in order that the bereaved need not beat his breast in public, calling out upon all to witness his grief. When one is born or dies or is married both the French and the Chinese have a printed card or a formal phrase of congratulations or condolence which takes care of the situation and permits people who are not especially interested one way or another to get on to other and more interesting subjects of conversation. By formalism they have encouraged sincerity. It was all part of an efficiency, Mrs. Parkington often reflected, which would long survive the dull mechanical efficiency of water closets and automobiles.

Aspasie was like that. In a time of calamity or tragedy she was always on hand, quiet, sympathetic, knowing the thing to be done and doing it perfectly, with taste and without ostentation. She did not take possession of the injured or the bereaved, exploiting him to demonstrate publicly her own sympathy and greatness of spirit. She simply went to work doing the dull, painful things which had to be done.

As Mrs. Parkington grew older she came to understand that only two women in her life had been very close to her, only two whom she loved and understood so well that communication between them and herself was rarely necessary. The two women were her maid and a woman who had once been her husband's mistress.

Even in that role Aspasie was wonderfully and humanly efficient. Whatever there had been between herself and the Major was ended when he married Susie and the new relationship was begun upon a new basis. There remained no sloppy tags and ends of sentimentality, of faded memories, of implications and intimations. What was ended was ended; in it there had been happiness for which Aspasie was grateful, knowing that there is very little perfect happiness placed at the disposal of the poor human race. Despite the scene in which she had given so pictorial a performance in the red and gold sitting-room at the Brevoort, she did not see any reason why the past should slay her friendship with a woman like young Susie Parkington for whom she felt affection and respect. Her heart had not been in the scene because she had believed none of the conventional speeches she made nor the conventions upon which they were founded. This was very French; it was also very civilized. Because of it the Major respected her more than any woman in the world except his own wife, and there were even times when of the two Aspasie seemed to be the more practical and sensible.

Long after that scene between the two women, Susie often considered how much of intelligence, of guidance, of understanding, or richness, she would have missed during her life, if she had been a fool and said, "No, since you were my husband's mistress, we must never again see each other." She had not the human efficiency of Aspasie, nor the background of deep civilized wisdom, but she had a sound instinct which she trusted and Leaping Rock had spared her the sentimentality she might have acquired in a half-civilized community. At one end of her experience lay Leaping Rock, an utterly barbaric community, rooted in harsh reality; at the other end stood Aspasie, a monument to complete civilization. Both were good; the bad half-civilized ground between them she had never trod, in all her existence. For that she was grateful.

So it was Aspasie, very smart in dark clothes, more handsome at sixty than she had been at twenty, who met them at the pier. Everything had been arranged by her. The house was open and the servants expecting them. There were no newspaper men because Aspasie had given them a performance which so distracted and enchanted them that they were willing to forego seeing the great Major Parkington until he had landed and was settled in his own house. The memorial service at St. Bart's had been arranged.

She did not rush forward gushing tears, crying out, "My poor darling Susie!" There was a swift perfunctory kiss on the cheek, a pressure of the hand, and she began brightly asking about the voyage, telling bits of gossip, arranging with the Major's secretary, Mr. Billingsley, concerning what was to be done with the luggage. What she said without saying it was, "This is something so deep one must not talk of it now. That will come later on. Now, the immediate thing is to go on living, picking up the small threads. That alone will help the pain and bring back the knowledge that there is tragedy in life which we must endure and put into its proper place in the scheme of things, into that perspective from which one will see it much later in life. In all things, in all human experience, even in tragedy, there is a richness which must not be denied, lest it turn into a cancer which devours you."

And so when in that same "terrible summer" the news came that Alice could no longer endure the humiliation of her marriage and had asked for a divorce, it was Aspasie who said, "Dear Susie, I think I should go with you to Paris. There are things about the French that I know which you could not possibly know."

It wasn't possible for the Major to leave but he and young Eddie came to the boat with Susie and Mattie and Aspasie. The Major was efficient in the grand manner, committing them to the care of an American international lawyer in Paris named Bates who was a friend of his.

On the dock, she took Eddie aside and said, "Try and take it easy, Eddie. You don't look well. You've lost weight. Try not to stay up all night. Try to drink less." She said nothing about women because she knew that it would be no good and he would only resent it and thrust out his lip stubbornly. And it was women who troubled her most.

He looked at her, grinning, and said, "Sure, Ma. I'll slow down. I promise it. I'm going out to the mines in the fall. I'm only having a good time until I go. Out there I'm not expecting much fun."

She could understand why he was so successful with women. There was something engaging and boyish about his red hair and freckles and blue eyes but really there wasn't anything boyish in him. He was too precocious and knowledgeable; in his tough young body was all the violence, the vitality, the capacity for desire, which was in all the

Parkingtons, but with Eddie there was no direction but that of his own pleasure. It wasn't often that a woman found in a young man all these things, along with money, all the money of Eddie's father, money which he gave his son with a lavish, extravagant generosity.

It wasn't as if Gus tried to restrain Eddie or give him good advice. Gus, whose own youth had been both wild and hard, thought a young man should sow his wild oats. He found a kind of pride in the fact that his son should be keeping a show girl as beautiful, as famous, as Shirley Seagram; at his son's age, Gus had been courting waitresses. If it had only been Shirley, Susie wouldn't have minded so much but there were others too. It wasn't something you could discuss with Eddie; Susie would have discussed it if the choice had been left to her alone, but she knew that neither Gus nor Eddie would have tolerated it. To them it was a subject a wife and a mother never spoke of; it was something concerning which a good woman should remain in ignorance, or at least in the pretense of ignorance.

The two men, husband and son, stood on the pier until the big ship had slipped away into the river, waving their straw hats until they were no longer distinguishable among the crowd on the pier. Susie felt a pang at leaving them and a pride that two such splendid specimens belonged to her.

As the evening closed down on the ship, she walked round and round the deck, arm in arm, in silence with Aspasie, trying to fight off the depression that settled over her as America slipped away behind the ship into darkness. It was a depression filled with self-reproach and a belief that she had failed as a mother. She was on her way to Paris to see through the divorce of a daughter whose marriage was a failure. One son had made a foolish marriage and been killed, leaving behind two little girls, and the other, for all his charm and good looks, was only a wastrel.

In the thickening darkness, she tried to discover where she had failed. She had been as good a mother, as wise a mother as it was possible for her to be, yet somehow it had come to nothing because outside the realm of her influence, where she herself was powerless, there were forces too strong for her, pulling forever against her. There was Gus himself with his wild generosity and egotism and pride in his own wife and in his children, and Mrs. Ogden, and the huge fortune and the great houses in Newport and New York and the yacht and the newspaper reporters whom Gus was forever encouraging.

The very schools to which Gus had insisted on sending the children had ruined them by their peculiar vulgar snobbery and emphasis on wealth, on family, on importance. In spite of anything she could do, the schools had implanted, in the two boys, at least a sense of being possessed of some special privilege, of being outside the rules which governed the conduct of ordinary people. Neither Eddie nor Herbert had, thank God, been snobs; there was too much vigor, too much Parkington in them, but they believed they belonged to a world especially blessed and privileged. In a way, that was the hidden result if not the purpose of St. Bart's and schools like it with their feeble traditions and imitations of everything English.

All of these things had conspired to defeat her — these things and that curious passion for Gus which always softened her and made her yield to him and his ideas against her instinct and judgment. It seemed to her that there had been a time when, if she had asserted herself, she could have changed the whole course of their lives. It was during the summer in the little red house at Long Branch after the awful business of the ball. She could have fought then to go on living as they had lived that summer, quietly and well and above all, simply. Then the children would have had a chance. She could have kept them outside all the forces which had in some slow and mysterious fashion, deformed their lives.

But when she went on thinking, reproaching herself, she knew that such a course had been impossible so long as she was married to Gus, because a quiet, respectable life would have been insupportable to him. He had to take everything he possessed, even his wife and children, with him on his way, or leave them behind forever. Gus had wanted what he had got; he was pleased with it. After the first shock it seemed to her that he had forgotten even Herbert's death. He did not live in the past, but only in the present and future. What was gone was gone. She did not doubt how deeply he loved her but neither had she any illusions as to what would happen if she died. For a little while he would grieve, but only for a little while, and then there would be another woman and after a little while he would never think of her at all unless by chance he saw her picture or someone spoke of her. Gus was always a kind of wonder to her; he was a natural man, perhaps therefore a lucky and happy one. Gus was perhaps what nature intended man to be — a creator, a breeder, violent and healthy and unreflective. It seemed to her at times that man had complicated and deformed his own existence and perhaps even doomed himself by believing in civilization.

And she knew that as soon as Gus and Eddie left the pier, they would go together, father and son, to Delmonico's or Rector's to eat and drink well and meet a couple of girls, Shirley Seagram perhaps and a friend, and at the end of the evening Gus would perhaps be faithful to her and perhaps he would not. The odd thing was that somewhere, in some remote part of her being, she loved them both for loving life so much. In some remote part of her there was a little envy of them because they were men and full of the enjoyment of life. In Bad Gastein she had understood them. In some strange fashion it made her love them all the more.

Then the ship passed from the harbor into the open sea and the wind came up sweeping the open deck and screaming through the rigging and Aspasie who perhaps divined what she had been thinking and so kept silent said, "We had better go and dress for dinner. It will make you feel better to change."

It was the Frenchwoman speaking again, drawing her back into the frame of everyday existence which made life in times of disaster endurable.

* * *

Alice had left the Duke's great house in the Rue de Varenne for the Hotel Meurice. It was a famous house designed by Gabriel with a great garden at the back. At the time of the marriage, the great house stood empty for, bit by bit, the Duke and the Duke's father had sold the furniture and sculpture and pictures and tapestry deposited there generation after generation by the descendants of the first Duc de Brantès, peer of France and treasurer of Francis the First. The house was restored now with the money Major Parkington had made out of railroads and mines and oil in a country discovered about the time the first Duc de Brantès received his title. But its splendor held no attraction for the Major's daughter. There was in her, as Susie well knew, a streak of commonness which rendered her uneasy in the presence of splendor. There was in her none of the adaptability of her mother to circumstances, none of the flair of Susie for living up to a situation, of *acting* as she had acted in response to Aspasie's performance in the Brevoort long ago. Alice merely remained awkward and uneasy. Only bitterness and disillusionment and long habit of worldly associations gave her, late in life, a kind of brittle poise and a kind of malice and wit. In the year she divorced the Duke she was merely an awkward, stubborn and provincial young woman who surprisingly spoke the classic French of the Théâtre Français taught her as a child by Aspasie.

It was this rather dreary young woman, dressed in expensive clothes by Worth which she wore badly, who met Susie and Aspasie at the Gare du Nord. She had the air of a bedraggled, beaten puppy. Her pleasure and excitement at seeing her mother and Aspasie was more unbearable than the misery in the eyes.

Remembering what Aspasie had said on the day of the wedding — that Alice might as well go through with the marriage since if she did not marry the Duke she would marry someone just as bad — she thought, Perhaps it would be better for her to stay married to the Duke no matter how bad it was. But almost at once she saw the weakness of that idea. She was assuming that Alice was like herself — that she had resources and could build up a life of her own outside the realm of her husband's existence. Alice was not clever and resourceful; she was dull and dependent and without initiative. And the story was much worse, when she heard it, than anything she had imagined.

At the end of the summer, the Meurice was filled with Americans and English, buying clothes, returning from summer holidays or on their way to Austria or Hungary for grouse and pheasant shooting. It was filled with people whom Susie knew. They were everywhere, in the great halls, in the restaurant and in the lift and Susie saw at once that it was impossible to think of staying on there in circumstances so humiliating. In the taxicab Alice had said, "He has decided to fight the suit." And Susie knew at once what that meant — dirty linen, recriminations, all the horrors of a scandal in an age and a country where a divorce scandal was more than a scandal of any other sort could possibly be.

Susie had asked, "Are you still determined to go through with it?" and Alice answered with an astonishing intensity of feeling, "I want to be free of him! I have to be! I will never feel clean again if the whole thing is not finished completely!"

Across Alice, Susie's eyes met Aspasie's black ones. It was worse than either of them had ever expected.

In the hotel sitting-room Aspasie, once they were settled and Mattie had the unpacking underway, said that she was going out to look up some old friends and relatives. She would not return until after dinner. There *were* friends and relatives and Aspasie meant to see them, but that was not the reason she went out. Susie discovered afterward that she went out in order to leave mother and daughter alone, and also on a kind of scouting trip. She went out to purchase all the newspapers, the gossip papers, the *revues mondaines* to discover the state of mind of Paris itself — French Paris as well as international Paris.

When Aspasie had gone, Susie ordered lunch and while she and Alice ate, Susie talked of things at home, trying to establish a casual feeling which would permit Alice to tell her all that was clearly shut up in her heart. She was not very successful for she felt between them almost at once that curious undefeatable strangeness which had obscured, like a fog, the relationship between them since the time Alice was old enough to talk. It was as if they were no relation to each other, as if Alice were a foundling of some strange blood. Sinfully and filled with shame, Susie sometimes thought, If she had been pretty and gay and amusing, it would have been different. How much I would have enjoyed that kind of daughter. Because this was not so, Susie had tried all her life to make up for it, conscientiously straining to establish something which could not be established; the effort perversely only heightened the sense of strangeness.

Halfway through the lunch, it became slowly evident to Susie that Alice had become even more remote and difficult to reach. She sat there, sallow-faced and plain, her eyes dark with misery and hurt pride, wanting sympathy and kindliness but thrusting it away the moment it was offered. It was the misery of a person whose whole world was encompassed by her own ego. If the weather was bad, the fact was of importance only in its effect upon herself. It was the misery of a person destined always to suffer because she remained enclosed in a shell, shutting out all sympathy, giving out nothing, uninterested in anything beyond the limits of her own self-imposed and gloomy prison. It was in a strange way the fierce egotism of Gus himself, inverted and devouring not other people but itself. Watching her, Susie thought shamefully that it was a strange and bitter world — that if one of her children had to die, why had it not been Alice, who found so little pleasure in life, rather than Herbert, bright Herbert, who loved life so passionately and gave back more than he received from it.

She sighed and looked at the dusty tops of the chestnut trees in the Tuileries gardens. This Paris, dominated by the disaster of Alice, seemed a strange, gray city, cold and unfamiliar. Even the station and the streets did not look the same, but dimmed and misted over by the fog of Alice's private misery.

When the waiter came, Susie ordered champagne with the dessert, hoping wildly that somehow it would release the sense of strain and permit Alice to talk. But Alice only refused it, saying something about her liver — an organ which Susie thought it unnecessary and unattractive to mention save in the presence of one's doctor.

Then unexpectedly, when the waiter had taken away the table and Susie stood looking out of the window into the Rue de Rivoli, it happened. Alice began to cry, silently, the tears rolling down the sallow cheeks, and she began to talk; the whole story, shut up for so long deep inside her lonely spirit, poured forth now without check, like water from a shattered dam. Susie, standing by the window, turned for a moment toward her and then thought, No, I must not look at her. I must not touch her! If I try to console her, it will spoil everything! So she turned away again and with a casual air of listening absent-mindedly as she watched the street, she heard the whole of the sordid story, never once interrupting Alice, but saying "Yes" now and then or murmuring some indistinguishable phrase so that Alice would believe that she was hearing it all and continue to unburden what clearly had to be told if she was to save her sanity. Without being told, Susie knew the girl had kept the whole story locked up inside herself, telling nothing beyond the simple record of the Duke's infidelities, even to her lawyer.

It was a dreadful story, filled with dark intimations which shocked Susie and which she was certain Alice herself did not understand, a story of humiliation both public and private, a story of mistresses and obscure debauchery. Much that Alice told innocently fitted together with Susie's knowledge and experience into a pattern of perversity and vice. What Alice knew was bad enough; what she did not suspect was far worse. The Duke had not lived with her for more than two years. Quite openly he had shown all Paris that in fact she was no longer his wife and that he felt only contempt for her. Susie, listening to the end, was aware that she had always known what the end would be; she had hoped that somehow Alice could defend herself or at least build a life independently, of her own. But she knew now, as she had known in her heart all along, that this was a vain hope. The strength was not in Alice; poor Alice who would always be dependent upon men, would never be able either to hold them or to discipline them. The end had come much more quickly even than she feared.

And as she listened, she realized how helpless the girl was — that she had really learned nothing at all since she had left home on the day of her marriage. She had gained nothing from experience, nor was it possible to explain or teach her anything. It was as if she were determined to be miserable, and found a kind of perverse satisfaction in it, the satisfaction denied her elsewhere in life.

The story finished at last in a burst of hysterical sobbing. Then Susie crossed the room and sat beside her daughter and drew the shaking body of the girl against her. She said very quietly and in a matter-of-fact way, "From now on you must leave the whole thing to Aspasie and me. You must try not to think of it any more. Are you certain that he means to fight the divorce?"

"He has it all planned. He has even worked out evidence to show that I have been unfaithful."

Susie considered this for a moment and then asked, "Have you?"

Alice looked at her in astonishment. "No. Of course I haven't. I have had friendships with one or two men who were kind to me. That is all."

"You haven't been indiscreet?"

"I don't know. I am not a lawyer."

It was clear enough that Alice would not know what indiscretion might mean to a lawyer or a court. It was quite clear that she was altogether helpless in a strange country whose laws were very strange and different from those of America. Susie thought, It's all Gus' fault in a way . . . Gus' wild generosity and his passion for doing everything in a big way . . . as if to advertise his success and his wealth. If he had not settled so much money on the Duke, the Duke would not have dared to threaten a countersuit.

They might, of course, still be able to buy him off, but that was not what Susie wanted. Deep inside her there was a sense of profound and bitter outrage, very like the outrage she felt at the behavior of Norah Ebbsworth. The story Alice had just told her was impregnated with evil, with deliberate cruelty and perversity, and these were things which Susie had never been able to tolerate. Now she would not try to buy off the Duke, she would do it only as a last resort. She had a better plan, but before she acted she needed the advice of Aspasie.

She said to Alice, "You had better lie down now. I'll get tickets for the theater and when Aspasie comes in we'll make arrangements to take a flat or a small house. It's quite impossible for us to stay in any hotel at this time of year. There are too many people about we know. Go now and rest and leave the whole thing to Aspasie and me."

Then suddenly, for the first time in all their lives together, Alice kissed her spontaneously and with feeling, so much feeling that there was in the gesture a sense of hysteria, almost of madness. She said, "You don't know how much difference it makes to have you here. It's changed everything. I feel now as if I wasn't completely alone any longer. I can trust everything to you."

It was the first time there was understanding between them, the first occasion on which the sense of strain between them was broken. It would take a long time for them to understand each other completely; the understanding would not be complete until Alice herself was an old woman.

At teatime Aspasie unexpectedly returned burdened with newspapers and periodicals reporting that the whole thing was worse than she had feared. The divorce was the talk of Paris; every *revue mondaine* had references to it. Some took the side of the young American woman against the dissolute Duke; others said that she had got her just desert for buying her way into an ancient French family. But it did not rest there; imaginative and blackmailing journalists wrote dark intimations of orgies, of lesbianism, of androgynous activities on the part of the Duke. The divorce found its way even into serious and solemn political newspapers; the conservative ones cited it as an example of the evil results of the breaking down of old traditions; the Roman Catholic papers attacked it as an example of the evils of Catholic-Protestant marriages; the radicals used it as a brilliant example of the evils of wealth and capitalism. It was clear that Paris had had no such scandal since the accusation and suicide of the Duc de Praslins.

Together Susie and Aspasie went drearily over the whole sheaf of papers, Aspasie ashamed of her own people for the peculiar vicious pettiness of the journals, Susie astonished by the notoriety which a person so dull and unspectacular as Alice had somehow managed to achieve. The odd thing was that Alice seemed unaware of the attacks; it was as if, buried in her own personal misery, she were utterly indifferent to the opinion of a world in which she had at best played a small, pale role.

When they finished with journals the two women set themselves to planning a campaign.

"C'est honteux," said Aspasie. "The French can be at the same time the most elevated and vulgar of people."

Susie did not mind so much the French journals; she was aware that Alice's life in France was ended, that Alice felt no regrets at the fact. It was the American papers she feared, the awful, sensational Sunday supplements and their stories about "Another American girl who bought a title." For a moment she wished that the Major was in Paris to deal with the situation, but after a little reflection, she realized that nothing could be worse than the presence of Gus; he would grow furious and contemptuous and violent and only make everything far worse. This was a thing for herself and Aspasie to handle.

There was no theater that night. Alice did not even waken at the hour for dinner and Susie did not wake her. It was as if the release of telling the whole story to her mother had brought the first relaxation she had known in many months, and with it the first sleep she had known in all that time.

Susie and Aspasie dined in the sitting-room and after dinner they laid their plans for action. It included the spending of much money, the use of unscrupulous people, much knowledge of the world in all its aspects, not a little blackmail and above all, promptness of action. There was, they decided, not a moment to be lost.

Tomorrow Susie would see all the lawyers in the case and Aspasie would find a house or a flat and engage four or five private detectives, as unscrupulous as she could possibly find. It would be simple enough to find them, they were everywhere in Paris. Most difficult of all was the task of Susie herself; it was necessary for her to arrange a meeting with the Duke. In all of it Alice must be kept quiet and out of the picture.

And so the two women set to work. The flat was easy to find and after Susie had interviewed Alice's lawyers she understood at once that very little was to be expected from them. The American lawyers were elderly and uninspired and respectable and more concerned with their position at the Traveler's Club and at the embassy than with fighting for their client; it was clear almost at once that they wished, but for the huge fee they expected to receive, that they had never become involved in so scandalous a case. Their French partners, nice, elderly and funereally respectable, were no more than bookkeepers; both were listed in the telephone directory not only as *avocats* but as *hommes de lettres*. The detectives were much more what Susie needed. One of them looked like a fashionable undertaker and kept dry-washing his hands throughout the first interview as if he had some stain upon his soul from which he was unable to cleanse himself. The other was a short, dark man with a brutal face and a tic. One was named Monsieur Blanc, a perfectly innocuous name, and the other, the undertaker, was called Monsieur de Trevillac, a noble enough Breton name concerning the falseness of which neither Aspasie nor Susie had any illusions. The two gentlemen promised to turn up whatever was desired. As their business caused them to spend a great deal of time among the more vicious elements of the Paris underworld, they already had, they said, a considerable *dossier* on the Duke. One collected such things and filed them. One never knew when they might be of use. When they brought what impromptu things they had already collected so casually, Susie and Aspasie went over the whole record with them and Susie concluded that already she had all she needed for her purpose When they had gone, bowing their way backward out of the drawing-room, Susie sat down with the aid of Aspasie to write a letter to the Duke requesting an interview. They sent it by messenger and the answer came by messenger.

The Duke would be delighted to see his

mother-in-law again, nothing would give him greater pleasure, but he could not possibly accept her proposal to call upon him; it was his duty and correctness demanded that he call upon her. It was for her to set the time. She did not like the note. It was, she thought, not the moment for suavity, not the time for flattery.

He arrived at four on the following afternoon. Susie was alone in the flat. She had wanted Alice out of the way but there was another more important reason; she meant to do something which was shameful to her, which violated profoundly her whole nature. It would be difficult enough to do it alone face to face with her son-in-law; she could not possibly achieve what she meant to achieve in the presence of a third person, even Aspasie who knew all the details of the plan.

When she came into the drawing-room of the flat she had taken in the Rue Tilsit, he was standing at the window looking down into the street. He did not hear her come in and she stood for a moment in the doorway, the awful *dossier* furnished by Monsieur Blanc and Monsieur de Trevillac, under her arm. When she spoke she did not call him "Jacques" nor even address him as "my son-in-law." She said in a low voice, "Monsieur le Duc." There was both mockery and insult in what she did.

But as soon as he turned and she saw his face, she felt her bitterness weakened by something which was beyond her control as a woman; he was a very attractive man, as dissolute men can sometimes be. It was as if his mere presence, his mere mocking, flattering smile broke down barriers of resistance, of moral principle. It was not the overwhelming physical attraction of a man like the Major; this one's charm was more insinuating and evil, more destructive, as if inviting you, seducing you — the charm of a good-looking and utterly abandoned man who stopped at nothing.

He crossed the room and kissed her hand, saying, "I am delighted to see you again, *belle-mère*. It is not flattery when I say that you are one of the women I am always eager to see."

She was aware again that she was only a little older than he and that there was something grotesque about her being his mother-in-law. She was aware too, with shame now, that she had made a special effort to make herself attractive for the meeting. She felt suddenly ashamed of being feminine and vain and almost whorish. Yet she was secretly pleased that he found her attractive.

She said, "Thank you, Jacques. You needn't be flattering. It's scarcely a time for that."

She asked him to sit down and said, "This is a painful business. I did not expect the marriage to be happy but I had hoped that it might outwardly be decent." She put the *dossier* on the table beside her and noticed that he watched the action even while she was speaking.

He said, "I assure you, *belle-mère,* that I tried to make the best of a bad situation. You may believe me or not."

"It has turned out very badly."

He looked away from her and the dissipated, good-looking overbred face grew serious. The seriousness brought sadness into it. He said, "I did my best. Perhaps it was not a very good best. Have you ever lived closely with Alice? Have you ever spent an evening alone with her?"

She saw where he was leading her and determined to avoid the trap. It was impossible to argue that Alice was brilliant or amusing or even companionable. She said, "After all, Alice is my daughter."

"There is a curse on her," he said. "Please believe me, I have no feeling of hatred for her. If I feel anything at all it is pity, but a pity which I wish to avoid having awakened by her presence. Pity may be an estimable virtue but it is also sometimes a painful emotion to the one who experiences it. I make no pretense of virtue on my part. I only believe one thing — that I have but one life to live. I am already thirty-nine years old. That is very old for a man who has lived as I have lived. I do not believe specially in self-flagellation. I tried with Alice and one or both of us failed. It was misery from the beginning. Nothing is worth that."

Then Susie said, "Not even with a hundred thousand dollars a year?" She had meant to be nasty. Now she was forcing herself and the effort filled her with shame.

"It might buy my body for a little while but never my soul. There are times when the violation of the soul renders the body impotent and incapable."

She said nothing to this. She thought, What he is saying is at least honest, however unscrupulous may be the motives, however depraved the character. It made it difficult for her that in her curious honesty she could not deny what he said of Alice.

She heard him saying, "Alice does not want love, *belle-mère*. She does not know how to receive it or respond to it. I am not an unattractive man. Nor an inexperienced one. At least experienced women do not consider me so; yet each time I made love to your daughter she treated it not only as an indignity but, what is much worse, as a bore. What she wanted was not a lover or a husband, but someone to sit with her doing nothing, nothing at all, during long interminable evenings. She wanted someone, a man to exhibit to the world as belonging to her. It was intolerable, *belle-mère*. Believe me I tried. I am an impatient man, but I tried."

There was a kind of honor and anguish, a shadow of genuine suffering, in his voice that moved her despite all her bitterness, and she saw that to him the painful egotism and lack of spirit in Alice must have been an agony. It would have been the same with herself, if she had married some man who was dull and passive and conventional, instead of Gus. The man opposite her, however unscrupulous he might be, however depraved, was of those who had been blessed with wit and intelligence, those in a strange way who were the elect.

She said, "If all this is true, why then do you want to bring a countersuit against Alice?"

He was thoughtful for a moment, covering his face with his hands. At last he said, "That is difficult to answer, perhaps more difficult for you as an American to understand. I do not hate Alice. Divorce for me presents a problem which scarcely exists in your country. That Alice did not bear me an heir, that she seems incapable of having a child is something, but less important to me than to some men. There will be men in my family to carry on the title. I have, as you know, two nephews. I am not certain that I want to bring children into a world which I have never found especially satisfactory and which I see deteriorating to a level at which all men will be reduced to a uniform mediocrity. I do not believe in divorce. Even though Alice wins a divorce in the civil courts, it means nothing to me. Only an annulment in Rome can free me. For that I do not need a divorce. But for that, I am frank to say, money, perhaps much money, may be needed."

She was beginning now to understand. He was being remarkably honest, as only the French can be honest. In spite of everything she found satisfaction in dealing with a man who had no hypocrisy. She thought, Now the time has come. Now is the time to do it.

Quietly she said, "There isn't going to be any money, Jacques. My husband was too generous to you in the first place. Money doesn't mean anything to him. It's just something to have around. He has no idea how rich he is, and so he throws it about. He doesn't understand what good money can do or what evil — what colossal evil."

Watching him, she understood what had happened in his mind. He had come cheerfully believing that she meant to buy him off, and then he had noticed the *dossier* lying on the table beside her and became alarmed. It appeared to fascinate him, for despite himself he kept glancing at it all through the conversation. She thought, He has seen a *dossier* before. It isn't the first time he's been blackmailed!

She went on talking in the same level voice, filled now with a kind of evil amusement at what she was doing. She said, "It would probably be cheaper to buy you off, but that isn't what I intend to do. You understand, money doesn't mean much in the whole affair. It's very likely that my husband at this moment has available as much as two billion francs. There's no need for him to save it. He makes money all the time. Every day more comes rolling in from all over the world. You can understand that he wouldn't mind spending a billion francs just on this case alone."

She was being deliberately vulgar because it suited her purpose, and she saw that her course was having its effect. The astronomical figures she mentioned chilled his thrifty French heart and his logical French mind.

"You are aware, I am sure, that a billion francs could buy all the newspapers in Paris, and also you are aware that most of them — and certainly the scandalous ones — are perpetually for sale." (This was on the sure information of Aspasie who had given her much good advice just before the interview.)

He began to smile as he divined what she was up to, a curious smile of amusement and admiration, and again she felt a liking for his perverse honesty; he had planned to blackmail her into buying him off, very politely and in a gentlemanly fashion, and now he realized that the plan had failed and that she was about to turn the game against him. And he did not mind very much. He was enjoying the meeting and the conversation and admiring her quite sincerely for what she was doing. He was hopeless but somehow likeable.

"Yes, *belle-mère*," he said. "I'm aware of all that."

"And you understand that Alice has no intention of staying on in France or of carrying on any life here. Nothing that happens can affect her in relation to France. I doubt even that she would ever come to France again, even as a tourist."

"Yes, *belle-mère*."

Now the time had come. She reached for the *dossier* and his smile grew more radiant.

"That," he said, "is possibly a *dossier* on the subject of my evil doings."

"That is exactly what it is."

She untied the string very slowly, and he said, "You are very good at your game." And again he smiled in frank admiration, as if he were admiring a fine performance by a great actress.

"The trouble with you, Jacques," she said, "is that you have no morals at all . . ."

"No, *belle-mère*, none." His face grew serious suddenly, "Morals come out of moral background and I never had any moral background. My mother was a frivolous woman. I am not even certain who was my father. I never believed that I shouldn't enjoy myself in life. The body causes us great pain. It is only proper that it should give us in return great pleasure. It withers and dies all too soon. One had best enjoy it while it is still capable of providing enjoyment."

"What a philosophy!" she said. "It is one in which self-respect plays no part."

"What is self-respect? It is founded only upon conformity with what others have set up as a standard of behavior. That has no interest for me. I am an individualist, perhaps an anarchist."

"You are a *voyou,*" she said, conscious again that she was enjoying his company far more than she should.

The *dossier* lay opened now in her lap. Monsieur Blanc and Monsieur de Trevillac had done a very neat, efficient job. It was even cross-indexed, according to vice and according to names of persons involved. It was a perfectly fantastic record, but rather fascinating.

She said, "I think we had better go on with the business. Do you know a Madame Lazare who has a strange establishment in the Rue Blanche?"

He smiled without answering and she turned a page, "A Madame Celestine in Marseilles. She had an establishment there as well as in Tunis. Her business is criminal under the Code Napoléon and her clients as well as herself are liable to prosecution and imprisonment." She looked up at him and continued, "In all this you must remember that it is not only yourself who is involved. An exposé would drag in the names of other important people — bankers and at least one cabinet minister. It would make a really horrible scandal and you would be responsible. It would not make you popular. It might make it almost impossible to live in Paris. Certainly it would be the end of the Jockey for you and the Traveler's and a good many other things."

The smile grew broader and she was aware that he was scarcely listening. He was simply watching her.

"*Suivi,*" he said.

And turning the pages she said, "There is a *voyou* in the rue de Lappe commonly known as Pepé Le Marteau. That is a singularly *un*pretty story . . . especially for a professional lady-killer in a country where lady-killing is a profession."

He stood up and said, "Never mind. I see your point. You might read me a few more names just to see how good the record is, but I won't take your time. I am forced to say that your two investigators are remarkably good and they worked very quickly."

She closed the *dossier*. "They had most of it on file. It appears that in their business they keep records of prominent people. You must occasionally remember, Jacques, that you are the Duc de Brantés and very fashionable and that you married the daughter of an immensely rich American *milliardaire*. These facts I've been reading mean business at some time or other to gentlemen like Monsieur Blanc and his friend. It's a kind of investment they keep in their safe-deposit boxes waiting for an occasion like this to turn up."

He said, "*Vous gagnez, belle-mère*. And you

gave a fine performance. My lawyer and yours will get together." He smiled again. "There is only one thing?"

"Yes?"

"How did you know about what to do? How did you know where to find your friends the private investigators?" She did not answer him. "Was it Aspasie who found them?"

"It is of no importance who found them."

He kissed her hand, "Good-bye, *belle-mère.* I am sorry that things could not have been different. I think that you and I might have made a remarkable couple. Together we could have gone a long way. I shall write to you now and then."

"Good-bye, Jacques." She tucked the *dossier* under her arm. "Good luck."

And then he was gone and she was aware of a desire to call after him, "Don't go yet. Stay a little while and talk. Now that the awful business is over we can enjoy ourselves." It wasn't often you met someone like Jacques; too many people were bores, whose conversation was without spirit, only turgid, void and vapid mumblings.

Then she heard the door close and knew that he was gone and suddenly she was very tired and filled with an unaccustomed sense of profound loneliness.

It was the last time she ever saw him, although afterward, he had from time to time written her flattering and amusing letters that came year after year, three or four times a year until be was killed at Verdun. He did not even appear in court for he told his lawyers not to contest the case and she never knew whether he had given up his plan because of the blackmail or because of herself. It was one of the unsatisfactory, unfinished things which tormented her for the rest of her life.

But "the terrible summer" was not ended with the divorce. She sailed with Alice and Aspasie at the end of September. It was a dull voyage marked by apathy and weariness, one of those periods in which nothing at all happened, which later in life seemed to have been utterly lost out of the span of existence.

The Major and his secretary came aboard at quarantine. She had not expected him and so was in her cabin and he sent for Aspasie before he saw her, for what he had to tell he was without the strength or the courage to accomplish. For the first time in all his life, even his greal vitality, his great egotism, were not enough.

He had no son left, for Eddie was dead now too in a mining town in Montana. It was not until a month afterward that she knew for certain that her boy had shot himself and not until years afterward that she discovered he no longer wanted to live because he was sick with a disease which in those days no one mentioned in decent society. That had been the end of all his wild hysterical enjoyment of life.

It was after the funeral she went away to Portsmouth with Mattie to the Rockingham Hotel to hide away, alone, where no one knew her, like a hurt animal. There were many things she had to face, many things she had to think out for herself before she could return to live again with Gus. When she returned, she was aware of a new strength she had never had before; after that summer she knew that nothing again could ever really hurt her.

Lying there alone, tired and wakeful in the comforting darkness, Mrs. Parkington knew suddenly that at last the wounds had healed, for now at eighty-four, the memories of "the terrible summer" no longer had the power of giving her sharp pain that was almost physical. It was at last all very remote and hazy like a distant landscape veiled by mists. In a strange way it was a part of the extraordinary richness of her life. She thought, Perhaps one day I will meet Eddie and Gus and Herbert again. Who knows? Perhaps in another world I shall know them not as themselves but as creatures more perfect. Perhaps I myself will be in that world a better woman — less vain and less hard, more understanding and stronger and wiser than I have been in this world.

Toward morning she fell asleep.

XI

She was wakened by Mattie placing the tray with her tea on the table beside her bed. When Mattie said, "Good morning!" Mrs. Parkington noticed that she seemed more cheerful and this pleased her for Mattie's own moods had an extraordinary powerful effect upon her despite anything her reason could do about it. When Mattie drew back the curtains, she saw that it was a beautiful day and that too cheered her. It would be a busy day but there were times when it was better to be busy than to think too much. That knowledge, she knew, had been Gus's greatest strength; he never reflected; he was always busy up to the very end. He understood very little even of business for he was above all a gambler, but he knew how and when to act.

Considering that she had slept very little, Mrs. Parkington felt remarkably brisk, perhaps because in those long dark hours while she lay awake living over again the unbearable hours of "the terrible summer," she had achieved at last a certain release from the past. She had awakened, cleansed and purified, with an extraordinary sense of freedom. It was almost like being reborn, like feeling as she had felt long ago as a young girl on waking, before there was any past to fill her with forebodings regarding the future.

She said to Mattie, "You had better call Miss Beasely and ask her to come at ten instead of ten-thirty. It will give us an extra half hour to go over things."

Mattie gave her a sudden searching look as if she were saying, "What has come over you since last night?" And then said, "Do you think that wise, madame?"

"Yes, Mattie. I feel remarkably well this morning. Almost gay."

"You certainly beat anything, Mrs. Parkington" said Mattie and her mistress felt a great sensation of satisfaction that she had won Mattie's approval for once. The day was indeed going well.

The newspaper was not cheering. The war was going from bad to worse, and she thought, There is no way of our keeping out of this thing. It has been coming to us for twenty years and more — oh, much more than that.

Looking backward, it seemed to her that she could out of the past recall signs of it as far back as 1910 or 1911 or even before that in the days of their friendship with the

Prince. The Prince too had seen it coming, although there were many things that he had not reasoned out that were not clear to him then or to any of them and had since become clearer, long after he was dead.

Because this morning she felt exceptionally well, it was one of the occasions when Mrs. Parkington wished that she might go on living forever in order to see what came out of this tormenting, depressing, chaotic confusion. It might be that a bright new world, brave in its decency and understanding might be born of all the agony, and that would be something to see. There were other times when, feeling less cheerful, she hoped to die quietly in her bed before her country too was swept into the misery of war and the confusion and bitterness of peace.

But this morning she felt almost frivolous and even the depressing news of fresh defeats for her friends the British and fresh misery for her friends the French, did not depress her. Nowadays, she reflected, people took far too immediate a view of everything. It was, she knew, difficult not to do so with news bulletins and commentators and headlines pounding at you every hour of the day. In the making of history it was not the short view which was important, the immediate defeats and victories, but those great turbulent waves of feeling which swept whole peoples to achievement or destruction. In this modern complicated world one could not see the forest for the trees. Everyone thought for a day or two that the fall of Crete or the retreat from Dunkirk was all important and decisive, but these things were only a part of a much greater whole, pebbles beneath a great surging wave pounding upon the beach of time itself — just as the war itself was not in itself an end but only a manifestation of a vast revolution engulfing all the world, a revolution of which Amory himself was a strangely minute and insignificant victim just as Gus if he had been alive now would have been a victim.

As she drank her tea she turned away from the accounts of the war and deliberately thrust aside the heavy weight of the *Times*, taking up in its place the more sensational papers which she asked Taylor to get for her since the judge had made his remark about reading everything in sight in order to understand what was going on. In these she knew that she would find the first hint of what was going to happen to Amory. But in their pages she found no hint of disaster.

Mattie returned presently and helped her with her bath and dressing. She had just finished as Miss Beasely arrived and came up to the boudoir.

She was a quick squat woman of thirty-eight, like Harriette Livingstone, a lady and consequently not too efficient, but Mrs. Parkington put up with her out of kindness because Miss Beasely's mother had no means of support but Miss Beasely and it was extremely unlikely that Miss Beasely could have long held a job in the world outside. Her very dress betrayed her character. She set out in the beginning to costume herself in clothes befitting a mannish, energetic, efficient woman, but sooner or later frills and ribbons and bits of lace had a way of attaching themselves to various parts of her plain person, so that in the end there emerged a picture, neither of an efficient nor of a feminine woman, but only of one atrociously dressed. There were times when it seemed to Mrs. Parkington that the inside of Miss Beasely was very nearly as silly as the inside of Harriette had been up to that moment when she found expression in the salvage of stray dogs and cats. Miss Beasely, especially in the matter of checking accounts, possessed an immense power of irritating her employer, but Mrs. Parkington put up with her since Miss Beasely tried so hard and so desperately to overcome the profound sense of suffering and confusion rousedby the mere sight of a column of figures.

Now Miss Beasely, in a confusion of tweed and lace, opened her dispatch case and took out pencil and notebook and awaited orders. Mrs. Parkington first of all gave her a list of things to be done. Call Judge Everett and ask for an appointment. Ring up the South Street Settlement to discover if they had yet got the estimate on the new playground. Ring Miss Janie and ask her to come in at teatime. Order fresh flowers sent to Mrs. Sanderson and flowers to old Mrs. Edgerton who was dying at the Doctor's Hospital. Call Mr. Montgomery who was writing a life of Edward VII and wanted her impressions and anecdotes and tell him that she would see him on Friday at four. Make the usual monthly checks for the British War Relief, the British Book Fund for soldiers (on the London account) and the France Forever Fund for short-wave broadcasts and the Chinese Relief. Ring up Doctor Chung at Hampshire House and ask him for tea for Monday.

She recited them all as they came through her head, all the endless, dull, sometimes annoying tasks which devoured so much of time and of thought. Besides all these there was the great pile of letters which had to be answered, letters of every kind and sort from fawning ones begging for help for someone she had never seen, through letters which had to do with business, to the semi-personal ones which were the most tiresome of all because the senders presumed upon friendship or acquaintance to ask you to do impossible things.

Mrs. Parkington was aware that many people said she was a wonderful woman and how wonderful it was that at her age she remained so interested and conscientious about so many things, but she had no illusions; she was not wonderful at all. If she had been really strong she would have chucked the whole lot into a wastepaper basket to lie there forgotten and impotent to wear down her vitality and disrupt the pleasant routine of existence. She was not wonderful at all; she was simply the victim of a compulsion from which she would not save herself.

In the midst of her morning's work, Taylor knocked at the door and came in to say that there was a woman belowstairs who wished to see her. He carried a note which he said the woman had given him to deliver to her. Mrs. Parkington took the note and told Taylor to wait.

She tore it open and read:

Dear Madame:

I realize that what I am doing is not a correct thing to do but the case was so urgent that I overstepped the bounds of etiquette. I must see you. It concerns Mr. Stilham and myself. I am frantic and do not know which way to turn. Only a moment of your time would make a great difference to me. I apologize profoundly for intruding upon your privacy.

Hoping that you will grant this favor, I am

Yours sincerely,
Esther Hobson
(Mrs. J. W. Hobson)

Even while she was reading the note she conceived a picture of Mrs. Hobson — that she was vulgar, that she was timid, that she was frightened and that she had a pitiful awe of wealth. Possibly she occupied some small niche in life which was sheltered but also limited. Who she was or what she wanted, Mrs. Parkington did not know. From the letter she judged that the woman was both pretentious and toadying and beyond question a bore. But her curiosity, she knew, would force her to see the woman, and in any case the way things stood now she would have to see anyone who knew anything whatever about Amory. If he was to be saved, the salvation must come accidentally now from some unexpected quarter.

She said to Taylor, "Take her into the small sitting-room and tell her I'll be down directly."

Then very quickly she finished the immediate business with Miss Beasely and went downstairs.

The woman was almost exactly what she had expected and the discovery made Mrs. Parkington feel both clever and pleased.

As she entered the room, the woman rose quickly and came toward her. Before Mrs. Parkington was able to say anything, she said, "I apologize for having intruded upon you." (It was the wording out of a column given as advice on etiquette.) "My name is Esther Hobson."

"How do you do?" said Mrs. Parkington, and then saw that Mrs. Hobson's eyes were red from weeping. "Please sit down."

Mrs. Hobson appeared to be in her middle forties, a pretty woman in a banal fashion, with too-small features and more than inclined toward plumpness. Mrs. Parkington divined that as a young girl she must have been extraordinarily pretty. She was dressed in the kind of clothes which are a poor imitation of smart ones, which somehow go awry in line, in pattern, in material, resulting only in an effect which is neither bad nor good but only mediocre.

She seated herself in anxiety on the edge of her chair. Mrs. Parkington sat down opposite her and said, "Now, what is it I can do for you?"

Mrs. Hobson did not look at her. Instead she regarded the red handbag she carried, her fingers fondling the clasp. She said, "It is very difficult to explain. I don't know quite how to begin."

"I am a very old woman," said Mrs. Parkington. "You need not mind saying anything you like."

Again the woman hesitated and Mrs. Parkington, aware of the busy day ahead of her, wanted to say, "Do stop being silly and get on with it." But she held her tongue and Mrs. Hobson said, "It may seem very strange, my coming to you of all people, but I was desperate."

"So you said in your note." Mrs. Parkington had no desire to be unsympathetic but the woman did seem sillier and sillier.

Then suddenly with an effort so great that her face became quite red, she said, "You see, Mr. Stilham has been my friend for a long time."

"Oh!" The expression came out despite Mrs. Parkington. So that was it.

"And now it's all finished." She began to cry. "That's what I can't bear. It's not the money so much as his throwing me over now, after all these years."

Mrs. Parkington said very quietly, "I wouldn't cry if I were you. That never does any good. Just try to relax and tell me about it."

"You're very good to me . . . to let me take all this time."

"Never mind that. I should like to hear about it. I shan't be able to understand if you don't tell me about it. Where do you live?"

"In New Rochelle. I have a nice house there and I belong to several clubs. Nobody there has ever known anything about it."

She looked up now, a little encouraged by Mrs. Parkington's curiosity which she misinterpreted as sympathy, "You see he never came there. He always had to make a good many business trips and I used to go ahead of him and stay at the same hotel . . . in different rooms of course . . . in places like Rochester and Cleveland and Kansas City. We never saw each other in New York except a few times when he wanted to see me and then it wasn't really New York. It was in Newark or Brooklyn. But he gave that up. He thought it was too risky."

"Are you married?" asked Mrs. Parkington.

"No. I'm a widow. I've been a widow for fourteen years since before I met Amory — I mean Mr. Stilham."

"How did you meet?"

The woman looked again at her red handbag. "In Atlantic City," she said. "It was just after my husband died. I went there for a rest. Mr. Stilham was there at some kind of convention and somebody introduced us in the bar." A sigh interrupted her and she said, "He was so good-looking then."

Mrs. Parkington thought, What a fool! Aloud she said, "He is still a very good-looking man . . . only gone a little puffy and red in the face."

All the time Mrs. Parkington was listening, she kept seeing Amory, taking up the collection in St. Bart's on Sunday, acting as governor of St. Bart's school, appearing always as a model husband, father and citizen. It wasn't simply that he was all these things; he was a prig as well, always talking about standards and behavior and such stuff. He had dared to disapprove of people like Gus who, God knows, whatever else he was, had never been a hypocrite.

She said, "What is it you want me to do? Do you want me to persuade him to return to you?"

Mrs. Hobson's face turned scarlet again. "No, I didn't expect that. That would be too much." She coughed and held her gloved hand before her mouth. "It's about money." And then stopped talking again. Considering that she had to ask favors it seemed strange that you were forced to pry the request out of her now.

"Yes?" said Mrs. Parkington, wondering whether this dull, commonplace little woman contemplated blackmail.

"I don't know whether you've heard about Mr. Stilham's trouble. He's lost just about everything."

"Yes. I know all about that."

Mrs. Hobson looked down again at her handbag. "It's been very hard on me. It was bad enough having him break off with everything. That just about finished me." Suddenly, it seemed an idea came to her. "You understand, Mr. Stilham never gave me money. It wasn't like that." The face turned red again. "He paid for the expenses of the trips and gave me a present now and then but he didn't give me money. It wasn't like that." She seemed passionately anxious to cling to the last shreds of respectability, to establish in the eyes of Mrs. Parkington the conviction that she was not a real kept woman.

Opposite her Mrs. Parkington was listening with equal passion to this further revelation of Amory's character. She was thinking that it was always unbelievable how consistent most people could be. If she had invented a mistress for Amory and devised a code of behavior for her it would be exactly like this. Mrs. Hobson, with her passionate desire for respectability, her pride in her position in New Rochelle as a clubwoman, was absolutely safe. She would never be indiscreet or attempt blackmail. She was exactly the sort Amory would pick. It must, she thought, have been a very pedestrian, dreary affair. What did they talk about, sitting in dark corners of "tea shoppes" and taprooms in Harrisburg or Newark or Kansas City. Amory must have been a very dull, uninventive lover, but no duller than the woman sitting opposite her.

"You see," Mrs. Hobson continued, "I was always independent. My husband left me the house we lived in and quite a good income. I didn't need to accept anything from Mr. Stilham even if he had offered it. But now my income is gone and I don't know what

I'm to do." She began to cry again, helplessly now, like a meek and not very clever child. "Now I'll have to give up the house and leave New Rochelle."

Her anguish was genuine. Eve, thought Mrs. Parkington, could not have suffered more anguish at the expulsion from the Garden of Eden than Mrs. Hobson at the prospect of having to leave New Rochelle.

"What happened? How did you lose your money?"

"Mr. Stilham asked me to loan him my securities. He told me that he would make a lot more money for me, and now they're gone and he says he can't pay me back."

Mrs. Parkington tried to remain calm. She asked, "How much did you lend him?"

"At that time," said Mrs. Hobson, "they were worth about a hundred and forty thousand dollars." She took out her handkerchief and blew her nose in a very refined fashion.

"And why did you come to me?"

"I thought you might help me. I didn't know where to turn. I was desperate. I could have married again but for Mr. Stilham. During the years we were together I had two offers . . . very good suitable offers. I refused them because of him."

There was no doubt of it, the woman was a fool, but that, Mrs. Parkington knew, did not make Amory's case any the better nor Mrs. Hobson's situation any the less pitiable. She thought suddenly, She is like hundreds of others who were ruined by Gus' manipulations. They all want to get rich quick and they haven't any brains and when they lose their money they're helpless. But Gus had never seen the women he ruined; they were ciphers, remote and hazy and unreal, "widows and orphans" on the periphery of his vast machinations. And Gus had certainly never robbed his own mistresses.

She said, "The whole business is very unfortunate, Mrs. Hobson. I don't know what is to happen. It may be that things will work out so that we'll be able to pay you back."

Mrs. Hobson's face grew bright and expectant. "Do you really think so?"

"I don't know."

"You see, it isn't as if I could sue him. If I did that I would lose everything too. I might get back my money but I'd have to resign from my clubs. I'd have to leave New Rochelle. I'd have to give up all my lovely friends."

She was safe all right. Amory had certainly picked shrewdly. She was safe as a church.

"I know you'll forgive me, Mrs. Hobson, if I don't give you any more time," said Mrs. Parkington, "but I have a very full day and I'm already late. I'm quite sure something will be worked out. If I were you I'd go home and not worry about it too much. I think I can assure you that you'll get back your securities or others of the same value. If you'll give me a card, I'll send it to my lawyer and he'll keep in touch with you."

Mrs. Hobson opened the handbag and began fishing in the disorder of lipstick and matches and cigarettes it concealed. Without looking up she said, "You're very good to me. You've changed everything." She found the card at last and gave it to Mrs. Parkington. One more thing seemed to trouble her. She asked, "Do you think everything can be arranged so that Mr. Stilham won't get into trouble? I wouldn't want anything bad to happen to him . . . I mean really bad, if you know what I mean?"

"I know what you mean. I can't answer that. We can only hope for the best. In any case I don't think you'll have to give up New Rochelle or your clubs."

"They mean a great deal to me," said Mrs. Hobson. "I have so many lovely friendships and a lovely home. If you're out driving some day I would love to have you see it."

"Thank you," said Mrs. Parkington graciously but with utter insincerity, "I may take up your invitation." She rose and asked, "Have you enough money to carry on with?"

"Yes," said, Mrs. Hobson, eagerly, "Yes. It's just the future . . . You see I'm not as young as I once was."

Mrs. Parkington held out her hand and Mrs. Hobson took it. Then suddenly in a swift gesture she swept Mrs. Parkington's beringed fingers to her lips and kissed them.

"You've been so good to me . . . so generous."

Quickly Mrs. Parkington snatched her hand away. "Don't do that," she said with sudden ferocity.

"I didn't mean to offend you. It was only that you've been so good to me . . . so kind."

"I haven't been anything at all," said Mrs. Parkington. Never, it seemed to her, had she hated all Gus' money so much as in that moment, because it had the power to degrade a fellow human creature. "You must understand I wasn't angry with you."

She went with Mrs. Hobson to the outer door and watched her plump buttocks quivering as she tottered on her too-high heels, down the steps into the street. Then she turned away and instead of taking the lift, walked up the stairs because she was not yet prepared to face Miss Beasely and Mattie. She had first to understand and analyze her own anger and contempt. The groveling gesture of Mrs. Hobson left her feeling sick, and the revelations about Amory had filled her with contempt. Amory, she thought, was the pattern of a "gentleman," the kind of "gentleman" who had been trained to pay his gambling debts and let the grocer sing for his money. But Amory hadn't even paid his gambling debts. Certainly there was something very awry with a system which produced men like Amory. You gave them every advantage of education and background only to have them develop the psychology of pimps.

As she reached the top of the stairs the telephone was ringing and as she entered the room she heard Miss Beasely saying, "Yes, Doctor, I'll call her."

He was speaking from St. Luke's Hospital. He had just brought Mrs. Sanderson there from her flat. She had developed symptoms of pneumonia and was better off, he thought, at the hospital. No, up to now she seemed to be doing very well but it was too early to tell how serious a case it would be.

Mrs. Parkington put down the telephone and turned to Miss Beasely. "Ring up Mr. Brearly and say that on account of illness in the family I shan't be able to go to the Symphony Board meeting. It's Mrs.

Sanderson. She has pneumonia." Then she called into the next room, "Mattie, get your hat and coat and go with me. We're going to St. Luke's."

She did not want to go alone. She wanted a friend with her. In her heart she knew that it was all finished. The Duchess was getting at last what she wanted. There wouldn't be any more need of drink or drugs.

The Duchess died quietly and quickly, slipping out of life without pain in a dim fog of delirium in which she recognized no one about her. All the last night until early in the morning Mrs. Parkington sat beside the bed, knowing perfectly well that there was nothing she could do and that there was no hope. At the end, in order that Alice might die quietly and without struggling, they gave her again for the last time the drugs which for so long had dimmed the edges of daily existence and blurred the unhappy memories of the past.

Mattie stayed with her mistress all through the long night dozing off and waking suddenly now and then to apologize for having dropped asleep. Twice Mrs. Parkington suggested that she go home to her own bed, but Mattie knew that the old woman wanted her to stay there and nothing on earth could have driven her away. Mrs. Parkington was not afraid;

she was not even troubled, for she was aware by midnight that no skill, no knowledge, no amount of money could save her daughter from death. But she was lonely.

There were many things which Mattie, out of their long intimacy, divined and understood. She knew, sitting there on the uncomfortable chair, her head nodding on her plump body, that Mrs. Parkington was thinking that the last of the children born of her own flesh was dying. When the Duchess was gone, she would be alone, for not even Janie who was so close to her, could ever take the place of her own child.

Just before midnight Mrs. Parkington sent for Dr. Fletcher. He knew very little about pneumonia; his field was psychiatry, but Mattie knew that her mistress had not sent for him in any hope that he could save the Duchess, but because he was a very old friend and his presence there helped her loneliness and the conscience which even now still had the power to torment her with the faint, querulous reproach that somehow, long ago, she could have helped the woman dying there in the room with them. When the doctor arrived, tall and gray and slightly stooped, Mattie said, "I think I'll go out and get some air. I'll just walk around the block and come right back." She knew that there was something her mistress wanted to say to the doctor alone.

There was never any need to say it, for Dr. Fletcher knew what it was she wanted of him. He knew Mrs. Parkington very well and had known her for a very long time. He had dined with her many times alone, while they talked of all the strange dark tangles of the human mind which he knew so well, perhaps better than any other man on earth. And he knew Mrs. Parkington's mind, its quietness and sureness, its honesty, its quick intuition and the long experience and understanding which lay beneath its brilliant surface. For a long time he had preferred her company to that of any other woman, even that of his own wife to whom he was devoted.

Now as Mattie closed the door he said, simply, "I am sorry, Susie. It is hard for you. In spite of everything death is always hard. You've been told the truth — that there is nothing to be done. There is another truth that I can tell you — that it is much better this way. Above all, it's better for Alice herself." He took Mrs. Parkington's hand. "It is always hard for a mother to survive her child but Alice is already an old woman — much older than you, dear Susie. There are things you know as well as I do — things you know by intuition which I have had to work hard to learn. One of them is that Alice has already been dead for a long time. She had a will to die. Nothing can bring her as much happiness as death. It is the only thing that can bring her peace. For a long time she has been seeking peace and oblivion. She was a very tired woman."

She said nothing but looked away from him, aware that tears were filling her eyes, not tears of sorrow or even now of pity, for Alice was already beyond the need of that, but of gratitude for something which she did not quite understand. In the quiet silence she heard the slow labored breathing of the dying woman.

Then Louis Fletcher spoke again, "And above all, dear Susie, you mustn't reproach yourself. The things which destroyed Alice were beyond your control. They were in Alice herself, when she was born, in her very glands when she was a tiny girl. The doom was already there. And it was there too in the world into which she was born, an ugly, harsh world in which only strong and willful or hard or clever people could survive."

Then she looked up at him. She was a small woman and he was a very tall thin man. She said, "It was very good of you to come. It was very silly of me to have sent for you.

I don't know why I did. Perhaps I sent for you not as a doctor but as a friend. You have always been a very good friend."

She took her hand out of his and added, "Now go home. You have told me what I wanted to hear. It was something I knew already but I needed to hear you say it before I would believe it."

"I think you know me well enough to know I wouldn't be stupid enough to try to make you believe anything your intelligence rejected. What I have said is honest and it is the truth. There are people in life who are doomed by the very stars. There are others like ourselves to whom God, or whatever it is that controls this universe, has given special favors, special reserves of strength and understanding. Why this is so I do not know nor does anyone else, but you yourself have lived long enough to know the truth of what I am saying." The tears had wet her cheeks now. Very quietly she said, "Please go, Louis, quickly. You have done what I wanted you to do."

He picked up his hat and quietly without another word he left the room and when he had gone she walked to the window and standing there with her back to the bed as if she were ashamed lest the unconscious dying woman should see her tears, she quickly dried them. Below her in the street, two cars passed each other. In the doorway opposite, a sailor and a girl stood in the doorway, their bodies pressed together in the eternal embrace which marked the beginning of all life. It had been raining and the reflections of the yellow street lights were drowned in pools of water gathered on the uneven surface of the asphalt. Far off down the river the lonely whistle of a freighter sounded through the fog, and suddenly the strange, unearthly feeling of gratitude for life burst forth again from Mrs. Parkington's heart. There were no words, or even thoughts which could translate what she felt. Only through music perhaps could it be clarified and given form.

How long she stood there she did not know, for it was one of those moments in life when there is no time, when one's very existence seems suspended in space.

The sound of Mattie opening the door quietly roused her and she thought, Perhaps that is what death is. Perhaps in the end it is only death that brings complete understanding, for in that moment it had seemed to her that she understood all that had ever happened to her, that all the tragedy, all the pleasure, all the satisfaction, the suffering had come together like a single superb tapestry in which every fragment, every line had a meaning and a beauty related to the whole.

She asked, "Is it cold out, Mattie?"

"No, Mrs. Parkington, it is much warmer."

While the two old women sat there, thinking and dreaming, the nurse came in to take the pulse of the dying woman. She said nothing. She was a clever woman; although death was familiar to her she still respected it. It was one of the few things in life which, for every man and woman, partook of dignity. Watching her through half-closed eyes, Mrs. Parkington thought, All she is doing is futile, yet she is going through it because somehow we must go on, making gestures so long as the heart beats, so long as the breath stirs — gestures made in the very face of fate itself.

Since Louis Fletcher had gone, since the curious moment of revelation at the window, there was peace in the room. The doubts, the fears were dissolved. There were people who in themselves had the power of bringing peace. Louis Fletcher was one of them; the power had made him a great physician.

This was the only one of her children she had seen die. Now suddenly it seemed strange to her that both her parents had died in violence away from her. So too both her sons had died. And then she thought of Gus, who had died quickly in the arms of a woman she had never seen, whose name she never even heard, in a hotel bedroom in Cannes, an old man fighting to the end against old age and death.

Quite suddenly she understood that too — that to Gus the prospect of growing old and tired was beyond endurance. It was not peace he had sought, but violence and sensuality and power. In the end, she understood now, with a sudden clarity, he had been unfaithful to her not because he did not love her, but because in the beginning he could not help himself and in the end because he had tried to defy weakness and death with the gesture of a vigorous young man. And in the very gesture of life, death had taken him. That was something perhaps only Louis Fletcher of all people in the world, would understand — that there had always been something magnificent about Gus which made her forgive him everything, that there were times when she was grateful for the curious quality of extravagance and splendor with which he had invested all their life together. That was a gratitude and forgiveness many women would never understand.

XII

Outside on the river, the whistle sounded again, this time nearer at hand, and quite suddenly she was back again on the yacht in the basin at Cannes and it was early morning with the mist still hanging over the blue line of the Mediterranean and Mattie was in the room waking her and saying something about Captain MacTavish and when she had arranged her hair and put on a dressing gown and gone outside the cabin door, Captain MacTavish, red-faced and uneasy was standing there with a little fat, pock-marked *sergent de ville*. Captain MacTavish said, "I apologize for disturbing you, Mrs. Parkington, but something has happened to the Major."

Instinctively she started toward the door of the Major's cabin but MacTavish, his face now scarlet as a poppy said, "He's not in there, madame. He's at the Carlton." He was a blunt man but now he was suddenly tactful. He said, "It seems that he played at the casino until very late and then went to the Carlton for some champagne with friends and stayed on the night."

She knew immediately what had happened. It was the thing she had feared for a long time. She knew that he was dead and she knew how it had happened and she understood that whatever the sequence of events she must pretend that she did not know or understand anything, if for no other reason, only to save poor Captain MacTavish from embarrassment.

Quickly she dressed. Mattie helped her, saying, "I can go with you, Mrs. Parkington, if you like." But she refused Mattie's offer. Mattie's presence would only complicate things. She thought, Somehow we must get him back on the boat so that no one ever knows. And quickly she glanced at the clock and saw that it was a little before five o'clock. No one would be about, no one they knew. Through the chill mist she went with MacTavish and the *sergent de ville* to the Carlton, all the way on foot since she could not wait until they sent for a car and in any case the Major's driver must not know of what had happened. In the hallway of the Carlton two old women were scrubbing the floor. The manager, unshaven, his hair still uncombed, was there in his frock coat and striped trousers wringing his hands and talking French as rapidly as he was able to articulate.

She tried to check the wild flow of his speech. He kept saying, "I do not know how it happened. Such a thing has never happened before. It is very unfortunate. Such a thing has never happened before in the Carlton. I apologize, madame. I apologize."

Quite coldly she said, "Never mind all that. I should like to go to the room." There was something monstrous and grotesque in the idea of his apology.

MacTavish tried to prevent her because, for all his gruffness he was a nice man, but she was aware that, with his incredible French and his lack of tact, he would never be able to manage the stupid *sergent de ville* and the hysterical manager. The thing would have to be done by herself.

The manager kept wringing his hands and the door of the office nearby was opened suddenly and a fat short woman of fifty with a mustache came out. In the second the door was opened, there came from the room the low wailing sound of a woman's voice, sobbing hysterically. The manager said fiercely to the mustachioed woman, "Get that *grue* out of here. Why is she still hanging around?"

The mustachioed woman disappeared again into the room and the others went with Susie in the lift and when they reached the door of the room, she said, "I would like to go in alone," and they stood aside.

It was only when she had closed the door

behind her and stood there looking down at him that the fact of his death had any reality, and even then what she saw was not Gus. Gus was life and vigor and enjoyment. Gus was good humor and recklessness and warmth and tenderness. Gus wasn't there at all. There was only the body of a man lying on the floor covered with a sheet, a stranger with Gus' giant physique and strength, grown cold now and lifeless. It had nothing to do with Gus. She need never have come to the room at all.

Quickly she turned and opened the door and to the manager outside, she asked, "Have you a *brancard* — a stretcher," and in a silly way he replied, "No, madame. We have only a wheel chair."

"Can you get a stretcher?"

"Perhaps, madame, at the hospital."

"It would require a requisition," said the *sergent de ville.*

She knew what that meant — red tape, perhaps for an hour or more — the endless red tape without which the French seemed unable to exist. There was no time.

In English she said to MacTavish, "We must get him back to the yacht into his own cabin."

MacTavish thought it a good idea, but difficult. The *sergent de ville* had not even allowed him to move the Major's body from the floor to the bed. There must be a report first, an investigation.

That was exactly what they must avoid.

She turned quickly to the *sergent de ville* and said, "Could you use five thousand francs?"

The blue eyes widened in the pink face, "Five thousand francs! Of course, madame. Five thousand francs! Who could not use five thousand francs?"

"It's for you if you make no trouble. The circumstances are perfectly simple. I want the body of my husband taken to the yacht."

"It can be done," said MacTavish. "We can manage it if we have a stretcher."

"There is no stretcher. There is no time. There is only the wheel chair."

It took a moment for MacTavish to gather what it was she meant and he said, weakly, "Yes . . . I see."

The *sergent de ville* was now scarcely noticing them. He seemed to be dreaming, perhaps of what he meant to do with more money than he had ever seen before in his life. To the manager she said quickly, "No one must know anything."

His hysteria was gone suddenly, translated into admiration. He said, "Of course, madame. Of course. No one will ever know," and he seemed suddenly to become weak with relief.

To MacTavish she said, "I will go back to the yacht and you will come to my room and waken me when you return. What about the crew? Will they be about?"

"I think I can manage that. I will go ahead and if there is anyone about I will send him below. If there is any slip-up, I will say that the Major had a seizure while gambling."

Then she left them and hurried back down the stairs and through the corridor into the garden. As she passed the door of the office, it stood open. Neither the woman with the mustache nor the woman who had been wailing were there. It was quite empty.

The whole thing went off admirably. A man washing the streets and two gardeners watering the cinerarias around the newly-erected statue of Queen Victoria, saw an invalid being wheeled across the street toward the basin by a man in the uniform of a ship's officer. The invalid lay back in the wheel chair, the hat pulled low over his face to shut out the rays of the rising morning sun. The workman and the gardeners were scarcely aware of what they saw. Invalids were common enough in Cannes and besides in few places in the world could the human race behave more strangely than in Cannes.

Mattie had never been more magnificent. When her mistress returned to the yacht she was waiting and she asked no questions, accepting the statement that the Major was dead.

When Susie said, "I'd like to be alone now, Mattie," she went away without a word. She was there in the passageway when MacTavish arrived and helped him with his grim task. When they had placed the body of the Major in his bed MacTavish took the wheel chair off the ship, to the end of the pier and pushed it into the blue water. Then he went back to the hotel and sent a messenger for the hotel physician.

In her own cabin Susie threw herself down, her face away from the light, buried in the pillows. No tears came. She was suddenly very tired and she was aware of a feeling of great emptiness as if only part of her were alive. The death still had no reality. She only knew that something magnificent had gone out of her life, something she had loved, which had brightened all her existence, something too powerful for her which had brought her some sorrow but much happiness, was gone. It was something she would never again find. For the rest of her life it would be as if she were only half alive. In the Major's cabin there was a body but Gus was gone forever. At last the tears came, quietly, searing her eyes. They came out of her heart, out of the very depths of her body — out of her soul and her spirit for in a strange way all of these had belonged to him.

The newspapers in every part of the world reported that the famous and fabulously rich Major Parkington was dead at seventy-one years of age in bed on his yacht "Navajo" at Cannes, France.

Dimly she heard again the sound of the boat's whistle through the fog and was aware that someone was standing before her and knew that she had been dozing. She heard the voice of the nurse saying quietly, "You can go home now, Mrs. Parkington. There is no longer any reason to stay. I have telephoned for your car."

She thanked the nurse and suddenly noticed Mattie, sound asleep in her chair, her head sunk in to her short plump neck, her hat a little over her eyes, and she thought, "I must get Mattie a new hat. She is so tiresome about spending money — saving it all for that niece of hers. She rose and crossed the room and laid her hand gently on Mattie's arm. Softly she said, "Come Mattie. We'll go home now."

XIII

It was her granddaughter Helen who took over. Helen was like that. For all the drooping mouth and the listless unhappiness, she could be, except for Mrs. Parkington herself, the only really efficient member of the family. She was especially good at weddings and funerals. At times Mrs. Parkington thought that much of Helen's unhappiness and futility came of her having been born at the wrong time and in the wrong station in life. In a small village, a small world, where there were endless small fragments of gossip and loose ends of living, Helen might have been happy, she might even have been a splendid citizen. She was meant for a petty world, cluttered with details, and she had been born into a large world whose responsibilities she neither understood nor accepted.

Now she was in the house quietly doing all the dull tiresome things which go with funerals — the telephoning, the announcements, the grim business of the undertaker, the calls and notes and flowers of friends and acquaintances. She went about quietly, engrossed in her task, the sagging mouth rising a little at the satisfaction of all the petty activity. She managed even Miss Beasely who resented orders from anyone but Mrs. Parkington. And Janie helped her; Janie was in and out of the house bringing brightness to Mrs. Parkington merely by her presence.

If the funeral had been left to Mrs. Parkington she would have said, "Let us have a cremation and a quiet quick burial without fuss." But the thing was not entirely in her hands. It was clear that Helen and Amory believed there should be an important funeral at St. Bart's. It was a curious thing, Mrs. Parkington thought, how people whose importance was waning should always be so insistent upon "importance" for themselves. Gus had never needed to worry about such things as importance; it was thrust upon him; whatever he did was important and exciting.

But there was another element which softened Mrs. Parkington and that was the thought of the kind of funeral Alice herself would have liked. It was a subject that they had never discussed but Mrs. Parkington knew that Alice would like her own funeral to be important as she had liked a long time ago the importance of her wedding to the Duke. Birth and marriage and death had been after all the only moments of importance in all the life of Alice. Public funerals like public weddings had long ago become for Mrs.

Parkington barbarous affairs, remnants of some less civilized era in which there was time and place for primitive spectacles and festivals. Now she thought, I shall hate it all — the walking down the aisle, the odious show, the tiresome drive to Woodlawn, the whole business of putting what remains of Alice into the earth beside her father and brothers. I shall hate it all but no matter, it will give pleasure and satisfaction to a great many people. It would be like a christening of which Gus had said long ago, "It can't do the child any actual harm and it will give a lot of people pleasure."

There were, she knew, actually people who *liked* funerals, who went to them almost professionally. She only wished that she need not be the central figure, that she might go incognito to watch all the people who came out from under stones, the forgotten once important people whose only contact with the great world any longer was through funerals, all the forgotten, rather decayed people from obscure, dingy brownstone houses who would come to St. Bart's as to a kind of village homecoming because they knew that the ceremony for the daughter of the rich and fashionable Mrs: Parkington would attract great crowds. They would see people there whom they had not perhaps seen in months and years, not since the last fashionable funeral.

So to Helen she said, "My dear, I will leave it all in your hands, willingly."

And so Helen did a really splendid job. The obituaries were splendid and occupied a great deal of space, especially in the *Times,* the *Tribune* and the *Sun.* There were pictures of Alice, years old, taken from the newspaper "morgues" and an account of her marriages to the Duc de Brantès, Lionel Swinford, the remittance man, and Alfred Sanderson of Pasadena. But the odd thing was that nearly half the space was given over to the Major who had been dead for nearly thirty years, to his achievements, his fame, his spectacular history. Even in the grave he was more "important" than most people who were living, far more important than any of his descendants.

Flowers came in great sheafs, in baskets and blankets and set pieces and Mrs. Parkington, annoyed by the great number of them, was coldly aware that they were offerings not to Alice or the memory of Alice but to herself because she was rich and important and powerful. If she had died first, the offerings to Alice who had been almost forgotten by the great world, would have been miserable indeed. When she herself died everything, she knew, would fall apart; in a few years after her death, the whole family would disappear into obscurity and only in history would the memory of the Major survive.

Only once did Amory come to the house and then she managed to see him alone for a moment. The disturbance of death had made her forget for a little time the trouble of her grandson-in-law. He was still drinking and although his eyes were swollen and bloodshot and his handsome empty face the color of mahogany, he seemed to make sense.

He did not know what the Grand Jury meant to do, nor how far the hearing had advanced, but it was clear that he had given up hope and was making no effort to save himself, trusting only to some turn of luck which by a miracle might save him. He was sullen and morose and said, "It does not matter. In any case it is the end of everything — for all our class. The whole world is going to hell. I might as well have a peaceful time of it in jail."

It was a silly statement and she asked, "What do you mean by our class, Amory? I am not aware of belonging to any class. I happen to have a great deal of money, but that is an accident."

"I mean," he said heavily, searching for words, "all the people who have standards, who were brought up to believe that tradition and decency and responsible government were important."

She did not answer. She only thought, The man is completely crazy. There was no use in talking to him. The very words he used had no meaning to her, or a meaning so distorted that the conversation could only become empty and without significance.

He grinned at her, showing one of his rare traces of humor, "At least," he said, "Helen is happy. I think she should have been a caterer or a female undertaker or something."

On the day before the funeral, Janie had tea with her great-grandmother in the boudoir. Mrs. Parkington managed it so that they would be alone and in the middle of the half hour they spent together, Janie suddenly said, "Do you think, Granny, that Great-Aunt Alice was ever happy?" And Mrs. Parkington answered, "No, my dear. Now and then perhaps for a little while. She once had a Cairn terrier she loved very much. Its name was Sally." And after a moment she said "Happiness is an odd thing. Perhaps people who have never known it are not really unhappy. I do not know whether Alice ever knew that she was unhappy. Sometimes I think only that life was intolerably dull for her always, and that is something which comes from the inside. The outside, other people, have very little to do with it."

"She wasn't happy in any of her marriages?"

"No. I don't think that she was. You see people are really happy I think, in proportion to how much they give out. Sometimes I think it doesn't much matter what it is so long as they give out something. Your grandfather wasn't always a good man but he gave a great deal. In a way he gave a great deal more than he took from others, and I don't mean money. Money is easy to give away whether it's a penny for a beggar or a million to charity. That's nothing. It's what you give of yourself that matters in time, in amusement, in stimulation. You see your great-aunt Alice never gave out anything and so she never got anything back. She just existed. I doubt that she was ever happy or unhappy. She might have been happy, she might even have been different but for all the money her father had. It spoiled all her chances. It deformed her whole life."

Janie was silent for a time watching the tip of her cigarette burning away. Mrs. Parkington regarded her, secretly, wondering what all this could mean to her. Presently the girl looked up and said, "Granny, I've been thinking a lot lately and sometimes I've thought just what you've been telling me. I think my mother's unhappy because she's never had any fun. Everything was always arranged for her. Everything was always easy for her. She's never had any excitement. She's never had to fight for anything. Nothing that ever happened to her was ever an adventure."

Mrs. Parkington said nothing and suddenly Janie began to talk again, rapidly as if what she was saying had long been shut up inside her. "Granny, I don't want money. I don't want any money at all except what Ned and I earn. You can leave it to all the others. They'll need it because they couldn't get on without it. I'd like to marry Ned and do my own housework or get a job and go away with him somewhere into a small town somewhere . . . like pioneers. I'd like to get away from everything I've known." She looked shyly at her great grandmother, "Maybe I sound very childish to you."

Mrs. Parkington smiled, "No, I don't think so. Only I wouldn't underestimate money. In a way it's all in how you use it, what you buy with it. It's not worth anything in itself, but only what you can exchange it for. Most people exchange it for rubbish and so it doesn't bring them either wisdom or satisfaction or self-respect. You cannot buy these either, nor what comes out of your mouth, nor what is inside you." The old woman put down her teacup and said, "Did you ever talk about this to Ned? He might like you to have money. It's for him to decide too."

"I've never talked to him about it directly, as we're talking, but he worries because some day I may be rich. He doesn't like it. He'd like it a lot better if I just worked for my living like anybody."

They got no further with their talk that day for Janie's mother knocked and came in. She seemed calm and pleased about something, "I succeeded in arranging it," she said. "Bishop Burchard himself is going to read the service. I think Aunt Alice would have liked that."

"That's very nice," said Mrs. Parkington. "I'm sure Alice would have liked it. Thank you very much Helen."

But she wasn't thinking really about whether Bishop Burchard read the service or not. She was thinking suddenly about the bishop's grandfather whom Gus had bought with a new heating plant and a gift of fifty thousand dollars; and his horsefaced wife who had called on her long ago at the Brevoort. It was in a way a racketeer family, running a racket inside the church — three generations of bishops. Gus had been right when he said that the Reverend Burchard would get along. His grandson shook hands with the same false enthusiasm, with the same show of teeth which looked false in the fierce intensity of the smile. He talked in the same mealy-mouthed way . . . In some ways it was fun to live so long, just to see how things turned out if for no other reason.

On the afternoon of the funeral it rained, but the rain did not prevent a crowd from filling St. Bart's and standing on the sidewalk outside to watch the fashionable people arrive. The family entered the church by the vestry room but as Mrs. Parkington's car passed the main door she lifted her veil a little to look at the people who stood outside the entrance. There were no young people among them, they were mostly women, elderly or middle-aged, who could still remember that the woman for whom the service was being said had once been the Duchess de Brantès and the daughter of the great Major Parkington. Some of them no doubt had read the accounts of the wedding long ago at the house in Newport.

She was glad of the mourning veil. You could look through it without people being able to see your face. They couldn't see that there were no tears in your eyes; there was no necessity for feigning an air of tragedy and grief. It permitted her, too, to study the faces near her without their being aware of it.

As she walked down the aisle from the vestry door near the center of the church, she saw that it was all exactly as she knew it would be. The church was filled, mostly by people who had come out of curiosity. There were all sorts of faces — old Mrs. Sackville and her old maid daughter. (Their money had vanished long ago. She had not heard of them for years. Annie Sackville had once been very pretty and smart.) And the Manson twins, both widows, who must be nearly seventy, and Jim Donaldson, a whiskey-faced old pauper whom Gus helped long ago when he had gotten into difficulties in the Hercules mine business. And Sarah Goodson who, they said, never left her home among the Fifth Avenue shops except to attend funerals. In the fifty feet she walked on the arm of Amory, she saw perhaps a score of faces that she recognized and a dozen others which were vague and distantly familiar, and each one of them involved something of the remote past, memories, stories that were by now legends.

This was one of the last of the fashionable funerals and she regretted that she happened to be one of the principal performers; she would have preferred to be in the audience itself where she could study the faces. She understood suddenly that the remnants of a world which was vanishing, which was almost gone, had gathered here like sheep to attend the funeral ceremonies of one of the last of their number. In a few more years most of them would be dead, their houses closed or pulled down. The horses and yachts of most of them had gone long ago, along with all the tinsel and glitter, the snobbery and vulgarity and promiscuity of their era. The world had long since passed them by; some of them it had mocked, some of them it had ruined, most of them it had already forgotten. She had lived long enough to have seen the world out of which these relicts appeared come into existence, flourish, wither and die. Once she had been a part of it but somehow she had escaped and gone on into a new and other world which was beyond the reach of most of them, a world which included people like the judge and Louis Fletcher, a world which was everlasting and indestructible because it was founded upon the eternal qualities of man's civilization.

In the expensive showy church, the spectacle was a bitter footnote upon the shabbiness of mankind. Alice had been rich and a duchess, but that was not why they had come to her funeral; they had come because the occasion was an excuse to bring them all together once more. Like sheep, huddled together, they felt less lonely. She saw suddenly that although she and Gus had spent a large part of their lives in their world, neither of them had ever really been a part of it. They had seen it all; they had lived in it like lodgers in a lodging house and in the end rejected it. Long before Gus died they had chosen other worlds — Gus his gay and raffish one filled with declassé but human people and herself a world in which beauty and things of the mind were the standard. What both of them chose had nothing to do with money. What they attained could not be bought; they would have had it if they had been beggars. They had escaped the ultimate vulgarity, that of buying things. As she reached the pew, she was suddenly very proud of Gus and of herself. They had been very lucky.

She had come down the aisle on the arm of Amory because that was the conventional thing to do and since the whole funeral was the apotheosis of conventionality, it had to be done however distasteful it might be. Once she arrived at the pew, she managed to place Mattie on one side and Janie on the other.

It was a pity, she thought, that Alice couldn't see the magnificence of all the flowers, or perhaps she did see them and knew about them. She did have a curious feeling that Alice was not far away, that she was somewhere just on the other side of a curtain, taking part after a fashion in her own funeral. And she found herself wondering whether all very old people, like herself, had no fear of death nor any special desire to embrace it, but only regarded it with indifference, as a fact like the rising or setting of the sun. Perhaps others too had the same curious certainty which she was experiencing in this moment, that the death of the body was not the end of spiritual entity, but only a break in a journey, like transferring from one tramcar to another in the old days. Once when she had been younger, as at the moment of the boys' deaths, the pain had been not over the physical fact of death but over the certainty that she would never again, in this life, know the pleasure of seeing them smile, of hearing their voices calling to her up a stairway, of hearing Herbert's funny chuckle and Eddie's loud laugh that was so like that of Gus. This pain she had not felt when Gus died. Then she had felt lonely and once or twice, when she was very tired, she would have welcomed death. And now at the funeral of Alice she felt nothing at all, either at the death of Alice or the prospect of her own death which could not be far away.

And while they waited for the service to begin, she thought that perhaps she had no resentment because her own life had been so filled with human experience that it had, like a good book which one has enjoyed, to come at length to the last page. It might be that she experienced this serenity now only because in the past she had known as much suffering as pleasure; and grotesquely she remembered the curious philosophy the Duke had uttered the day she had blackmailed him into behaving like a gentleman — that "the body causes us in our lifetime great pain. Consequently it owes us the debt of all the pleasure we can wring from it." That might be true too of human experience — that if one had too much happiness and satisfaction, or too much suffering and sorrow, the spirit itself became deformed and in the end there was a lack of serenity and a sense of incompleteness which made one resist the fact of death. In her own life she had known extremes both of suffering and of happiness; looking back upon it now, she was aware that in it there had been an even, a complete balancing of the scales.

And presently through the veil she was aware of the figure of the bishop crossing toward the lectern and at the same time she became aware of the hymn being played by the organist. Until now she had not heard it with her mind although somehow it had penetrated her consciousness and perhaps had its effect upon the strange thoughts going through her head. There was a magnificence in the music, a splendor which filled her with a sense of elevation. There was no hymn more beautiful in its splendrous assertion of faith, no hymn as beautiful in the sense of music. Her heart sang, *Ein feste Burg ist unser Gott* and she was no longer at the funeral of her daughter in fashionable St. Bart's but in a tiny baroque church in Bad Gastein.

XIV

It was a Church, she had thought even then, such as churches should be, all pink and blue and gilt with gilded cherubs winging into space from the cornices.

Outside it was a sunny autumn day and at the keyboard sat Eric, the late afternoon sun shining on his gold-red hair. He had gotten permission from the priest to use the organ and had been playing Bach fugues, explaining them to her, for at that time she was only in the midst of learning all about music. And quite suddenly he had turned from Bach into *Ein feste Burg* saying, "This too is great music — the greatest!" And while she listened something happened inside her heart. She knew with a curious certainty that the thing which she already knew existed between them was somehow right . . . that it was a beautiful and good thing and that if she denied it she would live with regret until the end of her days. It was something which might come to a woman once. It was not at all like her feeling for Gus. This feeling for Eric was quite different, so different that in yielding to it, she was doing no wrong because it was something she could never give

Gus because he would neither understand nor desire it nor even be aware of its existence. And yet it was something she had to give if she were honest with herself and were ever to know the richness of existence which she must achieve.

It was not that she said these things to herself; they were said to her out of the fading sunlight, out of the splendor of the music itself. Out of the music a voice to which her body and spirit paid eager heed, said, "This is a beautiful world. It is filled with beauty which was meant by God for man's enjoyment. The men who built this gay little church knew it. The man who wrote the splendor into the music you are hearing knew it. The painters knew it. The artists knew it. All those especially beloved by God have always known it. To deny this splendor and beauty is evil." She knew that Eric had brought her to the little church to woo her with music because all else had failed and he was young and ardent and in love. But it was very odd that it should be a hymn which seduced her.

She saw him now very clearly as he turned from the keyboard to smile at her, a curious enveloping smile which seemed somehow a part of the music which still echoed in the little church. She saw the straight nose, the wide mouth and the dark eyes set in a face that was heavily tanned through his passion for mountain climbing.

They went back to the hotel past the little rushing stream which divided the village. And that night they dined together as they had done on the three preceding nights and afterward they sat drinking brandy on the terrace above the rushing little river and then in the moonlight she went back with him to the little hotel where the young men lived who climbed mountains in summer and skiied in winter.

Until now, sitting here between Mattie and Janie, she had never understood the madness of what happened on that night and in the days which followed. Afterward, even when the news came to her of Eric's death, it seemed to her that in Bad Gastein she had been another woman, a stranger; that she herself, Mrs. Augustus Parkington, wife and mother, was utterly incapable of what had happened, that in some way it had never happened to her at all. It had come at a time when Gus was more passionately interested in his vast manipulations than he was in herself or in any woman, when for the only time in his life women existed for him in the abstract, as a convenience, nothing more or less. She was in Bad Gastein because he had sent her there for the cure to keep her out of the way, perhaps because he wanted, through shame, to conceal from her manipulations that were rather more ruthless and shady than usual. That was something she would never know for Gus had never told her and now he was dead. She had arrived in Bad Gastein, ill and depressed, troubled that perhaps the thing which had always existed between them was at last waning, at least on Gus' side. She had thought (She could remember it well even now, sitting here in the front pew at St. Bart's), Perhaps he no longer finds me attractive. Perhaps, after all, the understanding between us had its roots only in a passionate physical attraction. Perhaps that is waning and with it the confidence, the simple pleasure, the zest we find merely in each other's company.

She was wrong, for that part of their love had survived everything, but she did not know it until she had said goodbye to Eric and the whole thing was finished between them. What she did not know then and knew now because she was much wiser, was that men — especially tremendous men like Gus — could at times, when their plans or ambitions obsessed them, lay aside love and even women for a time, turning to them again when what they sought was realized, turning to them again with the same or greater zest than before. Of such a thing no woman was capable, since for a woman in love, love invested whatever she did — her plans, her dreams, her work, her very breathing. It was not a thing apart — Man's love, she thought, beginning the old quotation is of man's life a thing apart . . . It was extraordinary the truth which underlay all banalities, perhaps because they contained, each one of them, so much of human experience.

Yet even now the memory of Eric had the power of bringing a sudden warmth to her old body. He had been many things that Gus was not, careless and free and without ambition beyond draining from each day, each hour, each minute, all there was of enjoyment and sensual delight. She had learned much from the adventure of Bad Gastein, much much wisdom which Gus could never have taught her, which she could not have learned alone. She learned that one must not calculate too much but seize the pleasure and the beauty of the moment, and Eric, somehow, in that little time had taught her to see *inside* many things, that you could not live at all by mind or by will alone, no matter how clever you were. The cleverest people she knew were very often the most empty, the ones who drew the least from the rich springs of satisfaction from which one could, if one knew how, drink one's fill. Perhaps because of what she had learned from Eric she had afterward suffered no remorse. Certainly because of Eric she knew what magnificence lay *inside* the splendorous chords of *Ein feste Burg*.

But these were things you could not go about preaching because they would be dangerous to those without wisdom or appreciation. It was like giving fine wine to a drunkard to whom alcohol of any sort brought equal satisfaction. Perhaps that was why churches existed and fierce codes of morality and restraints and stupid admonitions — to protect those who were not strong and wise from a wisdom and a knowledge too heady for them. And she remembered suddenly a coarse, vulgar, lusty story which Gus had told her ". . . It is too bloody good for the common people . . ." and at the same time she heard Bishop Burchard's voice reading. "I am the resurrection and the Life . . ." and thought, I am a wicked old woman, unrepentant and unregenerate, thinking such things at the funeral of my own daughter. Yet a voice told her, "All this is more important than the barrenness of the life of poor Alice who died in the end by her own desire because there was in her life none of the richness and warmth which came from people like Gus and Eric — those people whose relation to life and nature was so simple and sound and direct." Poor Alice for whom nothing could ever be done . . .

But because she disliked the bishop and felt a contempt for his worldliness, she could not go on listening to his voice and she drifted back again to Bad Gastein, seeing Eric again as he was the last time she had ever seen him, when he came to the station at Salzburg to see her off on the Orient Express, dressed in *Lederhosen* and a shirt open at the throat because when her train left he meant to go to Berchtesgaden to climb the very peak which Hitler had chosen long afterward as his vulture's nest. He had not kissed her because of the other people in the station and because of Mattie who went on pretending she suspected nothing, but he had gone through the farce of shaking hands and saying, "I'll be in Paris in April. Until then . . ."

The train pulled in and after she was in her compartment, she had gone to the window to look at him again for the last time as he stood there looking up at her, one lock of hair fallen over his forehead, thinking, He is bright and beautiful and healthy and I will never again see anyone like him, for she knew perfectly well that this was something which could not be carried over the interruption of weeks or months or years. Once she was out of this pretty bright Austrian world, there would be no returning to it. What had happened was perfect, but it was finished now. If she could manage it, she would never see him again. If she did see him again, perhaps in months, perhaps in years, she would greet him as an old friend, for the madness would be gone, and in its place only a sentimental sadness.

When the train pulled out she pretended to be absorbed in the landscape because she could not look at Mattie, but the pretense was no deception because nothing could check the tears that came flooding until she was forced to dry her eyes and blow her nose — tears not so much at the sadness of parting as of happiness and gratitude that the thing had happened to her. And Mattie who then still had a faint accent which she could hear again now, said, "A small bottle of champagne might help, Mrs. Parkington."

That was the only time Mattie ever betrayed for a moment that she understood all that had happened, that she too somehow saw *inside* things. From that moment until this when she sat here in the pew, an old woman, Mattie had never spoken his name or mentioned Bad Gastein. Only on the occasions of the Christmas parties when the little band came in to play Viennese waltzes, Mattie would never look at her. Sometimes she managed to disappear during the whole time the band was there and when that happened Mrs. Parkington never called upon her or made any effort to find her. There were times when Mrs. Parkington thought that Mattie had lived through those bright days of her adultery vicariously, half-believing that it was herself whom Eric loved.

She had never seen him again for she heard, quite casually and by accident, through a letter from Annie Pulsifer who suspected nothing, that he had been killed climbing in the Tyrol near Innsbruck. But by that time she knew that the thing between herself and Gus was beyond waning or destruction and the figure of Eric had become unreal like something in a dream.

And now she felt a nudge in her ribs and heard Mattie saying, "It's over, Mrs. Parkington." The others had risen and the undertaker's men were bustling about carting out the great bundles of flowers. She felt a sudden desire to say to Mattie, "You couldn't imagine where I have been during the services," but restrained herself. But she thought, How wonderful it is to have had a satisfying life, full of excitement to which one can return at moments of boredom.

There was still the dull business of the drive to the cemetery and the brief service at the grave. She felt that she must say, "Come along, Alice, and see the rest of it. It's very dull but a lot of people are enjoying it." Only of course you couldn't say that, because people would simply think you were crazy.

The organ was playing, but the magnificence of *Ein feste Burg* no longer filled tie church. It was an insipid evangelical hymn, vulgar and limited, and she thought again, And the king said, "But it's too bloody good for the common people."

XV

The death and funeral were a kind of interlude which interrupted the steady, busy flow of Mrs. Parkington's life and provided in a curious way a kind of holiday from responsibility. During those three days, the committee meetings, the appeals for help and funds, the troubles of all the family, had been put aside and nearly forgotten. For three days because there was death in her house, old Mrs. Parkington was permitted to lead a lazy life without cares, without the perpetual annoyance of the telephone and Miss Beasely's good intentions. She hated the telephone most of all and never spoke over it save when it was absolutely necessary and then only to communicate or to obtain information. The telephone she said, was the invention of the devil. It permitted people to intrude upon your privacy, to poke into your affairs, to derange your existence. There was no more reason for people to expect you to answer a telephone call than to expect you to welcome their barging into the room while you were in the midst of a bath.

But the morning after the funeral, it all began over again with the arrival of Miss

Beasely. There was a long list of things for Miss Beasely to do, and worst of all, Amory's trouble returned — more menacing than ever. Mrs. Parkington realized that really she had done nothing at all to cope with the situation and now Amory, as if paralyzed, had simply folded up and taken refuge in drink. While she had her breakfast she went quickly through the newspapers but found there nothing, not even a gossip paragraph, which had any bearing on the situation. The news of the world was not good; it was a sick world, it would go on being sick for the rest of her life and probably for the rest of the life even of a child like Janie. A little later she said to Miss Beasely, "I want to give a dinner. Will you send out notes to Dr. Fletcher and his wife, to Judge and Mrs. Everett, to Herbert Edmonds — he is in Washington now at the Mayflower — and to Count Sforza and the Dutch Minister. There will be some other names later as I think of them."

She thought, I'd like to be rid of the wives but there's nothing I can do about it. Wives of well-known men so often suffered from a deep sense of inferiority and took to asserting themselves, as they grew older, in all sorts of impossible and tiresome ways. I'm getting slack and lazy, she thought, it's time I pulled myself together and got interested again in the world. I've had too much of the family lately.

Miss Beasely, waiting with her pencil poised, asked presently, "What day, Mrs. Parkington?"

She reflected for a moment, "Make it in ten days. People are busy nowadays." She turned the pages of the date calendar on the table beside her. "Let's see. That would be Thursday the twenty-third. And please say that inasmuch as I am in mourning, the whole thing will be a simple dinner and no formality — simply a gathering of friends to talk." She gave a long list of other instructions and said at last, "And call Judge Everett and ask if he could come in about four o'clock. If you want me I'll be downstairs. I want to clear away some of the flowers. I can smell them all the way up here."

It was the fragrance of the lilies, heavy and rich, which troubled her. They were, in her mind, associated with funerals, and now that all the sad dreary business was finished, the sooner it was forgotten the better. Alice would not be forgotten; Alice would always be with her, a kind of perpetual reminder that somehow in spite of everything she had failed to help her own daughter. She had a curious feeling that Alice had at last moved into the house and was sharing it with her. At last, in death, Alice had come home.

A great many of the flowers, in pots, had been sent, not to the funeral but to Mrs. Parkington herself, and Taylor, proud of the tribute had put them everywhere, on tables, on the floor, in the fireplaces, while she had been occupied with other things. They were handsome expensive flowers but there were far too many of them. The house looked like a florist's shop and had a strange, exotic, suffocating smell.

She opened the pantry door and said to Taylor, "Will you call up the florist and ask him to send his delivery truck. I want to clear away some of the flowers. There are too many of them. If you'll help me I'll move out those I want sent to the hospitals. Some of them are too heavy for me."

Resentfully Taylor called the florist and then came to help her move out the heavier pots. He hated to see them sent away; it was as if somehow she was sending away her own prestige.

While they worked, Taylor said, "It was a fine funeral, madame. Very distinguished."

"Yes. Very distinguished." But by what she did not know.

And then suddenly she remembered that Madeleine and her cowboy had not been there. Madeleine had sent a wire from Nassau saying that she would come by plane but she had not arrived. She was sorry, not because of the family slight or because she missed Madeleine, but because she wanted to see Al again. As they moved out the last of the heavy-scented lilies, it seemed to her that she wanted to see Al's tanned, lean face and clear blue eyes more than anything in the world, more even than Ned and Janie.

Judge Everett came punctually at four but he brought no good news. As her lawyer he had talked with nearly all of the clients whose securities Amory had used and he had discovered a surprising thing — that most of them, even one or two who had been schoolmates of Amory, felt bitterly toward him. Out of eleven, two were out of town and could not be reached, four were willing to let the matter drop if Mrs. Parkington paid their loss but the others were for pushing the prosecution.

"It was very puzzling," the judge said. "I had not expected that attitude, especially from some of them. I imagine that all of them would have been even harder but for you. They were all very sorry that you should have this trouble. What is it Amory has done that has so set them against him? Most of them are friends or at least more than acquaintances."

Mrs. Parkington said, "Do you know Amory very well?"

"No . . . only casually."

"I think it was his pompousness. Only stupid people are ever pompous . . . no matter how high a station they occupy in life, you can always be sure that a pompous man is a stupid one who, sooner or later, will be found out. A few years ago Amory made a lot of money. He was insufferable. Caesar or Napoleon or Alexander the Great or God became less important to Amory than Amory Stilham. Now when he is in trouble, he has collapsed. Amory is, I'm afraid, a very tiresome fellow."

"Dick Weston," said the judge, his eyes twinkling with humor, "was very bitter. He said Amory should be punished for having let down his whole class at the very time when his class was being attacked."

"That's Harvard Club talk," said Mrs. Parkington.

As she spoke someone knocked at the door and Mrs. Parkington said, turning, "Come in."

The door opened and Mattie stood here. Mrs. Parkington noticed that her face was deep red. She was carrying a tabloid newspaper tightly folded as she came toward her mistress. She gave Mrs. Parkington the newspaper and said, "Cook just brought this in. I thought you would want to see it at once."

"Thank you, Mattie."

Mattie went out the door, closing it behind her and Mrs. Parkington opened the tightly folded paper. She knew exactly what she would find but she had not divined the bitter wording of the headline. It read:

GRAND JURY CHARGES RICH CHURCH AND CLUBMAN WITH GRAND LARCENY

Beneath it was a picture of Amory and Helen entering the ornate doorway of St. Bart's — a picture which must have been taken on an Easter Sunday, and a caption which read:

Amory Stilham, vestryman of St. Bart's Church, charged with theft by Grand Jury, accompanied by his wife as they entered the church last Easter Sunday.

She handed the paper to Judge Everett.

It had happened and now she was immediately troubled, not by the disgrace but by the vulgarity of the paper and the fact that she had been too late to warn Janie before it happened. She must find Janie at once; she might be anywhere on the street or in a shop or a hotel with people saying, "Her father has just been indicted!" They might be saying it even before Janie herself knew it.

She rose and said, "I'm going to leave you now, Judge. I must go to see Helen and Janie. There isn't anything we can do right now." Then she said, "Will you help with the trial?"

"I'm not a criminal lawyer and Amory hasn't asked me. You can count on me to help all I can."

"It would make a great difference in prestige and respectability."

He was thoughtful for a moment. "I'd rather be out of it, Susie, but if you think my name would help, I'd do it for your sake."

"I think it would help."

"My car is outside. I can drop you at Helen's."

"No, thanks. I'd rather go alone. There are so many things to think out."

She refused even to take Mattie. This time she was quite firm. There was quite a quarrel about it.

In the hallway of the Stilham house she was met by a chambermaid, one she had never seen before, for Helen was always changing servants. The girl looked at her in a stupid, frightened fashion as if there were murder in the house and then scuttled up the stairs.

While she waited, Mrs. Parkington thought, This is a gloomy house. It's as if there were invisible dust and cobwebs clinging to everything. What is it that makes it so dreary? She began to study the furniture bit by bit. There was nothing wrong with any of it, yet the whole was terrible. She thought, Poor Janie! and then the maid appeared again to say that Mrs. Stilham asked her to come up to her sitting-room.

The door was open and Helen was standing by the window looking toward the door, her face gray, even in the lamplight. The mouth sagged bitterly and there seemed to be new sharp lines drawn from the nostrils to the lips. As Mrs. Parkington came in, she simply said, "It's unbelievable. Why did Amory do it?"

It was curious that she did not even express a doubt concerning his guilt.

Mrs. Parkington said, "I came right over. Where is Janie?"

"I don't know. She lunched out today. She didn't tell me where. She never tells me anything any more since that boy came into her life."

"I want to find her."

Helen did not answer her. She said in anguish, "Why did he do it? How could he do it to us?" She blew her nose and added, "Do you really believe he did it, Grandmother?"

Mrs. Parkington sat down, "I'm afraid so, my dear. He told me so himself."

"You knew it all the time! And you never told me!" The fretful look turned to one of anger. "You might at least have tried to prepare us."

She saw that Helen was going to be difficult. Firmly she said, "Now try to pull yourself together, Helen. It's bad enough as it is. I didn't tell you because we hoped until the last minute that everything could be arranged."

"I suppose everyone in New York knew about it before me."

"I'm afraid a great many people knew something about it. Certainly the ones who had the money taken knew. And I don't imagine they held their tongues altogether. Even Cook heard about it. Judge Everett was working to straighten it out. He was working until the last minute. He was with me when Mattie brought in the newspaper."

Helen began to walk up and down. Suddenly she cried out, "It's that woman. I knew it would happen. It's that God-damned woman!"

"What woman?" Mrs. Parkington asked innocently.

"I don't know her name. She used to meet him in hotels in places like Buffalo and Kansas City."

"How did you know that?"

"I hired detectives. I knew something was happening. Twice they got the evidence."

"That was a vulgar thing to do. Why did you do it?"

"I had to know. I couldn't stand it any longer."

"Were you planning to get a divorce?"

"You know I don't believe in divorce."

"Then you were a very foolish woman as well as vulgar. Was it because you were jealous? Do you love Amory?"

"I wasn't jealous. I just had to know." She flung herself on the chaise longue where Janie had found her reading at four in the morning. "No, I don't love Amory. I don't think I ever loved him."

So it was like that, and here was another woman who had not loved at all, who had never given or forgiven anything. What if she had been married to Gus? But a man like Gus would have had no patience with her. He would have thrown her out. Aloud Mrs. Parkington said, "We are getting very far from the point. I can put your mind at rest. It wasn't the woman who ruined him. He never gave her anything and he took everything she had as well. It wasn't even as good as that. It was all just plain sordid."

Helen stopped crying and looked at her sharply, "How do you know that?"

"Because I've talked to her."

"Do you mean that you received her and tolerated her after you knew?"

"That's a ridiculous word 'tolerate.' I tolerate a lot of people worse than she is."

Helen was drying her eyes and blowing her nose. She was really a very sour, unattractive woman now. She asked, quietly, "What was she like?"

"A dull, commonplace, provincial little woman who must have been pretty once in a waitress kind of way."

"And he preferred her to me!"

"Maybe he didn't prefer her, Helen. I imagine she was restful and satisfied him. Amory isn't exactly what you'd call an intellectual." Then after a moment she asked, "Where is Amory?"

"He's with his lawyers."

"Do you know whether there will be any trouble about bail? That's one of the disagreeable things we have to consider."

"I don't know. I don't know anything about it. I don't want to know. I'm going to leave the house. Can I come and stay with you?"

Mrs. Parkington reached out and touched her granddaughter's hand. "Come now, Helen. You must keep your head. You can't do any of those things. You can't run out on him when he is in trouble."

"I won't see him. How could he have done this to me and the children?"

"I certainly can't have you in my house. I'm too old and cranky for that. And I think your place is here. If you don't believe in divorce, you can't consider leaving now."

"This is different."

"If you feel like this, divorce would have been a much more honest and honorable business."

She was aware that she was wasting time. It was Janie she must help, not this peevish, unreasonable woman whose life was already over, who would only undo everything you did to help her, who would only defeat herself eternally.

She said, "I am going to do three things. I am going to call Amory's lawyers to see about the bail business and then I'm going to call Janie's young man and then I'm going out and look for Janie."

Helen, she saw, would be of no use to her. She said, Where do you keep the telephone book?"

"It's there. Under the lower part of the table."

Mrs. Parkington picked it up. "Will you find the number, please?"

Sullenly Helen found the number and repeated it to her.

"You had better dial the number," said Mrs. Parkington. "I'm not certain that I'd do it correctly. I never telephone if I can help it."

But before Helen was able to take the telephone and dial the number, the bell rang and Mrs. Parkington said, "Shall I answer it?"

"I wouldn't. It might be those awful newspapermen. They've already called twice."

Mrs. Parkington only said, "I think I can manage them. I've done it pretty well all my life." The bell rang again, more insistently this time, and she took up the telephone and said, "Hello. This is Mrs. Stilham's house."

A familiar voice came back, "Is Miss Jane Stilham there?" and suddenly she felt a great sense of relief. It was Ned's voice, a deep voice, eager and anxious but comforting to her because it made her feel that she was no longer alone. The whole thing wasn't, as always all on her shoulders.

She said, "Is this Ned? This is Mrs. Parkington." And the voice came back, "Oh, I'm glad I got you, Mrs. Parkington. I'm trying to find Janie."

"She's not here. I'm trying to find her myself. Do you know where she had lunch?"

"She had lunch with me, downtown here. I left her about two o'clock. It's very important that I find her."

Mrs. Parkington saw that Helen was watching and listening, with a certain catlike intensity, so that she could hear Ned's resonant voice as well as her own. There was a curious expression of bitterness in her eyes.

Into the telephone Mrs. Parkington said, "It's the most important thing in the world. I was about to go out and look for her."

"Did you tell her anything?"

"No. I had meant to but I hadn't yet done it. Can you get away now?"

"That's what I'm counting on doing."

"You had better come to my house. She may come straight there." Across the telephone she saw the bitterness in Helen's eyes deepen and the drooping mouth twist with contempt. It was no time to save Helen's feelings. Only Janie mattered. Janie was young and would be hurt and bewildered and frightened. She said, "I'll leave word here for Janie to call me the moment she comes in."

"I'll come straight up . . . or I'll stop first at my flat. She might just have gone there."

"I'll be waiting for you."

As she put down the telephone, Helen said, "I don't see why you think she wouldn't come straight to her mother first."

Mrs. Parkington felt suddenly irritated. She asked, "Do you think she'll come straight to you first?"

Helen did not answer at once, then said, "That's where she should come. I've done everything for her. I've always tried to be a good mother."

"That has nothing to do with it," Mrs. Parkington said sharply. There was much more that she could have said but she held her tongue. If Helen chose to be truculent she could be more than a match for her.

"It's that boy," said Helen. "She's not been the same since she lost her head over him. He's brought nothing but bad luck to all of us."

Mrs. Parkington stood up, "I think that's a very silly attitude to take, Helen. The boy is certainly going to be your son-in-law. Behaving like that is not going to bring Janie any nearer to you." And even while she was speaking, she understood that behind the whining of Helen there was more than irritation. Helen was afraid. The whole of her empty secure life was falling apart and what she saw beyond frightened her. She was neither a clever woman nor a resourceful one. Mrs. Parkington for the first time felt sorry for her. Helen was alone now and she knew it. She was aware that she could not turn to her husband, her son or her daughter.

Mrs. Parkington said, "I think you ought to know that of course I'll go on doing all I can to help Amory. Judge Everett is going to help if Amory wants it and I'm going to pay back all the money, no matter what happens."

Helen's eyes were filled with astonishment. "Pay it back *now?* Pay it back even if they go on prosecuting Amory?"

"That has nothing to do with it. Amory stole the money. He as good as confessed it to me. I'll pay it back. It can come out of your share of the inheritance."

"I don't think that's fair."

You don't expect to ask Madeleine and Janie and Jack to pay it."

"I don't see why not. *I* didn't take the money."

It was fantastic, Mrs. Parkington thought, but there was no use going on with the discussion.

But Helen meant to go on with it. She said, "You certainly don't intend to pay back that woman?"

"I certainly do. Amory took everything she had."

Helen's mouth turned hard, "I certainly don't understand you. If the whole world was like you there'd be no morality at all."

Mrs. Parkington started to speak and then checked herself. There was no use in going on with the conversation. What was there in Helen's background, and the world in which she lived that had perverted all reason and common sense? She was quite as smug and amoral as Amory himself and just as bitter. Why was it that people like this who made their own troubles always whined loudest about them?

She said, "I'm going now, Helen. Call Amory's lawyers for me and say that I'm ready to do anything at all to help." Then she asked, "Where is Jack?"

"I don't know. He has had his own flat now for two weeks. I've scarcely seen him."

"What do you think he'll do?"

"How should I know?" asked Helen. "Nothing perhaps. I don't understand him, I'm afraid."

There seemed to be nothing more to do or say. Mrs. Parkington turned toward the door, "Tell Amory he can count on me in every way. I think you should both go out of town until it is necessary to come back. Only let me know where you go and what name you'll be using. It's the only way to avoid newspapermen and more trouble. Tell Amory to hire someone to look after that end of it. I don't trust him not to make a fool of himself." At the doorway she turned and said, "I certainly advise against your leaving him. It might just be that out of this will come a chance for you and Amory to come together again. It's something to consider. You're not yet forty-five. You have a long time to live yet, Helen. It might not be a bad idea to make something of it."

Then, before Helen could gather the full significance of what she had said, Mrs. Parkington left the room. She had left a good deal unsaid. She might have added, "In a way you're as much to blame as Amory. If you'd been a gay and amusing wife, if you'd ever tried to show him a good time, find for him things he'd enjoy and share with him the things he already enjoyed, he wouldn't have gone to the 'God-damned' woman and he might have understood that making money wasn't everything in life. He might not have gone out stealing because he found life so dull that making money was his only interest. You could have taught him many things but you didn't. There are so many things you didn't do. Even your sister Madeleine with all her husbands and lovers has done a better job of living than you. She at least doesn't live by denial but by affirmation."

The startled maid appeared from the back of the house to open the door, looking more wild-eyed than ever. I suppose, thought Mrs. Parkington, this is the first time she has served in the house of a major criminal.

In the car outside Hicks, the driver, was deeply absorbed in a newspaper, so deeply absorbed that he did not even hear the closing of the house door and jump down to open the door of the car. She knew what he was reading. No doubt at home Taylor and Cook and the kitchen maid were all doing the same thing — reading about Amory's disgrace and discussing it.

Taylor, like Mattie, she thought as the car drove off, had no liking for Amory. They resented his bluff, patronizing way of greeting them, his condescension when he talked with them. No one detected insincerity more quickly than a servant; no one resented it more. Amory's manner was a professional one, the manner taught at St. Bart's of a gentleman toward servants. It was bogus through and through, bogus and hearty and false because it was not founded upon simplicity but the affectation of it. Each time Mrs. Parkington saw him speaking to Mattie or Taylor, she felt slightly sick. It had never occurred to Amory that servants might also be friends. His social outlook was a very simple one, all in neat layers. No, neither Taylor nor Mattie would feel any sorrow for Amory's predicament.

In front of her own house, Hicks got down and opened the door and helped her out and then ran up the steps to ring the bell. She had never asked Hicks for these attentions. She had never asked anything of Mattie or Taylor or even Cook. There were many small extra things they did out of the kindness of their hearts. This touched Mrs. Parkington but not so much as the knowledge that if any of them was worried or in trouble they came to her before they went to any other friend. They had done so many times. They were both wise and kind, for they had never allowed the fact of all her wealth to create a barrier between her and themselves as vulgar people often did. They were neither awed nor impressed by it.

Now Hicks said quietly, "I'm very sorry about all this trouble Mr. Stilham is having.

I'm sure it will turn out all right."

"Thank you, Hicks. I hope it will."

"If there's any little thing I can do to help, Mrs. Parkington . . . I mean any special extra thing. I'll be glad to do it."

She smiled at him and said, "Thank you again. I know that." Then as he was turning away a sudden thought came to her and she said, "Would you like to go on quite a long trip with me out West a little later?"

"Yes, of course, Mrs. Parkington."

"Your wife wouldn't mind your being away two or three months?"

"No, Mrs. Parkington."

"Well, it's not definite. It's just an idea I had. I'll let you know if it develops."

Then she entered the house and Taylor said, "I'm very sorry about the trouble, madame. Cook said to tell you that's the way she felt too."

"Thank you, Taylor. No one has telephoned?"

"No one, I think."

"Mr. Talbot isn't here?"

"No, madame."

"When he comes take him into the sitting-room and let me know."

He went with her to the lift, saw her inside and as he closed the door, she asked, "Is there champagne on ice?"

"Yes, madame."

"When Mr. Talbot comes I'll have a split in the sitting-room. I'm a little tired. I don't know what Mr. Talbot will want. You might ask him when he comes."

Then he closed the door and pressed the button.

Upstairs Mattie was waiting for her, pretending to be occupied with putting fresh tissue paper in the drawers. Mrs. Parkington knew why she was hanging about instead of having her rest. She wanted to talk, so Mrs. Parkington said as she took off her hat and fluffed out her hair before the glass, "It's an unfortunate business, Mattie. I doubt that we can do anything to save him."

Mattie went on with her work. "I've never liked Mr. Stilham," she said. "I always thought he was a pompous humbug. But it's very hard on all the others. He had no right to bring all this trouble on the rest of you, especially you and Miss Janie."

"I'm afraid people don't think about that before they get into trouble. If they did there'd be a lot less of it."

Looking at herself in the glass she decided that she looked sallow and tired and, skillfully, so that Ned would not notice it, she put rouge on her cheeks and powdered her nose. In the mirror she saw Mattie was no longer making a pretense of working but was standing by the bureau watching her, and suddenly she knew what was troubling Mattie. Mattie was being devoured by curiosity about the woman who had called on the morning Alice was taken to the hospital. Since then there had been no time for Mattie to hint or practice her sometimes devious ways of finding out things.

So Mrs. Parkington, as she went on with her prinking, said quite casually. "That woman who came to see me just before we went to the hospital was a Mrs. Hobson. She lived in New Rochelle. Mr. Stilham had been living with her off and on for fourteen years." In the glass she saw in Mattie's reflected face a look of pleasure and release.

"I suppose he squandered a lot of money on her," said Mattie.

"No. On the contrary, he lost all *her* money."

Mattie made a clucking sound. "It's a very funny story," she said. "Mr. Stilham had every advantage in his life and look how he turned out."

"I'm afraid it was the advantages which ruined him, Mattie. He was taught by his family and school to believe that he had special privileges. Most men grow up and unlearn all that after a time but he never did. He still believes there's something wonderful and special about being a Stilham and belonging to all those clubs."

Mattie considered this for a time. Then she said, "I must say the woman seemed very ordinary and common. I should have thought he would have had better taste . . . that he'd at least have found something flashy. It has always seemed to me that if you were keeping a woman you ought to get something for your money. Of course with a wife it's different."

"I'm afraid," said Mrs. Parkington, "that she was just about his speed." She turned and stood up. "So you peeked that morning."

"Yes," said Mattie. "I peeked. I thought she must have had something to do with Mr. Stilham's trouble."

Then Taylor knocked and said that Mr. Talbot was downstairs.

The sight of his face filled her with extraordinary pleasure almost as if she had been a young woman meeting the man whom she loved very much. There was something so straightforward and nice about him, his face dark now with anxiety, the grave blue eyes troubled and full of pain. He held an envelope in his hand and as she came in, he said, "Janie had been to the flat but she had gone away again. I found this letter in the box." He opened the envelope and took out a sheet of paper marked with the name of the Ritz Hotel.

The note read:

> Darling Ned:
>
> It's no good. It isn't possible now. I can't go through with it. It would spoil everything for you. You certainly cannot marry me now. The whole thing would be too sensational. Don't try to find me. I promise I'll come back when I get used to the idea and talk it over with you. But if I were you I'd just try to forget the whole thing. Just pretend you never met me or knew me. Love,
>
> Janie

Without raising her eyes, Mrs. Parkington said, "It reads like something out of *True Love Stories*."

When she put down the note she found herself looking into Ned's blue eyes. They were questioning her, pressing her for some sort of an answer. She said, "It's a very foolish childish note. Sometimes Janie can be very childish."

"You don't think she'd do anything foolish?" he asked.

"No. I don't think that. She isn't that kind. She's an emotional girl but very steady too with a great capacity for pain." She did not say exactly what she was thinking. What she thought was that Janie was extraordinarily like herself and that at Janie's age she would possibly have acted exactly as Janie had acted. Look how easily she had accepted Gus, so easily that he married her without meaning to. But that was very lucky. . . . She said, "I think the important thing is for us to find her as quickly as possible."

"What shall we do? I've tried to think of everything. Maybe you have some idea where she might have gone. I hate to think of her alone on a train somewhere or in a hotel bedroom."

"There's only one thing. The police mustn't know anything about it. We can't go to them. The papers would love a story like that — 'Clubman's Daughter Flees Father's Disgrace.' I haven't the faintest idea where she could have gone."

Then Taylor knocked and brought in the champagne and when she asked Ned what he wanted, he said, "Nothing at all, thanks."

"But that's foolish," said Mrs. Parkington. "You'd better have some champagne in any case." And without waiting for his answer she told Taylor to bring more champagne.

When Taylor had gone out she asked Ned, "How do you feel about it yourself?" But knew at once that it was a silly question.

"I mean to marry Janie," he said. "This doesn't make any difference at all. She had a lot of crazy ideas about her being rich making a difference, but I could manage that. That didn't worry me. It only worried me because it seemed to make her unhappy. She worries about a lot of silly things."

Mrs. Parkington smiled, "One or the other of you has got to give up worrying. Two worriers in a family is impossible."

Then Taylor came in with more champagne and went out again and Ned said, "I'll stay away from the office until we've found her. I'll go every place she might possibly go to hide."

"Can you stay away from the office?"

"I'll send word that I'm ill and can't come in."

An idea began to take form in Mrs. Parkington's brain. She asked. "Who is your big boss in Washington?"

"Holman Drury."

She said, "Oh, yes, of course." She did not say that she knew Holman Drury, lest she make the boy suspicious. She only said, "Of course, it was stupid of me to have forgotten that. Is he very difficult?"

"He's always been very nice to me. I think he likes me."

"Then if it was necessary, it wouldn't be too difficult to arrange a leave of absence — I mean if we didn't find Janie right away?"

"No — probably not. I wouldn't want to ask it unless it was necessary."

And while she was speaking she was putting together all the things she knew about Holman Drury — that he was untidy in appearance but had a brilliant mind, that he had gone to Princeton and had a rich father, that all this was why Amory had always reserved for him a special spite and hatred. Amory said that Holman Drury had betrayed his class, that he was therefore one of the worst men in Washington. She remembered Holman Drury's mother and his grandparents who thought he had lost his mind when he turned out to be a crusader.

Her nimble wits were leaping ahead, planning what was to be done after Janie was found. Janie, she suspected, would be abysmally stubborn as she herself had sometimes been stubborn with Gus.

Aloud she said, "I think the best course would be to engaged the services of a detective bureau. They could put three or four men on the job. Sometimes they are very good at such things."

At this idea he seemed to brighten and the misery to go out of his eyes.

"I doubt if it's any use counting on Janie's parents," she said. "They seem too much upset by everything. I'll call my lawyer and arrange it. You had best stay here and dine with me."

"Could you call your lawyer now?" he asked. "I could call him for you."

"He's Judge Everett. His number is in the little book there by the telephone."

While he turned to the number she said, "You know I think it would be a good idea if you came here and stayed in the house until we find her. There is plenty of room and it will be more convenient for both of us." For some reason, perhaps because it was still difficult for her to feel that she was an old woman, she felt shy and waited for him to become occupied with the telephone before she made the suggestion.

He dialed the number and while he was waiting he said, "Thank you. I think it's an excellent idea. Then we wouldn't have to be calling each other all the time."

In a moment she was speaking to the judge, apologizing for always causing him trouble because of her family. He agreed to come to dinner. He would try to come early and bring the head of the detective bureau with him. They could go to work at once, the sooner the better. Had they any idea of where she might have gone? No. That would make it difficult.

It was nice having Ned in the house. And it pleased Mattie. After the judge had gone and Ned had gone out in the wild hope that he might find someone somewhere in the city who had seen Janie, Mrs. Parkington and Mattie sat up for a long time talking. They always found a great deal to discuss but to-night both of them, each with a fear of betraying it to the other, sat up hoping that Ned would come in before they were in bed, that he might have news, that they might talk with him. It was almost as if the two old women had gone back forty years to the time when Herbert and Eddie came home late from parties to look for the light under their mother's door and come in to talk about the evening. They had left the door of the boudoir ajar so that they might hear the street door open when Ned came in.

Mattie was worried about Janie. She kept saying, "It's not like her. She's such a sensible girl."

Mrs. Parkington smiled, thinking about herself at Janie's age, about how dove-like and quiet she had appeared to be. She said,

"She's that way on the surface, Mattie, but underneath she's a seething torrent of romance. And she has too much imagination. How what has happened affects her is very difficult for us to understand. We're both old and tough and in our hearts we both know that even if Mr. Amory goes to prison it won't make very much difference in Janie's life, if she chooses to keep control of things. She's at the age when people suffer most, when little things become overwhelming tragedies. After all what is happening to her isn't easy to take."

While they sat there, Mrs. Parkington found herself wishing Aspasie was with them. Aspasie always gave you a feeling of confidence because she had a clear sharp realistic way of dealing with everything. She always considered all the elements, made an analysis, and acted in a straightforward resolute fashion, just as she had acted at the time the boys died and when Alice was divorced and it became necessary to blackmail the Duke. But Aspasie had been dead for fourteen years, dead in her bed of a stroke in the great château in Fifth Avenue. When she died, something went out of Mrs. Parkington's life which could not be replaced, something of wit and intelligence and bravery and style. It was extraordinary how chic Aspasie had remained, even as a very old woman. She was chic even lying in her coffin, leaving behind a debt for Susie Parkington which could never be repaid. There were many things in her life which Mrs. Parkington could not perhaps have survived or even endured but for the wisdom of Aspasie. Aspasie always preached that no woman should ever put all her egg in one basket, since if one dropped the basket everything was lost, and so Susie had learned to spread her affections over many people and her interests over many fields, and by doing so had come, like Aspasie, to find the world a wonderful and fascinating place in which there was so much to be enjoyed and understood that the wise never despaired and were never defeated.

Opposite Mrs. Parkington, Mattie had begun to doze in her armchair and Mrs. Parkington, feeling there was no longer any reason to pretend that they were sitting up because they were fascinated by each other's conversation, said, "I think I'll go to bed, Mattie. There's no use sitting up any longer. There's no telling when he'll come in. If there had been any news he would have telephoned."

While Mattie was helping her mistress get ready for bed, they heard the sound of footsteps on the stairway. He had come back but he had no news. He had found no one who had seen her.

For the first time Mrs. Parkington was frightened, although she was careful not to betray her feelings. Bravely she said, "I'm sure she's simply hiding out in some strange place like Philadelphia or Atlantic City. Try to get some sleep. I'm sure there will be good news in the morning."

And as he left she thought, Janie mustn't lose him. She mustn't lose him. She mustn't be a little fool. And she mustn't go back again to that awful house.

She had forgotten until the moment she entered Amory's house how bad it was, how terrible for the children who had grown up there and had been forced to live in it. She herself never went there if she could avoid it, but she saw now that somehow she should have rescued Janie. Until Helen stood there, whining and bitter and naked suddenly of all pretense, she had never known how bad it was. It was terrible how a house could be affected by the people who lived in it, and how in turn it could affect them. Houses certainly had auras, created by what had happened within their walls. As she grew older she had become aware of this. The house in England where Gus had taken up with Norah Ebbsworth had had an unhappy aura, as if there were a curse upon it. Within its walls "the terrible summer" had begun. If she had known then what she knew now, she would never have taken it. From the moment she and Gus walked through the door she had known, even then, that it was, like Amory's house, an evil one.

As she said good night to Mattie she added, "Don't bother to call me, Mattie, unless there's news of Miss Janie. I'll sleep late. I could do with a little sleep."

"I'm glad you're showing some sense."

Then as she went out Mattie turned and said with a sudden extraordinary passion, "You won't let him get away from her, will you, Mrs. Parkington? It would be terrible if she lost a boy who feels as he does. You can see it in his eyes. You can fix it if you try. You've fixed a lot of things in your life."

"I'll do all I can, Mattie."

She got into bed and put out the light at once, for she was very tired, more tired, she thought, than she had ever been in all her life. At last she fell asleep wishing still that Aspasie were here to help her.

All the next day there was no news. In the morning Helen, apparently alarmed at last, came in to spend a peevish hour with Mrs. Parkington. She was still fretful because

Janie had not turned to her instead of running off alone, and then just as she was leaving Jack appeared.

It was the first time his mother had seen him since the awful news and she asked at once, "Where have you been?"

"In my flat mostly. I couldn't very well go out where I'd see people."

"That's a strange attitude to take and very disloyal. There's no reason to suppose that your father is guilty. He's the victim of persecution."

Mrs. Parkington said nothing, waiting for them to finish their squabble. Jack did not answer his mother. Instead he addressed Mrs. Parkington. "I don't think Mother understands," he said. "I don't really owe my father anything. He never forgave me because I didn't make his damned clubs. He always forced me to do things I didn't like, things I didn't want to do. He wouldn't let me go on with music. He wanted me to be a football player and be elected to all the clubs. I don't give a damn about that and I never did. I'm really not any relation to him. I'm like the crazy Blairs. From now on I'm going to do as I please."

"You see what he's like?" said Helen, her mouth drooping.

"I've really come to say good-bye to you,

Granny. I'm going to Canada this afternoon to join the air force."

Mrs. Parkington's heart gave a great leap. He, too, then, was going to escape before it was too late! There was in the handsome, rather decadent face, a look of bitterness and dissipation that was horrible in so young a boy. Perhaps, she thought, he'll manage to lose that. Perhaps he wasn't as bad, as worthless as he seemed. Perhaps it was only Amory and Helen and the frame into which they had tried to force him that had made him wild and vicious — that idiotic frame which had deformed their own generation with its snobbery, its imitation of English standards, its utter lack of relation to anything real or American. It was as false as Amory himself and now it was being smashed with all the wealth which had made possible its imbecility.

She heard Helen saying, "At least you're going to say good-bye to your father."

"I'm not going near him. I wouldn't care if I never saw him again. You can tell him that for me. You can tell him I'm sorry that I'm any relation to him."

"Jack!" said Mrs. Parkington, softly.

"It's true, Granny. He never did anything for me. He was always a humbug, always even in the days when I was a kid in school and he would lead the school in prayer and then back in my room he'd knock me around because I hadn't made the football team. He used to yell at me, 'I'm ashamed to have such a sissy for a son. I was a big man in my school. Why can't you be?" He turned suddenly to his mother. "You never knew that, did you? Well he did all that and a lot more. And look at him now. I knew he was like that all along." Then he looked away from Helen and said in a low voice, "And so did you."

He glanced suddenly at Mrs. Parkington, "You see, Granny, I never had a real home. I used to go on visits to friends whose families were happy and everyone had a good time. In our house no one even smiled. Sometimes we'd sit through a whole meal without anyone at the table speaking. And all the time everybody was pretending to the outside world that we had a lovely devoted home life when it was about as lousy as it could be." Helen did not answer him. After a moment Mrs. Parkington said quietly, "What about Janie?"

He looked up at her and she saw that his eyes were filled with rage and tears. "You mean about her getting lost? She'll turn up. Janie is tougher than I was. She has more sense too. She's always known enough to do what she wanted, without asking him. Only let me know when she turns up. I'll wire you from Canada as soon as I know where I'll be." He came over to her and shyly bent down and kissed her cheek. "Good-bye, Granny. Write me the news sometimes."

Then he took his mother's hand and said, "Good-bye, Mother, I'll let you know my address," and went quickly out of the house.

When he had gone, Helen began to cry in a curious, childish, helpless fashion and suddenly she seemed very like Alice, although Alice, even in her most unhappy moments was never shrewish.

For a time Mrs. Parkington sat watching her, saying nothing, thinking, Perhaps if she cries, it will calm her. But the crying only seemed to grow worse until Mrs. Parkington said, "What are you and Amory planning to do?"

"We can't do anything until we find Janie. Then we'll go away to the Bensons' camp in the Adirondacks. You see Amory can't leave the state."

"No. Of course not."

"You don't think Janie has done anything foolish, do you?"

"No. That kind of thing isn't in Janie." But she wasn't so certain now after the outburst of Jack. Suddenly he had lifted a curtain and let in the light and what she saw there was terrifying.

She said, "I think you'd better go home now, Helen. Is Amory at home?"

"Home!" said Helen bitterly. "Home? That dead house with Amory sitting in his room drinking himself insensible!"

"He'll get over that."

"It doesn't much matter." Helen spoke with a dull indifference and Mrs. Parkington thought, It isn't possible that she is as dead as that. And then she saw what really lay behind the remark — that Helen, without being honest enough to admit it, would not be displeased if Amory drank himself to death before the ultimate disgrace of a public trial. There were people who believed that one had one's hell on earth, and it seemed now to Mrs. Parkington that this was what she was witnessing in the lives of her granddaughter and her husband. She thought, Nothing that ever happened to me — not even the death of the boys — was as bad as this. Death was sharp and clean and made no compromises and in the end one learned to accept it, but this other thing was hideous because it went on and on devouring happiness and health and decency and self-respect.

She heard herself saying, 'I was wrong the other day when I said I didn't want you in this house, Helen. I was worried and overwrought and I apologize now. If ever you should want to come here I hope you will come and think of this house as your own, just as you did when you were a child. Whatever is mine is yours." She could not help herself. It had to be done just as one had to help a stray dog wounded and suffering in the gutter.

Helen stared at her for a moment and then her eyes filled with tears again, "Thank you, Grandmother. I shan't come now. I'm going to stick with Amory until this is all finished one way or another. If . . . if . . . the worst should happen I would like to come here. I should like to be under your wing for a little time anyway. It's very good of you." She stood up and said, "I think I'll go home now."

"I'll call you the minute there's any news of Janie."

"And thanks for taking all the trouble about her. What she did is very selfish and it's really my responsibility but I appreciate all you've done."

"I haven't done anything really. It's all been done by Ned." They were moving toward the door now and Mrs. Parkington went right on talking. It seemed the best way to say what she had to say, very casually, "I think, too, Helen, that you should know the boy better. Janie is very lucky . . . as lucky as a girl could be. You must remember that the world is very different from what it was when you were her age, and Janie is going to live her life in a world which is still more different. The old things are breaking up. What has happened to Amory is a part of it. The advantages Amory had — what people called 'advantages' — have become disadvantages in this new world."

"Perhaps," said Helen dully, as if she wished to dismiss the whole thing, because she was desperately weary of it. There was little use in talking to her in this vein. It was as if one spoke Greek. It occurred to Mrs. Parkington that nothing on earth was so provincial as the New Yorker of Helen's and Amory's sort.

Evening came and there was still no news or even the faintest clue as to what might have happened to Janie or where she might have gone. It was a busy day, for which Mrs. Parkington was thankful. She saw Judge Everett again and told him about Mrs. Hobson and how the money Amory had lost for her must be paid back, and she had to go through the tiresome business of arranging for the restoration of the stolen funds to all the other clients and friends. And there were many things to do with Miss Beasely. For a time she considered calling off the dinner she had planned, but in the end she rejected the idea. Despite the scandal she must go on living exactly as she had always done; she must, above all, preserve the prestige she had won and the place she had made for herself, since these things would provide a shelter for Helen and be a help to Amory when it came to the point of seeing the thing through to the bitter end. She saw very clearly the dread duty which lay before her. When the time came she would have to go and sit in the courtroom beside Helen day after day until it was over. Whatever Amory had done, however great a hypocrite he was, however great a scamp, he was a part of the family and the father of Janie and Jack, in whose veins flowed her own and Gus' blood. The least she could do was to bring him as much dignity as possible.

And through the whole of the busy day between appointments and plans and dictating letters, her mind kept returning to one thing — what was it that had blighted the lives of nearly everyone in her family? She had done her best, however poor that was, and yet somehow, she felt, she had failed. Gus and even she perhaps had spoiled their own children day in and day out. Parents had done so since the beginning of time, yet spoiled children sometimes turned out to be satisfactory and brilliant. It was certainly a pity that Alice had started off her career with the Duke, but perhaps it was a blessing that she had never had any children, just as it was unfortunate that Herbert had chosen to marry a Blair with the eccentric, melancholy taint that ran through all that family. How Herbert and Eddie would have turned out, she would never know, since fate had cheated her there during "the terrible summer."

The more she considered all her life and the lives of the family, the more the finger of evidence pointed always toward money. But for Gus' great wealth and ambitions, Alice would never had met the Duke and married him. He would not even have wanted to marry her. But for the money, Alice would never have had a remittance man for a second husband and an idle feeble man for a third. But for the money Alice might have carried through her idea of becoming a nurse. She might have found a husband who suited her and with him found a peaceful useful existence. But for all the money, Herbert would never have met and married the Blair girl or bought the automobile which killed him at the time when automobiles were fantastic luxuries. But for the money, Eddie would not have gone wild and come to a tragic bitter death. But for the money Madeleine would not have been able to lead her wild, empty vicious life nor satisfy in a shameless open fashion her insatiable desire for men. And Helen would never have met Amory with all his "advantages" and married him because he was the catch of the season. It was always the money; down whatever alley or bypath her mind wandered during the long day, always at the end of it was the money. It was there still, increasing faster than she could give it away or taxes could devour it. It was like a monster created by Gus which had destroyed all the things the son of a vilage grocer had wanted most in life for himself and his descendants. He had wanted to be a founder, a great figure who left behind him descendants who would be distinguished and a glory to his name and memory.

And now look at the damned thing!

There was, she thought too, something wrong with American life during the long span of her existence, something wrong with American education, creating a tradition which confused automobiles and water closets with civilization, which corrupted decent standards and set up monstrous values. It was like Amory thinking there was something distinguished in being a stockbroker, like automobile manufacturers who believed they were messiahs and had brought about the millennium, like men believing that intelligence and honor, civilization and wisdom could be bought at so much a pound.

Dimly, as through a mist, she began to see that there was some logical connection between all these things and the creaky straining collapse of the world founded upon their falsity that was going on all about her. She thought, That is something I would like to discuss with minds clearer and than my own. And she called Miss Beasely and added to the list for dinner the names of one philosopher and one economist. There was so much still to be learned and understood, and the time was so short.

Four times during the day Ned called to say that he had no news nor any clue and the detectives had been no more successful than himself. His voice sounded tired and dead and she knew that he, like herself, was beginning to have dreadful doubts — that perhaps Janie *had* done something foolish, that perhaps in the end they would find not Janie but only a body floating in the river. But neither of them even hinted at such doubts in the conversations over the telephone. There was an extraordinary understanding between them. Mrs. Parkington sometimes felt when they talked, that they would have understood each other just as well without words. He had a kind of instinctive wisdom and an intuition with which only a few people, she knew, were blessed.

At seven he called to say that the detectives had found a man at the Pennsylvania Station who thought that he remembered selling a ticket to Philadelphia to a girl who fitted the description of Janie. He noticed her, he said, because she seemed to have been crying.

"I'm sure we'll find her very shortly," said Mrs. Parkington, over the telephone. "I have a feeling in my bones."

When she put down the receiver she called Taylor and said that she would have dinner in bed.

While she ate Mattie hovered about the two rooms performing all sorts of needless tasks and fussing over the tray. It was, Mrs. Parkington knew, her way of saying that she too was troubled and that she understood all the anxiety of her mistress.

She said again, "When Miss Janie is found you must go away on a trip. What you need is to get out of town and away from the whole family."

Mrs. Parkington laughed. "It always seems to be one more thing. After Mr. Amory it was Janie and after Janie it will no doubt be something else."

"You've got to be strong. You've got to walk out on all of them."

"That isn't always easy to do, Mattie."

"You're too soft — that's what you are."

So Mattie was going to begin all over again.

She tried not to listen to Mattie's grumbling. She was thinking, I only hope Janie is as much like me as I think she is. If she's really like me she'll be all right. She'll come back. It was odd that never once in her life, never even at the moments of bitter unhappiness, had she ever thought of suicide. The idea just wasn't there . . . very likely because she had a very sound liver and a well-balanced set of glands.

Then she heard the distant ringing of the doorbell. The sound came to her from the outside through the windows on the garden, as it always did when Cook left the pantry door open on a warm evening. The bell rang again and again urgently, before Taylor reached the door to open it.

Sitting up in bed Mrs. Parkington thought, It's something to do with Janie. Oh, please God, let it be nothing bad. Please God! And for the first time in her life she thought, This is the one more thing I cannot endure. If this was bad news, she would simply take to her bed and die because she had no more force to go on.

Through the doorway into the boudoir, she saw that Mattie's curiosity had overcome her. She was standing in the hallway peering down the stairs. From Mattie's stolid faithful body she could tell, perhaps, what it was. The seconds passed, unbearable seconds, each one heavy and slow and unendurable. And then she saw Mattie turn toward her and come hurrying across the boudoir, her broad face smiling. She could not even wait until she entered the room but called out, "It's Miss Janie! It's Miss Janie herself, Mrs. P.!"

She looked pale and tired and a little sheepish as she came through the doorway with Mattie following her. She came directly to the bed and without saying a word kissed her grandmother and said, "I'm very ashamed of myself, Granny."

"Sit down . . . here on the bed beside me. It doesn't matter now."

"Where's Ned?"

"Where do you suppose? Out looking for you. You won't be able to reach him anywhere. He's living here in the house. He'll be in some time tonight. Here, give me your hand."

Mrs. Parkington was trembling now, simply from excitement as if, instead of being a very wise old woman, she was herself a young girl alarmed and a little bewildered at the prospect of all the living which lay ahead of her. And Mattie was standing there trembling too and crying like an old fool. Now Mattie said, "Maybe you'd like something to eat, Miss Janie. A sandwich and some tea. I could make it in a minute."

Janie smiled at Mattie. "I'd love a sandwich and some tea. I didn't have any dinner. You see I ran out of money."

"You poor little darling," said Mattie.

"Come! Come! Mattie," said Mrs. Parkington, "get yourself in hand."

"I'll go right now and fetch it. Cook will be glad to hear you're back. Taylor was glad too, wasn't he, Miss Janie?"

Janie laughed, "He looked as if he thought he was seeing things."

"Then run along, Mattie," said Mrs. Parkington, "so you can hurry back and not miss anything."

So Mattie hurried out and Mrs. Parkington said, "Here, kiss me again." And she put her thin arms about the girl and hugged her. "I knew you wouldn't do anything silly. I knew you were *my* Janie." She said, "And now I think you'd better call your mother."

"Oh, Granny. I don't want to go back to

that house. I can't. Will you let me stay here?" There was real fear in her voice and now, after the talk with Helen, Mrs. Parkington understood the fear. The poor child had gone on and on all this time never once betraying what really took place in that gloomy house.

Janie picked up the telephone and with her free hand she held tightly the thin blue-veined hand of her great-grandmother. When her mother answered on the other end of the wire, she said, "It's Janie. I'm all right. I'm at Granny's."

Then Helen said something and Janie answered, "No. Don't come over tonight. Granny's in bed and I'm going to have a bath and go to bed too. I'll be home in the morning."

Again Helen said something and Janie answered, "But I'm all right. There's nothing to worry about: I'll come over early in the morning." Then Helen interrupted and Janie said, "Don't be difficult, Mother. Everything is absolutely all right. Please don't begin all over again."

Mrs. Parkington knew what Helen was saying. Her voice would be full of reproach and injured vanity. There was only one thing that mattered now and that was for Ned and Janie to come together again. Nothing must prevent that. Silently she shook her head at Janie and her lips formed the words, "Don't give in."

At last Janie was able to speak. She asked, "How is Father?" And after a moment Janie said, "Then I'll see you in the morning. Good night and don't worry."

As the girl turned from the telephone she seemed limp and exhausted as if somehow, even by way of a telephone wire, her mother had managed to drain all her vitality.

"You're not going on with this foolishness about not marrying Ned," said Mrs. Parkington.

"I don't know. He's so queer. He'd want to marry me even if it ruined everything for him. That's why I came straight here to you. I wanted to talk it over with you. I don't want to give him up. I can't Granny . . . I can't . . . I don't know what to do."

"You were a foolish girl to run away. It never solves anything and it was very hard on Ned."

Janie didn't answer her. She only sat there like a naughty child being scolded, looking down at her hands. And suddenly Mrs. Parkington understood that Janie really *was* a child, that the strangeness of her life had kept her a child. Now her great-grandmother thought, At her age I was already a woman. I knew hardship and worry and responsibility. I knew all the things that went on the length of Main Street in Leaping Rock, in the gambling dens and brothels. I knew people as people — good, bad, tough, rotten, decent and indecent. I could look at a man or woman and know pretty well what they were up to. But Janie — Janie didn't really know anything much. Everything in her life had conspired to shut her away from reality. Whatever had happened to her was enveloped in falseness.

"Tell me," said Mrs. Parkington, "what happened? How did you come to run away?"

She knew that the answer would cause pain to Janie, but that would be good for her, like cauterizing a wound. She would have to be cured of the impulse to run away from things.

The girl swallowed and looked away from her great-grandmother. Then she said, "I had lunch with Ned and afterward I went to the British War Relief and about four o'clock I left to go home and write some letters and I was walking along Fifty-fourth Street when I heard a newsboy yelling something about 'a prominent clubman indicted' but I didn't pay much attention to it. I hardly heard it. And then at Madison Avenue I stopped, waiting for the light and I happened to look at a newsstand and there I saw on the front page of the *Globe* a big picture of mother and father." She stopped suddenly and began to cry and Mrs. Parkington took her hand and said, "I know it's hard, my dear. But go on and tell me. It will clear up things in your head."

With a great effort Janie began again, "I knew the picture because it was one that appeared in the *Times* on Easter but I couldn't believe it. I looked at it again and then saw it was certainly mother and father on the steps of St. Bart's." She stopped again and Mrs. Parkington patted her hand gently, "I thought I was going to faint and then I thought, I can't do that. It would only make it worse. So I went into the drugstore and ordered a soda. I don't know whether I drank it or not. I just sat there. I couldn't even think. All that went through my head was, I must go away and hide. I must go away and hide somewhere . . . anywhere! I don't know how long I stayed there but after a time I knew what I meant to do. I went to the Ritz and wrote a note and took it to Ned's flat and put it in the mailbox and then I went to the Pennsylvania Station and I thought, I'll go to Atlantic City! They'll never think of looking for me there. And everywhere I looked was that picture or some newsboy yelling about 'prominent clubman' and I was afraid of meeting someone I knew who would be sorry for me and want to talk.

I didn't meet anyone. I don't think anyone saw me. On the train I went into the day coach because I knew I wouldn't see anybody there I knew and because I didn't have much money. And when I got to Atlantic City I went to a hotel. I didn't eat anything. I couldn't have eaten. I went to my room and locked the door and tried to think things out. And the more I tried to think, the worse it got. It wasn't only the thing about Father itself, but there was Ned too. He couldn't marry a daughter of Amory Stilham. The newspapers would make a terrible story of it. The whole thing would be notorious and awful, with newspapermen and cameras and everything. I wanted to die but that wasn't possible either. And I didn't want to give up Ned. Oh, Granny, it was terrible! And this afternoon I came to the conclusion that I didn't have enough sense to decide anything for myself and that I ought to come and talk to you, so here I am.

As she finished the story, the figure of Mattie carrying a tray appeared in the doorway. There was much more on it than a sandwich and a cup of tea. There was a cup of broth and buttered toast and an omelet under a china cover, and cold chicken and lettuce and mayonnaise and fruit and a large piece of cake.

Mattie brought it over and put it on the table beside the bed and as she put it down, she said, "There now, Miss Janie. You mustn't cry like that. It's all going to turn out all right. I've brought you something to eat. Cook said you ought to have something hot so she got up and fixed this for you. You must eat it or you'll hurt Cook's feelings."

Janie said, "Thank you, Mattie. I think I can eat it. I haven't had anything but a chocolate bar since yesterday."

"That's a good girl," said Mattie. "You'll get your young man and everything will turn out all right."

Mrs. Parkington, watching Mattie, tried not to smile. She said, as Mattie prepared to leave, "You needn't go, Mattie. We're trying to arrange things. You might be able to help." And Mattie seated herself happily to watch Janie eat and hear what was going to happen. She said, "Cook says if that's not enough, she'll make up another omelet."

"It's plenty, thanks," said Janie.

She was already eating, hungrily. Mrs. Parkington thought, That's fine. When she has some food in her she'll make more sense. Once she stopped eating to say, "Do you think Ned will be in soon?"

"I don't know, my dear. He might not come

in till after midnight." Then Mrs. Parkington thought, I've got a big job to do. I've not only got to make her marry Ned but right away — tomorrow. And I've got to fix it so that no one knows and they've both got to get out of town quickly.

To Janie she said, "You are going to marry Ned and there's to be no nonsense about it."

"I don't know how he feels."

"I do. I know very well. There's nothing to worry about concerning his future. You'll have plenty of money."

Janie looked up at her. "Don't talk about the money, Granny. I hate it. In that dreary hotel I thought about a lot of things. And I thought about money too and I hated all the money we've always had. It was money that got Father into trouble. Anyway money isn't any good so far as Ned is concerned. That isn't what he wants."

"I know that isn't what he wants. I'm merely being practical, my dear. You can't starve to death and sleep in the gutter. Money has never meant anything to you because it was always there, and now you want to get rid of it . . . but unfortunately you have to have it now and then."

There was tartness in her voice, partly born of irritation roused by Janie's highfalutin' speech and partly born of the knowledge that she had to destroy this whole fantastic point of view. She remembered herself at Janie's age; she knew then what money was and what it was worth. She knew about mortgages and interest and debts and the possibility of being turned into the street out of the Grand Hotel in Leaping Rock, and she knew how much work it took to produce that money, work which broke the back and calloused the hands and dimmed the eyes. She remembered her own dreams of great houses and restaurants and jewels and all the things that could be bought with money.

"If you had to work for money, you would know what it is worth." She added, "You mustn't be a little fool."

"I wish I could work for money," said Janie. "I've always wanted it more than anything. But it seems sort of silly to work for it when you've already got more than you knowwhat to do with."

"Yes," said Mrs. Parkington, feeling that she had been answered, "there is a great deal of truth in that. Indeed the whole thing is fairly obvious, but that doesn't solve anything. It's like a lot of other things in the world . . . people sit around telling you that obvious disaster is obvious, but frequently they don't do much about it."

* * *

It was Mattie's slightly deaf ears which heard the sound of the bell in the yard below the window. Perhaps the others failed to notice it because they were both lost and enchanted by the new intimacy which had arisen between them. For a long time, since Janie had ceased to be a little girl, she and her great-grandmother had been feeling their way toward the Janie who was no longer a child or a *backfisch* but a grown, sensible woman. The relations between very old and very young people are simple enough; the one should have acquired simplicity and directness, the other has not yet had his simplicity corrupted. Adolescents only understand each other and are misunderstood by all the world because to children they seem incomprehensible and to older people merely comic or silly. Their sufferings, more tragic, more hopeless than are any sufferings which ever come to them again seem, like childbirth, to be dimmed in a kind of haze in the memories of older people. Afterward, as with women who have passed through childbirth, people like to talk of their adolescence, perhaps because in both adventures there is an ultimate clarity, an ultimate reality of suffering which they never again attain.

And so Mrs. Parkington, watching Janie change from a child to an awkward bumptious young girl, too plump, with braces on her teeth (which came from the Blair side) had tried to understand all the morbid, ingrowing suffering of a creature who was miserable without understanding why she was miserable or being able to do anything about it. But this, with Mrs. Parkington's wisdom and hardness, was not easy to do. She had a feeling that somehow she had failed as long ago she had failed with Alice. Adolescence, she knew, was in some ways the loneliest, saddest time in one's existence, especially if one was a woman. Unless one was simply marked for futility or sluttishness. Amory had probably had a very happy, triumphant adolescence, so successful indeed that for the rest of his life he had clung to it, seeking always to return to that period in which he was a leader because he had great physical strength and could bully others. And Madeleine, earmarked for sluttishness since the age of ten, had found adolescence uncomplicated because her purpose in life was always clear and simple. It was men she wanted, men who were to be her whole existence. And so she had never been complicated or unhappy or given much trouble save for using lipstick at the age of twelve and leading boys out onto the fire escape at assemblies. It seemed to Mrs. Parkington that a carefree adolescence marked you later in life for stupidity or sluttishness. And she had never been very interested in Amory's kind of achievements nor Madeleine's direct assaults upon men.

But Janie had troubled her and so, when Janie stood in the doorway and said, "I'm very sorry, Granny. I've been very stupid," the old woman was happy because she saw suddenly that Janie was emerging from the fog of uncertainty and misery which had held her captive for a long time. Janie was becoming a woman. The running away was perhaps her last childish act. And now when Mattie said, "There's the bell. Perhaps it's Mr. Ned," Mrs. Parkington thought, It's all right now. I can leave her to make the decision without being bullied.

Janie sprang up, her whole face alive with excitement and said, "Do you think it could be?"

"You'd better go and see, Mattie," said Mrs. Parkington. And Mattie, pleased at the chance to break the news of Janie's return, hustled out of the room across the boudoir into the hall.

To Janie, Mrs. Parkington said (just in case she might need a *little* bullying), "Now, don't be silly, my dear. Ned matters more than anything in your life . . . not because you love him so much but because you're lucky to have found the right boy. Don't think too much about what you want or how noble you'd be to give him up. Do what *he* wants. Now go on and see him . . . I'm sure it's Ned. Nobody else would be coming at this hour. I'm going to sleep now. I'll see you both in the morning. We'll have some planning to do."

Lying back in the pillows, she watched the girl hurry out of the other room into the hall and heard her cry out, "Ned! Ned!" from the top of the stairs, and in spite of everything she felt a sudden small pang of envy and she remembered again the first night at the Brevoort with the red curtains and the gold *baldaquins*, the white roses and the champagne on the marble-topped table and the snow falling outside. She had been lucky. In spite of all the bad things, she had been lucky. If Janie could only be as lucky . . . perhaps she and Ned could start afresh . . . Perhaps they could take the curse off the family.

Then Mattie reappeared, her big round face shining. She said, "It's going to be all right, Mrs. P. I think Miss Janie's found her head again."

"It isn't her head she's found, Mattie. It's her heart and that's much more important." She pulled herself up very straight in bed and said, "Close both doors, Mattie. I've got a job to do. I've got to call Mr. Ned's boss in Washington and neither of them must know anything about it."

When Mattie had closed the doors she dialed very efficiently the long-distance operator and said, "I want to speak to Mr. Holman Drury in Washington. He lives at the Mayflower Hotel."

What she was about to do was one of the most difficult things she had ever attempted in all her life. It was not only that she risked refusal and humiliation; she might even have to humble herself, a thing which did not come easily to Mrs. Parkington even at eighty-four. She, the widow of Augustus Parkington, immensely rich, entrenched in wealth, the relict of another age, the product of a world which had been ruthless and unscrupulous, was about to ring up a man who was the avowed enemy of everything she represented, who had set himself to destroy it, and ask him a favor in behalf of the daughter of a man whom he had run to earth. While she waited, she tried to remember exactly how Holman Drury looked and how he had behaved on the two occasions when she had encountered him casually at great dinners in Washington. For this was important; if you knew something of a person, how he looked and how his mind worked, it was a great help in getting what you wanted from him.

She did remember his face fairly clearly — a dark face with a high, domelike forehead, a thin, tight mouth, a receding chin and burning, fanatic eyes. It was not an impressive face, not the face of a powerful man whose ideas were big, whose power of accomplishment was without limit. It was an unhappy face, at times almost feminine and peevish, the face of a nagger who felt the mantle of God had descended upon him. There were many faces like that in Washington nowadays; they were there because of the things Gus and men like him had done long ago. The pendulum had swung to the other extreme from the days when Gus had only to go to Washington with a fat checkbook to get done what he wanted. Washington was nowadays overrun with little messiahs, each with a pocket formula for the salvation of the world. The pendulum had swung now to the other extreme, and somehow good, honest, sane citizens were always caught in between.

She dreaded having to speak to this particular, pocket-sized messiah for other reasons. If he had been a scoundrel she could, she knew, manage him, or if he had been a poor man of simple origin who had raised himself to a position of importance. But Holman Drury was neither of these things. He was a fanatic who had no scruples so long as he got what he wanted, and he came of exactly the same background as Amory himself, only long ago, perhaps in boarding school, because he had been ill-treated or unpopular or nonconforming, he had revolted and out of the bitterness of the revolt was born an unscrupulous pocket messiah, set upon the destruction of the world which he hated and which in a way had created him. Amory had gone one way and Holman Drury the other, but in a curious fashion they were the same. Holman Drury, the reformer, was as destructive in his way as Amory Stilham the crook.

Such men, Mrs. Parkington reflected while she waited, could be very dangerous, and they were difficult to approach and difficult to manage especially if you were called Mrs. Augustus Parkington. In her heart she had a contempt for Holman Drury, not because he was the natural enemy of Gus nor because he was as much a product of a system as Amory, but because he was feminine and vengeful, and because there was something never quite reliable or authentic about the radical produced by revolt against a Tory background. The very process implied frivolity and resentment and hysteria as if all the time the force behind his revolt was no more profound or dignified than to get back at the boys who had persecuted him at school.

Then the bell of the telephone beside the bed rang and when she answered, the operator said that Mr. Drury was on the wire and would speak to her. She thought quickly, I must not let my feelings color my voice. I must show him great deference. It will please him to think he has brought the widow of Augustus Parkington to her knees.

When she heard his voice she said, "This is Mrs. Augustus Parkington speaking. Do you remember me?"

The voice of Holman Drury came back, rather deep and pompous, a kind of false voice like a false face.

"Of course I do. Yes, indeed. How are you?"

She thought quickly, He believes I'm going to ask him a favor in behalf of Amory and he is treating me as if I were a doddering old fool. And she answered, with exaggerated briskness, "Very well, thank you. I'm sorry to trouble you at this hour but something urgent has come up."

"I hope I can be of service to you."

She was old enough and wise enough to know that he would be certain to answer her call because he thought it concerned Amory's case. He would not want to escape her because he could not say "no"; on the contrary it would give him pleasure to say "no" because it would give him the opportunity of delivering a small lecture on the side. She must make clear her purpose at once.

She said, "You have a boy called Edward Talbot in your department."

"That's right." The voice came back, colored by enthusiasm. "He is one of our best young men."

"What I have to ask is simple enough. It happens that he was going to marry my great-granddaughter, Amory Stilham's daughter, and all this unpleasant business has very nearly wrecked everything."

"I'm very sorry to hear that."

"My great-granddaughter and Ned Talbot are very much in love with each other and it seems to me there is one way out. You could help them a great deal."

"I'd be delighted to help if possible. What do you suggest?"

She was certain now that she had passed the worst point. She had established the fact that she was asking nothing in behalf of Amory, and she discovered his liking and enthusiasm for Ned. So she went directly to the point.

She said, "I think they should be married as quickly as possible, but that isn't possible in New York. You know what the newspapers are. It occurred to me that if he were transferred to Kansas City or San Francisco or some place like that, it could be accomplished without any fuss. No one would know about it. Do you understand what I mean?"

"Yes, I think I do. You want Ned sent somewhere where no one will know his wife or know who she is."

"That's it. Exactly. Could it be done?"

She felt her heart beating more rapidly now, for as she talked this thing had become to her the most important thing in the world. It was as if she herself were Janie.

The voice of Holman Drury came back, more pompous than ever — the voice, she thought, of a despot bestowing a favor.

"Of course. Nothing could be simpler. Ned was in line for that in any case."

"There's one more thing. Could it be done very quickly — by telegram yet tonight so that he'll receive it in the morning?"

"I'll send a wire at once."

"Could you send it here to my house?"

"Certainly."

She gave him the address and then said, "I can never say how much I appreciate this. If there is anything I can do . . ."

His voice interrupted her. "I'm delighted to do it, Mrs. Parkington, I'm delighted to do anything for you."

"Of course you'll never let Ned know that I called you."

"You may count on me."

"Good night and thank you again."

"Good night."

It was done then. Quickly she put out the light and lay back among the pillows, feeling very tired. It had been easier than she hoped.

It seemed to her that somehow all the troubles of the family were being solved, all its tiresomeness eliminated, partly by the inevitable turn of fate, partly by her own efforts. Mattie's idea was a good one; once Ned and Janie were out of the way, a trip would be the thing. It would give her the strength to go through the agony of Amory's trial and the misery of having Helen under her wing for a long time.

She was pleased over the way the interview with Holman Drury had turned out. What she did not know was that she had succeeded because Holman Drury remembered her, extremely well, as the most witty, charming and amusing old lady he had ever met, and he had wanted to help her so that he might have an opportunity of seeing her again. That was one of the dividends on a life which had been long and human and sometimes wise.

And she did not know that Holman Drury

loved old ladies like herself. He had never married and he worshipped the memory of his own mother.

In the morning Mattie brought her breakfast and wakened her at nine o'clock. She knew by the look of the bed that Mrs. Parkington had slept well and was probably in a good humor. So she said, "Have you been thinking more about the trip, Mrs. P.?"

"Yes. As soon as the date of Amory's trial is settled, we'll know how much time we have."

"It won't be for three or probably four months," said Mattie. (She was very knowing this morning and sure of herself, a little as if she'd swallowed a canary.)

"How do you know that?"

"From Mr. Ned. He says Mr. Amory's lawyers want the trial put well ahead on the calendar." (And now she was talking like a lawyer.)

"Have you seen Mr. Talbot already this morning?"

"Yes, Mrs. P. They're going to be married."

"When?" asked Mrs. Parkington.

"I don't know. Some day when everything is straightened out."

"That's not soon enough."

"Mr. Ned has some good news."

"What sort of good news?"

"He says he's going to San Francisco at once."

Mrs. Parkington was silent for a moment. Then she said, "That's good. Will you ask Miss Janie to come here as soon as she's dressed?"

"She's dressed already. I'll tell her to come in."

Then Mattie went away and Mrs. Parkington began thinking how she could send a wire of thanks to Holman Drury without anyone's finding out about it, and she thought at first that it might be a good idea to include with the thanks an invitation to the dinner, but almost at once she saw that this was impossible since it was Drury who directed the investigation which trapped Amory. It was very tiresome having a relation like Amory.

Janie came in presently but she wasn't alone. Ned was with her and Mrs. Parkington saw at once that something had been settled. She saw it in their faces, in the way they walked, in the way their voices sounded when they wished her good morning.

She drew a lacy peignoir a little higher to hide the bones in her neck and said, "Mattie tells me you're going to be married."

"Yes," said Ned.

"When?"

"As soon as people have forgotten about the whole thing. The newspapers won't bother us then."

"That isn't enough," said Mrs. Parkington. She looked at Ned. "Mattie tells me you've been ordered to San Francisco."

"Yes. The telegram arrived about an hour ago. It was sent here. I don't know why. Nobody knew I was here."

"That *is* odd," said Mrs. Parkington. "How could they have known?" Then she said, "Sit down. I have a better plan than yours. I want you to consider it carefully."

Like small children they sat down on the edge of two gilt chairs.

"It's this. You're going to get into Ned's car and leave town, before noon if possible. And you're not to tell anyone where you're going or that you're going away together. And you can get married in Maryland if you like or when you get to San Francisco or along the way if you can find a place where you can get married right off. I've heard they do that in Kentucky. The point is that you must get out of town without anybody's knowing it and together, and you can turn up in San Francisco as man and wife and Janie need never say who she was and nobody will know anything. You'll just be two nice, attractive new people arriving in San Francisco to do a job. Do you see the point?"

Ned certainly saw it. His face betrayed his delight, and watching him Mrs. Parkington thought, He must learn to control his face better than he does. It isn't safe like that — as if someone had set off fireworks inside him.

Janie looked puzzled. She asked, "What about Mother and Father?"

"I'll take care of them. You're to tell them I've sent you away to stay with friends — with Mrs. Rodney at Aiken. I'll fix it with Molly Rodney to forward mail and telegrams. I don't trust your mother not to let out the news."

"She won't like that."

"It doesn't matter what she likes now," said Mrs. Parkington. She wanted to add, "She and Amory forfeited long ago the right of consideration from their children." But she held her tongue. To Ned she said, "You'll have to straighten out things at your office, so you'd better be on your way and get it done. And Janie will have to go home and get some clothes, and now come and kiss me."

Janie kissed her and said, "You're wonderful, Granny."

"I'm nothing at all but I hope I've learned some sense in eighty-four years."

Then Ned kissed her shyly and said, "Thank you, Mrs. Parkington."

"Just write me when you get to San Francisco and tell me about the trip."

Then they went out and as they reached the doorway of the other room Mrs. Parkington called to them, "Tell Mattie to come and talk to me while I dress."

She felt suddenly old and lonely. But there was no time to be lonely because when Mattie returned, she said, "Miss Madeleine's husband is downstairs."

"At this hour?"

"Yes. He said he had dropped in to say good-bye."

"Why 'good-bye'?"

"He didn't tell me," said Mattie, going off to turn on the bath.

Mrs. Parkington called out, "How does he look?"

"Peaked . . . a little peaked," said Mattie above the sound of running water and Mrs. Parkington thought, I suppose that's the last of this marriage too.

The cowboy was standing with his back to the door studying the Boucher nudes that hung over the fireplace and when she said, "Good morning, Al!" he turned nervously and said, "Good morning, Mrs. Parkington." The morning light was not good in the small sitting-room and she could not see whether he blushed or not.

He said, "Maybe I came too early. Maybe I should have telephoned."

"No . . . no. I'm delighted to see you."

There was something solid and reassuring in the trim wiry figure and the honest blue eyes set in a face which had not lost its tan beneath the luxurious sun of Nassau and Miami. She noticed at once that his manner seemed easier and more assured. That would be, she thought, because he has seen plenty. He's got the numbers of a great many people who once awed and frightened him.

Almost at once he politely expressed his sympathy over the death of Alice and the ugly business of Amory. He did it with dignity and feeling, quietly and simply, so that his earnestness touched her.

Then he said, "It's all broken up between Madeleine and me. I'm going back to Nevada.

"I'm sorry to hear that. It didn't last very long."

He looked down at his feet. "No, it didn't. I don't say it was anyone's fault. It was just the way Madeleine wants to live and the kind of people she sees. I said I couldn't go on leading that kind of life and she said '*What* kind of life?' It wasn't really that she was pretending. She really didn't know what I meant. She really meant what she said when she asked that. She really doesn't see anything crazy about it. You see, that's the trouble. I'm sorry. I liked Madeleine. I still like her. When I saw her out there in Nevada, she was different. She could ride all day and drink and she was good with the cattle — real good, better than most of the hands. And she never got tired either. I thought she was a pretty swell woman and that mebbe together we could build up a ranch that would be the best in the country. She was going to be a partner and put money into it and I was going to do all the organizing and buying and selling. Out there we had a lot in common."

While she listened, aided by experience and a knowledge and understanding which in his simplicity he could never possess, she began to see the whole story in its true light. Knowing Madeleine too, she understood many things which puzzled him. She saw it all suddenly as it must have been, not as it appeared to be. She divined clearly how Madeleine had operated. Madeleine had cast her eye upon Al and decided that he was what she wanted, and then almost at once his simplicity must have baffled her. She would never understand that Al would feel very simply about their relationship — that if they found each other agreeable and sympathetic, then marriage was the solution. And as Al became more difficult to possess, she worked herself into a passion over him, and held out all sorts of bait and bribes which very likely she never meant to pay. In the whole affair, armed by sophistication and trickery, she had been the wooer just as she had been as a little girl when she took boys out on the fire escape at assemblies. In most ways poor Al could never be a match for her, least of all in the beginning; it would only have been in the end that he might have won out as he was winning out now by his simplicity and integrity. Al wasn't a callow boy; he was a man who knew what he wanted and what things were worth.

And he had stood up under Madeleine's demands, better than the Argentine or any of the others. The trouble with Madeleine was that she had a split personality. On one side she was a good, hearty sort who would have made an excellent cashier in a Las Vegas gambling establishment. On that side she was kindly and bawdy and insatiable. But on the other side she was a fool, a kind of half-baked Messalina with an appalling taste in friends and in life itself.

But Al was going on with his story. "Here in the East," he was saying, "she seemed like a different person . . . like someone I didn't know. She didn't seem to have any sense. She just wanted to stay up all night and lay in bed until six in the evening. I ain't made that way, Mrs. Parkington. I guess I couldn't take it. I tried to make a good husband. I gave her everything a husband could give her . . . within reason, but it wasn't enough."

Mrs. Parkington thought, I wonder if he's trying to tell me discreetly what I already know. There was about him a simple air of astonishment.

"She wanted me to be a lot of other things than I am. I'm just me. I'm smart in a lot of ways, Mrs. Parkington, but I couldn't keep up with Madeleine and her friends." He put his head on one side and grinned, "You know, I never met women like her friends. I never met women who tried to take men away from their best friends. One of them — maybe you know her, a Mrs. Posley — just came right out cold and said" — the tanned face grew darker as he blushed and hesitated — "I couldn't say it in front of a lady like you what she really said. I said to her, 'But I only met you last night' and she said, 'What difference does that make? I just wanted to know what it would be like.' And when I said, 'But you're a friend of Madeleines,' she said, 'So what? Do you think she wouldn't try the same thing on me?' " The blue eyes became grave and shocked. "You know, Mrs. Parkington. We have some pretty tough women out there in a place like Las Vegas but we haven't got anything like that."

Mrs. Parkington felt an irresistible desire to chuckle. She only smiled and said, "I'm sure you haven't."

"So when I said we were going back to the ranch, Madeleine said, 'Oh, no, we aren't. We're going to stay three or four weeks in New York' and I said, 'Who says so?' and she said, 'I do!' So I said, 'All right. Then you're going to stay alone.' And then we had quite a fight and I packed up and went to another hotel."

He looked down at his hands. The big horny fingers twined and untwined and that was the only sign he gave of any inward emotion, but Mrs. Parkington understood the curious gesture. It was the only way he betrayed what he was feeling, the shame and disillusionment he experienced, the certainty he had that he had been made a fool of, that he had been used until Madeleine's curiosity was satisfied. His pride was hurt as well as his sense of decency.

"It'll be kind of nice to get back there again. I'm sorry about Madeleine but I guess there was nothing I could do or nothing she could do either. Sometimes I think it's a sickness with Madeleine. Maybe if she'd had to work or had a family, it would have turned into something else . . . something good . . . all that energy."

And Mrs. Parkington knew that he understood the whole thing, simply and profoundly, and that he was sad because he had once been fond of Madeleine and knew now that she was a lost woman and that nothing could ever save her from an end that it was better not to think about.

"You don't think she might come back, do you?" he asked. "You don't think anything might change her?"

"No," said Mrs. Parkington, "I'm afraid it's too late for that — she got started off on the wrong foot long ago."

All the time she had been listening and thinking about the sadness of these two people who had both wanted something and failed to find it, who had hoped, even Madeleine herself, for a little time, only to be disillusioned, she had been thinking too of something else — an idea which had been there, half-realized, in the dim reach of her mind since the moment he had crossed the room to say, "Good evening, ma'am," on the night of the Christmas dinner. It became clear now as she watched the honest, tanned face and blue eyes, as she watched the hands twisting over and over upon themselves. She knew what it was she wanted — to go back, far, far back, beyond all the triumphs, the tragedies, the satisfaction and bitterness and brilliance of her life, back to the very beginning. She had known that for a long time. Almost without being aware of it, she had been searching for some key to unlock the door of the past, some means by which she could escape the accumulated thicket of wisdom and cynicism, of knowledge and experience, which enclosed her. And now by a curious twist of circumstances, Madeleine, in her insatiable desire, had delivered her the key. It was Al, sitting there opposite her, miserable and hurt. Al could do her great good and perhaps she could help a little to make him forget his hurt pride and disillusionment. She liked Al very much. She hadn't seen a man like him for more than half a century; even good friends like Louis Fletcher and the judge did not have his quality of simplicity which was like the simplicity of a nice and faithful dog. She hadn't really seen a man like him from the day she left Leaping Rock until Al crossed the room at the Christmas dinner. Something had happened to men like that, or perhaps it was only that her life had led her into worlds where they did not and could not exist. No, she liked Al very much. He touched a part of her which had been lonely for a long time.

Quietly she said, "When are you planning to leave?"

"As soon as I can go. I don't know what to do with myself here."

"I've been thinking for a long time that I'd like to see Leaping Rock again.

He smiled at her as if he understood what was in her heart. "There isn't much left of it, ma'am. A few deserted, run-down buildings."

"I'd expect that. It wouldn't be a disappointment." Now she herself felt shy. It required an effort to speak. She said, "I have an idea and if it doesn't suit your plans, I want you to be perfectly frank and give me an honest answer. For a long time I've wanted to make a trip somewhere and I didn't go because I couldn't make up my mind. I've been so many places and I've seen so much. But now I know where I want to go — to see Leaping Rock again and to see your ranch."

"It would give me great pleasure, Mrs. Parkington. It might not be as comfortable as you'd like, though it's pretty good."

"I'm sure that wouldn't trouble me. I like to be luxurious when it's possible but if it isn't, I'm just as satisfied — especially if it's something I want to do." She looked away from him and added, "But that isn't all. It would give me great pleasure if you'd come with me in my own car. It's a big car, and very comfortable. I like traveling at a good speed. It wouldn't take us more than a week. I could be ready in two days if you could bear to wait that long."

There was an eagerness in her voice like the eagerness of a timid child which must have touched him, for he grinned and said, "Of course, ma'am. I could wait two more days. I'd like to go with you. I could show you a lot of things once we got to Denver and beyond. I'd like to show you that country . . . it's great country."

His eyes were shining so that she could not doubt his sincerity. She thought suddenly, Perhaps it's true that age has nothing to do with years — that people separated by years can be the same age in spirit.

Then she said, "Maybe it would be less lonely for you to come here and stay in the house."

But this plan he rejected and she knew suddenly that it was because the luxury made him feel awkward and shy and she thought, What a fool Madeleine is to lose a man like this! But then poor Madeleine was lost. She was long past exercising any sort of sane judgment. Already she would be searching for some other man.

"But you will come for a meal or two," she said.

"Yes, I'd like that."

"I could be ready on Friday morning. We could certainly get as far as Pittsburgh on the first day."

"That would suit me, ma'am. I think it's a mighty fine idea." The weathered face contracted in a frown, and he said, "I'm worried about Madeleine, Mrs. Parkington. I'd like to do something to help. But I don't know how. That's what I really came here to talk about."

She was thoughtful for a moment, trying to decide what it was best to say in reply. She thought, He is a simple, direct man. There is no use in being highfalutin' with him. So she said, "There is nothing you can do for her, Al. There's nothing anyone can do for her. All I can do is to see that her money is taken care of so that she'll always have enough to save her from poverty and misery. That's about all anyone can do."

He rose from his chair and said, "I'm sorry, ma'am. I felt that way myself but I thought that maybe I was wrong. It is a frightening thing."

That was it — a frightening thing. He had

said it simply and directly. It was a frightening thing when a soul was deformed, when obsession obscured judgment and decency, when a human ceased any longer to understand decency and shame. Yet Madeleine could be at times so generous and agreeable and plausible.

"We meant to come back at the time your daughter died," said Al, "but the weather was bad and the plane couldn't take off. It wasn't just an excuse. It was the only way we could have got here in time for the funeral. I wanted you to understand that."

"I did understand it, but thank you for saying that."

"And now I'll go. I apologize again for not telephoning first. I just didn't think of it."

That was it. He had just dropped in, the way people did long ago in Leaping Rock. Suddenly for no reason at all she remembered the kindness of the trollops on the morning her parents were killed.

"Would you like to come to dinner tonight?"

"Yes, ma'am."

"We could go to the theater afterward if you like."

"It would be something to do."

That gave her the clue. It would have to

be a musical show.

"We'll have to dine then at seven."

"I'll be here."

She went with him to the door and at the door she said, "It was very good of you to come and tell me about it. If you hadn't come, I might never have seen you again and that would have been a pity." She did not add, "It would have been a pity because I think we get on, that we understood each other from that first moment, and that does not happen often in life. It is a thing to be glad of, to be cherished."

"I almost didn't come," he said. "I thought maybe you'd be angry and wouldn't understand what happened exactly. And then I thought, Yes, I think she'll understand better than anyone. And then I wanted to see you and say goodbye. So I came." He picked up his hat, the smart, expensive gray felt Madeleine had forced upon him and which suited him so little, which looked so wrong above the leathery face.

"I'll see you tonight then at seven," he said awkwardly and went out the door. As he opened the door she had an odd feeling that outside in Sixty-seventh Street there should be a hitching rail with a cayuse tied to it. That was what God meant him for — not Madeleine.

* * *

Miss Beasely had a busy morning, indeed there was far more than her unclear head had the power to cope with. First of all, the whole dinner had to be called off. Mrs. Parkington dictated the form of this note which was to be sent. She regretted that "she would have to put off the dinner until her return from the West because of circumstances beyond her control." And Miss Beasely had to call the judge and Louis Fletcher and find an hour during the next forty-eight when they could meet with Mrs. Parkington. And there were committees to be called and checks to be made out in advance for various charity and relief organizations, and invitations to be refused.

Miss Beasely appeared not only to be flustered by the amount of work and detail but also by the knowledge that a woman of eighty-four could change all her plans so quickly and set out upon a transcontinental journey as if it were no more than driving downtown to the florist's. She kept boring Mrs. Parkington with such remarks as, "You are wonderful, Mrs. Parkington," and, "I don't see how you do it," her dull eyes taking on a glimmer of vicarious excitement. Like Harriette Livingstone long ago, Miss Beasely was a groveler. In her own exaggerated humbleness, she worshipped clever people and energetic people. She was unendurable because there was no envy or spite in her soul; that at least might have added spice to her character and made her less tiresome.

As she dictated and gave instructions, Mrs. Parkington thought, I must get rid of her when I get back. I can't endure her cowlike glances of admiration any longer. But I shall have to find something in which she is interested and safe as Harriette was. The difficulty was that she could never discover anything which could rouse Miss Beasely out of apathy into interest.

When she had finished with Miss Beasely she had to talk to Hicks to tell him about the trip. He was delighted with the idea. He said, "My wife and Johnny will go and stay with her mother in Trenton. It's a visit she's been wanting to make."

"Is the big car in order?" she asked.

"It's in good shape," said Hicks. "Ready for anything."

"There won't be much luggage — only three or four suitcases and the dogs."

A shadow crossed Hicks's face at the mention of the Pekingese. He didn't really dislike them; he only hated them for their yapping and their occasional mock-savage attacks on the cuffs of his trousers. Long ago he had come to accept them as the fly in the ointment, the only thing which marred his utter devotion to Mrs. Parkington.

Apologetically she said, "I'll have to take them, Hicks. It's impossible to leave them with anyone. You know how they are?"

"Of course, Mrs. Parkington," he said, without enthusiasm.

Mattie was violently excited by the news. She, like her mistress, like all her own ancestry, was a born traveler. At the prospect of a voyage, however difficult, her blood pressure rose, her cheeks grew pink, the years dropped from her. On a journey you never knew what might happen; and for a long time, all too long a time, her whole life had been inside the four walls of the house.

Cook and Taylor were pleased too, not only at the prospect of a holiday but at the idea that Mrs. Parkington was going to have a change which they thought she needed badly. It was not that she seemed ill or even older but at times she seemed bored and listless. And always they were haunted by the fear of Mrs. Parkington's death because they knew that never again would they find places in which they were so happy, where they felt the house in which they worked was their house, that they were a part of all that took place within its walls, where what happened to their employer or what happened to them was of equal importance. In their hearts they wanted to keep Mrs. Parkington going on forever, because she was their friend and because if she died something would be gone from their lives which could never again be replaced. They knew, too, that with the world what it was, there would be very few Mrs. Parkingtons in the future. In a way she was the last remnant of a world which was already almost destroyed — a world which to them was everything because it represented dignity and security and strength. They knew too that they had been very lucky to have found, in the long pattern of their lives, a woman like Mrs. Parkington. It was Taylor himself who once unbent enough to say in vulgar slang that "Mrs. Parkington knew all the answers."

Now that Mrs. Parkington was going on a trip, Cook would go to stay with her sister who was married to a mill foreman in Bethlehem and Taylor would go to visit a cousin who was a farm manager in North Carolina.

The house would be left in charge of Mary Jenney, who brought up Janie and Jack, and her husband. It wasn't merely that a trip was being taken by Mrs. Parkington. It was a change and a holiday for everyone. A whole small world was involved.

At last all was in order and everything and everyone arranged for save the matter of the will and as, one by one, she checked off the list of things to be done with Miss Beasely and things to be done by herself such as writing to Molly Rodney at Aiken to hold all letters addressed either to Jane Stilham or Mrs. Edward Talbot, Mrs. Parkington felt younger and younger. There were a great many small things, having to do with committees and directors' boards, which others would have to take over while she was gone, things which had tied her down, day after day, week after week, like so many tiny cords. And now they were broken by one simple decision and she was going away to forget them all because Madeleine had picked up a rancher and married him and brought him into her own life, making her know at last what it was she wanted.

There were times when her life and all that it encompassed seemed in a curious fashion like the life of her own country — that its melodrama, its color, its fantasy, its opportunities, its tragedy, was like a history in miniature of the huge incredible opulent nation which she had loved without ever wavering for so long. Now at last something like Al might come to help and free it, as Al had come to help and free her, showing her the way back to those simple things upon which all the rest of her existence had been based, out of which she had drawn the strength, the wisdom and the wit to survive and perhaps even to triumph over all the turmoil, the disappointments, the fears and the shattered hopes.

On Thursday evening the judge and Louis Fletcher came to dinner. It was a good dinner for Cook had done her best, and the talk was good, of politics, of neuroses and medicine and the war, for here were three people who knew what conversation was, three people who had done well not only by themselves but by their fellowmen, who were just and honest, who had never cheated nor evaded a responsibility. Most of all they had rarely been guilty of the great American error of deceiving themselves. And so they belonged to that small world of those who were permitted to know and understand the inwardness of things and the brilliance of the spirit.

It was altogether one of those rare evenings which raised the mere privilege of breathing and thinking and speaking, indeed the whole of existence, to a level which one day all of mankind might attain. And Mrs. Parkington, aware of this now and then in a brilliant moment of satisfaction, understood that the foundation of all the satisfaction lay in simplicity. Pretentious people were inevitably shut out from such a world as theirs. Watching the two men whom she had known for so long, she divined the ultimate secret of their curious splendor — that at heart they were not much different from Al. Circumstances had provided them with perhaps a better brain than his, and greater opportunities and experience had brought them the wisdom which only experience can create, but all of these things would have been futile and dead save for the goodness and simplicity which gave them solidity and purpose and direction.

After dinner in the small sitting-room, she said presently, "It is growing late and I think we had better get down to the business I wanted to talk about with you both. I want to make a new will before I go away."

Both men, aware of what was in her mind, found no words for an adequate remark and so, wisely, they kept silent, waiting for her to continue.

"I've had a lot of new ideas during the past year and I want to put them into effect now." She rose and took out of a drawer of the table a pad of fresh white paper and a pencil, and giving them to the judge, she said, "I'll tell you what I want and you can have it ready for me when I get back from the West." She smiled suddenly and said, "And until I've finished I don't want you to interrupt me to tell me that I'm being foolish or fantastic. What I am doing, I have considered carefully for a long time. In fact, in a way, I've been moving toward all this all my life. It's just become clear to me lately."

Then she turned to Louis Fletcher and laughed, "I suppose you don't know what part you play in all this."

Fletcher grinned and said, "No, I don't, Susie. I'm not a lawyer."

"I want you to make a statement, drawn up legally, that I am in my right mind, in full possession of all my faculties, and not the subject of undue influence. You do believe all that . . . don't you?"

"I've never seen anyone more in their right mind or more in possession of their faculties."

"Very well. Then we can go ahead. Are you ready, Judge?"

"Yes, Susie."

She picked up the small bit of paper she had taken from the drawer along with the pad and pencil and glanced at it.

"First of all, there is the family — that is to say, Madeleine and Helen and Helen's children. I want to leave trust funds which will yield thirty thousand a year each to Madeleine and Helen." She glanced at Judge Everett and saw his expression of surprise. "I think that's about right. They can do on thirty thousand. If I left them everything outright they'd be sure to lose it sooner or later and neither of them would be able to make fifteen dollars a week if they had to go to work. Amory is finished. He'll never make any more money even if people came to trust him again. They have to be taken care of. In a way, all three are useless members of society. I don't say it's their fault. It's partly my fault and the fault of Gus and the fault of the age they were brought up in. It conspired to make them useless. It was a trashy era. With thirty thousand a year they'll be able to live very well and at the same time they won't be able to make fools of themselves. You understand that Helen and Amory are getting really a great deal more than that. I'm paying out about seven hundred thousand to take care of the money Amory misused . . . Have you all that?"

"Yes," said the judge.

"Do you approve?"

"They won't like it considering the huge amount of money they count on."

"I don't mind that. If I thought they had even the faintest idea of how to use so much money, I'd feel differently. They have to be taken care of but they shouldn't be entrusted with money. They don't understand what money is for nor how to use it."

She turned over the small bit of paper. "And I want to leave ten thousand a year to Jack. He has a little Blair money. Maybe he won't need it. Maybe he'll be all right. I don't know yet and I may die before I find out. He's one of the leftovers . . . bewildered by everything. He doesn't know what anything means or where he is bound and that's not his fault either. He's never had a proper chance. There are a lot of young Americans like him."

She saw the judge's eyebrows move a little and his eyes brighten with curiosity. Louis Fletcher was smiling as if he had already caught the clue to what she was doing.

"And Janie," she said, "I'm not going to leave Janie anything now . . . not for fifteen years, and by that time things will be all right. She'll have had the fun of working up to something with the young man she's marrying. They'll have made their life together. She'll know what that is like. It won't be spoiled for her — all the sacrifices and the economies and the sense of reality upon which a good life is founded. She'll know by that time what everyday people are like. She'll know the things which money can't buy, the things which money would keep her from ever acquiring."

She turned suddenly to Louis Fletcher, "You use words very well. You'll know how to write what I'm trying to say. It would be a great favor to me if you'd write the paragraph about Janie. She'll understand what I meant. We've already talked of it. You understand what I'm trying to say, Louis . . . don't you?"

"I think I do . . . perfectly," he replied with gravity. She had known that he would understand.

She turned back to Judge Everett. "I do want her to have a fund which gives her thirty thousand but not now . . . not until she's nearly forty. Then she's to have the right to the whole amount. By that time she'll know how to use it properly." Her small face grew stern as she said, "You know, Janie's the only one who's worth a tinker's dam. She's bewildered too but she tries to understand. And that boy Ned has a good head on his shoulders."

She was thinking of them as she spoke, somewhere on the way to San Francisco, together now as they should be, as they were meant by God to be. And in her heart she felt again the faint sharp stab of envy because they still had before them all that for her was in the past.

Judge Everett was saying, "I understand that you want the fund to be set aside immediately upon your death and the interest to accumulate until Janie is forty years old."

"Yes. That's right. That's it exactly."

"And if anything should happen to her?"

"Then it's to go to her husband and children if any."

The judge had been making figures, neatly and precisely on the edge of his pad of paper. He looked at her and said, "And the rest? What are you going to do with the rest? There's still a huge amount of money."

"How much?"

"At the last audit and appraisal in January, the total estate amounted to about forty-seven million dollars."

She smiled, "Yes, that's a lot of money . . . so much that it doesn't mean anything at all to me. For a long time now, for about fifty years I've never had any sense of money. I always knew that there was all I wanted, all I could possibly spend even with all that Gus gave away toward the end of his life. It seemed to come in faster than he gave it away, faster than he could spend it, and Gus could spend money. Sometimes it used to frighten me. It seemed to me that there was something wicked about it, but I didn't bother to worry about it any more. After Gus died I didn't need much. All the things Gus spent money on didn't mean much to me. I just keep giving it away and when I die it will all go back where it came from."

"And where is that?"

"Back into the country itself. Gus did a lot of good but he did more evil. He did a lot of plundering."

"How are you going to do this?"

"I don't know. That's where I want you both to help me. Giving away forty or so million dollars is a job in itself."

The judge took a sip of brandy and then said, "of course the simplest fashion would be to set up a foundation . . . something called the Parkington Foundation to the memory of Gus and yourself."

Her face grew serious and her voice turned hard. "No, that is exactly what I don't want. I want it to be given away without any bronze plaques, without any fanfare. I'm not interested in creating a legend at this late date that Gus was a great American who devoted his life to the good of his country. Gus did a lot of good but most of it was done accidentally. He was always thinking about Gus first, along with power and making money, like all the other rich, successful men of his day. I've no desire to have them white-washed. His partners tried that when they hired that miserable hack to write up his life so that he sounded like a saint. I couldn't even read it. It made me want to vomit. If Gus had been like that I wouldn't have stayed married to him forty years. I'd have left such a pious husband after a couple of years. I stayed married to Gus because he was a scamp on a gigantic scale and because he was fascinating, and because I was in love with him right up to the end." The faint echo of a chuckle came into her voice and she said, "I was a kind of a gun moll to the very end. And that's the truth. You know what I say is true, Judge. I heard you practically tell him that one night long ago in the house in Newport. You probably don't even remember it. It was when you first came to be his lawyer. We had dinner together . . . just the three of us and afterward you two went into the library to talk and the window was open and I could hear what you said on the verandah."

The judge smiled, "I remember the night because I remember thinking, If I say this it'll either mean that I'm out of a job, or that Gus Parkington and I will understand each other and we'll get on. I thought that night, The way he's going he'll need good advice. Maybe I can keep him out of trouble, if only for the sake of his wife Susie, whom I liked very much." He grinned and added, "I didn't know that you were listening. If it had happened later on, when I knew you better, I'd have known that when you were around, even the walls had ears. I liked Gus in spite of all I knew about him. That's why I stuck to him to the very end. There aren't any more like him."

Mrs. Parkington said, "Then you understand what I mean when I say that publicly there was little about Gus that ought to be memorialized but that privately I was in love with him always. I suppose that either he or I or both of us had what are called split personalities." She turned to Louis Fletcher, "Am I right, Louis?"

"Split," said Louis. "Split into fragments, both of you."

"What we know, we know," she continued, "but that is no reason for trying to make future generations believe Gus was a saint and his whole period the acme of American civilization. There's too much of that already, too many foundations to the memory of men who were crooks like Gus and ruthless and thoroughly bad citizens while they were alive. I doubt they'll succeed in the whitewashing process. Sound historians are likely to be fairly accurate men who can't be bought like hacks." She lifted her brandy glass and said, "But to get back to business. I want to leave something to the symphony and to St. Mary's Hospital and the MacKenzie Street Settlement and enough to keep Harriette's Cat and Dog Hospital going as long as money means anything. For the rest I want you and Louis to make me out a list of things which would benefit most, and institutions that would do the most good. I'd like some of it to go where it would undo two great American falsities — that making money is distinguished and important and that automobiles and water closets have anything to do with what is called civilization. You two can figure that out. You've had more experience than I have. If you do it wisely, maybe Gus' money will do some good after all. It's certainly done his own family little but harm for nearly seventy years. You can send the list to me. I'll wire you my address from time to time in case you need it. I'll okay the list or make any changes I think advisable. But I want the gifts made as anonymously as possible."

Louis Fletcher smiled, "You don't think that when you die the papers are going to let you off lightly. Your whole life is too good a story."

"No, I don't suppose I can expect to be able to just die and be buried, but I hope you both try to make it as much like that as possible. I just want to die and be cremated and put away beside Gus with as little fuss as possible."

She remembered the show and vulgarity of Alice's funeral and the ghosts who appeared there out of the brownstone houses and second-rate apartments, and she added, "I suppose there will have to be some sort of services to satisfy Helen, but I hope it will be short and sweet. Put that in the will as well." She laughed suddenly, "I suppose it doesn't really matter. I remember when old Mrs. Morton Ogden insisted that Herbert be christened properly, Gus said, 'It can't do the child any harm and it will give a lot of people pleasure.' Maybe I'm being selfish."

Louis Fletcher joined her laugh, "You might as well let them have their fun. In any case, you'll probably live to bury us both and then we won't have anything to say about what is done."

"I might at that." She looked at the watch on her wrist. "Have you got everything straight, Judge?"

"I've got the idea. I'll draft a form and send it along to you."

"I think we'd all better go to bed. I have to start on a long journey tomorrow."

The two men stood up. Louis Fletcher

grinned at her suddenly and said, "There's one question I'd like to ask you."

"What's that?"

"Are you going to Leaping Rock?"

"Yes, of course. Why?" There was a little irritation in her voice as if he had surprised something she had meant to keep secret.

"I knew you'd have to go back there before you died."

"So I'm a specimen to you?"

"Yes," said Louis Fletcher gravely, "all people are."

She was silent for a moment and then said, "Maybe you would have had a great success as a clairvoyant."

"Yes, that's quite true. So would you. In a way, we've always been in the same business, only you've always been an amateur."

The judge felt suddenly out of it and interrupted by saying, "Good night then, Susie. And thank you for an excellent dinner and an entertaining evening."

"Give my best to Margaret. I hope she understood that this was business and not pleasure this evening."

The judge smiled. "I'm sure she understood."

To Louis Fletcher she said, "Give your wife the same message."

"Of course."

Then they went out and when they had gone she walked slowly up the stairs feeling that nearly everything was now wound up, neatly and efficiently, all but Amory's trial. At the thought of that she sighed. *Everything* would probably never be wound up and settled until she died.

Mattie was waiting for her and asked, "Was it a pleasant evening, Mrs. P.?"

"Very pleasant, Mattie. Are you all packed and ready to go?"

"I've been all ready since four o'clock."

"That's good. You had better go off to bed now and call me early — about seven. We'll have to make an early start if we're to make Columbus by evening. Mr. Swann is in a hurry to get back to the ranch and Hicks doesn't like to drive above fifty. It makes him nervous."

The employees of THORNDIKE PRESS hope you have enjoyed this Large Print book. All our Large Print titles are designed for easy reading, and all our books are made to last. Other Thorndike Large Print books are available at your library, through selected bookstores, or directly from us. For more information about current and upcoming titles, please call or mail your name and address to: